THE EAGLE TURNS

THE EAGLE TURNS

JAMES GREEN

Published by Accent Press Ltd – 2014

ISBN 9781908262936

Acknowledgement

I would like to acknowledge *The Paranoid Style in American Politics* by Richard Hofstadter, first published in *Harper's Magazine* in November 1964, as the source of the speech made by the orator in the New Knickerbocker Theatre in chapter two. The original article, as quoted in 'The Paranoid Style', first appeared in a Texas newspaper in 1855. I have altered only slightly its essential message to fit its new context. The play-acting interlude is, however, completely from my own imagination.

The sentiments concerning the Mexican-American war placed in the mouth of Sam Grant in chapter fifteen are his own and are taken from *The Personal Memoirs of Ulysses S. Grant*.

All articles in italics are genuine quotes.

In July 1790 the US Congress established the Contingent Fund of Foreign Intercourse in response to a request from President George Washington for funds to finance intelligence operations. The fund was granted $40,000 which within three years had grown to $1 million, more than ten per cent of the federal budget. Successive administrations developed and expanded this fund until, in 1947, President Harry Truman signed into law the National Security Act and the CIA was born.

In 1846 Congress demanded from President James K. Polk an account of how moneys from the Contingent Fund of Foreign Intercourse had been spent in the annexation of Texas and the period leading up to the Mexican-American War. Here is a part of the president's response …

The experience of every nation on Earth has demonstrated that emergencies may arise in which it becomes absolutely necessary for the public safety or the public good to make expenditures, the very subject of which would be defeated by publicity. In no nation is the application of such funds to be made public. In time of war or impending danger, the situation of the country will make it necessary to employ individuals for the purpose of obtaining information or rendering other important services who could never be prevailed upon to act if they entertained the least apprehension that their names or their agency would in any contingency be revealed.

James K. Polk, US president 1845-1849

This reply effectively removed the use of the Contingent Fund from any congressional oversight for almost a century and left the uses to which it could be put entirely and solely in the hands of the president.

Chapter One

The Yellow Oval Room, the White House, Washington

July 9th 1850, dawn

The heavy, velvet drapes of the Yellow Oval Room were drawn back and through the windows the pale, first light of dawn could be seen spreading over the South Lawns. The gas lamps still burned brightly and the light reflected from the walls, papered as they were in deep yellow with gilded stars, gave both men in the room a somewhat jaundiced tinge.

The man standing at the window looking out was fifty years old and wore a baggy black suit. Of middle height and full figure, his thick fair hair, fleshy jowls, and plentiful chin gave the impression of a man who would smile and chuckle easily, a comfortable, jolly man. But not imposing. In no way could he be described as a man whose bearing alone would command attention, respect, and obedience. His aspect was, if anything, avuncular. Yet in a few days this man would command considerable attention though not, regrettably, respect or obedience. It would be paid to him by the highest in the land in no less a place than Capitol Hill where he would be sworn in as the thirteenth president of the United States.

Millard Fillmore turned away from the window. He looked tired, as indeed he was. He had been working non-stop through the night and when he spoke there was no disguising the weariness in his voice.

'President Taylor won't last the day. The medical men are all agreed that he will probably die sometime this

1

morning.'

'Thank God they are finally able to agree on something.'

The man who spoke stood by the presidential desk. Daniel Webster was a man whose appearance very much might commanded attention and, among some, respect and obedience. Of no great height he was sixty-eight years old and thin, but he stood ram-rod erect in a superbly cut, dove-grey suit. He looked at the world through sunken, dark, eyes shaded by heavy eyebrows. What straggly hair he still possessed lay brushed back flat and his high, prominent cheekbones emphasised a cruel mouth. His face, his bearing and manner gave him an air of supreme arrogance. And they did not lie.

Vice President Fillmore nodded in agreement.

'Aye, they haven't covered themselves in any glory in this business.' He let his eyes wander abstractedly around the room. 'You know, once it was clear that Taylor would die, almost the first thing Abigail said was that she wanted to turn this room into a library. She wants me to ask Congress for the money.'

'A fine woman, Abigail, but impetuous and disconnected from the greater affairs of the nation as women are. For myself, I doubt that upon the death of President Taylor a new presidential library will be one of your most pressing concerns.'

'No, I don't suppose it will.'

The vice president turned and gazed out of the window once more and the man by the desk waited in silence for a short while, but he was not a patient man.

'Well, Mr Vice President, are you going to gaze out of that window much longer or will you tell me why you have brought me here at this ungodly hour?'

Millard Fillmore came back to the desk and sat down.

'I want President Taylor buried.'

'And when he's dead he will be. When he's gone his

body will be put in the public vault in the Congressional Cemetery until it's taken back to Kentucky.'

'I mean I want him buried in every sense of the word. I want his remains in the ground with every ceremony proper to a president and a hero of the Mexican War.' The new president-in-waiting sat back, folded his hands together, and looked at Webster, 'And then I want him forgotten.'

Webster looked down his nose at the comfortable man gazing up at him.

'As for putting him in the ground, that's for his family. I suppose they'll get round to it when they're ready. But as to getting him forgotten, that's a different matter and I'm not sure to whom one might apply to see it achieved.'

Millard Fillmore smiled, looking more than ever like a favourite uncle.

'No?' The smile disappeared and the tone became businesslike. 'Well, more of that later. Now there's other things to consider. For instance the late President Taylor's Cabinet intend to resign *en masse* and they'll do it as soon as I've taken my oath of office.'

Webster raised his ample eyebrows.

'Are you sure?'

Fillmore nodded.

'They want to show me where I stand, that once sworn in I will be as much their puppet as the country's president. In everything but name I shall still be vice president. It is their intention to become the real power when Taylor's gone.'

'It would be a bold move.'

'They think I can't run this Administration without them, that I will have to refuse their resignations and concede to them becoming the ones who run the White House.'

'And how, exactly, do you know of their intentions?'

'Because I have always, since taking up office, made it

3

my business to know what Thurlow Weed intends.'

Webster tried to keep the surprise out of his voice, but failed.

'Weed? Has he put them up to it?'

'Oh yes. He's been manoeuvring to get me out and his own man in as vice president at the next election ever since Taylor was elected. As soon as Taylor's condition looked like it might become terminal he got Bill Seward to set it up.'

'Seward? A clever choice and fast work indeed on his part. I could almost admire it.'

The smile returned.

'Could you, Daniel? Could you indeed?' He gave a small, derisive laugh. 'Weed, he thinks he owns the whole Whig party. He sees Taylor's death as his chance to nominate both the next presidential candidate and the vice president on our ticket and through those nominees he intends to become the most powerful man in America.'

'I see.' Webster gave the news some thought. 'With Seward and the anti-slavery movement at his disposal he'll be a difficult man to oppose. What exactly do you intend?'

'To accept their resignations and appoint my own Cabinet.' Any hint of a smile was gone as the vice president looked up at Daniel Webster. 'I've been working on it all night and now I have all the names I want but one, that of secretary of state. I want men about me who can get the Compromise through Congress, men I can trust. As for Taylor's Cabinet, they despise me and I have no use for them, so we'll be well parted. But there's another reason I want them all out. I don't want any of them in a position to press for an investigation into the circumstances of Taylor's death.' The smile returned and Webster found it more than a little uncomfortable as this new Millard Fillmore continued. 'Now tell me, Daniel, seeing as how you're the country's sharpest constitutional lawyer, why do you suppose I wouldn't want that?'

4

Webster shifted uneasily. This, he had begun to realise, was not at all the man he thought he knew. Vice President Millard Fillmore had been a cipher to fill a slot on a presidential ticket. A nobody to play the role of a nothing. The man, sitting back and smiling at him with his hands folded together, was someone new and it was this Millard Fillmore would soon be president of the United States.

Webster's reply when he made it was suitably cautious. He had cross-questioned witnesses often enough, all the way up to the Supreme Court, so he recognised the question for what it was. He was being offered the position of secretary of state but, he felt, and rightly, his confirmation in that office was in no small way dependent on his answer.

'Well,' he paused, 'Mr President,'

Fillmore's smile widened and he gave an approving nod.

'Go on, Daniel, you're doing fine.'

'Well, the circumstances which gave rise to President Taylor's present condition are confused and unclear. He has been ill only a short time, a matter of a few days. As I understand it he seems to be suffering from some sort of abdominal fever brought on by something he ate or drank. All his doctors say his condition is the result of some sort of digestive malaise.'

'As they've been told to say.'

'Yes, perhaps so, but that changes nothing. They are unanimous in the general outline of their medical opinion. When the president is dead, to challenge their opinion as to the cause of death, what I'm sure will be their unanimous opinion, would be to suggest that something was,' he paused, searching for the right words, 'being withheld. That President Taylor may have died under questionable circumstances.'

'Go on, Daniel, you're still doing fine.'

'Were such a suggestion to be framed by unscrupulous

minds and placed before an uninformed public severe damage could be done to the proper running of the engine of state.'

Fillmore nodded encouragingly.

'Proper running of the engine of state? I like that, powerful phrase. I might use it myself. Go on, go on.'

'To sponsor, to support any such line of un-American activity would be to strike at the very security of the country at this difficult time, this very difficult time in our nationhood. In fact, with the divisions between North and South as fraught as they are, it would be tantamount to treason. No president could permit enemies of the government to cast such calumnies against Taylor's physicians, all loyal men whose only wish was and is to serve their country ...'

Webster stopped. He was a renowned speaker, one of the foremost advocates of the American Bar. Yet here he was before this chubby buffoon, babbling like a schoolboy. Why? Because this man, this petty man, was somehow about to become president of the United States and it was in his gift to make him secretary of state.

'Finished, Daniel?' Webster stood in sullen silence glaring. That look, however, which had intimidated so many, seemed not to discommode Millard Fillmore at all. He stood up, still smiling, placed his hands behind his back, and walked again to the window where he turned. 'Finished? Yes? Good, because there is still much for me to do and much that I want you to do also. Firstly, as I said, I want Taylor, when he's good and dead, safely back in Kentucky and in the ground. I want his reputation as a president intact and his status as a military hero perpetuated. And that's all I want of him. Once that's done I want him, and more especially the manner of his passing, forgotten. Understand, Daniel?' Webster nodded. 'I hoped you would because I am in great need of a co-operative and understanding secretary of state. You see, I'm not

6

going to be a very popular president.' That drew a look of surprise from Webster. 'But that doesn't bother me. I am not the stuff of greatness and I shall not try and use my office to change that. I won't even make a speech at my inauguration at the Capitol. Such things as a place in history I can safely leave to others,' the smile returned, 'like you, Daniel.' Webster was beginning to hate that smile, and be a little fearful of it. 'You and others like you, I have no doubt, will make sure you are remembered. I am satisfied that, having done my duty, I shall, like Zachary Taylor, be forgotten.'

Webster had the good grace to recognise the truth of what the still-vice president had said about both of them. He certainly intended that he should be remembered, as much as Millard Fillmore seemed ready and even willing to consign himself to historical oblivion.

'I'm sure your country will always remember and honour you as a good and worthy president.'

'My country won't get the chance. As I said, there are already those like Thurlow Weed and Senator Seward working hard to see that my name is not on the next Whig ticket either as president nor vice president. Weed has already selected his man, General Winfield Scott.'

'Winfield Scott?'

'I see that surprises you.'

'It does.'

Weed persuaded Scott that he is the natural successor of Zach Taylor, not that he needed much in the way of persuasion. Weed wants another military hero, someone the people will see as a strong leader, a man of action, experience, and decision. But he also wants someone who will be completely guided by him once in the White House. Winfield Scott might have been made for the part. You know what he likes people to call him?' Webster shook his head. '"The Grand Old Man of the Army". You know what Zach Taylor said his senior fellow officers called him?' Another shake. '"Old Fuss and Feathers". No matter, Weed will try and replace me with Winfield Scott as Whig candidate for president when my term expires. I hope to God he fails, either in getting him on our ticket or, if managing that, getting him elected, for if by some miracle Scott was to become president the Cherokee Nation won't be the only ones who will have had to endure a trail of tears at his hands.' Fillmore shrugged his shoulders. 'Well, I leave Weed and others to their plots and connivances. My job, the only job that matters when I am president, will be to do all I can to keep the North and the South off each other's throats. Taylor liked people to see him as a bluff, straight-spoken military man incapable of guile, '"Old Rough and Ready".'

Fillmore gave a genuine laugh. 'Simple and straightforward? He was as straight as a corkscrew and as devious as the best of them. But he was strong. A strong president. He could have held this country together. He knew how to give orders and how to get them obeyed.' Vice President Fillmore came back to his desk and sat down heavily. The weariness returned in his voice. 'I'm not that strong, Daniel. I can give orders but I'm not at all sure I can see that they're obeyed so I must play the politician rather than the soldier and compromise. If Taylor had died only a week earlier I could have seen that Henry Clay's bill got through Congress. As it didn't I must re-present it myself.'

'Including the Fugitive Slave Act?'

'Of course.'

'You know I gave it my support in the Senate and it cost me my seat?'

'I know. But the slave states won't let the bill pass without it.'

'There are those in the North who call it the '"Bloodhound Law".'

'And those down South who call it taking their property

back.'

'Quite. But as you yourself have just said, Mr President, you can frame the law and perhaps get it passed. But can you make the people obey it?'

Fillmore's face took on a mock surprise.

'Me? I will be president. The unenviable task of enforcement will fall to the secretary of state. Seeing it gets implemented to the hilt will be his task, not mine.'

Webster took the point.

'Not an enviable one, as you say.'

Fillmore's fist hit the desk.

'Damn and blast, Webster, the Compromise is the only way I can keep this country from tearing itself apart and the best men on both sides slaughtering each other.' His flare of temper subsided as quickly as it had arisen. 'Or would you prefer to be remembered as the secretary of state who helped me take this country into a civil war?' Webster didn't reply. 'No, I thought not. So, Daniel, on to foreign affairs, something else that might soon be your department. Taylor managed in an amazingly short time to ruffle the feathers of just about everyone, Portugal, France, Spain, most of them. I want those feathers smoothed again. Then there's the damn Clayton-Bulwer Treaty, his last act of state, and his most consummate blunder.'

'You want to renege on it?'

'No. At the moment we're on as good terms with the British as we're likely to be for some time and I want it to stay that way.' Fillmore paused. He had dangled the carrot of high office, now it was time for the stick. 'But before any of that, before any appointment is announced, there is a little task I would like you to see to.' Daniel Webster at once knew that this was why he had been summoned. There was to be a test. Something which would confirm in Millard Fillmore's mind that he was the sort of secretary of state he wanted and could trust. 'I want you to see that no one raises any questions over the circumstances of

9

President Taylor's death. As I said, Taylor's Cabinet will, without realising it, give me their full co-operation by resigning. They will assume, wrongly, that I cannot begin my presidency without some sort of continuity. Once they're gone I can easily see to it that they can't do any real damage here in Washington. But there is the press. I need to be sure that nobody uses the newspapers to mount some sort of campaign or enquiry. I need a bully-boy to lay his stick about and make sure the main newspaper owners fall in line to a man. Do you understand, Daniel?'

Webster understood. The question he asked himself was, could it be done?

'How do you suggest ...'

'Oh I don't, Daniel. I suggest nothing and want to know nothing. I just want it done, done by you and done now. There's a man already here waiting to talk to you. You'll find him helpful in this matter, very helpful. His name is Jeremiah Jones. You won't be familiar with the name, I know, but talk to him anyway.'

'Who is he?'

'Right now he's no one. But he was the comptroller of the Fund of Foreign Intercourse under President Polk. He's already aware of what is needed. Let him advise you. I will approve the use of any money needed from the Contingent Fund and see that it is available to you. You're a well-connected man, respected, a gifted talker; organise a bit of persuasion. And if persuasion won't work put the fear of God into any newspaper that tries to raise the idea that Taylor died of anything except natural causes. I can hold the official announcement of his death until late tomorrow. That will give you two or three days.'

'That's very little time.'

'Yes, isn't it? But don't they say the very best men do their best work under pressure? And I'm sure you consider yourself one of the very best men, Daniel, so I expect this thing to be done.'

10

'But why involve this Jones? Why not use the present comptroller?'

'Dammit, Webster, I need a willing and compliant secretary of state, not one who questions my every decision. Make up your mind whether you want the job or not, and make it up now, this instant. I've no more time to spend on you.'

Daniel Webster disliked the position in which he found himself. He wanted to tell this clown of a man to go to hell. But he also wanted, nay, needed, to be secretary of state. The impassioned speech given in March in support of the fugitive slave law had lost him all of his Northern support and forced his resignation from the Senate. As a result, his finances, never robust given his tastes and lifestyle, were in a more than usually parlous state. Unless he did something to retrieve his fortunes he faced the very real prospect of bankruptcy. When he spoke it was almost humbly.

'I will do my best.'

'Good. You've made the right decision. And when I see that all our newspapers print the same story, that President Taylor died from whatever the doctors finally choose to call it, I shall announce your appointment. Now, Daniel, go and get it done.' Webster was about to leave. 'Oh, and when you meet with Jones, tell him I'm thinking of reviving the Polk Plan.'

'The Polk Plan?'

'Just that. He'll know what I mean and, when you're secretary, so shall you, Daniel,' the smile returned, 'so shall you.'

President Fillmore pulled some papers to him and Webster, realising he had been dismissed, went to the door where he paused to look back. The Yellow Oval Room was now filling with early morning sunlight and the gas flames had almost become redundant. Daniel Webster gave a brief, unflattering thought to the mysterious ways of divine providence. Today, in God's good time, there would be a new president of the Union, this stranger sitting at the desk, ignoring him. He took hold of the door handle and quietly let himself out.

Chapter Two

The New Knickerbocker Theatre, 37-39 Bowery, New York City.

July 11th, 7.30 p.m.

A single word was sent soaring into the lofty gloom.

'Friends.'

It was followed by a dramatic pause. Then with a voice full of emotion, two more words followed.

'My friends.'

And at once stamping, wild cheering, and waving of hats burst forth welcoming the third, final, and most important orator of the evening's programme.

Having spoken his first three words the orator now let his gaze sweep the crowd, packed tightly on the plain, tiered benches which surrounded the sawdust-covered floor of the amphitheatre. He stood, lit up by limelight flares, on the makeshift stage at one end of what, on other nights, was usually a circus ring. Having waited a moment to savour his welcome, he held up his arms dramatically and the audience, dutiful to his actions, fell silent and waited with eager anticipation.

'My good friends all.'

The lime-lit figure paused with one hand raised to show that no more cheering was, for the moment necessary. Once more he looked around the ill-lit seating of the great, but rather shabby interior of the New Knickerbocker Theatre. This crowd had come together from many parts of New York to hear him speak, to receive his message. They would not be disappointed. He lowered his hand.

There was an almost tangible thrill of anticipation.

'It is a notorious fact that the monarchs of Europe and the pope of Rome are at this very moment plotting our destruction and threatening the extinction of our political, civil, and religious institutions.' The figure paused and this time the crowd, realising it had received its cue, reacted with more wild cries and shouts. The figure raised a hand and the noise once again subsided. 'And we have the best reasons for believing that this horrible corruption has found its way into our executive chamber and that venerable place of government is already tainted with the infectious venom of Catholicism.'

As he uttered these words the speaker held up his hand and slowly closed his fingers into a fist as if to show how the very heart of the US government had been gripped by this poison of the pope in Rome. The crowd, well rehearsed by the previous two speakers, responded with renewed cries, angry jeers, boos, hoots, and much stamping of feet. Any nervous soul in the audience might well, at this point, have been forced to give serious consideration to the safety and solidity of the boardings supporting the benches on which the crowd acted out its part.

The orator held up his arms once again and the mob fell silent.

'The pope has recently sent his ambassador of state to this country on a secret commission.'

Now there came a necessary pause, for the speaker moved slightly to one side and adopted a supercilious air by throwing back his head, placing his hands on his hips, and sticking his elbows out. He was now not the orator, but taking the part of some opponent to this last statement. In this new character turned to the audience and, in an offensive and sneering tone, addressed them.

'And *how,* pray, are we supposed to know of this secret commission?'

Moving back, adopting a statesman-like stance, he once

14

more became the orator. His hands held the lapels of his coat, partly in the manner of an attorney addressing a jury and partly as an elder might rebuke the people. Thus clearly instructed the crowd knew that he was once again his own honest self.

He looked at the space he had vacated and dismissed his imaginary opponent's question with an angry frown and a gesture of contempt.

'Never mind, it is sufficient that it is known.'

He moved back and resumed the arrogant pose of the opponent. There was an audible low gasp.

Did this opponent truly dare to return and attack once more? Surely such pride, such arrogance, were incredible in the face of such honesty and nobility.

The sneering voice assumed by the speaker confirmed that it was.

'If the secret is known, then pray, how can it be seen?'

With a few steps and a change of pose the speaker was himself again, proud and confident with the final, demolishing answer ready.

'Why, anyone with open eyes can see the truth of what I say.' His arms swept the arena. 'Look around you, see the boldness of the Catholic Church throughout the United States. Its minions, minions of the pope, boldly insulting our senators, reprimanding our statesmen, propagating the adulterous union of Church and State, abusing with foul calumny all governments but Catholic, and spewing out the bitterest execrations on all Protestantism.' He stopped and, moving slightly, stood with legs wide apart straddling the space of both characters. Now he was the conquering hero, the nation's saviour, and his opponent lay, albeit invisible to all except himself, vanquished beneath his feet. The orator stood defiant, with his chin up, his head back and his fists thrust hard onto his hips, bestriding scene of the recent, mighty struggle. He was victorious and unconquerable.

The crowd rose and a great and prolonged howl filled the air.

One young man standing like the rest of the all-male audience and clapping wildly, turned excitedly to his neighbour who, strangely, had remained seated with his hands inactive.

'Isn't he great, Matthew?'

The young man beside him looked around at the standing, stamping, waving, cheering throng.

'Breathtaking. Truly unbelievable.'

But though his words fitted the occasion, his manner of speaking them suggested that he was distinctly less enthusiastic in the giving of his answer than had been his friend in the asking the question.

The speaker raised and lowered his arms several times. At this signal the noise diminished and the audience subsided. The young man sat down and looked at his friend doubtfully for a second. The words, he felt, were right, but there was something, he wasn't sure what, lacking in the manner of their speaking.

The colossus of the platform raised and lowered his arms one final time and silence slowly fell. The young man turned again to listen to the speaker.

'Catholics in the United States receive from abroad more than $200,000 annually for the propagation of their creed. Add to this the vast revenues collected here ...'

The young man's friend, Matthew, took his watch from his waistcoat pocket, looked at it, put it away, and nudged the young man with his elbow. His friend turned.

'What is it?'

'I must go. I have an appointment.'

'But he'll be speaking for at least another hour.'

Matthew tried to look disappointed.

'I guess so, but it's a story. I have to follow it up. You know how it is in my line of work.'

His friend shrugged. He wasn't a journalist himself but

he understood. A story was a story.

'Well, go if you must.' As Matthew rose his friend grabbed the sleeve of his coat and held him. 'But say you're glad you came. Tell me you've had your eyes opened tonight.'

Matthew found that this time he was able to answer his friend's question with total conviction.

'John, I can honestly say that tonight I have indeed had my eyes well and truly opened.'

A voice came from the bench behind them.

'Stay or go, friend, but don't stand there blocking my view.'

His friend let go of the sleeve and Matthew shuffled his way passed the men on the bench to the aisle, headed off up towards the exit and made his way to the front doors of the theatre.

Outside the summer evening was pleasantly warm and the Bowery was looking its best. Elegant, well-proportioned terraces of late eighteenth-century buildings rose up above sidewalks which, burnished by a million boots, had taken on an almost polished appearance. Matthew stood for a moment at the top of the stone stairs that led down to the street. Along the dry, hard-baked dirt of the broad thoroughfare some of the more affluent citizens were driving in their carriages, taking the evening air. Young ladies in bonnets with fluttering ribbons, wearing dresses of brightly coloured silks and satins, sat with parasols still open even though the sun was now well below the rooftops. Beside these dainty demoiselles sat dashing young gentlemen in shining top hats, sporting fashionable whiskers which, eschewing the upper lip, met under the chin.

Wide, soft shirt collars, it seems, are being worn open and turned down this year and fashion also dictates that the coats worn by these young Lochinvars are of many colours, greens, blues, browns, nankeen, and even, by some of the bolder bloods, wide stripes.

Most of these younger folk favour sprightly, two-wheeled gigs pulled by a single horse. The older generation, of whom there is also a goodly number, favour the more solid four-wheeled phaetons often pulled by handsome matched pairs. The gentlemen of these carriages still wear tight neckerchiefs with their stiff collars high. They also prefer more subdued colours for their jackets and their coats are mostly black, brown, or dark blue. But the ladies, even those admitting to thirty-five in society but, dare one say it, will not see forty again, rival their daughters in an exuberance of bright colours, flowing ribbons, and dancing tassels.

All, young and old alike, travel with the hoods of their carriages dropped to allow their occupants to enjoy the warm evening air and in taking their own pleasure give pleasure in turn to the many loungers and pedestrians who, like Matthew, gaze upon the scene, all enjoying the end of a fine Manhattan summer day.

Across the thoroughfare from the New Knickerbocker stands another palace of entertainment, the more prestigious and considerably more successful Bowery Theatre, a monumental building in the ancient-Greek style although now with a flat roof consequent on its partial destruction by fire and rebuilding five years previously. It has, however, retained the six great Doric columns at its entrance as befits such a temple of art. Still imposing though the Bowery Theatre undoubtedly is, and still successful, one has to admit it has come down somewhat from the high point of its glory days when it could claim rivalry with that most prestigious emporium of high-culture for the affluent, the Park Theatre.

These days the Bowery audiences are no longer so exclusive, being drawn predominantly not from the upper classes but rather from the more successful and upwardly mobile of the Irish immigrant community. Despite this, the noble Bowery Theatre stands as a constant reminder to the New Knickerbocker, if one were needed, of its own varied history and precarious present and uncertain future. The Bowery looks across at the New Knickerbocker, sometime theatre, sometime menagerie, sometime, alas, home of low, black-faced minstrel shows, and seems to say condescendingly, "there it stands, ladies and gentlemen, not much perhaps, but nonetheless a humble element in the hierarchy of art and entertainment that is Manhattan's Theatre-land".

Matthew looked across the road admiringly, drawing his own private comparisons between what he had just sampled and what the crowds pouring into the Bowery Theatre would soon enjoy. As he stood, looking, thinking, and breathing the sweet air, one of the many lumbering, horse-drawn omnibuses travelling on the double sets of rails down the middle of the road came to a stop. It was crowded, even the upper deck filled. He watched it empty its cargo of pleasure-seekers who made their way to join the pedestrians flocking past the great columns and into the Bowery Theatre's doors. From the numbers going in Matthew deduced that Hamblin had scored another success with his latest Dauber musical, *Azael, The Prodigal*. Not so surprising, he thought, when one remembered that he had brought in John Gilbert to play the lead, as his posters had trumpeted across Manhattan for some weeks, "Without Regard for Expense".

On this side of the roadway standing on the sidewalk at the foot of the Knickerbocker steps was a large group of loungers. Like Matthew they were young men in their late teens and early twenties. Their manner of dress at once showed them to have originated not from the immediate locality but rather from a nearby neighbourhood of more dubious social standing.

Their costume varied from light, linen jackets of a somewhat soiled appearance to – despite the warmth of the

19

weather – long overcoats. But all wore tall, black, stove-pipe hats in various states of repair.

One of this group turned to Matthew as he came down the steps and stopped him by the simple but effective procedure of placing his hand flat on Matthew's chest.

'Leaving early, friend?' The inquisitor dropped his arm and stood back as if to get a better look and his manner of address, when he continued, was mildly censorious. 'What's the matter? Ain't you enjoying yourself? Ain't you moved to your soul by what you hear in there?' Now a certain menace entered his tone. 'Or perhaps it's that you find yourself disagreeing with what's being said?'

At this question some of the others in the group, all of whom had been watching the crowds make their way into the Bowery Theatre, turned their attention to Matthew. These young men had all the hallmarks of thugs and rowdies looking to have the sort of night out which would send respectable folk hurrying off the streets. They were not a pretty sight, nor friendly, but they *were* impressive, and Matthew, born and brought up in Manhattan, had no trouble in recognising these toughs as members of that most notorious New York Gang, the Bowery Boys.

Another of the group took up the questioning nodding to the crowds across the road.

'Maybe you'd like to be over there with that Irish scum, hey? Maybe you'd like to go and breathe the poison of their Popish air instead of the clean, free air of America, hey, friend?'

Now Matthew was no coward, at least he didn't think of himself as one, but neither did he consider himself a fool. Trouble was obviously brewing. The Bowery Boys had come because the Order of the Star Spangled Banner, who had organised the meeting, intended that a substantial part of the night's business would be transacted later, after the meeting had ended. It would take place in the open-air, in those streets of the Bowery District which were now

20

Irish-immigrant enclaves. These young men were looking for trouble and Matthew had no doubt at all they would find it. When the final speaker of the Order of the Star Spangled Banner finally orated himself to a close the words would cease, but thereafter the action would soon begin. The Bowery Boys' Irish counterparts, the Dead Rabbits, would be on the streets to accommodate these thugs with all the trouble they wanted or could handle. Matthew's aim in leaving early was to ensure that he would be safely in his lodgings well before the main fun and games of the evening got underway. That was still his aim.

The crowd of aggressive faces looked at him. It was time to say something.

'Gentlemen ...' that got a laugh, 'I have been privileged tonight to hear something I would never have thought to hear spoken out loud in this our city, which I regard as the jewel in the crown of this land of the free.' The thugs looked at him doubtfully. It all sounded grand enough, mighty grand. But what, exactly, did it mean? Matthew pressed on. 'Sentiments have been expressed tonight, brave sentiments, great sentiments, and, I have no doubt, sentiments that will lead to action.'

That got a response.

'By hell they will.'

Matthew, encouraged, felt he was getting to grips with his audience.

'When a man can stand up in public and say words such as those as I have heard tonight, then I know, nay, I am certain, that America must and will listen.'

One of the thugs took off and waved his stove-pipe hat.

'Hallelujah, friend. You just spoke a mouthful.'

Another stepped forward and slapped Matthew on the back, smiling.

'Well said, brother. But if those words spoke in there are so mighty powerful, how come you're leaving early?'

21

'Alas, an appointment. As a journalist on one of the great organs of news here in …'

Another surly individual whose face looked as if it had been rearranged more than once by inexpert hands pushed himself forward.

'What the hell you talking about, fella?'

The back-slapper intervened.

'He's a reporter, Sam. A newspaperman.'

The inquisitive Sam accepted the explanation, but only with reluctance. He'd come for trouble not polite conversation and he was getting impatient.

'Well why didn't he say so?'

The back-slapper edged between Sam and Matthew. No one wanted things to get started too early, with the wrong people and in the wrong place.

'What paper, brother?'

'The *New York Herald*.'

As Matthew suspected the name thawed any last remaining suspicion. True, the truculent Sam seemed disappointed rather than pleased that Matthew had indeed turned out to be a genuine friend, but even he went so far as to raise a sketchy smile.

The back-slapper continued.

'Then stick around, friend. There'll be plenty to report hereabouts tonight.'

'Yes, indeed, brother, plenty. Blood and mayhem, just as much as your paper likes.'

'Unfortunately I have an appointment.'

One of the thugs who had stood silently a little distance off spoke.

'Let him be on his way, boys. The man says he has an appointment.' He cast his eyes over Matthew who, watching the eyes, felt as if he were being marked down as prey by some dangerous beast. 'And he don't look the sort who goes in for our kind of entertainment.' The gang separated to make a space for Matthew to leave. 'On your way, friend.'

Matthew touched his hat to the man who had just spoken.

'Thank you, sir. I'll wish you and all the rest of your friends good evening.'

The man's mouth formed a smile, if anything more chilling than his gaze. A dangerous animal indeed.

'Do so, friend, for a good evening it will be. Aye, a good evening indeed, eh lads?'

This question evoked much laughter and mutual back-slapping among the thugs and Matthew took the opportunity to be on his way and walked quickly down the street.

Sam came and stood by the man who had just spoken.

'What do you make of him, Bill?'

Butcher Bill, for it was none other than the leader of the Bowery Boys himself, looked at the back of the retreating Matthew.

'I smell green shit, Sam.'

'Damn my eyes, I thought so. I smelled it myself.'

'And as to what I'd make of him? How about a cadaver? That's what I'd make of him.' And Sam, as fond as the next man of a well-made joke, laughed. 'But I ain't got neither the time or the inclination tonight. Tonight the Order of the Star Spangled Banner has brought free American air back to this Irish midden and I guess the rats who like to live in shit will come a-scurrying out when they get a sniff of that free air.'

Sam gave him a big grin.

'They will, Bill, and when they do we'll be happy to oblige.'

'And our reporter friend's newspaper will have its story, how a fine neighbourhood is now a place of blood and violence, where free Americans fear to walk, and Catholic scum ...' and here he paused for a moment remembering, '... where the pope's minions plot the destruction and threaten the extinction of our political, civil, and religious institutions.'

And the thugs, to a man, burst out laughing and took to waving their stove-pipe hats wildly in the air.

On the other side of the road many of the people making their way to the Bowery Theatre looked across apprehensively at the rowdy gang. One middle-aged couple, respectably dressed, he in check trousers, cut-away coat, and shiny top hat, she in bonnet, shawl, and wide skirts, stopped.

The husband turned to his wife.

'Come, Philomena, we'll give the show a miss tonight. We'll go home now.'

'But, Eamon, we've paid for the tickets.'

'So we have, dear. But I suddenly find the price of the show has become more than I'd be prepared to pay.'

His wife looked across at the Bowery Boys and, considering the street where she and her husband lived and the route home they would have to walk after the show, suddenly she found that she agreed with her husband. The price of attending the show, John Gilbert or no John Gilbert, was indeed more than she cared to pay. Taking her husband's arm they turned and hurried back the way they had just come.

Chapter Three

Who were these thugs, these rowdies, these dangerous Bowery Boys and their sworn enemies, the Dead Rabbits? They were the product of New York's worst district, Manhattan, and both they and their philosophies were the spawn of its grinding poverty.

But New York was more than Manhattan's slums, it was a city on the move, a hungry city feeding on the seemingly endless stream of humanity that poured into it. Thanks to the Erie Canal it had already replaced Boston as America's premier East Coast port. Yet even with so much already gained it wanted more. New York was still as ambitious as it was successful and equally heartless, for with greater prosperity came greater demands. It wanted a bigger, better harbour, new roads, taller buildings, new industries. It wanted it all. From far and wide they came, the workers who were looking to claim their a share of New York's ever-increasing wealth, and once arrived they slaved for a pittance to see that New York, their city, got all that it wanted.

But where was this ever-growing mass of labour to live? It lived, if you can call it living, packed together in conditions unfit for animals awaiting slaughter. They flowed into those parts of the city whose use and value had diminished almost to nothing. Decrepit and defunct premises which should have been torn down or left to fall down of their own volition were converted into dwellings. Old Coulthard's Brewery, ruinous and derelict from before the turn of the century, found a new lease of life when it was turned into a warren-like habitation by one of the city's many successful entrepreneurs. By 1850 Colthard's Brewery, to the amazement of everyone including its developers, not only still stood, but had even achieved some small fame as the most notorious tenement in that most notorious Manhattan district, Five Points.

And did these slums in any way put a drag on the money-making machine that was New York? Not at all. The city was not short of clever men who had found that nothing made money quite as easily as poverty and they set about turning rotting dereliction into human habitation. With what result? The masses of newly arrived poor found themselves competing for dwellings in the worst slums with those born and bred New Yorkers who had been left at the bottom of the social and financial ladder.

To add to the regular outbreaks of cholera, yellow fever, widespread consumption, and a horrific infant mortality rate, the people of the Manhattan slums added violence and vice to the daily round of degradation. The slums bred in equal parts despair and anger. Mostly the slum dwellers preyed on one another, they vented their frustrations and their bitterness on any neighbours who could be identified as different. And the newcomers were nothing if not different. They spoke differently, dressed differently, ate differently, and, worst of all, worshipped differently. And out of this lethal mix of inhuman poverty, violent hate and religious intolerance, the gangs of New York were born.

And they prospered. They became famous as thieves and thugs. But villainy, the simple villainy of violence and vice, has its limitations and the leaders of the gangs, though uneducated, were not unintelligent. They saw that the gangs could be of use to those whose villainy was considerably more sophisticated and infinitely more rewarding, men like Weed. These vicious, daring young men, dead to all morals except money and their own animal code, had achieved an important social purpose. They had become the street soldiers of political money.

As the creeping tide of humanity spread out from

Manhattan, the rich stayed well ahead of its advance. They sold their neighbourhoods to the developers to be adapted to accommodate the successful second and third generation immigrant who wanted to turn their backs on squalor. The rich moved away and found some new, pleasant, and unspoiled spot in the countryside, somewhere like Greenwich Village. Here they made their homes in the clean, fresh, uncontaminated air. And when, eventually, restless New York neared they sold again and moved on. In due season Greenwich Village was swallowed, developed, and became yet another high-rise, tight-packed, respectable middle-class urban district.

It was among the most wealthy of New York society that the gangs found their sponsors, for it was among the serious money that political ambition flourished. In the great houses on fine avenues and in peaceful squares, safe from Manhattan's slums, lived the men who vied with one another to control the growing city. They had money and words in plenty at their disposal. When they made their fine speeches, their newspapers printed them, and the people read the newspapers.

But New York was no European monarchy, nor had it any time for despots. It was the foremost city in the Land of the Free and here the rule of God and democracy was supreme. That being so, each candidate for high city office needed votes and the gangs knew all about that great democratic principle: One Man, One Vote. Gang members could, when well marshalled by leaders like Butcher Bill, vote as one man up to twenty times in a single day. Not only that, they could, when in a group of several men, frustrate the democratic ambitions of their patrons' adversaries by wreaking violence on their opponent's voters. Any City Hall election day was a day of frantic activity for the gangs, a day of voting, violence and money.

So it was that the slums poured out their wealth, both in

rents and choice City-Hall appointments, into the already well-filled pockets of New York's politic bosses and their friends.

And what of New York's great organs of free speech, the newspapers? Did they blazen forth the iniquity of the slums? Did they point the finger, fearlessly, to where the blame lay for the stinking mess that pock-marked so much of Manhattan. Alas, the owners of New York's newspapers were too busy riding the tide of wealth and success to let their publications criticize what lay behind so much of it. The newspapers took sides with the various parties and did their utmost to show how their candidates were saints and heroes, while their opponents' candidates were devils and the foes of humanity.

The *New York Herald*, for instance, backed groups such as The Order of The Star Spangled Banner, one of many secret societies who stood four-square behind the supremacy of native, Protestant, white Americans. The *Herald* was a pipeline of propaganda for those who blamed all ills on those immigrants who happened to be Catholic. Did they not fill the slums? Were they not subservient to the pope in Rome? Were they not idolatrous? Did they not undercut wages and take the bread from the mouths of poor white Protestant New Yorkers? Did they not, by violent and unlawful means, infest City Hall with corrupt placemen? Of course they did, it was plain for everyone to see.

And from all of this was born the Bowery Boys, nurtured from birth on brutishness and force-fed on hate. They turned on the newcomers whom, they had allowed themselves to be convinced, were intent on stealing their city and frustrating the God-given supremacy of white, Protestant Americans.

And the young men of the Irish immigrant community responded in kind. Among them arose the Dead Rabbits, so named by their leader, Daniel Cassidy. Dead, slang for great, and rabbit from, Ráibéad, a man to be feared, thus, Great Men to be Feared. So it was that the gangs of New York had arisen, each nurtured by that same clever money which had grown rich on developing the slums from which the awful violence came.

And the rich? The rich prospered as the rich always do. But they were not without their own rivalries and antagonisms. Old Protestant money vied with new Catholic money, but all of it was clever money. That being so, it fought for power by fair means through the newspapers, and by foul through the gangs. The gangs became the armies in the proxy-wars fought in the foul places that fair means couldn't or wouldn't go.

And no doubt Jesus, like many a Protestant and Catholic mother, looked on and wept.

Chapter Four

Matthew hurried away down the Bowery, leaving the Knickerbocker Theatre to the Order of the Star Spangled Banner and the Bowery Boys to their lounging and anticipation of a jolly evening of mayhem with their Dead Rabbit counterparts. He wanted to get back to his lodgings and settle down for the evening. If a street battle was to be fought in earnest that night some other intrepid reporter would have to cover it. He wanted to be safe and sound inside.

Matthew was a respectable young man who lodged at a respectable address and had a respectable, though minor, position on the *New York Herald* newspaper. And if he was somewhat prosaic, what of that? A great city's real wealth is truly built on the Matthews of this world, not the likes of Bill the Butcher. Matthew was, as had been suspected by Bill, second-generation Irish, but his family had climbed from the slums long ago and now numbered themselves among the lower middle class. Matthew had never needed or wanted to acquire the skills or wisdom of the slums. His learning had come from books and teachers. He was an educated young man, the pride of his parents, and more than a little proud of himself.

Matthew's father, Daniel, had been one of three brothers brought up on a small farm in the west of Ireland. It was little more than a subsistence life and could never support more than one of the sons if they married and Patrick, the eldest, took precedence of course. The farm would one day be his so he was seen by local mothers as a good catch. Sean, the middle brother, accepted his lot, resigned himself to celibacy, and would stay on working for his elder brother. Daniel, the youngest, was a handsome but somewhat wild, spoiled youth who left tomorrow's problems to tomorrow and got on with today's enjoyment today in those hours he wasn't working. His life of freedom and fun, however, stopped dead when he got a local girl into trouble and, when the trouble began to show and could no longer be hidden, the two sets of parents arranged for the nuptials to take place. It was of necessity a quiet affair and the couple returned from church having received the sacrament of marriage and a scalding sermon from the parish priest. After the wedding breakfast at Daniel's home his father had taken him to one side.

'You can stay on here for a while until I can get passage for you both to America. I can ill afford it but I'll see if I can borrow the money. There's nothing here for you now that you have a wife and child on the way and when it's all arranged I'm afraid it's the Prodigal you'll have to play, only I doubt I'll ever set eyes on you again. I hear they're building a monstrous great canal over in New York and there's work a-plenty for strong men. Go to the New World, son, and if it's God's will you'll land on your feet. But if you do, don't make the same mistakes as the Bible chap. Stay away from drink and loose women. You've had your fun here, now you must settle and make some sort of life for you and your family. Look after your wife, work hard, and make something of yourself. You'll be a father soon enough so put your wild ways behind you and may God go with you, all three of you.'

So it was that Daniel O'Hanlon and his young new wife, Betty, made their way on foot to Cobh Harbour in County Cork and from there took ship to America. The boat was already almost full on arrival at Cobh which was the last embarkation point before the Atlantic crossing. From across Europe thousands were making their way to the Promised Land, some fleeing hunger, oppression, and violence, some seeking new opportunities, some running away from the law, and not a few trying to run away from themselves, but all in search of a new life. Many of these huddled masses knew their European homelands only as a place of starvation and injustice and had given up all hope that somehow it might change. For them America was seen as a land where they could realise dreams of freedom and equality.

And, for the vast majority who crossed the Atlantic and poured into the poisonous slums and tenements of New York, the dream would to some extent come true. They would escape the nightmare and find it possible to dream, if not for themselves, then for their children.

And they worked, my God how they worked. They sweated from dawn to dusk on building sites, on docks, in cellars, sheds, and factories in all manner of buildings not a few of which any self-respecting farmer would have rejected as unfit for his beasts, let alone human beings. But the work paid. To the respectable middle and working classes of New York it may have been savage exploitation and the wages a disgrace, but not to the newcomers. So many of these immigrants had grown up in a harder, more unforgiving poverty, and had seen more than hunger; they had seen starvation. Regular wages, a home to live in, and being part of a community allowed them to live, eat, and bring up their children: those who survived the first cruel years.

To decent folk these people and the way they lived brought shame to their great city. But even the most outraged of the decent folk accepted that they were an essential part of the lifeblood of their cramped, crowded bustling, ever-growing city, so they lived with it. But nobody could make them like it.

For themselves, all the newcomers cared about was that they were free and that their children might reap in laughter what so many of them were sowing in tears. And that was enough.

What kept many of them going were the neighbourhoods: the Italian, the German, the Irish, the Jewish. Here whole communities spoke the same language, ate the same foods, shared the same customs, followed the same religions, and harboured the same bigotries and superstitions. These neighbourhoods might have more than their share of disease, violence, crime, and debauchery, but they also had more than their fair share of that most adhesive of social attributes – familiarity.

And the children of these immigrants, did they understand how much their lives in New York had cost their parents? Alas, to children parents are always a mystery, people with no past, no individual history, and no future. They are simply parents, an ever-present fact of life. The new generation, those born in New York and never knowing what had driven their parents into exile, grew up and began to make their own world of the neighbourhoods.

Daniel's journey from the family farm to Cobh had to be made slowly because of Betty's condition and by the time the ship arrived Betty was heavily pregnant and near her time. Daniel O'Hanlon became a father only a week into the voyage. Experienced women, who had children of their own and had attended at deliveries, gathered round her in her labours while the men-folk stood away talking quietly and smoking pipes until the new life was brought out to them, swaddled and crying.

Daniel was slapped on the back and heartily congratulated on his success. It was as if he, rather than his wife and her attendants, had done something wonderful. Daniel accepted their congratulations and praise and passed round the small cigars he had brought with him against the day of the happy event. That night, the first night of new birth on the voyage, the music began and the national costumes came out and all was joy and laughter while Betty O'Hanlon, a proud new mother, lay and crooned over her new son, little Daniel.

On the quay at Cobh Harbour Daniel had met another man from the same county as himself who also had a pregnant wife, and they and their wives had fallen into a friendship while awaiting the boat and in the first week of the journey.

Eugene Oliver Bigane – Gene Bigane, or Big Gene as he was soon to become known – was a man with a vision. He was almost six feet tall and of powerful build. But he was not only possessed of bodily strength and stone fists but brains and ambition too. On arrival in New York, he confided to Daniel, he did not intend to break his own back in physical labour but to be a provider of labour. He would let others break their backs while he made the money. He wanted to be a gang-master.

But life on the voyage started badly for the Biganes. When, three weeks out, his wife Nora's time came, the delivery was long and difficult and the child died after two days. For a time Eugene Bigane walked the crowded deck with his friend, Daniel. He was worried for the health and even the sanity of his young wife. But Betty O'Hanlon, herself so recently a mother, became for the distressed, grieving woman a tower of strength. Both husbands, big strong, fearless men, stood around for days in each other's company, helpless as small children as their women tried to come to terms with what had happened. By the end of the journey Nora Bigane had recovered and was as much a mother to little Danny as was his real mother, and she and Betty O'Hanlon were firm friends.

Eugene Bigane had a contact in the New York construction industry: a cousin who had a hardware shop which supplied, among other things, building materials and tools to jobbing workmen and the general public. This cousin was currently a single man, though walking out regularly with the widow of an omnibus driver who, lunching too well one day from a flask he carried, somehow managed the difficult feat of falling under the wheels of his own vehicle. This man had been a neighbour of Eugene's cousin and his fatal thirst had left a widow forced to fend not only for herself but two young daughters. The widow, a sensible and practical woman, had at once set about looking around for a suitable and available replacement breadwinner and settled on Eugene's cousin.

Her first move was to put it about in the neighbourhood that Eugene's cousin was, and always had been, sweet on her. The women of the neighbourhood immediately grasped what was afoot and began, as an act of sisterly solidarity, to badger their menfolk. Eugene's cousin liked a pipe and a glass of beer at the end of the day and it was his habit to visit a quiet local tavern before returning home for a simple supper and bed. One evening a small but determined delegation of his male neighbours visited him as he sat, alone as usual, in the tavern, and put it to him directly. He had made his intentions clear when the woman's husband was alive, had he not? He had flirted with a respectable married woman, had he not? Well then, now she was available he would do the right thing, would he not? Eugene's cousin was stunned at this news of his philandering, but he was also acutely aware of the thews and sinews of the men who brought him the news of it. They were all fine physical specimens, hard-working, labouring men. Faced with a mad bull none of them would have quailed and probably felled it with a blow. But nagging wives were a different matter. They had been given a choice: see the widow righted or face scorn and derision from their own womenfolk. It was no contest. Eugene's cousin, a mild and retiring man by nature, accepted his fate and the following Sunday after morning Mass asked the widow if he might accompany her and her daughters home. The widow demurely accepted. The wives nodded to each other and their menfolk stood and watched as the victim began the first of what was to be many, many walks.

Eugene's cousin was no hero, but neither was he a poltroon. Between walking out and the awful state of confirmed matrimony there was a wide margin and, a clever man in business, he intended to use his brains to see if the final catastrophe might yet be delayed or even, God willing, averted.

Thus was the state of things when Eugene Bigane and Daniel O'Hanlon with their respective wives arrived from Ireland. To Eugene's cousin it seemed like a miracle. At the eleventh hour when all seemed lost God had stepped in and saved him. Above the cousin's shop there were two rooms which, as the widow had often pointed out to him, would accommodate them and the girls nicely. As soon as Eugene arrived his cousin proposed that he and Daniel, together with their wives and Daniel's child, should take up residence. Being still a single man, though walking out, he could make do with a truckle bed in the store room at the back of the shop. Eugene and Daniel were as amazed as they were grateful for this almost oriental hospitality.

'Eugene,' said his cousin once everything was arranged, 'Your mother was my elder brother's half-sister by marriage. You and this friend of yours are from the same beloved county as my second cousin Desmond O'Hare who became a priest. How could any Irishman do less and still call himself a Catholic?'

Of course put like that what could one say? That very evening, the evening of their first day in America, Eugene Bigane and his wife moved into one room and Daniel O'Hanlon and his wife and child moved into the other, and the cousin made up his bed in the back store room. The following day the news quickly spread. The cousin had worked it, he could walk out with the widow in safety so long as he had his guests occupying his house.

'When they go, my dear, we might be able to think of

37

ourselves. But the calls of family are, I'm sure you will agree, paramount. I doubt they'll stay more than a year or two. Three at the most. Will you wait for me?'

The women gave it up. He had played a master-stroke. The widow would have to sit it out or look elsewhere. The following Sunday she walked home alone with her daughters. Three weeks later she accepted the company of a widower of sixty with three grown-up sons, one still at home who was an idiot. It was all over. The men looked at each other with a wild surmise and began to treat the mousy, bespectacled shop-keeper with a new respect. Muscles and broad shoulders were all very well but when push came to shove and you had a pistol to your head, brains told every time.

The cousin's shop was not in a good district, it served a neighbourhood not far from Five Points, that most vicious and evil of all the slum neighbourhoods, but for Eugene and Nora as for Daniel and Betty and their baby it was a roof and privacy and they accepted it gratefully.

Eugene Oliver Bigane was a dynamic and impatient man and at once set about to cut out a place for himself in the New York's casual labour-supply market. This required him to use his fists and boots as often as his undoubted business skills. Other men were already well established in the trade who resented this interloper and made their disapproval felt. But Big Gene, with Dan O'Hanlon's help, responded so much in kind that negotiations eventually replaced violence and Mr Eugene Oliver Bigane was admitted to that small lucrative circle of entrepreneurs who controlled the supply of newly arrived, Irish, unskilled labour to New York's voracious construction business.

It was not much more than a year before Big Gene moved with his wife into their own house and Daniel, with his wife again heavily pregnant, moved into an apartment further away from Five Points. Eugene's cousin was not sorry to see them go, not least because three months previously the omnibus driver's widow had married her elderly escort and the cousin felt that his time of penance in the back storeroom could not come to an end too quickly. He accepted their thanks and undying friendship, bade them farewell, and moved back to the comfort of one of the upper rooms.

Big Gene expressed his gratitude to Daniel for the help he had given and the danger he had endured by obtaining for him a permanent post that befitted one who had so ably and so bravely assisted him in the establishment of his business. Dan O'Hanlon was a gang foreman on the construction of the Erie Canal.

The years passed for the O'Hanlons, more children arrived, and Daniel's application, honesty, and fairness to those under him made him a valued employee. His wages increased, as did his responsibilities, until they were eventually able to move into a fine terraced house in Bayard Street. It was here that Betty had eventually given birth to her twelfth child, a boy, Matthew Cornelius O'Hanlon who, she swore to herself, would be her last and would, one day, become a true gentleman and a scholar and make her proud.

Chapter Five

The day on which Betty O'Hanlon's dream had come true was Matty's seventeenth birthday, at the party held in his honour. Educated now and spoiled in equal measure, he had announced to his assembled family that he had decided on a career. His education, he told them, had shown him to have a bent towards literature, he had no doubts that he could, and maybe one day would, become a novelist. However, he begged to believe that he was as hard-headed as the next man so he had decided that the career of novelist must wait and the place at which he hung his hat had to be one which paid and, for the right man, paid well. Matthew's family and friends all waited to discover the lucky nominee for his talents. He saw their eagerness and did not keep them waiting any longer. He would become a journalist, and not the least of them. All that remained was for him to select on which of the mighty New York newspapers he would bestow his undoubted talents. Having made the announcement he thought about it for a whole week and finally selected *The Sun*, probably the most serious of the New York papers and, so Matthew thought, best placed to appreciate his intellect and keen insights.

The reply to his letter of application took only two weeks to arrive. *The Sun*, whose slogan was, "It Shines For All", had decided that it could rise and set in New York without the help of Mr Matthew C. O'Hanlon. It was a blow, Matthew admitted it, but the loss, he pointed out to his mother, was theirs. His mother enthusiastically agreed while his father sat quietly smoking a thoughtful pipe.

He liked Matty, he liked listening to his educated way of talking, although what he actually said seemed mostly nonsense to this practical, common-sense working man. But, he often admitted to himself as Matthew held forth on some topic of the day, he had a grand ring to him. Young Matty, he admitted in the privacy of his own mind, was of course a spoilt, coddled fool but, thank God, not the worst of them. Maybe after a few hard knocks and a little experience of real life he might actually make something of himself. He might indeed.

And the knocks soon came. The next two application letters proved no more effective than the first. One came back after three weeks with the curt reply that they were not taking on new staff. From the other there was silence, no response at all. The world of journalism seemed to be saying that it could, after all, do without Matthew C. O'Hanlon. Matthew's mother felt, in the absence of any better motive, that there was a conspiracy against her son. His father said nothing but smoked his pipe and nodded sympathetically. Even when his wife asked him point blank, 'Can't you get someone to help Matty?' Daniel shook his head. He could indeed have asked people for help and undoubtedly help would have been forthcoming. But favours like that came at a high price and Dan O'Hanlon wasn't prepared to pay what would inevitably be demanded of him merely to place his son in some comfortable job. Long ago he had left behind him the methods of Gene Bigane and those like him and had made his way on hard work, fairness, and honesty. There were plenty of well-connected men who would do him a favour, but it would be the men under him, those he was responsible for, who would bear the real cost of the repayment. So Dan gently lied.

'No, Mother, I don't have that kind of pull. I'm still no more than a glorified labouring man.' He turned to his son. 'Sorry, Matty, if you're to succeed in this newspaper business you'll have to do it on your own merits.'

Matthew was half disappointed and half glad. On the

42

one hand he desperately wanted a job with one of the big papers. But on the other hand he wanted to show his parents and the rest of his family that he was now a man in his own right, grown up and independent.

'Thanks, Dad, but I want to do this for myself even if you could have helped.'

And Matthew went up to his room to re-plan his campaign which he now realised would be a longer and more difficult one than he had at first anticipated.

Chapter Six

Up to now Matthew had tried the big, central papers. For his fourth attempt he decided to try somewhere a little further afield, the *Daily Eagle* in Brooklyn. In addition, Matthew changed his style of application. This letter was more humble in that, instead of offering the editor the inestimable prize of his invaluable services, he emphasised his willingness to learn, his long-held enthusiasm for journalism, and his belief that New York City was bound for great things and that he hoped that by being taken on by one of its papers he might, with diligence and effort, work his way up from whatever post he might initially be given to one day be a reporter and be allowed in some small way to chronicle some few aspects of the path of America's most exciting and promising metropolis.

It was, in its own way, as much a sample of his writing style as a letter of application, and in less than a week it drew from the editor Walt Whitman a most encouraging reply. It wasn't a job offer but, the editor explained, that was because he was about to leave the paper and any new appointments would be for his successor to make. But the editor encouraged him to re-apply as soon as the new editor was in place and to try other papers in the meanwhile.

Hugely encouraged Matthew had read the letter to his father and mother. His mother said, sniffily, that it was no more than the truth. His father had nodded and said,

'Keep it up, Matty, I think you've got them on the run.'

Matthew, unable to sit at home with the letter, took it to his oldest brother Dan's house and read it to him.

'What do you think, Dan?'

'I think you should do as he says and have another go.'

'I will. I'll try the *Herald*.'

'The *Herald*? Well, why not? But if you'll take a bit of advice I think you'd have a better chance with them if your name wasn't so Irish. There's plenty in this town who would throw a letter from someone with a name like O'Hanlon straight in the trashcan and spit on it. I'm not saying that's so of everyone, but I'd get a new name just in case. The *Herald*'s a paper that's no friend of the Irish.'

Matthew thought over what Dan had said and decided that it was good advice.

Dan had followed his father into the construction industry and, from what his sisters had told him, had racketed about quite a bit before Jenny Murphy had taken him in hand, straightened out his wild ways, and married him. His sister Eileen, who had stayed at home to look after the house for her parents rather than marry, had told him Dan had never run with the gangs but was a respected street fighter in his young days. She told him how, after an particularly difficult encounter, Dan, bloodied and bruised, had been on his way home when a young woman whom he knew by sight from around the neighbourhood and at Sunday Mass, had called to him from across the street and then come over and looked at him.

'Well, you're a fine sight. If you think I'd let myself walk out with a man who looks like a badly butchered side of beef you're mistaken. Go and get yourself cleaned up, put on a suit and hat, and I'll meet you at the church door at six this evening and you can walk me back to my house.' Then she had walked away only to turn back and say, 'And this will be the last time I want to see you looking like that so make up your mind; it's a street-rough or a gentleman. The choice is yours.'

Dan had arrived home where Eileen had cleaned him up before his mother could see him and he'd told her of the encounter.

'Grab her if you've any sense. She's worth twice and

three times those pretty empty-heads like Kitty McShane you're always flirting with. And I know for a fact she's had offers although God knows why she waited and has chosen you.' Dan had suggested that it was the man who was supposed to do the choosing. Eileen had laughed. 'Dream on, Daniel O'Hanlon, dream on.'

And Dan, after some brief thought, decided that his sister's advice was sound and duly presented himself at the church door at six. When Jenny Murphy arrived, a quarter of an hour late, she looked him up and down.

'God, I could make a better specimen out of a lump of coal and two carrots. But I suppose you'll do. Now you can walk me home.'

And Dan, watched unseen from a distance by his sister Eileen, had done as he was bid.

He had also done as Jenny had told him and become, if not a gentleman, no more a rough-neck. He became a hard-working and respectable husband and, after one year of marriage, a father, and although unlike Matthew he had no education to speak of, he was a man wise in the ways of the world and understood the city as Matthew didn't and probably never would.

So it was that on the letter applying for a post at the *Herald* Matthew's surname had been abbreviated to Halon, and it was as Mr Matthew Halon that he had been invited for an interview by none other than the editor himself.

Chapter Seven

Frederic Hudson, the formidable editor-in-chief of the *New York Herald*, was tall with penetrating eyes, short dark hair, and an imposing walrus moustache. Having greeted Mr Halon and asked him to take a seat, he said he was impressed by his letter of application and asked him if it was his first application to a New York paper. Matthew had not anticipated that the interview would begin with such a question and felt a sense of panic. What to do?

'Yes, the *Herald* was my first choice.'

Mr Hudson nodded.

'Good.'

Then he waited.

Matthew's sense of panic grew further. What was Hudson waiting for? He'd answered the question. He cast about for something else to say when suddenly his sense of being trapped by his own lie passed.

'No.'

'No?'

'No. That last answer wasn't true. I applied to *The Sun* first, then two other papers, and then the *Eagle* in Brooklyn. The truth is, Mr Hudson, I would work for any New York paper that would take me on.'

And he sat and awaited the inevitable dismissal.

Hudson also waited a moment.

'That's fine. Sometimes the bald truth just won't do the business and all you're left with is to bend it. *Herald* newsmen never lie, Mr Halon. But if you have to bend the truth, do it well and with confidence. And if you can't do it well then don't do it at all and stay honest.'

Hudson smiled and Matthew nodded enthusiastically.

'Yes, Mr Hudson.'

'Now why do you want to work on,' here he paused, then smiled, 'any newspaper that would take you on?'

Matthew took a silent deep breath. This was it.

'Newspapers are the future. Not the sort we have now,' and he rapidly added, 'though they're fine, of course, especially the *Herald*.'

Hudson smiled again.

'Of course, especially the *Herald*. Go on.'

Matthew, encouraged, plunged into his topic.

'With the magnetic telegraph developing the way it is people can already send messages over miles in an instant. Soon, the news that everyone reads won't be the letters and articles written by the great and the good and it won't be so local. Look at the way New York papers handled the Mexican War. They set up the New York Associated Press and brought that war right here onto the streets of New York. If that was what the pony express could do then think of what the telegraph will achieve. Why in a few years …'

Frederic Hudson held up a hand and Matthew stopped.

'I know son, I was one of those who set up the Associated Press.'

'Oh, yes, sir, of course. But what I mean is that things have changed and will go on changing and they'll change faster than ever. News will become national, international, and people will read it, well, perhaps not as it happens but damn soon after …'

And here Matthew stopped, realising that in his enthusiasm he had openly cursed.

But Hudson just nodded.

'I'm sure it will. Now, if you join the *Herald* there are a few things you ought to know.'

And the editor-in-chief, in concluding the interview, spelled out for Matthew what the *New York Herald* stood for.

It was pro-American, pro-Protestant, pro-Democrat,

anti-Catholic, and anti-Whig, and it was the owner Mr James Bennett's confirmed view that the role of a mass-circulation newspaper was not to instruct but to startle. Hudson invited Matthew to speak up if he found any or all of these things repugnant. Matthew decided at once that he could sufficiently amend his point of view on religion, politics, the social order, and the role of the press to accommodate Mr James Bennett. True, Mr Hudson had not actually said that the paper was anti-Irish, but Matthew felt that, if not explicit, it was implied, so he decided that, as the editor seemed quite satisfied that his name was indeed Halon, his bending of the truth had been sufficiently well carried through and could therefore stand. He would, from now on, stay Matthew Halon and take service under the banner of that great organ of news and entertainment, the *New York Herald*.

Matthew's parents were not readers of the *Herald*. As a matter of cold fact neither could actually read. Since coming over from Ireland Daniel O'Hanlon had worked hard, made his way, become respectable, and raised a family. All of this he did without being able to read and, having achieved some modest success in his life, he never saw any reason to regret his state nor to remedy it. Matthew's mother had learned as a girl at home how to pray, wash, cook, sew, show proper respect for the clergy, and generally run a house. That, as far as her mother and father were concerned, was all the education any girl needed. And if any lack in her education can be said to have played a significant part in her early life it wasn't an inability to read: that had not been what led her to become pregnant out of wedlock.

Married and a mother at sixteen, building a new home in a new land, a mother again by seventeen, and ten more times in nearly as many years, she found her time fully occupied. As the years passed and blessed with twelve children, seven of whom survived to adulthood, somehow

51

the necessity of learning to read had never climbed sufficiently high on her list of priorities to be begun, never mind accomplished.

But although themselves unschooled and illiterate, both father and mother were fierce believers in education. All of their children received some sort of schooling but it was the youngest, Matthew, who had shone. Matthew was the family's star, the one who would break away from the tyranny of physical toil and make something of himself.

And on the day he came home from his interview with Frederic Hudson and announced that he was now a newspaperman on the *New York Herald* his mother had wept and his father had knocked out his pipe, put it away in his pocket, stood up, and solemnly shaken his son's hand.

Matthew then went to tell his brother Dan about his success and thank him for his sound advice.

Dan was, of course, delighted by Matty's news as they sat in the kitchen drinking tea.

'No thanks needed, Matty. You're the only one of us who's had a proper go at the learning and we all want to see you get on in the world. Besides, maybe changing your name had nothing to do with you getting this chance. You're educated, sharp, and keen. I guess they probably knew a good man when they saw one and would have taken you on whatever your name.'

There Dan paused.

Matthew waited then gently encouraged his brother to say whatever it was he was obviously thinking.

'But?'

'This is an Irish neighbourhood, Matty, and as I've said before the *Herald* is no friend of ours. I don't say they're hand in glove with the likes of the Bowery Boys but they're always boosting the Know Nothing crowd and plenty of that bunch are in the Order of the Star Spangled Banner and they're tight with the Boys. They use them as their own private hooligans. It's just a thought and I don't say it will happen, but if the *Herald* find you're Irish-Catholic there's a good chance they'll bounce your green butt straight out of that fine building of theirs all the way down Broadway, and kick you and it into the East River.'

Matthew, filled with the new acolytes' enthusiasm and loyalty, rejected this slur on his new employers.

'Never. Mr Hudson is a man of honour. They all are at the *Herald*, I'm sure of it.'

But the lie, for lie it had to be considering Matthew knew no one at the *Herald* except Frederic Hudson whom he had met only once, was not well told, nor did it carry conviction, and it obviously failed on Dan.

'Suit yourself, Matty. It's your job not mine.'

Matthew pondered the proposition. Dan's previous assessment had been right. Or had it? He himself had just said that maybe his name had nothing to do with getting the job. This set him thinking. Would he have got the job as O'Hanlon? Were they anti-Irish at the *Herald*? How could he know one way or the other?

'What about this neighbourhood? You think I should move out?'

Dan had always felt protective of his baby brother. Little Matty was not bred for a rough-and-tumble life and calloused hands. He was destined for something better and it was Dan's duty as the eldest to steer him in the right ways of getting it.

'You've a job now, a fine job. You're a newspaperman. Can you walk among your fellows at the *Herald* with your head held high if you're living at home with your mother wiping behind your ears as you leave for work each morning? You're all grown up, Matty, get yourself a new address, new friends, and a new life.'

Matthew walked home thinking about Dan's advice and found it sound. He already had a new name, why not a new address? He thought about this new man he'd suddenly become and he liked it. He was independent now, his own man, a real man, a newspaperman. Newsmen didn't live at home with their parents.

He spoke to his mother straight away, fully expecting and prepared for tears and opposition but, to his surprise, she immediately agreed.

'Get out and get on, Matthew. Get away from all that holds you back. Make a proper life for yourself. It's what me and your father came here for, a better future for ourselves and our children.' Matthew was as pleased as he was amazed. But his mother had not finished. She also had been thinking. 'I'll speak to Nora Bigane tomorrow and arrange a room for you at her boarding house. You'll be comfortable there and I'll feel better knowing Auntie Nora will be looking after you properly. Now I'll off and get you your tea. I have a nice kipper for you.'

'Thank you, Ma.'

Matthew sat down at the table, somewhat deflated. It wasn't what he had planned walking home from Dan's. Not exactly how he saw himself now that he was a hard-nosed newsman. But what else could he say?

Matty's dad sat down and pulled out his pipe. Clearly he understood his youngest son's feelings.

'It's a beginning, Matty, settle for it and maybe after you find your feet you can arrange something more to your own tastes.'

Matthew brightened. He could, couldn't he? The great thing was to make the first move. After that, well, after that he could look around and …

But his thoughts were interrupted by his mother placing a plate on which steamed a pair of kippers.

'Eat up, Matthew, you're a working man now.'

And they all laughed, and none more heartily than Matthew himself.

Chapter Eight

As a matter of simple geography Nora Bigane's boarding house was not so very far away from Matthew's home in Bayard Street. It was one of a terrace of substantial, red-brick, four-storey houses towards that better-class section of Bleecker Street where it crossed 6th Avenue, and neither its location nor its name identified it as an Irish establishment.

Matthew's mother was as good as her word and arrangements were quickly made for him to move to Auntie Nora's. On the day he left home, even though the journey would take him only about twenty to thirty minutes to walk, she wept and his father had knocked out his pipe and once more solemnly shaken his hand. But despite the tears and the solemnity they were both intensely proud. Matthew was an educated man, professional, truly middle class. They had wanted him to do well and he had. Now he would make his way in life and they didn't want to keep him back. If he had to leave home, very well, plenty of others had done as much and gone on longer journeys to more uncertain futures.

His mother's final words at the front door were drawn from the store of wisdom it had taken her almost a lifetime to acquire.

'Keep the faith, son, stay away from loose women, and don't mix with Protestants.'

With much of the street looking on, she had then fallen weeping into the arms of Matthew's unmarried sister.

His father spoke sufficiently loudly for the audience who stood at their doors and windows.

'Remember your Bible, son, especially the story of the Prodigal Son. He took his money and some he spent on gambling, some on drink, and some on women,' then he lowered his voice and moved his head a little closer to Matthew, 'and the rest he wasted.'

Then he smiled, winked, and slipped a silver dollar into his son's hand.

Matthew, a little shocked and disconcerted by this unexpected side to his father, slipped the coin into his pocket and, finding that there was no more to say or do, set off wearing his best overcoat and Sunday hat, carrying in one hand a suitcase of clothes while from his other dangled a parcel of essential books tied together with stout cord. These were the sum of the possessions with which he set out into the world. All else that he valued he carried in his head and his heart. As he walked through Bayard Street he nodded somewhat condescendingly to the people who, up until now had been his close neighbours and had come out to wish him good-bye and good luck. He decided to take a route along the Bowery as far as West Hudson Avenue. This gave him a long, straight walk along which he could stroll and savour his new independence.

As he turned into the Bowery it felt as if he had turned the corner on the first chapter of his life and was now entering into a completely new chapter. It was a significant parting, not only the beginning of a new life but the beginning of an adventure. But his feeling of elation as he strolled through the mid-morning sunshine among the other pedestrians was not without a pang of regret. He was leaving the only home he had ever known, a place of safety and certainty, and setting out into the unknown. He walked on, a young man who was a strange mixture of conflicting emotions, excited at his new independence, sad to be leaving his home and parents, glad to be starting a new career, sorry to feel some sort of barrier now existed between him and his family, confident in his success at gaining a place in journalism but unsure of how to take his place as an independent man in an adult world, strong yet

56

also strangely vulnerable. The thing that slowly surfaced to be uppermost in his thoughts was that he was about to take up residence among strangers. True, his mother's great friend Nora Bigane would be his landlady, but although his mother referred to her as Auntie Nora the truth was that he knew her only very slightly, his contact with her little more than saying hello after Sunday Mass when she and his mother would stand together and talk for a while. And what of the other lodgers? What would he make of them and what would they make of him? Then there was the name. That was a problem. He had not thought it necessary to mention to his parents that he was to be known at the *Herald* as Matthew Halon. But that was at the *Herald*. What should he be at Bigane's Lodging House, O'Hanlon or Halon?

His mind was full of such thoughts as he suddenly found he had arrived at his destination, and he stood looking at the doorway of 174 Bleecker Street. He put down his case and looked at the bell-pull. What to do, O'Hanlon or Halon? He was seventeen, in many ways still a child but in an adult body. He was confused and confident, scared and certain, happy and fearful and who, with the child gone and the adult beckoning, has not felt the same?

Matthew stepped forward and pulled the bell. A moment later Mrs Bigane herself opened the door. She looked at Matthew for a second.

'Mr Halon, welcome. I'll get Rosie to bring in your case. Come this way please.' Mrs Bigane stood to one side and Matthew, surprised at her using his *Herald* name, but also mightily relieved, entered the hallway. As he did so Nora Bigane leaned conspiratorially to him and smiled. 'Young Dan came round last night and told me.' She nodded. 'Very sensible of you. Do your ma and pa know?'

'Er, well, as it happens …'

'Quite so, quite so.' Her voice returned to normal. 'This

way, Mr Halon, I'll show you to your room.' Then she called out. 'Rosie. Gentleman's case to be brought in.' From a back room a pretty young girl appeared and hurried past them to the door, picked up the case with both hands, and joined them.

'Isn't it a bit heavy for her?'

Mrs Bigane looked at him a little severely.

'Rosie is a strong girl and I'd be grateful if you left her to my management.' Matthew felt like a chided schoolboy and looked embarrassedly at the young girl who smiled and looked down at the tiled floor. 'Come along, Mr Halon.'

And Mrs Bigane, now very much the landlady rather than any auntie, led the way with Matthew following and Rosie bringing up the rear.

Well, he thought, I've arrived, so that's done at least, and he pulled himself together and mentally prepared to play the new tenant, the one who paid the rent, a man in a man's world who would stand no nonsense.

And Rosie, as if she could in some way read his mind, uttered a small giggle.

'Enough of that, Rosie,' came Mrs Bigane's sharp voice. 'Mr Halon wants none of your silliness.'

The giggle ceased and Matthew somehow, he wasn't quite sure how, felt caught in the cross-fire of the reprimand and was again a chided child, so he bowed his head and followed Auntie Nora up the stairs.

Chapter Nine

Mrs Bigane's husband, Big Gene, had fared better than even he had expected. He built up a thriving practice as a gang-master and then diversified into politics by the simple method of being put up for membership of that well-known, though not universally respected, Irish Social Club, the Society of St Tammany, better known throughout New York since the building of its fine-hew headquarters, as Tammany Hall. There he soon became regarded as a rising force in the political life of Manhattan and was mentioned as a man who might one day even stand for high city office himself. Unfortunately this accolade to was denied him due to the fact that he died rather prematurely as the result of an altercation over the nature of democracy. That is, Mr Bigane had been shot down in a tavern by a rival over a dispute concerning how many times men employed by Mr Bigane had voted in an important local election. It was not that the rival was in any way opposed to multiple voting. Indeed, he himself employed a significant number of men to do exactly the same thing. No, what he objected to was Big Gene's arbitrary restriction on the male adult franchise. For Big Gene's men, when not going from voting station to voting station to exercise their democratic right on behalf of Big Gene's favourite, moved in groups to anticipate the approach of rival men to the voting station, took them into alleys, back yards and other undisturbed places where they beat them almost senseless and thereby impaired their right to express their political preference at the ballot box. This intimidation was not American democracy in action as Big Gene's opponent understood it, and he decided to exercise his constitutional right to bear arms and took direct action. That is, he found Big Gene and shot him dead.

Nora Bigane mourned her husband and went about in bombazine black and long veil for a full week after the funeral before casting off her widow's weeds, selling up their house, and buying the property on Bleecker Street which she at once set about turning into Bigane's Boarding House.

Nora Bigane had remained childless since the death of her first-born on the voyage. Once Eugene had made enough money he paid for her to consult several good doctors but they all agreed that she had, unfortunately, sustained damage which meant she would never be able to conceive. The news devastated her although her husband seemed singularly unmoved when she told him. Eugene Bigane, sadly, was one of those men on whom sudden success and money have the worst effect. He stayed out of the house until late talking and drinking with the men whom he knew would bring further success and more money. He moved himself and his wife into a fine house at a good address, but in this new home Nora became little more than the house-keeper while also acting as occasional hostess when her husband felt it necessary to entertain guests. Their relationship became formal and distant although Nora, through that female intelligence system that is common to wives at all levels of society, was able to discover that her husband had at least three illegitimate children scattered around various parts of Manhattan.

But decency had been maintained. They lived as man and wife and went each Sunday to Mass together, and she acted her part with what charm and courtesy she could manage when Eugene brought guests to the house. They were regarded by many who knew them slightly as a devoted couple. To those who knew them well, of whom Betty O'Hanlon was one of the very few, the miracle was that Nora hadn't shot the beast herself years before.

Nora Bigane, suddenly free from her loveless marriage, set about making a real life for herself. On her husband's death she had become comparatively wealthy and could have settled to a life of leisure, but she straight away shunned the idea of becoming in any way involved with the people with whom her husband had dealings. They, she knew, would take her money and make it work for her, and them. But she didn't want more money; she had all the money she wanted and needed. What she wanted was a definite purpose in which to immerse herself, something that would give her life meaning and direction. Having decided that much she then had to decide what exactly her purpose would be and came to the unusual decision – unusual for a woman that is – that her definite purpose would be to build up a commercial business of her own. Nothing if not practical, and always honest with herself, it didn't take her more than a few days to decide that all she really knew was how to keep a house well. That being so she might as well continue at it and make it her life's work. It became her simple ambition to own and run the most successful boarding house in the whole of Manhattan.

Nora Bigane was a determined, efficient woman who, from the beginning, made the rules of the house clear to her tenants and made sure that both she and they stuck to them. Her Ten Commandments were simple: no politicals, no travelling men, no labourers, no theatricals, no Italians, no Jews, no strong drink, no swearing, no credit, and *no women*, not of any sort. They were not written in stone, as were those which God gave to Moses, but they might as well have been.

Strict though she was her gentlemen tended to stay. The rooms were comfortable and clean and there were one or two among the longer-term residents who thought her cooking alone was worth the rent. Bigane's wasn't cheap but nor was it expensive and no room ever stayed empty for more than a couple of days. All her lodgers were professional gentlemen in permanent work locally. All except one. The exception was Mr Diver.

Clarence Diver was a shortish, single, middle-aged gentleman of soft manners, quiet voice, comfortable figure and plentiful, wavy, silver-grey hair parted in the middle. He looked like a minor but moderately successful poet. But he was not. Clarence Diver travelled. When any bold spirit asked Mrs Bigane why she made the exception in his case she pointed out that Mr Diver wasn't a traveller as salesmen were. He worked for the government, and then tried to avoid saying any more. This inevitably caused such curiosity that finding out which department of the government employed Mr Diver inevitably became an obsession with her questioner and, if forced by persistence to reveal the information, the name always, when it came to her lips also brought a blush to her cheeks.

'If you must know he works for the office of the Contingent Fund of Foreign Intercourse. There, now you have it.'

And she would bustle off furiously doing something, anything, her cheeks bright pink and muttering to herself.

Intercourse! What sort of name was that for an American government department?

Only once, at the very beginning of his tenancy had she confronted Clarence Diver himself on the matter.

Mr Diver had smiled at her gently.

'It's only a name, Mrs Bigane, only a name. We are really no more than accountants. When I travel I assure you my boudoir is almost always a musty office, my paramour a ledger, and my sweet nothings columns of figures.' And he laughed. 'Good heavens, there's nothing in the world the least bit naughty about the office of the Contingent Fund, Mrs B,' and his eye had lit up with a roguish, poetical light, 'being a single man I sometimes wish there was.' Then the light was turned off. 'But there isn't, so I must settle for what I've got.'

And that, as far as Mrs Bigane was concerned, had been that. All was well and the office of the Contingent Fund of Foreign Intercourse forgotten, until some new, have to explain, blush, and furiously find something, bold, and curious tenant took up residence and Mrs B would anything, to do.

Chapter Ten

The large front room on the ground floor of 174 Bleecker Street was the breakfast and dining room. It had heavy dark blue velvet curtains, red and cream Regency-striped wallpaper, and three ornate gas lamps. The chandelier in the middle of the ceiling was genuine crystal but, being entirely without candles, served no practical purpose. Mrs Bigane's husband had bought it through an associate who seemed able to come by such things and charged absurdly cheap prices on the simple condition that the buyer asked no question other than the price. It had gone up in the dining room of their fine house to impress his more legitimate business friends. It was really too big for the room in which it now hung but Nora had brought it as a memento and a reminder. A memento of her husband's success and a reminder that some things can come at too high a price.

One day, she told herself, when she was ready, she would clean it and, in cleaning, let it fall and smash to smithereens. But not on the large, dark, rectangular mahogany table which stood underneath the chandelier. That, like almost everything else in the house, she had bought herself and she treasured it, for it had originally been made for a grand house in Dublin. The only other thing she had brought with her from her past was a large, silver-framed daguerreotype of her husband taken in the apex of his success, not long before his untimely death. He looked out from the frame standing in a rigid pose with one hand on a chair and the other holding the lapel of his cut-away jacket. His thinning hair was plastered flat and his ample moustache hung down at either side of his mouth. His expression was half angry, half embarrassed, and the overall impression mildly ridiculous. This picture served to remind Nora of what he had become, because there were still those rare occasions, usually late at night when sleep proved elusive, when she remembered what he had been in the days of their courting and early marriage, the years before New York put its mark on him.

The daguerreotype stood on the large sideboard, also mahogany, in which all that was needed for the table was kept, linen, crockery and cutlery, condiment sets, everything. Breakfast and dinner were served each weekday with a meat lunch added on Sundays. On Saturdays there was a late breakfast but no lunch or dinner; the gentlemen were expected to go out and provide for themselves. As Sunday required a proper lunch it could not be a day of rest for Mrs Bigane, so she had moved her day of rest to Saturday and did not expect to be disturbed in the third-floor front which was her private sitting room and bedroom.

On the floor above Mrs Bigane's private room, in a small but prettily decorated back attic, was the room of the only other woman in the establishment, Rosie. Rosie, the pretty young woman who had carried Matthew's suitcase, had come from the orphanage to the boarding house aged eleven to train as a domestic help. Mrs Bigane, having no children of her own, had agreed to take her on because the nuns at the orphanage wanted Rosie to go to a good home where she would be cared for. They were particular about the placement for the sad fact was that Rosie would not only need care but protection. When Reverend Mother had called and first asked Mrs Bigane to think about taking on Rosie she had not in any way hidden the problems that might, indeed would, arise.

'She came to us at about three years old. Her mother was a prostitute, an Irish girl who got into bad company and took to the streets. She was found one morning in a back alley with her throat cut. They found little Rosie by herself in her mother's room. It seems that some man had been living there with the mother and, well, you'll know the story as well as I do, heaven knows it happens often enough. We took Rosie in and at first everything seemed all right but slowly we began to realise that she wasn't developing properly. God alone knows what she must have seen in that room but whatever it was she must have locked it away in her head somewhere. She seemed to live in a private little world. She was a willing, well-behaved little thing but she got to seven and somehow stopped. Ever since then she's been a happy, innocent seven-year-old and it looks like she always will be. Unfortunately her body is growing perfectly naturally. Rosie will grow into a woman and very probably into a very attractive one. Already she's like her name, a budding rose. But she'll never become a woman in her head, there she'll always be a child. These things can happen. It doesn't show so much now, but it will as she gets older. She's loving, kind, obedient, everything a mother would want her little girl to be, but not at all what a young woman fending for herself in Manhattan or anywhere else in New York needs to be. We won't be able to keep her on at the orphanage once she's thirteen or fourteen. It's a cruel world out there, Mrs Bigane, and when she leaves us, as she must, I worry about what will become of her so I decided to try and find a home for her now. Not just a position, you understand, but a home and for life. If I can't then ...'

And the nun shrugged her shoulders.

Mrs Bigane needed no advice from anyone on the wickedness of New York and no imagination to answer the nun's question of what would happen to Rosie, a pretty, trusting, child-woman without family, friends, or protection adrift in Manhattan. No, no imagination was necessary.

'Of course she must come to me, Reverend Mother, and she must stay. From now on Bigane's will be her home.

I'll look after her as if she was my own.'

'May God bless you.'

And, as far as Mrs Bigane was concerned, God had.

Rosie had grown into a slim, pretty young woman with red hair and a fair complexion. At sixteen she was attractive, happy, and hard-working, and Mrs Bigane guarded her with what almost amounted to ferocity.

The truth is that Rosie had become a daughter to her, the daughter she always wanted but had never had. She taught her to help with the cooking, to sew, iron, wash, and to say her morning and night prayers, everything in fact that was within Rosie's limited field of achievement, and they were both very happy.

Only once was there a cloud. A new border, a Mr Wenger, a shy, diffident young man who worked in an insurance office, approached Mrs Bigane one evening and asked, politely, if he might accompany Rosie for a walk in the park the coming Sunday afternoon. The request was made with all due deference but received from Mrs Bigane the coldest possible of refusals. The following Monday when Mr Wenger returned from his office at six-thirty he found a vacancy notice in the street window and his belongings packed and waiting for him in the hallway along with his bill. That night he stayed with a friend and the next day began scanning the papers for new lodgings, and at Bigane's Boarding House a severe communal punishment set in. The breakfasts became a cold repast, portions at dinner became smaller, there was no gravy, and after dinner the dining room was locked on the excuse that Mrs Bigane wanted to do a thorough cleaning. The whole establishment took a distinctly penitential, almost Lenten turn for a full week at which point Mrs Bigane felt her message had sufficiently sunk in. The cooked breakfasts returned to normal, portions at dinner regained size, gravy flowed freely back and forth across the dining room table, which had in no way changed from how it had looked before The Incident. Best of all it was thrown open after dinner to be used once again as a communal social room.

After that, the first thing that any new gentleman was told by the existing lodgers on his arrival was that the pretty young woman named Rosie was absolutely off-limits and Rosie, unaware of anything outside her duties to Mrs Bigane, carried on being pretty, happy, and completely innocent.

In the evenings, when Rosie had cleared away the dinner table, it was the custom of those gentlemen who had no other calls on their time to gather in the dining room and turn it into a comfortable lounge. Here they could sit, talk, smoke and even, if they wished, partake of a glass of beer. Although Mrs Bigane had set her face against strong drink of any sort, in which she included both port and sherry wine, she was not opposed to beer in moderation nor tobacco in pipes. Mr Bigane had liked a glass of beer and had smoked a pipe when she had first known him as a young man and she considered smoking a pipe to be a manly pastime. But she would not tolerate cigars, which her husband had taken up in later life. Cigars she associated with wealth, pride, loose living, and general moral collapse.

Matthew had settled in well to life at Mrs Bigane's and adapted himself to the attitudes and routines of single men who earned their living and chose their pleasures. Despite having lived away from home for over a year he still did not smoke nor, he had found, could he ever accommodate himself to the idea of drinking beer in a domestic setting. He had never known his father to drink in or out of the house and his eldest brother Dan drank only on special occasions. Matthew didn't dislike beer, indeed, since becoming a professional man and assuming the condition and manners of adult independence he had liked taking a glass of beer, but only in the right conditions, in a respectable tavern or bar with colleagues from the paper or with other suitable company. He did, however, like conversation and was glad, on the evening of his return from the New Knickerbocker Theatre and his encounter with the Bowery Boys, to see that Clarence Diver, Samuel Dufferidge, and Lemuel Possett were assembled in the dining room.

Clarence Diver, during those periods when not travelling, held the role of elder statesman of Bigane's Boarding House and tended, if available, to preside over the after-dinner lounge gatherings. When Matthew came in and perhaps over-dramatically almost fell into a chair the conversation that had been taking place ceased. Samuel Dufferidge and Lemuel Possett, young men both, sat and waited for Diver to elicit from Matthew some explanation for his being missing from the dinner table and the theatrical manner of his arrival.

Diver's opening was, to the young men's minds, rather pedestrian.

'Working late, Matthew?'

Matthew, knowing he was the centre of attention, as he had intended, and knowing that he had a good story to tell, sat up and looked at his audience.

'Been with John Cutler at the Order of the Star Spangled Banner meeting at the New Knickerbocker. I left before it was finished and as I came out who do you think …'

But Clarence Diver was not prepared to concede the stage so quickly nor so completely.

'I can see how John Cutler, a young man of too impressionable a mind, might be drawn to such a meeting, but I wouldn't have thought it your idea, Matthew, of a decent evening out.'

'In my business, the news business, it's always as well to know what's going on.'

Matthew was about to go on when Samuel Dufferidge, who was second-in-charge of the haberdashery counter at

70

Philpotts Ladies Outfitters, took his pipe from his mouth.

'There'll be trouble over that meeting. Bound to be.'

Matthew, his news in danger of being spiked by a rival, nodded.

'Yes, sir, and big trouble. The Bowery Boys were outside as I left. I came down the steps and one of them …'

Samuel nodded wisely and pointed at Matthew with the stem of his pipe.

'Guessed they would be. Guessed it as soon as …'

Clarence Diver, unwilling to accept the Bowery Boys presence outside the New Knickerbocker as such a gripping topic, handed down his judgement.

'Thugs and thieves every one of them. They are no more than a rabble that needs cleansing from our social system, them and all the other gangs that come out of their rat holes and infest our streets.'

Lemuel Possett, who up until now had done no more than listen with a somewhat detached air and, when not working as a clerk in the New York branch of the Ohio Life Insurance and Trust Company, was both an amateur philosopher and aspiring writer, put down his tankard of beer.

'They must serve a purpose, Diver. If the gangs did not then how come there's so many of them? The Dead Rabbits, the Roach Guards, the Shirt Tails, the Chichesters, and that's just the ones from Five Points and thereabouts. Why if one cared to take a full count then …'

Diver turned aggressively on this sudden and dangerous assault on his position.

'Pah! Pah I say. Good heavens, Possett, one might as well say that thieves and murderers serve a purpose. There's enough of them as well in this city I suppose.'

But Possett, in his role as philosopher, met the attack philosophically.

'I don't say they serve a moral purpose, Diver, but I do

say that they serve a social purpose.'

Matthew, his hope of being sensational pretty much gone, was interested in this idea.

'What social purpose?'

Possett took up his tankard and made a gesture with it before taking a drink.

'Drama. Street theatre.'

Matthew grinned and Clarence Diver almost exploded.

'Drama! Street theatre!'

Lemuel was pleased with the effect he was having and waded on.

'They are part of the ever-changing kaleidoscope which is the pageant of life here in New York. They are, they are …' But here his words ceased as both his imagination and vocabulary failed to suggest to him what the gangs of New York were or might be so he took up another position. 'One day I may write something, an article or even a book. *The Gangs of New York*. The title would have a ring to it, don't you think?'

Matthew was disinclined to continue Possett's particular line of discussion.

'Yes, there's plenty of them, maybe even enough to fill such a book. One thing's for certain, the Dead Rabbits will come out onto the streets tonight and there'll be blood and mayhem. The bunch hanging about outside the New Knickerbocker said as much, seemed indeed to be looking forward to it.'

Clarence Diver, seeing his chance to reassert himself, responded.

'Why not? It's what they're paid for. Why do you think the Star Spangled bunch chose a place on the Bowery for their meeting? To provoke, that's why.'

None of these talkers took any notice of the doorbell when it rang and the conversation continued for a few moments until Rosie entered, crossed to Matthew, curtsied, handed him a folded note, and left.

Matthew opened it.

"Come office at once, repeat, at once. President Zachary Taylor dead. Repeat, President Taylor dead."

Matthew folded the note, put it in his pocket, and stood up.

'Excuse me, gentlemen, an urgent matter has arisen.'

Samuel Dufferidge, so much out of the give and take until now, took the opportunity to sally forth.

'Some old lady's cat stuck up a tree, Matthew?'

Matthew, now the holder of news that was really and truly sensational, looked at him.

'Not quite, Samuel. A little more important than that. Yes, just a little more important, I think.'

And with that mysterious response Matthew left.

Chapter Eleven

The *Herald*'s offices were on the corner of the Square formed by the intersection of Broadway, 6th Avenue and 34th Street. Although the newspaper called itself, and perhaps rightly so, "The Most Largely Circulated Journal in the World" they were singularly unimpressive. They occupied several floors of a large, slab-like building of little or no architectural merit. By the time Matthew arrived at nine thirty, most of the building was in darkness. There was, however, a light in the main entrance hall, shining through the window in the door that led into the small entrance hall. Sitting at a desk opposite the door was a man in a dark uniform who looked up as Matthew pushed the door shut behind him.

'Looks like something big, Mr Halon.'

'You could say that, Andrew.'

'Then I guess it's going to be a busy night.'

'That it is, that it is indeed.'

Matthew, feeling important by the news he carried and the solemn welcome of Andrew, guardian of the doorway, made his way up the staircase to the second floor and the editor's office.

The office wasn't so very big and the editor's cluttered, ink-stained desk took up a good deal of the available space. One wall was occupied with two bookcases which went from floor to ceiling and were almost filled with bound back-copies. Between these, in a dark, wooden frame hung a copy of the first front page of the *Herald*. Below this historic document was a smaller bookcase which held reference books and directories. On the top of this bookcase three books stood together, a new and revised edition of *Webster's American Dictionary of the*

English Language, John Locke's *Second Treatise on Government*, and Hazlitt's *Economics in One Lesson*.

The room was lit at either end by gas lamps turned up full and crowded into the room were the editor, Frederic Hudson, three senior journalists, and two young men, assistant journalists like Matthew. Hudson was standing behind his desk and the three senior journalists sat on chairs in front. Sitting behind and slightly to the side of Hudson, Matthew recognised the *Herald*'s owner, James Gordon Bennett.

Bennett was fifty-five with thick, wavy grey hair and bushy side-whiskers which met under his chin. His well-tailored coat was black and velvet-collared and he managed, intentionally or not, to give the impression of a rather vain Old-Testament prophet who had made good financially. Two of which were indeed the case.

Hudson had obviously been speaking for some few minutes as Matthew quietly entered and pushed behind the three senior men to the window, joining his two young colleagues.

'... Now, gentlemen, you who've managed to make it in tonight know as much as I do and, as we all get the news from our press association, we know as much as do all the other papers in New York. The president is dead and it's finally official. We need an edition out tomorrow that will show New York what the *Herald* can do when a story like this breaks.'

'No special?'

The question was asked by William Atherstone, one of the senior men.

'No, Bill, no point. We couldn't say anything in a special that any of the other five papers who use the Association won't say.'

Bill Atherstone obviously disagreed.

'Zach Taylor, Old Rough and Ready, the hero of Palo Alto and Resaca de la Palma, the president of the United

76

States, is dead. Goddam it, Fred, that's enough, surely? If I can't fill a one-page special on that alone then fire me now and let Jesse here do it or one of those young 'uns by the window.' He turned to Jesse Caulk, another senior man sitting next to him. 'Well, Jesse, a one-page special on a hero of the Mexican War and a dead president? Need it in half an hour, mind.'

'Sure, Bill.'

The third senior man of the row, Isaiah Potts, chipped in.

'A whole half an hour, Bill? Shoot, then I'll do it myself and make it a two-pager.'

And the room filled with laughter.

The door opened and another man slipped in, patted the senior men on the shoulders as he passed behind them, and came to the window where he squeezed himself in beside the younger men. It was Luke Jensen, the most senior of the *Herald*'s journalists.

He spoke quietly to Matthew.

'What's happened?'

'Don't know. Just arrived myself.'

Silence fell as Hudson stood aside and James Bennett rose from his chair.

All eyes in the room were on the owner as he began to speak in a strong Scottish accent tinged with New York.

'Gentlemen. I do not doubt that all of you could write one, two, or many pages on the death of President Taylor. As Mr Atherstone has reminded us, Zachary Taylor served his country in the army for forty years with skill and bravery before he became our president, so whatever any of you would write,' and here he looked around the men in the room and then smiled at them all, 'young 'uns or old 'uns,' his smile was answered with a polite laugh, 'would all be fine stuff, the best. I'm sure of that because I have made it my business to see that the staff of the *Herald* are the best.' Here he stopped and his eyes rested on Matthew.

'You son, how old are you?'

Matthew, suddenly the centre of all eyes, was both proud and embarrassed.

'Eighteen, sir. Been here just over one year.'

'There you are, gentlemen. Eighteen and I'd back this man ...'

Bennett looked once more at Matthew questioningly.

'Halon, sir. Matthew Halon.'

'I'd back young Matthew Halon here to write a better special on President Taylor's death than any other reporter in New York.' Bennett paused. 'Except Fred Hudson and you senior men gathered in this room, of course. Then it would be only as good.' And once again the room filled with polite laughter. Matthew forced himself to join in but a sudden fear gripped him. What if Mr Bennett decided to deliver on his wager and actually told him to go and write that brilliant one-sheet special? Could he do it? Fortunately his fears were immediately overcome as Bennett continued. 'But as Hudson here says, there'll be no special. We'll leave that to the likes of my great friend and rival Horace Greeley and those down at the *Tribune*. Let them have their moment. We'll wipe them off the street with our edition and, because we won't have lost time putting out a special, I guess we can have our first edition on the street pretty early.'

He turned to Hudson for an answer.

'It'll be out there as early as we can make it. Mid-morning at the latest,' and he looked round the room, 'if these men are as good as you say they are.'

Bennett turned to the men in the room.

'Well, gentlemen? You heard your editor. What do you say to him? Are you as good as I say you are?'

This time the room was full of cheers and hoots and Jensen leant his head towards Matthew and whispered.

'They make a great team, don't they? Bennett and Hudson. They could go on any stage in New York and make a fortune if they weren't busy making one here. And they wouldn't need any scribbler to write their material.' Then he straightened up and spoke through the noise. 'Fine, Mr Bennett, now tell us what we're to write and let us get on and write it.'

Silence fell.

James Bennett turned once again to Frederic Hudson.

'Take over, this is all yours now.' Bennett picked up his sleek, black top hat which was on the editor's desk and turned back to the reporters. 'I won't wish you good luck. *Herald* men don't need luck. Good evening, gentlemen.'

And he walked through the room, put on his hat, and was gone.

The door closed behind the departing grandee and Frederic Hudson stood forward once more and looked round the room.

'Now, men. What we have from the Associated Press all the other papers in New York will have. I've outlined the facts, that Taylor died of what they're calling bilious cholera ...'

'My God! Cholera in Washington? In the White House?'

The words were out of Matthew's mouth before he could stop them.

Hudson looked across at him, annoyed at the interruption. Isaiah Potts leaned back in his chair and spoke to Matthew over his shoulder.

'No. At least not the sort you mean. This bilious cholera has a broad footprint. If you vomit, sweat, shit fit to bust, and the medical men don't know how to cure you, then when you die they say you had bilious cholera. It's that sort of cholera.'

Luke Jensen joined in to ease Matthew's embarrassment.

'It a simple mistake to make, son. It's one of those names that sounds all right to the likes of you and me but

79

what it really means is the doctors didn't have a notion in hell what it was.' He turned back to Hudson. 'Taylor fell ill after that 4th of July jaunt at the Washington Monument. It must have been something he ate there. The weather was damned hot as I remember, maybe something turned in the heat and he ate it. Bad business, sure, but I don't see any angle for a story to put up against the other papers.'

'No? Then try this. Do you remember Taylor's visit in August of last year?'

Hudson waited but it was Bill Atherstone rather than Luke Jensen who remembered.

'Same thing happened in Erie. Fit as a flea all day busting out a busy schedule then struck down after dinner. Vomiting, diarrhoea, and put to bed with the shakes.'

Hudson turned his attention to Bill Atherstone.

'Remember anything about what went on before the day he took ill?'

But Bill's memory failed him and he shrugged.

'A lot went on, Fred. Taylor was touring the Northern States politicking. That kind of thing sort of blurs together.'

'Then I'll refresh your memory. In Mercer, Pennsylvania, the president made a speech.'

Bill's memory suddenly returned.

'Damn me, so he did, and he said a mouthful. That the Northern States didn't need to worry about any extension of slavery. That all the new Western territories would join the Union as free states.'

The drift of Hudson's argument dawned first on Isaiah Potts.

'By the Lord Almighty, Fred, are you trying to say that Taylor was poisoned in Mercer and again in Washington? Because if you are, you'd better have all the damn proof in the world.'

Jensen's voice was added.

'And then some.'

80

And Bill's.

'Amen to that.'

Hudson however was undisturbed by their reaction.

'Mr Bennett thinks we have enough and I agree with him. We have enough to run a story that will set this country on its ear and make the *Herald* the only paper anyone in New York wants to read.'

Suddenly the room was alive with anticipation and a solitary voice rang out from one of the younger men at the window.

'Halleluiah and glory be.'

It summed up the mood nicely and Matthew wished he'd thought of shouting it.

What Frederic Hudson was talking about wasn't a story. This was *the* story, the one and only story, the chance of a lifetime. A US president assassinated. That which could never happen in the greatest republic on the face of the earth, had happened. Not a man present, from the youngest, Matthew, to the oldest, Jensen, wasn't ready to go to hell and back to get it into the paper and onto the streets.

Hudson, obviously pleased with the reception of his news, carried on.

'Dr Robert Wood was Taylor's medical man in Erie. I want one of you to go and get all the details of what happened.' Hudson nodded to one of the young men by the window, the one who had shouted hallelujah. 'Kettleman, you go,' Matthew winced with envy, 'and have your copy to me in no more than two days.' Young Kettleman went to the door but stopped as Hudson called after him. 'Take whatever coverage we did at the time and make sure you know it by heart when you get there. I don't want any re-runs. I want new stuff, and details, plenty of them.' Kettleman nodded and left the room. 'Bill, I want you to get to work on everything that's gone through Congress since Taylor took office.'

Bill stood up.

'Hell's teeth, everything?'

'If we're going to point any fingers let's get it clear straight off who we're pointing at. I'll want everything Congress has debated on the slavery issue.'

'That's no help, Fred, slavery's about the only thing Congress has debated for the last God knows how long.'

Hudson had the good grace to give a small laugh.

'So it is, Bill, so it is. But we need to build the background, the in-fighting behind the scenes, and the fighting on the floor of the Congress. We need to make it absolutely clear what the stakes are, to show how this whole thing has come to the point that it could easily lead to civil war. If we can show them that, they'll be ready to believe that to some people the slavery issue is worth dying for, even if the one who has to die is the president. I want people to see that slavery is a boil that has to be lanced and that Taylor was about to do the lancing. I want all you can give me to fill pages two and three, a double-page spread on how this country's politicians stand on the issue and where their support comes from. Name names, Bill, and don't pull any punches. Who pays the men in Congress who oppose abolition.? Let people know what the price tag is these days to buy a Southern congressman or a Northern doughface.'

As Bill turned to leave Jensen asked a question.

'Is the *Herald* thinking of pointing a finger at anyone in particular or are we just going to scatter-gun the slavery politicians and the big slave owners?'

'Tomorrow we'll only lay the foundations. I don't want this to be a one-day grand hurrah. I want this story to run and run, so first we need to lay out our case. But once we get traction we'll begin by going for the likes of Henry Clay and Daniel Webster. After that we'll see.'

Bill Atherstone let out a low whistle.

'Well, like you say, Fred, there's been civil war talk in

the air for some time now but if the *Herald* goes for pro-slavery Whigs like Clay and Webster then their people will come gunning for us and I guess there'll be a war all right, even if it's only here, between the papers in New York. You sure Mr Bennett wants that?'

'Bennett's full-square behind this story.'

'Glad to hear it. I'm too old to start looking for a new situation if this thing blows up in our faces.'

'It won't, Bill, you have my solemn word.'

Bill Atherstone left the room as Frederic Hudson continued.

'Now you know where we stand at the *Herald*. Luke, I want you to write a front-page leader that comes down hard on the Whigs. Make them squirm. Let the people know it's all about money to them, that their God is finance and their only creed profit. That the ordinary man in the street is something to be milked like a cow, that freedom and justice can go to hell as long as the money keeps rolling into their pockets. Get the ordinary reading public on our side from the start, ready to bay for Whig blood as the story builds.'

Luke Jensen took his turn to walk to the door. He was the senior man on the reporting staff. The younger men watched him. He was their model. Each one wanted, one day, to be like him. If he believed, they could believe. At the door, with his hand on the knob, Jensen stopped.

'I hope you know what you and Bennett are doing, Fred. This will become life and death stuff, with real lives and real deaths. We'll be using real people. You know there'll be blood as well as ink spilt on this if we go ahead?'

Hudson's manner when he answered was as sombre in answering as had been Jensen's in asking the question.

'I know, Luke. But it's a story, the biggest one any of us is ever likely to handle. It's your choice. Want to walk away from it?'

There was a moment's pause and the room fell totally silent. Jensen looked at the floor, then raised his eyes to meet those of Hudson.

'I guess not, Fred. I'd say you'd have to prise the pen from my cold dead fingers to get me off this.'

And the door closed.

Matthew felt he should cheer, or shout hallelujah, or do something. But as no one else did anything, he remained silent.

'Now, the rest of you. Jesse, you're in overall charge.' He nodded to the two young men left standing by the window. 'Use these men to bring the front page together around Luke's leader, let them do the support writing for Bill's pages and scrape together what they can for the rest of the paper. Use them as you see fit, but use them. Let *The Sun*, the *Enquirer*, the *Tribune* and the others fill the streets tomorrow morning with specials. By mid-morning, lunch-time at the latest, I want such a broadside as will blow them all to kingdom come. Get me my front page, Jesse, and see you have two more damn good pages from Bill to back it up. After that I doubt anyone will notice anything else we print so don't waste too much time on it.'

The door opened and a young man's head came round the door shouting.

'Hey. Pitched battle going on in Broome Street between the Bowery Boys and the Dead Rabbits. Barricades and all hell broken loose. There'll be plenty of casualties and not a few of them bystanders. Saw one old man helped away head covered in blood and a woman went down near me with what I swear was a musket ball in her. I saw her drop.'

He stood and waited expectantly.

Jesse Caulk looked at Hudson.

'Could be useful, Fred, violence in our city, violence everywhere. Out on the streets here in New York, in the corridors of power in Washington. Sign of the times stuff, colour, right sort of background.'

Hudson thought for a moment then looked at the young man at the door.

'OK, write it up and get it to Jesse here. We'll use it to fill in somewhere. Maybe page three or four.'

The young man came into the office and looked around. Obviously he had not heard the news.

'Inside? But it's a regular battle, pistols, muskets, knives, clubs, you name it. There'll be a big enough body count this time to rattle City Hall and make them sit up and do something, and like I say, the casualties won't all be from the gangs. This is front-page stuff.'

Hudson's answer was a nicely blended mix of pity, weariness, impatience, and authority. He had been a young and eager newsman himself once, but that was long ago. Now he was editor-in-chief and nobody told him what to put on his front page.

'Yesterday maybe it was front page. Today it's not, it goes inside.' The young man's face showed his disappointment but he'd said all he had to say. The editor had given his verdict so he remained silent. He had run no small personal risks to get all the details of the action and to be buried on an inside page was not the reward he had anticipated. Hudson looked at him and relented a little as he picked up his hat, came out from behind his desk, and made his way to the door. When he was standing beside the young man he stopped. 'That's the newspaper business, son. Get used to it or change the way you earn your living.'

And the door closed behind him.

The new arrival looked around at those left in the room, then threw the hat he was holding on the floor and kicked it.

'Hell and damnation. I risked my skin tonight and all I get is some inside page. What's so God-almighty important that my story gets buried?'

Jesse Caulk, as the man now in charge, provided the answer.

'Nothing much. Only that Zachary Taylor, the president of the United States, has been assassinated. That's all.'

Chapter Twelve

Matthew was not given a writing job, nor even the task of assisting in the writing of anything. He was given the job of copy-runner. It was a disappointment, but he consoled himself with the fact that someone had to do it and the essence of bringing out a newspaper was teamwork. That was what he told himself more than once in the idle half hour when everyone else had gone off to various offices to get on with the writing. But after half an hour bells began ringing and Matthew had to hurry from office to office where sheets of paper were pushed at him. These he took to Jesse Caulk who would rapidly pass his eye over them and then mark them in blue pencil and hand them back with comments such as, "Tell the young fool he can't leave the *Herald*'s name until the third paragraph. Get the damn thing in the first sentence." Others he would drop into a wooden tray on the desk. These were the ones which eventually he might use. When he thought he had enough he pulled them out, sorted them, read them again, and put the rejects onto a weighted spike. Those on the spike, although rejected, were not thrown away. As the front page grew something that he had thought of as no use earlier might suddenly be found to fit in. Nothing, or almost nothing, was thrown away until much later in the process. The sheets in the wooden tray he arranged in some sort of order, re-arranging the order as more copy came in, until the time came when he marked them up and gave them to Matthew.

'Get Amos to give me a proof-sheet of this lot and tell him I want the headline as big as he can make it without losing anything but, if something has to go, I've marked the two that can be dropped. Wait until he's done it and bring it up.'

Matthew left the office and hurried through the corridors into the gloom of the barely lit stairwell. Risking his neck, he took the stairs two at a time. Speed was everything and his job was to get the sheets down into the bowels of the building where Amos and the compositing room awaited.

The compositing room was a low, windowless basement filled with wide tables and a hand-operated printing press at one end. The upper part of the walls were lined all around with shelves and each shelf was filled with shallow wooden boxes. Halfway down the walls, where the shelves ended, was a benchtop under which were drawers. In these drawers were more of the shallow boxes which contained type and all the other paraphernalia of compositing or typesetting.

The room was not windowless but as it was mostly below street level the windows were high up, small, dirty, and barred. Even during the day the bright summer sunshine penetrated very little into this basement and when in use it was always brightly lit by several gas lamps all turned up full. This was where the hand-written words of the reporters were turned into newsprint. After the speed of reporters in writing their articles, it was the speed of the typesetting by the compositors more than the speed of the presses that determined how quickly the paper could be printed and sent out.

Matthew handed over his sheaf of papers to a big, burly man in an ink-stained apron who was waiting with two other men, smaller but similarly attired. Amos Troop stood almost six feet, was broad in proportion, and had hands like hams. On looks alone you would have thought he earned his living by his obvious strength, a stevedore on the docks perhaps, a drayman or a labourer, but never someone whose work required the delicate nimbleness of fingers of a seamstress or lace-maker.

Big Amos was standing beside one of the tables and by him were an assortment of the shallow wooden boxes, each one subdivided into smaller compartments in which was the wooden type in various sizes. In another shallow box were flat, grooved sticks which the type could be slipped into. Amos already had one of the sticks in his massive hand and when Matthew arrived he said nothing but took the sheets with his free hand, spread them flat on space he had kept clear, cast his eye quickly over all of them, and then put them into the order he would compose them. Only then did he turn to Matthew.

'I heard there was something powerful coming on. You'll want the headline big I take it?'

'Big as you can. He's marked what you can drop if you have to.'

Amos nodded and passed one of the sheets to another of the waiting two men. This man, already holding a compositing stick, immediately began to select type and flick it into his stick. In what seemed to Thomas a matter of seconds the stick was full and passed to the third man who took it and began to fit it into a frame.

Amos was also building but in his case he was building shorter sticks with the larger type for the headings to the articles.

Matthew watched, fascinated, as the front page built magically in the deft hands of these skilled men. Today's newspaper was being born, a miracle repeated many, many times, but to Matthew always a miracle. Finally Amos pulled a tray of larger type to him and began to build the headline. Once completed it was given to the man setting the frame who slipped it in, tightened the whole thing, and took it to the proof-printer, the hand-operated machine at the far end of the room. The frame was inked and fitted to the machine, the bed of the printer with the blank page already in place was slid noiselessly under the frame, an upper leaver pulled to apply the frame to the paper, and the bed slid out again. The frame-setter lifted the page and held it up for Amos' approval. Amos looked, nodded, then turned to Matthew.

'Now, young Matty,' he knew everyone by their first name and used them, even for Frederic Hudson, 'who's Freddy left in charge?'

'Mr Caulk.'

'Then take that proof-sheet up to Mr Jesse Caulk with my compliments and see that it don't arrive smudged.'

It isn't easy to hurry up four flights of dimly lit stairs from the basement to a second-floor office with a flapping sheet of newsprint covered in wet ink without smudging it, and Matthew didn't manage it. At the top of the first floor the sheet flipped and one corner stuck. He stopped, laid the sheet carefully on the floor, and slowly peeled the corner back. It wasn't too bad, it was still readable, but there was a definite smudging to the type in the corner.

In the editor's office Matthew handed over the sheet to Jesse Caulk and waited for the blow to fall.

Jesse took the proof sheet, stared at it, then looked up angrily at Matthew. 'Damn.' He crumpled the sheet into a ball and threw it in the waste basket beside his desk. Thomas stiffened himself. The smudge, the fateful smudge. He had failed. 'The headline's fine but the lead article is lousy. I want you to go to Mr Luke Jensen, present my compliments, and tell him he's not writing some damn three-volume novel. He's writing a front-page leader. He's pushed three of the other articles off the page. Tell him to cut the damn thing in half.' Matthew didn't move. 'Well? What the hell are you waiting for?'

'You want me to tell Mr Jensen …'

'Blast your eyes, boy, he ain't Mr Jensen, he's just a damned cog, like you and me. We're a machine, understand? A machine that grinds out news and if one cog slips then the whole machine goes to hell in a wheelbarrow.'

90

'Yes, sir.'

'Then go and tell Luke Jensen that if his next one isn't any better then I'll have you do the damn thing.'

'Me?'

'Yes, you. Now get out.'

Matthew ran from the editor's office, along the corridor, and pushed open the door of the room where Luke Jensen and Bill Atherstone were both sitting in braces and shirt sleeves, writing, the floor round both of them scattered with crumpled balls of used paper.

'Mr Caulk says …'

Luke Jensen waved him silent.

'That it's too long. I know. Sit down, Matty, I'll have the re-write in a minute.'

Matthew sat down. After two minutes Jensen threw down his pencil, took up two sheets of paper, and held them out.

'There. That should hold him. It ain't great writing but it will get the whole show off the ground and let him get a sight of what his front page might look like. Off you go, Matty, and if he asks, tell him I'm working on the third one now.'

Matthew took the sheets and hurried back to the editor's office. As he handed over the sheets a bell rang from one of the other offices and Matthew hurried off into the corridor to collect more copy.

Jesse Caulk quickly passed his eye over the sheets, made a few marks and crossed out a few words, then put the sheets in the tray.

'Well, Luke, it ain't great writing but it'll give us a start.'

Slowly the copy came together and the story the *Herald* pages would tell took shape.

Chapter Thirteen

By the time the gas lights were being turned down the floor of the editor's office was covered with discarded proof-sheets and on the desk were the latest two. Luke Jensen and Jesse Caulk looked down at them.

'Which one, Luke?'

'Your choice, Jesse. Fred left you in charge.'

Jesse looked down at the two sheets, then picked up one.

'We go with this.'

Luke nodded.

'My choice as well.'

Matthew stood by the window. His work had been over for an hour and he could have gone home to his bed, but he stayed. This was a momentous occasion, the breaking of a great story, and he was a part of it. He'd been there from the beginning and he wanted to be there when the first edition hit the streets.

'How do you think Bill's doing? Hudson is going to want that page two when he gets back.'

Luke went to the door.

'I'll go and ask but if he's still at it he's in trouble and me butting in will probably lead to murder. Tell Maudy I died with my boots on, will you?'

Jesse laughed.

'Tell her yourself, she's your wife.'

Luke left and Jesse turned to Matthew.

'Some night, eh?'

'Yes, sir, some night indeed.'

'You're a lucky young Cuss, you know that? Copy-runner sees it all, sees the articles grow from scribbled sheets into pages and the pages grow into a paper and the front-page build. Yes, you're a lucky young dog, Matty, because you've seen it all and it won't just be a newspaper when it comes out, it'll be history, and you'll be able to say you were part of making it.'

That was right, thought Matthew. This isn't just a story, it's history, American history. In its own way it would be shaping his country's destiny. This was going to be …

The door opened and Fred Hudson came in. It didn't take a reporter's keen eye to see what sort of mood he was in.

He walked across to the desk, slammed his hat down, and looked at the proof-sheet.

'That the front page?'

Jesse Caulk nodded. Hudson picked it up and read it.

'What do you think?'

Hudson looked at Jesse Caulk then back at the page.

'I think it's fine. A fine piece of work, Jesse. You did a first-rate job, all of you.' Then he crumpled up the page with both hands and threw it into a corner. 'Now break it up and get ready for a re-set.'

Jesse Caulk was the first to manage any words.

'A re-set?'

'The president died after a short illness from an acute bowel disorder brought on by excessive exposure to the sun and from drinking copious amounts of chilled buttermilk and eating cold cherries.' There was a silence in the room until Matthew found, to his surprise, that it was his laugh which broke it. Hudson turned and glared at him. 'Something strike you as funny, son?'

Matthew stood, confused and embarrassed. Then suddenly he found words.

'Mr Hudson, sir, what you just said is about the biggest load of horse manure I've ever heard.'

The silence suddenly became intense, more than intense, oppressive, and Matthew was stunned, not only by what he had said but the way he had said it. People didn't speak to Mister Frederic Hudson that way.

Yet he had.

Hudson spoke slowly with an ominous calm. Everybody, he knew, had worked flat out all night. They were tired and frayed and he had just ordered all their hard work to be tipped into the waste basket. Sometimes you just had to make allowances.

'Is that so? Well learn to live with it, boy, because that's the story the *Herald* will be running.'

Matthew suddenly felt an immense anger. A moment ago he was part of the drama of history, someone who had a part, albeit a small one, in shaping America's destiny. And now Fred Hudson was trying to turn it all into some sort of low farce. Death from cold buttermilk and cherries! That wasn't the stuff of the *New York Herald*. It was more fitted to a New Knickerbocker Theatre minstrel show. That thought immediately brought memories of the meeting he had gone to and the rantings he had heard not so very many hours ago. He also remembered his brother Dan's words concerning the *Herald*, "they're in with the Know Nothing crowd", a collection of secretive societies whose agenda was to achieve the political supremacy of native-born, white, Protestant Americans who, on being questioned about their organisations or aims, always claimed to "know nothing".

What was happening to this story was a cover-up, a betrayal of the truth for narrow political purposes. Fred Hudson, the foremost editor-in-chief in New York, was killing this story because some political bosses wanted it suppressed. Matthew felt almost sick with the shame of it, as if he himself had been responsible. He could not and would not be part of such a thing.

'If you run it like that, Mr Hudson, you can do it without me.'

Jesse Caulk, embarrassed, looked down at the floor. Young men didn't speak to Fred Hudson like Matty had done and not even the most senior man would have issued such an ultimatum. Besides young men starting out certainly didn't walk away from a good job on the *Herald*.

Hudson's voice remained dangerously quiet.

'What's your name, son?'

'Matthew.'

'Oh, yeah, I remember, Matthew Halon.'

'No, Mr Hudson, not Halon, O'Hanlon. And yes, it's Irish. I lied on my letter of application because I thought my chances would be better that way and frankly I'm tired of pretending to be somebody I'm not.'

'I see. Well, Mr Halon or O'Hanlon, whichever you prefer, you're on a week's notice.'

Matthew suddenly felt slightly nauseous. What had he done, other than gone completely mad? The two men were looking at him and he felt he had to say something.

'Thank you, sir. Do you want me to work out that week?'

'No, I guess not. Collect your pay tomorrow.'

Hudson and Caulk stood watching Matthew in silence when the door opened and Luke Jensen came in.

'Bill's about done. He …'

Seeing Fred Hudson and Jesse Caulk by the desk and sensing the atmosphere he stopped.

Matthew found he had nothing more to say so he went to the door where Hudson's voice stopped him.

'For what it's worth, Mr O'Hanlon, I agree with you. The front page of today's *Herald* and most of what's inside about the president's death will indeed be horse shit. I know it and these two know it and every newspaperman in New York will know it. But it will be the same horse shit that gets printed in every other paper. That's the newspaper business, son, and if you don't like it you'll have to find some other way of earning a living.'

At last Matthew found words.

'Yes, sir, I guess I'll have to do just that. Good day,

gentlemen.'

And he left the room, pulling the door closed behind him.

Jesse Caulk broke the silence that followed Matthew's departure.

'A bit hard, Fred? He's only been here a year and I think he's showed promise. I put him on as copy runner. He did well.'

Hudson nodded.

'Did he, Jesse? Then I'm sorry to lose him. But he says he lied on his application.'

Luke joined in.

'Hell, Fred, everyone knows we're no great friends of the Irish. You can't hold that against him.'

'Maybe not, but I won't let him nor anyone else tell me how to run this newspaper and dictate what I can or can't print.'

Jesse Caulk decided to change the subject.

'OK, Fred. Why are we scrapping the assassination angle?'

'Because it's been assassinated itself, killed off by Washington. All the New York owners got a message saying toe the official line or take the consequences.'

'What consequences?'

'For the *Herald* it would mean closing us down.'

'Could they do that?'

'Yes. Could and would. Bennett called me over about an hour ago. William Cullen Bryant had been to see him.'

'The Grand Old Man himself.'

'None other. He was going to see all of the owners.'

Luke Jensen, who had remained silent since Matthew's exit, joined in.

'Bryant and the *Evening Post* are solid abolitionist. If Taylor was killed then I would have thought Bigelow would want the story out there even more than we do, and he's not just editor, he's co-owner, so I don't see even

Bryant giving him orders about what to print.'

'I dare say Bigelow's thought about it. But if it was an assassination, and I only say if, then trying to run to ground those responsible …'

'For God's sake, Fred, it was the slave oligarchy.'

'Pinning something like that on the slave owners would be well-nigh impossible and if we tried we'd be accused of fomenting the kind of trouble that could lead to the slave states seceding, and that would mean civil war.'

Luke disagreed.

'There's been talk of secession for years now. Nobody could put the blame squarely on us just for running the story.'

Caulk backed him up.

'Zach Taylor took no notice of their threats. When he went on that tour of northern states last summer he made his position clear. He'd be as quick and as happy to deal in the same way with any man who took arms against the Union as he did with spies and deserters in the Mexican war and he'd use the army to see that the law was upheld North and South.'

Hudson thrust his hands into his pockets. He wasn't happy with what these men were saying, not least because it was all true.

'And look what happened. He damn nearly died when he'd said it.'

Luke looked at Jesse Caulk.

'If we're right he was poisoned. But it didn't stop him.'

Hudson took his hands out of his pockets and banged the desk.

'No. But the second attempt did.' And, realising what he'd said Hudson slumped down into his chair. 'To hell with it. Bennett's been given his orders and he's given me mine, now I'm passing them on to you. The *Herald* goes with the Washington line. Taylor sat too long in the sun, drank too much cold buttermilk, and ate too many cherries.

Horse shit like our departed, young Irish friend said, but like I told him it will be the same horse shit in each paper so let's get it done and put a paper on the streets.'

'Do you agree with Bennett, Fred?'

Hudson paused a moment.

'Yes, Luke, I do. Taylor was a soldier, a popular hero, a strong and determined man.'

'A Southerner and a slave owner.'

'A man of principle who wanted to keep the country from tearing itself apart. He saw the way things were going, the way things had to go. He would have left the Southerners their slave States but he didn't want slavery to go west through what we won from Spain and Mexico. He wanted Texas, New Mexico and California, and all the Oregon Territory to be free states and he was ready to break heads in Congress to see that the laws to stop slavery spreading were passed.'

Jesse Caulk nodded in agreement.

'And he was the man to do it all right.'

'Yes, I guess Taylor might have pulled it off. But now our president is Millard Fillmore.'

This was greeted by a silence as all three men thought about their new president.

Luke Jensen summed up their views neatly.

'So it is, God help us.'

Hudson bustled on. Time was passing and there was a paper to get out.

'Now he's president he'll see that the Southern states get most of what they want and he sure as hell won't be able to do that if he lets his presidency start with someone accusing those same states of orchestrating the assassination of Zach Taylor. If we go up against the president we'd have to do it on our own, no other paper would back us and we'd finish up dead ducks.'

Sadly both Caulk and Jensen agreed.

'OK, Fred, if that's the way it has to be.'

'It does. So gentlemen, let's re-write today's edition.'

'What with?'

Hudson had already given it some thought. He'd had to.

'First the headline, "Mournful Intelligence from Washington", and before either of you say anything smart this has to be done the way it has to be done. Under that we put, "Death of General Zachary Taylor", make the name good and big, give it its own line, then "President of the United States".'

Jesse Caulk took up a pencil and pad and wrote it all down.

'OK, what after the headline?'

'His last moments.'

'Then?'

Hudson pulled out a paper and handed it across. Caulk took and read it.

'Well. It's mournful all right.'

'Dammit man, I've given you the headline, the tone of the thing, and the lead paragraph, if all I wanted was someone to take down notes from me I'd have …'

Luke Jensen interposed. Tempers were frayed enough and there was still a paper to put on the streets.

'How about after your paragraph we reprint a review of the bulletins that we've had since the illness began. How the fatal illness progressed.'

Hudson calmed down.

'That's good, Luke, go with that. Now let's get it out there,' he paused and gave a hard look at the two men, 'and if either of you agree with our young friend and think it stinks, well, that's the newspaper business. If you don't like it you'd better do like him and find some other way of earning your living.'

It was Jesse Caulk who answered, but with no great enthusiasm.

'You're the editor.'

Luke Jensen, though he had to agree, couldn't resist

adding a further remark.

'I guess it's like you say, Fred, nobody but nobody gets to tell you how to run your newspaper.'

Hudson looked at the two men. He could fire the likes of O'Hanlon, but these men he couldn't afford to lose.

'To hell with you both. Now get out. New York is waiting to know how their president died.'

Chapter Fourteen

Matthew returned to his lodgings at around nine when all the other lodgers had long since breakfasted and left to go to their various offices. He broke the news of President Taylor's death, that he had died from the stomach fever he contracted, all the papers would carry the details as they were known today. He himself and the rest of the staff at the *Herald* had been up all night on a special edition. Mrs Bigane was suitably solemn and offered to make him a late breakfast. Matthew declined. He wasn't hungry, he would go up to his room to rest. Mrs Bigane said she understood, it was a sad day for all true Americans but Matthew should make sure and eat. When he got up she would make something for him. Auntie Nora peeped through the efficient landlady exterior; his mother would expect it, she said. Matthew thanked her and set off up the stairs. Once in his room he took off his boots and lay on his bed to think. To his surprise he woke up three hours later feeling much refreshed and hungry. He got up, put his boots back on, and went downstairs. He found Mrs Bigane in the dining room cleaning.

'I'm going out to get myself lunch.'

'Are you sure? I can get you something in no time.'

'No, thank you, I need to walk and think and clear my brain.'

'Of course. You'll be in for dinner though?'

'Oh yes, everything back to normal tomorrow. Things have to go on, don't they, no matter what happens.'

'Indeed they do.'

Matthew left Mrs Bigane to her housework and went out to find a tavern and get some lunch.

Having eaten he spent the rest of the afternoon walking

aimlessly through the streets thinking over his situation until it was time to return to the boarding house and wait for the evening meal to be served.

After dinner he excused himself from any gathering and conversation by pleading residual tiredness after having put in an all-night session with his colleagues at the *Herald*, getting the paper out with the news of the president's death. It had, of course, been in all the papers and was the talk of the dinner table but, somewhat to Matthew's surprise, no one seemed in the least bit perturbed that President Zachary Taylor, Old Rough and Ready, veteran of innumerable campaigns in all weathers had succumbed to chilled buttermilk, cold cherries, and a hot sun. Such was the power of the press. That evening he kept to his room and, as no one in the boarding house could be aware of his predicament, decided to keep the matter of losing his job to himself for the time being. Mrs Bigane's views on unemployed boarders, he felt confident, would not be applied with her usual rigour to himself given her close friendship with his mother, but he would still say nothing until his plans became clearer. He decided that tomorrow he would get up as normal, go out at the usual time, collect his wages, then spend the day thinking of what direction his immediate future might take.

Next morning Matthew breakfasted, left with the other lodgers, and went to the *Herald* offices where he collected the money due to him, and walked away from the building for the last time. He didn't need to think about how he would spend the rest of the day, he knew exactly how he would spend it – deciding what on earth he would do now.

With a week's wages in his pocket and the day before him, he wandered pretty much at random to do his thinking. He didn't need to worry if he met anyone whom he knew, even other boarders. To them he would still be a newspaperman and not tied to a desk. He could always say he was out following up a story.

He walked and thought all morning. Did he want to stay in the newspaper business? And if he did, could it be done in New York? But if he turned his back on being a journalist then what else might he turn to? School-mastering he dismissed at once as far too dull for his nature and talent. Besides, his own years in education were not so very far behind him and the thought of returning to the classroom held little or no attraction. The summer morning passed in walking and thinking but produced no solid results other than a few more negatives. Over his lunch, a glass of beer and a steak at a tavern, he tried to be more positive and to fasten on to what possibilities other than journalism were open to him, and, by the time his steak was finished, it came home to him with some force that his options were distinctly limited. Manual labour of the sort his father and brothers did was, of course, out of the question. As for becoming a clerk, chained to a desk in some soulless office like John Cutler, or standing behind a counter peddling pins and ribbons in a store like Sam Dufferidge, well, no man of spirit could bear it. But then there was Lem Possett. He wasn't exactly a clerk; he worked in a bank. True, his position was minor and he may even have worked at a desk. Matthew's knowledge of what actually went on inside the offices of the New York branch of the Ohio Life Insurance and Trust Company was somewhat sketchy. But it was finance and finance was, well, different. What about a place in some good financial house? Matthew finished his beer, pushed away his empty plate, and mentally pencilled in Wall Street as a possibility. He sat back and gave his mind to the only other lodger whose employment he had not yet considered, Clarence Diver. Diver was a mature man, almost you might say, old, so his position could not act as a template for Matthew. But government work? 'Government man' had a ring to it, but what sort of government man? Not clerking like Diver, whom he knew was some sort of accountant, not the drudgery of ledgers and figures, nor anything else that would be no different from the thousand and one dull positions he might find at his doorstep here in New York. But a government man in some interesting capacity, some role that would fit his talents and his temperament.

Matthew stood up. He was pleased with himself. He had, near as a toucher and in only one morning, mapped out three distinct possibilities, another newspaper position, something in finance, or a government man. He considered his morning and lunch-time well spent, left the tavern, and spent the rest of the day walking and day-dreaming, balancing in rather glowing terms the pros and cons of the choices before him and finally, tired but satisfied, returned to Bigane's Boarding House at his usual time.

That evening he decided to go down to the dining room after Rose had cleared away. To suddenly change his habits might cause questions to be asked and as yet he had no definite answers he was prepared to give. Once he had made his decision and secured a suitable post he would make his announcement.

The only other occupant of the cleared dining room was Clarence Diver who looked up from his newspaper, the *Tribune*, as Matthew came in.

'Just been reading about the president. Bad business. Don't understand how they could have let him sit out for all that time in that heat without any hat on. There must have been some sort of cover available surely, even if only for the ladies present?'

Matthew responded absently.

'Yes, I suppose so.'

Clarence looked for a moment then laid his paper aside.

'You're looking a bit low, Matthew. Anything wrong?'

Matthew immediately tried to brighten up.

'Nothing. Just that I missed a whole night's sleep getting the paper out and didn't get to write anything for my troubles. I was copy-runner. It sort of knocked me a bit but I'm over it now.'

'I see. Well, I suppose your day will come.'

And he returned to his paper.

Both men sat in silence for a while until Clarence put the paper down again as Lemuel Possett entered, sat down, and immediately began on the same topic.

'Reading about the president?' Clarence Diver nodded. 'You know, I can't figure it out.'

'What?'

'Papers say the president drank copious amounts of cold buttermilk and ate several plates of cherries and that it caused some sort of attack.'

'And that he'd been in the sun too long without any hat or cover. They say that was part of the trouble as well.' Possett nodded his agreement with Diver but with obvious reservations. Diver lay his paper on his lap. 'Well, Lemuel, I suppose you have a contrary view as always?'

'Zach Taylor was a soldier, had been for forty years and lived rough, I suppose, for a good part of that time campaigning. Good God, he'd not so long ago fought through the Mexican War. He was used to the heat and as for buttermilk and cherries, pah! He'd campaigned on army rations and thrived on it.'

Matthew tried to sound nonchalant.

'So what's your point, Lemuel?'

Lemuel Possett edged forward on his chair and assumed an air of confidentiality.

'So how come a bit of southern sun managed to combine with things as mild as buttermilk and cherries to kill a tough old soldier who got out of bed that morning as hale and hearty as you or me?'

Possett sat back and looked at his companions expectantly. Clarence Diver responded.

'Bad luck, I guess.'

It was weak and it drew the laugh it deserved from

Possett.

'By God, Clarence, if that's your best effort I can see why you're well satisfied to be an accountant. What about you, Matthew? Anything better to suggest?' But Matthew only shrugged. He wasn't ready to enter into speculative debate about the circumstances of the president's death. Not here anyway. If the story he had worked on all the previous night was ever to be told he would do it as a newspaperman, not as a piece of idle after-dinner entertainment so, Matthew not speaking, Lemuel Possett continued. 'What does surprise me is that none of the papers seem to have taken it up.'

If Matthew wasn't prepared to pursue the topic, Clarence Diver was.

'Taken what up?'

'Now don't get me wrong, I'm not suggesting foul play,' he turned to Matthew once again, 'but you of all people will back me up that it's the sort of story the *Herald* would usually jump on. A bit of sensationalism to stir people up. Bread and butter to the *Herald* wouldn't you say?'

But Matthew once more declined to offer any comment so Clarence Diver continued.

'Don't you think that the death of a president is something that needs to be taken with proper gravity and not used just to stir people up and sell a few more papers?'

Diver's solemn response drew another laugh from Possett.

'By heaven, man, you're in good form tonight. I haven't laughed like that since I don't know when.'

Clarence Diver looked ruffled. As the elder man of the house he expected, and usually got, suitable respect.

'You may laugh, Possett, but I assure you I meant it. The death of a president should be neither a source of mere sensation nor treated as a joke.'

And he retreated huffily behind his paper.

Possett took out his handkerchief and blew his nose loudly then looked again at Matthew.

'I can see how Webb might take that line. He's become a fussy old woman and his paper won't move with the times. I can see the *Enquirer* taking the moral high ground on just about anything. That's why it's losing readers hand over fist. But the other papers, the *Tribune*, the *Post* and the rest, they're all in the business of making money. I would think a story is a story to them. Run the thing and apologise later if you have to.' But Matthew stubbornly refused to be drawn on either the death of the president or the manner of its reporting by the *Herald* and any of the other New York papers so Lemuel Possett gave up. 'Oh well, you're the reporter, not me. I'm just a bank clerk so what do I know of the news business? But I tell you this, it would make a damn good story and maybe one day I'll write it. *Death of a President*. Now how's that for a title?'

Matthew was only just saved the grave error of saying that very title had been the one nearly used by the *Herald* as Clarence Diver's paper dropped.

'About as damn silly as "*Gangs of New York*".'

And the paper snapped up again.

Possett looked at Matthew, made a face at the newspaper, and stood up.

'Well, it's time I think for a tankard. Want one, Matthew? You must need a drink to ease your throat after all the talking you've just been doing.' Matthew shook his head at Possett's satirical sally. 'No? Oh well, just as you please. I'll knock on John Cutler's door and see if he's a bit more sociable tonight.'

Lemuel Possett left and once again the paper came down. Clarence Diver looked at the door and said to the room,

'Damned upstart.'

'He's wrong, you think?'

'Wrong?'

'About the president's death.'

'Of course he's wrong.'

'You don't think he might have a point?'

Clarence Diver shifted uncomfortably and rustled his newspaper.

'Well, as a matter of fact the same thoughts did cross my mind. The circumstances, as they are reported, seem less than convincing.' Then he seemed to gather himself together. 'But what do we know? All we know is what we're told and we have been told that the death was due entirely to natural causes. We must accept that. We live in fraught times, Matthew, very fraught. But I cannot believe, nay, I will not believe, that any American worthy of the name would, could stoop to such a dastardly act.'

'But are all Americans worthy of the name?'

Clarence Diver gave Matthew an odd look, as if he were seeing him for the first time or in a new light.

'Matthew, are you sure everything is all right with you? You seem to be unsettled.'

Matthew forced a smile.

'No, it's nothing. It's just that sometimes Lemuel gets you thinking, doesn't he?'

'He may get *you* thinking. All he does with me is to bring on my indigestion.'

And the newspaper snapped up again.

Matthew sat and thought about what Lemuel Possett had said.

Possett had ambitions to be a writer and if he wanted to make a drama out of Taylor's death it meant nothing special. But if an old fuddy-duddy like Clarence Diver noticed how odd the reported circumstances of the president's death were, then there was a story all right and no amount of cover-up should be allowed to keep it from the people. If the *Herald* wouldn't carry it then maybe one of the other papers, after they'd been given a day or two to think about it, might be persuaded to run it. Especially if it was written by a free-lance and not a staff man.

Matthew stood up and the paper came down again.

'Leaving? Getting out of the way before Possett comes back? I don't blame you.'

'No, Lemuel's not driving me away. In fact I think maybe he's got a point. Maybe one of the papers should run the story.'

Diver gave Matthew that odd look again.

'Make the money and apologise afterwards? Wasn't that what he said? That's not journalism, Matthew, it's, it's ... well whatever it is, it's un-patriotic. More than that, it's damn well un-American.'

'Maybe you're right. But that's the newspaper business.'

'Then my advice to you is to get out of the business and find another way to earn your living.'

And the paper went up again.

Matthew left the dining room and went upstairs to his room. Earlier, on returning to the boarding house he had all but made up his mind to go into finance. But this evening's conversation had shaken that almost-made choice. It *was* a story, and the people had a right to know. Wall Street would have to wait for his services because now he was determined to do his damnedest to see that the people of New York *did* know. Lemuel was right and that fuddy-duddy, old stick-in-the-mud, Diver was wrong. He felt better. Now he had a purpose. Tomorrow he would go out and sell that story if he had to kick in every New York editor's door.

He'd show Fred Hudson that he wasn't about to find some other way of earning his living. He'd show him that he was still a reporter and not the worst of them. Not by a long shot.

Chapter Fifteen

The next morning Matthew set out on his self-appointed crusade. The previous evening in his room he had pondered where he should start. The *Post* he rejected. If one of its owners, William Bryant, the Grand Old Man, was a leading light in getting the story killed it was hardly likely that John Bigelow, the current editor, would run the story even though he was co-owner and noted for taking risks. Perhaps somewhere smaller, a paper hungry enough to take on something that the Establishment wanted to bury.

Before retiring Matthew had settled on the *Brooklyn Daily Eagle*. He had arrived at this choice not by some rational process of selection but because he remembered his early applications. The then editor, Walt Whitman, had been one of the few editors who had replied and in person. Not only that, he praised his letter and encouraged him to persevere. Matthew had kept that letter as a good luck token and, although Whitman had been gone from the paper for two years, Matthew felt that somehow the *Eagle* offered him his best chance.

Having taken his usual breakfast Matthew, confident of success but careful of his money just in case, didn't take an omnibus, all of which would be crowded at this morning hour, but joined the flood of pedestrians as New York made its way to work.

He walked the two miles down to the ferry which took him across the East River to Brooklyn and by the time he reached the *Eagle*'s Old Fulton Street offices it was just past ten. He gave his name at Reception and handed over a carefully composed note, outlining his proposal, which he asked to be taken up to the editor. He would wait for a

113

reply. And wait he did. He waited an hour before a small office boy came to him and told him, with a supercilious air, that no one would be able to see him today.

'I'll come back tomorrow.'

'If you like, but my guess is it'll be the same answer tomorrow and every day after that. Your name is known, my friend, and it's not known for the right reasons. My advice would be go to some other place where your name isn't known, Chicago maybe, or somewhere like that.' The boy turned to go, but added over his shoulder, 'If you want to stay in the newspaper business, that is.'

And he disappeared through a door marked 'Staff Only'.

This reversal sorely dented Matthew's enthusiasm but did not make him feel he was already defeated. He re-crossed the ferry and set off to his second choice, *The Sun*, whose offices were all the way back on Broadway.

The Sun was a conservative paper which aimed at the more discerning readers of the middle class. Matthew's reason for making this his second choice was that he felt *The Sun* might take a more independent approach to the death of President Taylor. Quite what he based this assumption on he wasn't sure but as he left the ferry and retraced his footsteps along the less crowded midday pavements back to Broadway his hopes, like the sun in the clear blue sky above, became higher once again.

After just over an hour of waiting in the lobby of *The Sun* offices Thomas was taken to see a sub-editor who listened to him patiently whilst chewing tobacco. Then spoke solemnly.

'Mr O'Hanlon, the president is dead. A nation mourns not only a great leader, but a great soldier and a great servant of our country.' He leaned to one side and expectorated into a spittoon that stood by the leg of his desk, then sat back with his hands behind his head and his manner became casual and conversational. 'Personally I think it's a bunch of horse feathers but that's *The Sun*'s story and I think you'll find it's the same story every paper in New York and right across the country is carrying. Don't fight the machine, Mr O'Hanlon, you can't win, no paper can, not yet. One day, when the telegraph runs from coast to coast and maybe even from country to country, news will travel too fast to smother it at birth. But, as I say, not yet. There's a dozen men on this paper who could write that story and probably do a better job than you, but none of them will. Give it up, Mr O'Hanlon. If Fred Hudson has kicked you out there's not a paper in this city that'll be in a hurry to put down a welcome mat for you as a staff man or as a free-lance. Go somewhere else, make a reputation, then come to New York, spit in Freddy Hudson's eye and come back here, then maybe there'll be a job for you.' The sub-editor waited but Matthew said nothing. When he continued it was with a noticeable sardonic tone. 'What's the matter, Mr O'Hanlon, can't spit?' And once again availed himself of the spittoon. 'Then I suggest you try some other line of work.'

The sub-editor sat forward and began to read the papers on his desk. Matthew stood, thanked the sub-editor and left.

By the time Matthew left *The Sun* offices the morning was well gone and it had been a morning wasted. He walked through the streets, busy and bustling again with late lunchers going to eat and early lunchers returning to their work. His enthusiasm had suffered two severe blows and it looked like they would prove fatal. He had nowhere to go and, he realised, nothing to do. If what the sub-editor had told him was true, and he rather thought it was, no paper was going to take either him or his story. His crusade had turned out to be a daydream, less, a mere fantasy. The words that rang through his head as he walked were those he seemed to have heard rather often at and since his dismissal, 'try some other line of work'.

It looked like Wall Street would, after all, have the benefit of his services but somehow, today, that idea seemed altogether flat. He stopped and looked around him. It was late but still lunch time. He wasn't hungry but the restaurants and bars were busy and he felt the need to be somewhere with people, to do something normal and ordinary, to sit and ponder on his situation. Suddenly he realised that, without thinking about it and out of habit, he had walked back to the intersection of Broadway and 32nd Street and was on the opposite corner to the *Herald* offices. He went into the nearest bar and ordered a beer. It was a bar that many of the *Herald* staff regularly used and he hoped there would be someone there whom he knew. He didn't want his recent colleagues to think of him as hiding from them somewhere licking his wounds and the sooner he met one of them and got the fact of his dismissal over with the better he would feel. As the barman pulled his beer he saw, at a table in a corner, Isaiah Potts. With him was a young, bearded man in an army uniform. As Matthew paid for his beer Potts looked across, saw him, and waved his hand inviting him to come to his table. Matthew picked up his glass, took it across the room and sat down.

Potts turned to his bearded friend.

'Sam, I want you to meet a bold young man and an ex-colleague of mine on the *Herald*, Matthew O'Hanlon although he sometimes passes under himself off under the alias of Halon,' and he gave Matthew a big grin. 'Matty, this is Sam Grant, lieutenant in the US Army, at present unattached and waiting posting.'

The two men stood up and shook hands. Matthew, although only five feet seven, was considerably taller than the bearded soldier and had to lean forward to shake his hand.

'Glad to meet you, Lieutenant.'

The soldier nodded but didn't smile. He seemed a

116

rather taciturn individual.

Isaiah Potts grinned at them both as they sat down.

'You two should know each other, you're both hell-raisers and both on your way to glory.' He turned to Matthew. 'Sam here is a war hero, brevetted for bravery twice in the late Mexican war. Served with Zach Taylor and Winfield Scott.' Sam Grant sat with downcast eyes, not looking up or commenting as Isaiah Potts spoke of him. 'And Sam, this young man should be brevetted as well.' At this Grant raised his eyes and looked at Matthew. 'Only the other day he as much as spat in the eye of Fred Hudson, the man-eating, fire-breathing editor-in-chief of the *Herald*. Not only spat in his eye, but told him his story was horse-shit and he could go to hell before he would soil his pen with such stuff. Quit his job and walked out. Yes, sir, walked out. Some fellow, this young Matthew O'Hanlon. There's quite few New York staff-men who would be proud to shake his hand this day and buy him a drink and I'm not ashamed to say I'm one of them.'

Matthew was considerably surprised by this unexpected encomium but, before he could ask Isaiah Potts if it was true or a joke, Potts turned away to wave his hand at the barman and, having attracted his attention, pointed to the glasses on the table. Sam Grant stroked his full, black beard with one hand and took advantage Potts' attention being elsewhere to ask a question.

'Really quit your job?'

Matthew nodded.

'But I didn't spit in the editor's eye.'

Potts turned back.

'Poetic licence, Matty, allowed to us scribblers.'

'Maybe I should have. Spitting seems to carry some weight in the news business.'

Grant asked another question.

'Got another job lined up?'

'No.'

'Easy to come by are they, jobs in the newspaper business?'

'No, but that's no matter. I think I've just about made up my mind to try some other line of work.'

The drinks arrived and Isaiah Potts took up his glass.

'A toast to celebrate a meeting of old friends and new. What shall it be, gentlemen?'

Sam Grant picked up his glass.

'General Zach Taylor.'

Isaiah Potts seemed disappointed but repeated the name and they both looked at Matthew who picked up his glass.

'To the late president.'

Isaiah Potts drank then put his glass down.

'Sam, if Matty here is thinking about another line of work what about the army? He's powerful strong on duty and service and when he believes in the truth of a cause he's as wild as a lion in following it up.'

Grant looked at Matthew and, finally, through the beard, a smile emerged.

'Then he can forget the army. In the army there's only one duty and one truth, obeying orders. The army's no place for an independent mind.'

Matthew was a little surprised, both at the words and the smile.

'What makes you say so ...' and he paused, unsure whether to say Sam, Mr Grant, or Lieutenant.

Isaiah Potts intervened.

'His name's Ulysses, Ulysses S. Grant. At West Point he got Uncle Sam because of his initials U.S. and the Sam stuck. Back when he was a kid and we were neighbours in Brown County, Ohio, he was just, hey you. Get it, hey U as in Ulysses?' As Matthew didn't respond, Potts pulled a pocket watch from his waistcoat pocket and stood up. 'Gentlemen, your company and conversation are as sparkling and soul-uplifting as always, but if you two are going to continue this wake I guess I might as well get

118

back to work.' He finished his beer in one long pull and put on his hat. 'Nice to see you again, Sam. Send my love to Julia and little Fred.' Grant nodded but didn't speak. 'Good luck, Matty. I hope you find a place for yourself, but take advice from a friend, if you decide you want to stay in the newspaper business then ...'

'I know, do it somewhere else.'

'Afraid so.'

And Isaiah Potts left them.

Grant took a drink and then looked at Matthew.

'So what will you do?'

'I don't know, find something I suppose.'

The words were nothing more than a mere formula. But as he actually spoke them Matthew found they had a profound effect on him. He realised that he was at something of a crossroads. Either he stayed in the newspaper business which apparently meant leaving New York or he stayed in New York and found some other way to earn his living. Did he really want to give up being a journalist? If what Isaiah Potts had said was true, then his stand had not only been noticed, but admired. If that was so, was he prepared to give up a reputation earned at so great a price, the price of his livelihood? Also, if it was true and his stance had been admired, some New York paper might yet take him and his story on.

The choices seemed to be, stick with his principles and try again, leave town and get a job on a paper in some other city, or change the way he earned his living? Sitting opposite him was a stranger, but a man who had faced personal danger and made brave decisions involving considerably more than his livelihood. Matthew decided to seize the moment and place his dilemma in front of this new and detached mind.

'Tell me, did you mean it when you said that the army was no place for an independent mind?' Grant nodded. 'So you believe that obeying orders, any orders, is your highest

119

duty?'

'As long as I wear this uniform I do.'

'So if it's an order, that makes it right?'

'It makes it an order. There's good military orders and bad military orders but morality, the business of right and wrong, don't come into it.'

'But Potts said you were brevetted for bravery, twice. Surely that meant you did more than just obey orders? Wasn't it because you believed in the justice of your cause that you were prepared to do all in your power, even to losing your life, to see it come to its proper end?'

'Friend, I'll tell you what we were fighting for in the late Mexican War. From its inception to its final consummation, it was a conspiracy to acquire territory out of which slave states might be formed for the American Union. It was no different from any European war, a war of conquest driven by greed.'

These sentiments, delivered in so considered a manner rather took Matthew aback.

'An unjust war?'

Grant nodded once more and continued.

'And it is my belief that nations, like individuals, are punished for their transgressions. The Mexican War will come back to haunt us one day and it will do so in a most sanguinary manner. But it's what we were fighting for, me and those who gave me my orders. As to your question about what I was prepared to do, I did my duty as a soldier, no more no less.'

Matthew thought this over.

'But if you felt the war was unjust, why not resign your commission? Wouldn't that have been the more honourable course to take?'

'Maybe so, but the man who obstructs a war in which his nation is engaged, no matter whether right or wrong, will occupy no enviable place in life or history. Better to advocate war, pestilence, and famine, than to act as obstructionist to a war already begun. The most favourable posthumous history the stay-at-home traitor can hope for is oblivion. I intend to make my way in the world, and for me that way is the army. I've made my choice and must stand by it.' Grant looked steadily at Matthew. 'Isaiah said you were similarly inclined. Was he wrong?'

'Similarly inclined how?'

'To make your way. To be remembered.'

Matthew thought about it. Was that what he wanted? Did he seek to be remembered? Then Potts' words came back, "There's quite a few New York staff-men would be proud to shake his hand and buy him a drink and I'm not ashamed to say I'm one of them".

Matthew had always thought rather well of himself but never as someone of consequence, a sort of hero. And yet ... He tried to remember how he felt when he had made his stand against Fred Hudson. All he could remember was that he felt vaguely nauseous. But however he had felt, he had stood his ground and acted with honour, even bravery. Why not a hero? Not of the same sort as this sombre lieutenant perhaps, but capable of an act of courage. Did he want to be a man remembered, a man people would be proud to say they'd known, a man who achieved something exceptional? It was an idea, and not the worst of them.

'Well, if the choice has to be glory or oblivion I guess I'd choose glory.'

Behind Grant's beard Matthew detected the smile once more as the soldier raised his glass.

'Well then, friend, to glory.'

Matthew raised his own glass.

'Yes indeed. To glory.'

Chapter Sixteen

Their drinks finished, the men left the bar together, Sam Grant to go to an appointment which he hoped would provide him with a new posting and Matthew with a renewed determination to resume his attempts to breach the wall of refusal he had so far met from editors. He spent the afternoon walking and thinking, trying to revise his approach. He needed a better note to be taken up to the editor and if he was seen by the editor he needed a more persuasive argument but one that could be delivered briefly and forcefully.

He had been considerably uplifted by his lunch-time meeting. Potts' praise for his stand against Hudson and Grant's approach to life had planted in his head the idea that he might be a man destined for something more than the commonplace. Matthew's thoughts lasted him until it was time to make his way back to the boarding house and it was with a confident step that he arrived there, sure that tomorrow he would once again be a newspaperman, and not the least of them.

That evening in his room he made the choice for his next morning's assault: the editor and co-owner of the *Evening Post*, John Bigelow. Matthew came to this unusual choice in the spirit of St George. William Cullen Bryant had been the one who had brought the assassination story crashing to the ground so Bryant's paper, the *Post*, therefore, represented the dragon. It was Matthew's firm intention to face that dragon, slay it, and then go on to glory.

The morning began well. Only an hour and a half after sending up the note he had carefully composed the previous evening Matthew was taken to the editor himself.

John Bigelow listened quietly, then, kindly but firmly, told him to forget it. Matthew had expected an initial rebuttal and refused to accept defeat. He said it was the duty of newspapers to bring the truth to the people, not merely what powerful, vested interests chose that people should read. He spoke fluently and well of liberty, justice, the rights of man. And John Bigelow sat back, listened and, when Matthew finished, looked at him sadly.

'Mr O'Hanlon, it is the duty of any newspaper to stay in print, and to stay in print means making money. Bring me a story that will make me money and I'll print it.'

'Does the story have to be true, Mr Bigelow?'

'It has to be believable, readable, and relevant and that's all it has to be.'

'Don't you think you have a responsibility to your readers and, yes, to history, to make the truth known? Even more so when others try to stifle that truth.'

'In my opinion, Mr Hanlon, and I'm a man who's studied the subject, all history is fiction, some completely so, some only for the most part.'

'In other words lies.'

'No, fiction. But nonetheless true for that.'

Matthew begged to disagree.

'How can fiction be called history especially if it's not the truth?'

'Because it's the only history we've got and it's based on the only truth we're likely to get, that's why. I'm sorry, Mr Hanlon. I wish I could tell you that I admire your courage and determination in trying to get this story out. But all I can honestly say is that I regret your foolishness in thinking for one moment that your view of things, even if it is true, will ever be told.' Bigelow stood up and held out his hand, in it was Matthew's carefully crafted note. 'Good day.'

Matthew took his note, thanked him, and left, defeated.

Outside the *Evening Post* offices the sun was already

high in the sky. Matthew stood in the warm sunshine and looked at the note which he still held in his hand. Was Bigelow right? Was he wasting his time, should he give up? Desperate men are given to desperate deeds and Matthew was desperate. When writing his note he had made a decision. He was a writer, a journalist, that was his talent and it would be a sin to bury in some other line of work. Little of the fire of that enthusiasm had survived his interview with John Bigelow, but enough for him to make one last attempt and, if he failed again, then he would give up.

For his last throw he chose the *Courier and Enquirer*. It was the paper that Lemuel Possett had disparaged as refusing to move with the times and had indeed been in steady decline for some years. Matthew and all the journalists he knew at the *Herald* agreed that its demise was inevitable so long as Webb was editor because he refused to adapt to the modern age of journalistic and technological change. It would not, for instance, make full use of the new Morse-telegraphy, it would not produce short, punchy news stories nor indulge in humour and satire as all the successful papers were increasingly doing. If its editor wanted to revive the paper's fortunes perhaps he would take a risk and run the story.

Having made himself known at the reception and handed over his note, to his surprise he was shown fairly promptly into the editor's office where the editor himself, James Watson Webb, was waiting.

Webb didn't ask Matthew to sit and came straight to the point.

'I've heard what you're doing, young man, and I'm telling you, here and now, to stop this nonsense.'

Matthew was taken aback by the words and the tone but he gathered himself quickly. He had had enough of editors and his blood was finally rising in revolt.

'You'd call the assassination of a president nonsense,

sir?'

'Yes, and damned nonsense, because there has been no assassination and anyone trying to bring such a story before the people can only be doing so for some mischievous end.'

'Mischievous end? I'm afraid I don't understand.'

'To scare-monger and sow discord. To harm the government and unsettle the minds of ordinary American citizens.'

'You think the truth might prove unsettling to ordinary Americans, Mr Webb?'

'Damn your impertinence, sir. Stop this nonsense I say or we will have it stopped.'

Matthew, deeply disappointed though not really surprised that his final effort had so palpably and so quickly failed, found himself happy to let his stoked-up anger coalesce around this blustering, middle-aged, self-important man and had been about to give him a broadside of searing invective, but Webb's last words suddenly gave him an almost uncontrollable urge to laugh.

'Stopped?'

'Stopped, sir.'

The desire to laugh evaporated. What did Webb mean? Was he actually being threatened?

'Who is this we, Mr Webb? And how will I be stopped?'

At Matthew's calmly delivered questions Webb seemed to become unsure of himself, as if he had said more than he had intended.

He made an angry gesture.

'Never mind the who and the how, sir. If you have a conscience and if you have any love of country you will have done with this, this ...'

'Assassination?'

Webb waved Matthew's note which he held in his hand.

126

'This pack of lies, this vile calumny, this lunatic fantasy, for, if you are not an out-and-out villain and traitor, then the only other thing I can imagine is that you are insane.'

And he crumpled the note into a small ball and threw it away from him.

Matthew allowed himself a small smile.

'No, Mr Webb, I am quite sane, I assure you.'

The smile seemed to infuriate Webb beyond his endurance.

'Then get out. I do not choose to breathe the same air as you, sir.'

Matthew went to the door, stopped, and looked back.

'Am I to assume, Mr Webb, that I have been threatened? That unless I stop pursuing this story some harm will come to me?'

He waited for an answer and Webb glared at him furiously.

'I have said all I intend to say. You can think what you like, sir. Think what you damn well like and get out.'

'I see. Well, whoever the we is that you represent, please tell them from me that they can go to hell. Good-day, sir.'

And Matthew left and made his way to the nearest bar to buy himself a beer and settle his nerves.

Having bought his beer and taken it to a table he sat wondering what, exactly, he was going to do. He had no job and it was clear that no New York paper would let him write his story. And he had been threatened. What on earth did that mean? Matthew tried to remember Webb's exact words, "stop this nonsense or we will have it stopped". That was no empty formula, Matthew was sure. Webb was delivering a message. And he had been ready for Matthew's visit. He expected him and was ready. All of which could only mean that somebody with enough power to control a New York editor had heard of what he was trying to do, thought him a threat, and had tried to warn him off.

So did that confirm that the assassination theory was true, or was it no more than him being warned off from being a nuisance? One thought slowly surfaced among the questions. Whatever the reason for the threat it was a sign that he had been noticed and had provoked a reaction. It was like his standing up to Fred Hudson, it showed him as someone of consequence, that he was indeed a man that people noticed and remembered. Perhaps his failures were Fate's way of leading him to this one significant, if unanticipated, success – that he had made powerful enemies.

That, surely, was something. Hadn't someone once said that you judge a man's stature by the greatness of his enemies?

Quietly, he raised his glass and whispered to it.

'To glory then, and a place in history.'

Chapter Seventeen

That evening Matthew had not gone down to the lounge at all after dinner. He didn't want company, he wanted to be alone with his thoughts. What to do? Well, first things had to be first. His week's wages wouldn't last for ever and so he needed a job and he needed one quickly. It was either that or return to living with his parents and that was definitely *not* the life-style of a man destined for glory.

The next morning he left as if for work as usual. To all outward appearances he was still employed and he felt sure his secret was safe from all in the boarding house. He had spent the first part of the day walking Wall Street although he was now fairly sure in his own mind that his future would not be as a banker. His family had not suffered any personal loss from the financial Panic of 1837 and the five-year long depression which followed but like all working families they had still felt the consequences. Costs had gone up and wages down. Two of Matthew's brothers and one brother-in-law had suffered bouts of unemployment and his parents had been forced to support them and their children until new work could be found. They also knew many neighbours who had fared considerably worse, losing their homes as well as their livelihoods. Many lives had been ruined and all-but-ruined by the financiers of Wall Street with their speculations and their greed. New York had eventually pulled itself together and now a new prosperity promised but bitter memories remained especially among the poor and the working classes who had borne the brunt of the consequences. Bankers were still largely a reviled and despised race in many homes across the city. As Matthew walked along the hub of New York's financial district he tried to imagine

129

himself as a captain of finance. He didn't doubt he could do it, but was mere wealth what he wanted? When you came right down to it, what was there that was glorious about bankers, even the wealthiest of them?

By mid-morning he had decided that finance could not fulfil his ambitions and left Wall Street behind him. Fate was at work in his life, he felt sure. Fate had pitted him against Frederic Hudson. Fate had introduced him to Sam Grant. Fate had followed him on his crusade for the truth and revealed to him that he had powerful enemies even if he had no friends. Very well, he would put himself in Fate's hands and take the first job offered to him. He bought a paper and scanned the positions open. Nothing struck him as so very attractive but he had acquired such a belief in his destiny that he now knew that whatever work he put his hand to, no matter how menial, it would lead to something. He would take a job, any job, and leave the rest to Fate.

Unfortunately, New York did not seem to share Matthew's new-found view of himself as a man of consequence. For the rest of that day and for all the next he followed up advertisements for various positions. He was an educated young man with a year's experience on a major New York newspaper who, he said, had resigned his position on a matter of principal, a personal disagreement with the editor, the nature of which he was not at liberty to reveal. But New York didn't seem prepared to co-operate with Fate and wanted neither a man of principle nor a man of destiny, however well educated, so Matthew returned on Friday evening to Bigane's at the usual time foot-sore and still without employment.

The following day being Saturday he visited his brother Dan and had dinner with him, his wife, and their three children. But he gave no hint of his current situation. On Sunday he met his mother, father, and sister at morning Mass and went home with them for Sunday lunch and again was silent about his situation, even going so far as, when asked how the job was going, to indulge in a direct lie.

'Great, couldn't be better. Doing fine.'

Matthew left the house in the early evening feeling somewhat guilty. He had lied to his parents, not only that, the lie had been told after going to Sunday Mass and must therefore be classed as a "mortal" placing his soul in peril of hell. He walked back to his lodgings determining that on the following Saturday morning he would go to early confession and in the meantime he would be very careful crossing roads.

On Monday morning, after what had been a thoroughly miserable weekend, he had gone out after breakfast with no clearly defined plan for the day and had not gone more than a few yards from Bigane's front door when he found Clarence Diver joining him and falling into step.

Matthew was more than a little disturbed at Clarence's presence. He was headed for no particular destination, indeed, he had no idea where he would go when he reached the end of Bleecker Street and he had no wish for company while he made up his mind as to his plans for the day. He tried to think of some way to part company without giving offence but Clarence Diver was the first to speak as they made their way among all the other pedestrians streaming from their houses onto the sidewalks.

'I'm afraid Mrs Bigane will have to be told.'

'Told? Told what?'

'That you're currently unemployed and were dismissed from the *Herald* last week.'

Clarence kept on walking but Matthew stopped dead and someone blundered into his back and cursed him.

'God dammit, man, what do you think you're doing?'

Matthew hurried on after Clarence and fell into step. He dismissed at once any idea of subterfuge. If Clarence

131

Diver knew that he was without a job, though God alone knew how, then he knew.

'How did you find out?'

'I was told.'

'Told? Who by? Why were you told?'

'Because I was asked to … how shall I put this? I was asked to put you out of action. If necessary to use my judgement, to dispose of you.'

'Dispose? Dispose how?'

Clarence turned and gave Matthew a friendly smile.

'If necessary, to arrange an accident. But that would be an extreme response. As I said, I was told to use my judgement.'

Matthew almost stopped dead again but remembered the last incident and continued. He was about to ask one of the many questions jostling each other in his brain and demanding utterance but decided to stay silent and consider what Diver had just so casually said.

He carefully looked sideways at the man walking beside him. Was he joking? Was this some sort of hoax? But Diver had never before shown any overly exuberant sense of humour. What's more, his manner of speaking, apart the actual words spoken, carried conviction.

Clarence Diver walked on among the crowd, looking straight ahead until they came to the junction where Bleecker Street met 6th Avenue and the stream of moving humanity increased. As they arrived Clarence slipped his hand round Matthew's arm.

'We go this way.'

'But …'

'No buts, Matthew. My office is this way and we're going to my office.'

Matthew felt the grip tighten and looked into Clarence Diver's eyes. No, there was no humour there. Whatever was going on it wasn't any joke, and this wasn't the Clarence Diver he knew. Suddenly Matthew felt a strange sensation – anticipation. Of course! This was exactly what he should have expected. The unexpected. This sudden and inexplicable behaviour of Clarence Diver was part of his destiny. He must grab it with both hands.

'Sure, Clarence, why not? I've nowhere else to go, have I?'

Clarence Diver let his hand drop and the smile returned.

'Very sensible, Matthew.'

They resumed walking although this time they walked against the flow of the main throng and speech for a time became impossible as they separated, rejoined, and separated again. Eventually the tide they were walking against lessened and more of the crowded pavement began to move with them rather than against.

'Are you going to explain?'

'Sure. Eventually. But not here in the street. We'll leave explanations until we get to my office. I'm glad that you can be sensible though, because that will be a great help to me. I need a man with sense and brains. Actually I need a man with more than sense and brains, but they'll do to be going on with. When I get to the office, after I've given you your explanation, I'm going to offer you a job, Matthew. I hope, when you hear what it is, you'll stay sensible and take it.'

Matthew tried to laugh.

'Or what? You'll have to arrange an accident for me?'

A young woman walking near them turned with a look of alarm on her face. Clarence Diver smiled and courteously raised his hat to her. The young woman turned away and hurried on.

'I might, Matthew, I might.' The words were not spoken in any form of jest and it seemed to Matthew that Clarence Diver truly meant what he said. Then Clarence turned to him. 'But let's hope it won't come to that,' and he smiled. 'No, I'm sure it won't, not if you're sensible.'

Chapter Eighteen

Clarence and Matthew walked together down 6th Avenue, the pavements bustling with pedestrians and the roadway busy with all manner of horse-drawn vehicles, heavy carts, hackney cabs, elegant phaetons, and rougher, more solid carriages built for roads where the city pavements ended. And in the middle of this mad throng, running along their rails, the noisy, over-crowded, ever-present omnibuses. A city on the move.

The buildings themselves seemed to be coming awake. Upstairs office windows were being opened at the prospect of another hot day and figures flitted to and fro across them. Shopkeepers were pulling out canvas awnings to offer shade to any customers who cared to pause and cast a glance into the displays in their windows. Other establishments had gone further and erected permanent wooden roofings across the whole of their section of sidewalk, offering shade from the summer sun and shelter from rain or winter snow. These flimsy wooden structures added a paradoxical air of frontier makeshift to the paved sidewalks and the massive, modern, stone buildings which lined both sides of the avenue and soared up three, four and some even five storeys high. Manhattan, it seemed, had determined that, as an island, if it couldn't for ever go on spreading outwards in its restless search for growth, it would go up, and no one doubted that one day the buildings which would line this very street would reach eight, nine or, yes, be bold, even ten storeys. Such was the miracle of Manhattan's drive and energy.

At Hudson Street Clarence turned. They walked on until they had almost reached the Hudson River itself then turned left into Greenwich Street. Here, immediately behind the buildings on their right, the great water highway ran parallel with their street was lined on both sides with all the buildings and paraphernalia of a waterfront; bars, lodging houses, shops, fenced yards, stables, closed workshops with grimed windows, open boat-yards where new craft were born and other yards where the old were broken up.

Light carts pulled by single horses moved slowly along the dusty roadway beside heavy carts pulled by teams of equally heavy horses and the pavements were busy with men and women nearly all of whom, one way or another, owed their living to the nearby river which, connected as it was to the Erie Canal, was New York's gateway to the Great Lakes and from there to the burgeoning interior of the mid-West.

Matthew was no snob, nor could he be coming from the district where he had grown up, but this was a waterfront neighbourhood and, like such neighbourhoods worldwide, it had its reputation. He was surprised that Clarence, whom he knew to be an accountant in the service of the government, should have his office in such a district, peopled, as it so obviously was, by river-men, longshoremen, and all those many others who were attendant on the waterway's trade.

Despite the fact that the original name, Greenwich Village, lingered for the whole area from the Hudson River to Broadway, this shoreline district had not been gentrified by any of the newer developments. Those more respectable and desirable streets began well back from the river, its people, and its industry. An office in somewhere like Hudson Square Matthew could have understood, inexpensive yet sufficiently central and convenient. But here? Good heavens, they were on the waterfront itself and almost *in* the river.

Spring Street came down from their left and finished in a wide gap between the buildings at the muddy reaches of the water's edge and here, just beyond the gap, Clarence turned into a detached, three-storey house which backed onto the river and on the ground floor of which was an apothecary's shop. He walked in, nodded to a man behind the counter, and crossed the sanded floor. The man, in a white, bibbed apron, returned the nod and continued about his business. Clarence led Matthew up a flight of stairs to the first floor and stopped at a very solid-looking door which had not one, but two locks. Diver took a key from one of his jacket pockets and unlocked the first lock, replaced the key, and took another from his trouser pocket, and unlocked the second. He turned to Matthew as he replaced the key.

'Come in. Welcome to my office.'

The house, from the outside, had been unremarkable and not dissimilar from many of its neighbours, plain and brick-built with large sash windows on the ground and first floors and smaller ones set into the roof for the third floor, all of which made Matthew's surprise the greater on entering Clarence Diver's office, for what confronted him wasn't strictly speaking an office at all. It resembled a cross between a scientific laboratory and a professor's study.

One thing it was not, of that Matthew was certain, it was not the office of a minor functionary in the service of some obscure government finance department.

Clarence Diver might indeed work for the government but whatever he did for them, he certainly wasn't an accountant.

Chapter Nineteen

Three sash windows ran across the wall facing the street; they were the only ones in the room and were barred on the inside. In the centre and taking up most of the available space in the room were two big desks. One had nothing on it except an empty, wooden paper tray. On the other there was a large, complicated, electrical-looking device which consisted of a substantial copper reel from which a thin tape of paper fed down into a metal box and came out the other side. Below the reel and box was a mass of metal coils and levers. The whole paraphernalia sat solidly on a heavy wooden base. On the side of the base were two small, brass connection points from which insulated wires were attached to a smaller machine which stood on its own wooden base. This smaller machine consisted of a brass lever with a black knob sticking up at one end. Below the desk and attached to the bigger machine by further wires was more equipment, some sort of heavy container.

It was all utterly strange to Matthew and obviously a world away from accountancy or any other office activity that he could bring to mind.

Clarence Diver took off his hat and jacket and hung them on a stand by the door while Matthew stood looking at the strange machinery. Diver came and stood beside him.

'It's a Morse magnetic telegraphic machine. Don't tell me that a modern newspaperman like you haven't seen one before?'

Matthew shook his head.

'Heard about it of course, but never seen one.'

'This machine and others like it are changing our world. Soon, it'll be as easy to send a message to

139

California as it is to say hello to your next door neighbour. And I'll tell you something else. It won't be too long before the wires of the telegraph will pass under the sea. When that happens London will be as close as Washington. What do you say to that?'

Matthew had nothing to say to that. He was, frankly, too amazed. Himself a great advocate of modernity in both social thinking and the role of science he was trying to comprehend a world where distances suddenly didn't exist, where machines talked to each other over distances of hundreds, nay, thousands of miles, even across oceans.

'Wires under the sea?'

Diver nodded a little smugly. He liked a suitably appreciative audience.

'Copper wires covered with a protective coat of gutta percha all bound together with a protective coating and laid in a cable. It can be done and it will be done. It's a new age, Matthew, the communications age.'

Matthew was impressed.

'That it will be, by God.'

'Which is why I've brought you here. Take a seat.'

Diver sat behind the free desk with his back to the windows and pointed to a chair opposite him.

Matthew sat down and looked around the rest of the room. On one side the wall was covered with various charts, diagrams, and maps. Below these was a deep, fitted dark-wood chest which ran the whole length of the wall. This chest consisted entirely of wide, shallow drawers with brass handles. Against the opposite wall, on either side of the door through which they had entered, stood two bookcases on which there were a great number of volumes of various sizes. Behind him, on the back wall that faced the windows, were three large, wooden filing cabinets of four deep drawers each. Each drawer had been fitted with a stout lock. Nowhere were there any ledgers or indeed any other evidence of accountancy.

Matthew turned his attention to Clarence Diver who had sat, patiently waiting while Matthew took in the room.

'You're not an accountant, are you?'

That drew a small laugh from Diver.

'I'm accountable, Matty, but as you say, not an accountant.'

'And do you work for the government?'

Diver nodded.

'Oh yes. I work for the comptroller of the Contingent Fund of Foreign Intercourse. Heard of it?' Matthew shook his head. 'No, I thought not. Not many people have.'

'It sounds ...'

Matthew searched for the right phrase but Diver neatly put his indecision into words.

'To Mrs Bigane it sounds downright sexual. But that's just her mind.'

Matthew hurriedly and with embarrassment countered this.

'No, that's not what I was going to say. It sounds like something diplomatic.'

'Well, sometimes it is and sometimes it isn't. It depends. But now you know who I work for let's get down to the business in hand. You. You've been making a nuisance of yourself, Mat, and I've been told to stop the nuisance.'

'By the comptroller of this Contingent Fund?'

'Not directly but as good as.'

Matthew left the evasive answer.

'What's he, whoever he is, got to do with me trying to tell people that President Taylor might have been assassinated?'

'Because to tell people that would not be in the national interest.'

'And this comptroller decided that?'

'No.'

'Then who?'

'God. God decided, Matthew. You're a Catholic aren't you?' Matthew nodded. 'A good one?'

'I try to be.'

'Then you'll know the difference between a venial sin and a mortal one.'

'What has any of this got to do with ...'

'Venial sins harm, do they not? Forgive a poor Protestant if I get the terminology a mite off mark. Venial sins are capable of correction. All that is needed is an admission of fault or error and a firm purpose of amendment. "Amendment"? That is the correct term, yes?' Matthew nodded once more. A firm purpose of amendment was exactly the correct term, just as it had been taught to him by parents and priests. 'Admit the wrong, put it right as well as you can, and you're forgiven. God grants you mercy. Right?'

'Get to the point.'

'That is my point. No admission of wrong, no firm purpose of amendment, then no forgiveness, no mercy. God must punish. That's the whole point, Matthew, and I hope I've made it clear to you. You've done wrong. Admit it, put it right so far as you can, and I, like one of your priests, will, in God's name, forgive you.' Diver smiled. 'I'd like to forgive you, Matthew. I would like to be merciful. But if you're stubborn. If you obdurately refuse mercy and forgiveness then the sin ceases to be merely venial and becomes more serious, in fact mortal. It becomes pride. And pride, Matthew, brings about a fall, a nasty fall. You understand?'

Matthew wasn't sure. All this talk of sin, of Catholic sin, confused him. He had tried to bring truth to the people, that a president may have been murdered. What had that got to do with sin and forgiveness? That was for Saturday confession, making you ready for Sunday Mass. It was nothing to do with ordinary life and certainly nothing to do with his work as a newspaperman.

142

'I don't know what the hell you're talking about.'

Clarence Diver pulled one of the desk drawers open, took out a large, strange-looking gun, and laid it heavily on the desk.

'I'm talking about life and death, Matthew. Your life and perhaps your death. You've done wrong. Accept forgiveness. If you won't or can't,' he tapped the large handgun, 'then expect punishment. You're Catholic, you more than anyone should see that's how it has to be.'

Matthew tried to laugh but, looking at the gun on the desk, suddenly found he couldn't.

'This is madness. You're talking like a lunatic.'

Diver shook his head sadly then, in almost one movement, picked up the gun, pulled back the hammer with his thumb, pointed it directly at Matthew's chest, and fired.

The noise filled the room and Matthew felt himself lurch back in his chair which nearly toppled over. Then he tipped forward and the chair settled.

There was a loud buzzing in his ears and, realizing he could hear it and was looking at Clarence Diver who was still holding the gun and still pointing it at him, was surprised to find that he was, after all, still alive. Then he felt a warm dampness in the front of his trousers, looked down and saw the darkening stain. The noise in his ears cleared and he heard Clarence Diver speaking. He looked up.

'… will come, Matthew. No one heard, no one who will do anything that is.' He nodded to the gun which he was still pointing. 'That chamber had no ball.' He pulled back the hammer of his pistol with his thumb. The chamber rotated. 'The next chamber is fully loaded, Matty, and it's time for you to decide. Venial or mortal. Forgiveness and mercy, or pride and a fall. Which is it to be?'

And Matthew watched as Clarence Diver's finger

closed on the trigger.

'I've wet my pants.'

It wasn't what meant to say, wasn't what he wanted to say. But it was what he said.

'That's natural. This betsy makes a powerful noise. But I still need an answer, Mat, and I need it now.'

If anyone had heard the explosion of the shot, and the man downstairs must have heard unless he was stone deaf, no one was coming.

'What do you want me to do?'

It was a capitulation, absolute and total surrender. It may not have been the response of a man who thought of himself as destined for glory, but it was certainly the response of a young man who had suddenly decided with absolute clarity that he didn't want to die.

Diver caught the hammer of his gun under his free palm, squeezed the trigger, and eased the hammer back into its seat, then held up the gun sideways in both hands for Matthew to see.

'Never seen anything like it, I guess. It's new, called the Colt Walker. Has six cylinders, each charged with powder and a forty-four calibre ball, and fired by a percussion cap. Too much gun to carry round of course but it's interesting and soon they'll find a way of making them smaller and lighter. Yep, sixteen inches long and weighs four and a half pounds, more of what I'd call a young cannon at the moment, but it's the shape of things to come.' He pulled the drawer open and put the revolver away. 'I take an interest in such things, it's part of my business to know what's going on in matters like weapon development. Now, if I need something of the sort on my person I use this.' He took another pistol from the drawer. It was small and filled no more than the palm of his hand. 'I had this specially made. It's a Derringer, two barrels and uses the new twenty-two calibre rimfire cartridge. Have to have the cartridges specially made, though, to give me

144

enough stopping power. Here, take a look. But be careful, it's loaded. It's small but up to ten feet it'll do the job well enough if you hit a vital spot.' Diver pushed the small gun across the desk to Matthew who sat looking down at it. 'No?' Diver reached across and pulled it back and put it in the drawer which he pushed shut. 'No interest in guns? I suppose as a newspaperman they're only of interest when other people use them? Well, no harm in that. Now, down to cases. You've made yourself something of a nuisance as I've said, but I think you're someone I can use. I've watched you, Matty, you're young and still a bit green,' he gave a small laugh, 'and by that I don't mean Irish. But there's something about you. You have a belief in yourself, you're willing to learn, and you want to make your way in the world. And today I found you could make up your mind quickly if you have to and, more importantly, come to the right decision.'

Matthew finally surfaced.

'Would you have shot me?'

'Absolutely.'

'Even though it would have been cold-blooded murder?'

'The people I work for don't abide by the normal rules. They have their own code of right and wrong. It had to be one way or the other, I told you that. I'm glad you made the right choice, by the way.'

Matthew tried to get some sarcasm into his voice. He might be down on the floor but he didn't want to become a door mat.

'Because you like me so much?'

That got a hearty laugh from Diver.

'Sure, Matty. But also because getting rid of a body here in New York can be troublesome and, as you'll find, I'm a man who'll go a long way to avoid trouble.' As there seemed no answer to the remark Matthew remained silent. 'Tell me, Matty, how does Panama sound to you?'

145

'Panama?'

'You know, northern state of Colombia. They're building a railroad there.'

'I'd heard.'

'Good, because I want you to go there. I have a job for you. New York's no place for you any more and you have to go somewhere. Why not Panama?'

'And help build the railroad?'

'Sort of. You might say so. But what you'll be is what you're good at. You'll be a newsman, a reporter.'

'And who'll I report to?'

'Me, Matthew, you'll report to me.'

'And the story?'

'Ah, the story. You comfortable? Trousers still bothering you?'

'They'll dry.'

'Well then, let me tell you all about Panama.'

Chapter Twenty

The Office of the Secretary of State
Washington, July 25th

The current comptroller of the Contingency Fund of Foreign Intercourse, Mr Oliver Blanchette, was a small, balding man with a drooping moustaches who had the dry and resigned air of an accountant, which by training and occupation he was. He was standing in front of the desk of Daniel Webster, for two days now secretary of state for the Union. Mr Blanchette was trying hard not to look alarmed, and failing rather badly.

'The Polk Plan! Oh dear me, no. No, no. I know nothing of the Polk Plan, nothing at all. No, oh dear me, no. Nothing.'

'Am I to take it then, that in answer to my question, "do you know anything of the Polk Plan?" you would say "no"?'

Webster's heavy irony, however, seemed lost on the little man who was too agitated to notice it.

'Yes. Absolutely yes. I know nothing. No, absolutely not.'

Webster's reply was as sharp as it was pointed.

'But you know enough to deny knowing anything?'

A look of confusion overcame the comptroller but, after a short moment, he seemed to pull himself together. He stood to his full height, such as it was, forced a tone of confidence and authority in his voice, and responded to the secretary of state's question.

'Mr Secretary, you may have my resignation, at once if you wish. In fact I would prefer at once. I never wanted my present position. I was happy in my previous situation

147

in the department of the treasury. I was forced into this present role, sir, absolutely forced by a person whose name I cannot and shall not mention, but who was at the time in a position of the utmost authority. The utmost. Yes indeed. As to any Polk Plan, or any other plan which the diseased imaginings of my predecessor as comptroller, Jeremiah Jones, may have dreamed up, I repeat, sir, I know nothing, want to know nothing, and can know nothing. There, sir. There you have it.'

And the little man stood, silent and defiant while Daniel Webster tried to decide on his best course of action. Bully? Browbeat and threaten? Coax and encourage? Or cajole?

He had faced this same choice many times when about to question hostile witnesses in one of his many court cases and it was his great talent to know when to play the bully and when to play the friend, and know how to change from one to the other in an instant, and back again if necessary.

'Come now, Mr Blanchette. I would no more dream of asking for your resignation than I would of offering my own to the president. I, like you, have been asked to take up the heavy weight of high government office. I, also like you, was content in my previous role. But, and again like you, someone of the utmost authority, the utmost, asked me to serve my country. Unlike you I was not forced. It was a question of my country so I took on my present burden willingly, most willingly.'

Here he paused, having injected into his last sentence a small hint of contempt.

The comptroller was, once again, subject to an attack of confusion.

'No. I didn't mean ... I am proud to serve. No. What I meant ... What, perhaps I should have said ...'

'Good. I'm glad we can agree that our duty is to serve, to be useful tools of the government. If we become blunted or broken tools our masters may cast us aside, that is their privilege, indeed it is their duty. Our duty is to serve until our services are no longer called upon or we break under our burdens. No. No resignations here, indeed not. Absolutely. No.' Webster's use of Mr Blanchette's own manner of speaking seemed to reassure the comptroller, as Webster had intended. 'Now, sir, the Polk Plan.' Mr Blanchette started. For a second he had begun to think the matter might be closed and, finding it was not, he was about to launch into another stout denial of any knowledge but Webster held up a pacific hand, 'of which you, of course, know nothing, want to know nothing, and can know nothing,' and Webster smiled a conspiratorial smile, 'so whatever you might tell me can go no further, cannot be in any way recorded, nor can it be used so that it might be traced back to you. It is one servant, new to office, seeking the help and advice of another servant who is now in service to his second president and therefore a man of wide experience.'

The comptroller gave the secretary's words some thought. Despite his earlier protestations he was not unhappy in his work. In fact he was quite contented to be comptroller of the Contingent Fund so long as the post was no more than its name clearly implied, full financial oversight, and no more. On being virtually forced into the position by one of the utmost authority, lately deceased, it was made clear to him by that person that the Contingent Fund had been used, indeed had been established to be used, for secret purposes. The same person made it clear that, in his view, too may presidents had not only used but misused the fund and none more so than his predecessor, President James K. Polk.

'Well, Mr Secretary, as I know nothing I don't see how ...'

'But *I* see how, sir, that is the point. For instance I see that there is indeed such a plan.' He waited a second. 'Is there not?'

'The name exists.'

'Good. You know the name and, I suspect, a little more than the name.'

'Mr Secretary, I am an accountant and, if I may say so, more than competent in my work. When I was employed by the treasury department my main task was to follow through possible cases of fraud perpetrated against the government by its contractors. I tell you this, sir, so that you may know that I have some considerable ability in following figures and documents and from them creating a highly accurate picture of how certain events unfolded.' Webster nodded encouragingly. 'You understand that it was never necessary for me to become acquainted with any of the parties I investigated. All I needed was full and free access to all the relevant account ledgers, invoices, bills of lading ...'

'Yes, yes, yes. All the necessary information and documentation. Please go on.'

'When I became comptroller of the fund I familiarised myself with its finances. I can only say that some of what I came across frankly horrified me. It would appear that, under my predecessor, Mr Jeremiah Jones, actions were funded and carried through which were not only highly illegal under American law but would be, in any society which claims to be civilised, abhorrent and loathsome.'

Webster pretended shock.

'Really? You astound me.'

'I was astounded myself, sir. That my own country could involve itself in such adventures, such nefarious adventures.'

'Yes, well, as you said, that was in the past. Under the present administration, of course ...'

And he left the sentence hanging.

'Of course.'

'So, the Polk Plan?'

There was a knock at the door which immediately opened. Webster looked across angrily, he was almost there and this interruption had come at the worst possible moment. The man who had entered ignored the look.

'The president wishes to speak with you, Mr Secretary.'

'Very well. I will be with the president shortly.'

'The president would like to see you now, Mr Secretary.'

Webster stood up and turned to the comptroller. He had been summoned.

'Thank you, Mr Blanchette, as you see I am called away by duty.'

'Will you need me again, Mr Secretary?'

Webster looked at him. Was it worth the effort? Probably not.

'No, I think we will leave the matter where it stands.'

'Thank you, Mr Secretary.'

And the comptroller sincerely meant those thanks and almost scurried to the door, slipped past the man waiting, and was gone.

Secretary Webster was led to the Yellow Oval Room where, standing by the president, was an elderly man with grey hair brushed back from a high forehead. His face was lined with age and illness but his eyes were clear and bright. This was the senator from Kentucky, Henry Clay.

'Good morning, Mr President. Good morning, Henry.'

Henry Clay shook Daniel Webster's outstretched hand.

'Good morning, Daniel, or should I say, Mr Secretary.'

President Fillmore sat down.

'I asked you to come, Daniel, to let you know that Henry is leaving Washington.'

'Now? At this time and after so much work on the compromise?'

Henry Clay gave Webster a sad smile.

'It's a simple choice, Daniel, one given me by my

doctors. Stay, fight on with the Compromise Bill, and be dead in a matter of months or even weeks. Or hand over to someone else and maybe live a few more years. What would you suggest?'

'I see. I didn't realise how much the fight had taken out of you. Of course you must hand over to someone else.' Webster turned to President Fillmore. 'Who shall it be?'

'Stephen Douglas. We need a strong figure, someone who will make himself heard and lead the fight in a way that others will follow.'

'Then Douglas is a good choice.'

Henry Clay began coughing and, when recovered, he put away his handkerchief and spoke slowly as if the attack had considerably weakened him, which indeed it had.

'And now, Mr President, with your permission I will leave Washington and go home to Kentucky. If I can make it that far.'

'Of course, Henry, and get well. Get well soon. The Senate still needs you.'

'Thank you, Mr President.'

Henry Clay left and Webster looked at the president.

'What is it, Mr President, just weariness or something more?'

'Consumption. He's already in his seventies so I'm afraid Henry's career is over.'

'And his life?'

'A year, maybe two if he's careful and lucky.'

'Well, Douglas is a good man, he'll fill Henry's place as well as anyone could.'

'Perhaps, but that's not why I asked you to come. I've had a letter from William Aspinwall.' He picked up a sheet of paper and held it out. 'Here, read it.'

Webster took the sheet and the president waited as his eyes passed over it.

'If he means what he says he's prepared to stop work

152

on the Panama Railway.'

'He means it all right.'

'But if he stops the work even for no more than a month it could mean an end of the project. Any extended delay would be fatal.'

'And that means investors here in the US will lose over one million dollars.'

'But that would trigger another financial panic.'

President Fillmore stood up angrily.

'Don't you think I know that? Any damn fool would know that. Just as any damn fool would know that if any hint of a cessation of work on the railroad was to get out there'd be a mass sell-off and that would lead to a run on half a dozen banks that are tied into this thing. If that happened we'd have to deal with something that would make the Panic of 'Thirty-seven look like a spat in a nursery.' The president walked to the window and stood looking out over the sunlight gardens. It was his favourite view from any of the White House windows, for he found it calmed him as none other did. Webster waited. Eventually the president turned. 'Did you tell Jones I might want the Polk Plan re-activated?'

'I did.'

'Did you ask him what it was?'

'Yes. He declined to tell me but he said I could say that things would be put in train if you asked.'

'What did you think of him?'

'I didn't like him.'

'No. Few people who had any dealings with Jeremiah Jones found him an easy man to like. Well, he did a good job in helping you squash any newspaper interest in Taylor's death so I suppose his finger is still pretty much still in the business of intrigue. Just as well seeing who Taylor left me as comptroller of the Fund.'

'I've just had him in my office.' That drew a look of surprise from the president.

'Have you, by God? Not going behind my back already, I hope, Daniel?'

'Just being ready. You said you might want the Polk Plan up and running again. I decided to see what the comptroller of the fund was like. He'll be no use to you, Mr President, if the Polk Plan is what I think it is.'

'And what's that?'

'The sort of plan that, if it ever got out, could bring down a president.' President Fillmore came away from the window.

'Maybe it could, if it was instigated by a president. Polk knew that and let it lie until he'd left office. He was going to take it up again with Jones as soon as his term had ended but the Lord Almighty had other plans before anything could be done.' Webster gestured to the letter on the desk. 'That's why this didn't surprise me.'

'You knew Aspinwall would make trouble?'

'Polk promised him full government support and protection for his railroad. Taylor all but reneged on that support but Aspinwall didn't want to go up against Taylor. Now he wants to know where I stand. Am I with Polk's view of the Panama Railway or Taylor's?'

'And which will it be?'

'Neither, Daniel. I will leave that decision to my secretary of state. And I won't ask him how he intends to carry out giving the railroad his full support,' he paused, 'if that's what he chooses. I will simply approve Contingent Funds if he requests them. You *will* be requesting funds, won't you, Daniel? After you've made your decision, of course.'

'Very probably, Mr President.'

'Good. I want you to tell Aspinwall of your decision straight away, that he will have the same full support from this administration as he was promised by President Polk. Do you understand, Mr Secretary? That my secretary of state has endorsed whatever President Polk promised?

154

Then get hold of Jones again.'

'I see. I assume what we are talking about is a clandestine project?'

'Oh very much so. And not only clandestine but inflammable and highly combustible, the sort that's likely to go up in flames and blow up all and any who are at all close to it if it in any way misfires. So you see, do you not, Daniel, that the president must have no knowledge of the details whatsoever.'

'And secretaries of state?' President Fillmore smiled and shrugged.

'Presidents are elected by the people, while in office they become the mind and voice of the nation. Secretaries of state are appointed, they are a tool the president must use and, like all tools, can and should be changed if they fail to function, as Henry Clayton will be changed. Do you not agree, Daniel?' Webster nodded. 'Then go and see that Aspinwall has his assurances and the Panama Railway continues to go ahead exactly as planned. Good-day, Mr Secretary.' Daniel Webster was dismissed.

'Very good, Mr President.'

As he reached the door President Fillmore called to him.

'Remember, Daniel, the Polk Plan is highly inflammable. Try not to get singed. You've got shares in this project I suppose?'

'Yes, Mr President, some.'

'Then you're stuck with them. I don't want any sell-off started by a bit of insider dealing. Get me my Polk Plan and maybe they won't be the scrap paper they're looking like at the moment.' President Fillmore smiled at him and Webster reminded himself how much he now loathed that smile. 'How comforting it must be to you, Daniel, when one's own interests and those of one's country so happily coincide. Do you not agree, Mr Secretary.'

'Absolutely, Mr President. Absolutely.'

Chapter Twenty-one

Almost as soon as Daniel Webster was back in his office the door opened and a visitor was announced. Webster told him to be sent in. A few moments later an elderly man dressed in a fashion that was ten to fifteen years out of date limped into the secretary of state's office, aided by a stick.

'I thought you might want to see me after your meeting with the president, Mr Secretary, so I made sure I was available. May I sit? My leg has always been weak but now, with the infirmities of age, I'm afraid standing soon becomes very painful.' Daniel Webster motioned his visitor to take a chair and Jeremiah Jones sat down. 'Thank you.'

Webster was not surprised at this visit. He had not liked Jeremiah Jones when they had met but he had been impressed with him and even more impressed with the way he had virtually taken over the task of silencing the newspapers, and had accomplished the task with what appeared to be not only efficiency but ease. Officially he might be retired but unofficially, despite his lame leg, he was obviously still very much on active service.

'It's the Polk Plan I suppose?'

'It is.'

'And now, as the matter will definitely go forward, do you still wish know the details?'

Webster, as had been the cast at their last meeting, felt his anger rising at this old man's calm but maddening manner.

'The matter will definitely go forward, will it?'

Jones looked at Daniel Webster for a second then leaned on his stick as if about to rise and spoke in an apologetic tone.

'If I am mistaken. If my information is in error I apologise. The choice will, of course be yours, Mr Secretary. When you have made your decision I will return, if you have need of me.'

Jones half rose and Webster snapped angrily at him.

'Sit down. The matter will, as you say, proceed.'

Jones resumed his seat.

'And you wish to know the details?'

'Do I?'

Jones gave the question some consideration.

'That depends on the possible outcomes. If the plan succeeds then to be seen as its author would make you someone beyond the ordinary, albeit among the very limited number of men ever allowed to know that the plan existed. You would become exceptional even amongst those who justifiably regard themselves as of some consequence.'

'And if it fails?'

'In ventures of this sort the political norm is reversed. Success ensures silence, failure ensures publicity. If the Polk Plan were to be implemented and fail, questions would inevitably be asked and answers would have to be given. I have no doubt that President Fillmore would, himself, remain above any unpleasantness and allow Congress to allocate the blame and decide the consequences as they saw fit.'

'I see.'

'That being the case it is for you as secretary of state to decide how much you can know,' Jones paused, 'officially.'

'And unofficially, as Daniel Webster?'

Jeremiah Jones' manner subtly changed. Previously he had been all false deference. Now he spoke in a more relaxed manner, one man to another, a conversation between equals. The change was not wasted on Daniel

Webster.

'You are an accomplished lawyer, Mr Webster, you will know that as long as a thing cannot be positively proved in a court of law men can and do say, "I have done nothing wrong" and the formula is accepted. If you have a casual conversation, away from your official office, with a person who once held a minor position in a previous administration, what does that constitute? No more than a wish on your part to understand the better what those who have gone before you thought and felt about certain issues. You would be availing yourself of background, a new secretary of state indulging in informal discussions, preferably with several individuals, which might or might not have touched upon any of many topics. Hardly evidence of conspiracy or anything else untoward in court-of-law terms.'

Daniel Webster, always a haughty spirit, resented this man's familiar tone.

'Don't try to teach me the law. How illegal would you say this Polk Plan is?'

'Oh I wouldn't say. But a secretary of state, if asked a direct question in such matters, would have to say, and the answer would be that any covert action against a friendly, sovereign nation, mounted without congressional knowledge or approval, would be treasonable. But as you observed, I mustn't try to teach you the law, Mr Secretary, especially not Constitutional Law.' Daniel Webster lost patience. This man's infuriating complacency was now bordering on arrogance but before he could speak Jeremiah Jones, despite his weak leg, was on his feet. 'And now I must leave you, Mr Secretary. I'm tired and my leg hurts. If you wish to see me again in your official capacity, in this office or anywhere else, then summon me formally and I will attend with my lawyer. If, however, you wish at any time to take tea with me at my residence I would be honoured. My store of knowledge of the world and its

159

ways is limited but it is at your disposal. I wish you well in your new office, Mr Secretary. The Union needs wise, strong, and honourable men at its helm. Good day'

And Jeremiah Jones limped to the door and left.

Daniel Webster sat for a moment reflecting on the strange, elderly cripple who had, he thought, just snubbed him in his own state office. Webster was a man of supreme self-confidence, both proud and haughty. But he was also an excellent judge of character and he felt that the man who had just left, President James K. Polk's comptroller of the Contingent Fund, was just the man he needed to set the Polk Plan, whatever it was, in motion. He rang the bell on his desk and his aide entered.

'Make an appointment for me to take tea with Mr Jeremiah Jones. He seems an interesting old gentleman and an amusing one. I liked him. I'm sure he has a fund of anecdotes he could relate on previous administrations. Note it in my official diary. Informal visit to Mr Jeremiah Jones for tea and conversation. Use those words.'

'Very well, Mr Secretary.'

'And make it soon. In fact make it as soon as possible.'

'Very well, Mr Secretary.'

And the aide hurried from the office sure he could catch Mr Jones before he left the building. But, to his surprise, his haste was unnecessary. Standing by his desk when he got there was Mr Jones, leaning on his stick waiting and smiling a gentle smile.

Chapter Twenty-two

It would not be overstating the facts to say that Matthew O'Hanlon was stunned. It wasn't that Clarence Diver had turned out to be some sort of real government agent; the new Matthew had been able to adjust his mind to that. It was all part and parcel of what he now expected, that something out of the ordinary was going to happen for him. What stunned Matthew was the job Clarence Diver had offered – special representative in Panama for the New York Associated Press.

Of course when he explained Matthew understood.

'You're a newspaperman through and through, Matty, and will be a good one given the chance. I'm giving you that chance. You're aware that William Aspinwall is building a railway across Panama?' Matthew nodded. 'If he succeeds it could be the most important railroad in the world. It will link the Atlantic with the Pacific but, more importantly, it will link our new states in the West with those here in the East. California and the Oregon territories need settlers and this railway line, when it's built, will not only make the journey fast but safe. We need families going out there, Matty, good settling folk who want a future for themselves and their children.'

Matthew chimed in enthusiastically.

'And there's the gold rush. From what I've seen of ships leaving the ports here in New York men can't get to California fast enough. They're pouring in from everywhere, the whole world seems to have got gold fever.'

'Yes, there's the gold too. That new railroad of Aspinwall's is going to be the new Camino Real, a royal road in every sense of the word. Settlers and prospectors going out and gold coming back. It's going to be a phenomenon.'

'If it gets built.'

'Oh it will, Matty, my boy. America has the know-how and the drive to get these great things done. Why, one day there'll be a railroad right across this great country from coast to coast. Railroads are like this magnetic telegraph here, they're going to change the world, and this railroad in Panama that joins one great ocean to another will be news. New York newspapers are going to want a blow-by-blow account of the building of it, the men, the machines, the difficulties, the failures and successes. And the human stories. They tell me it's a hell-hole down there, a white man's grave, so you'll have no problem with what to send. How many lives did each mile of track cost? How are their medical facilities coping?' Diver paused. 'That's if they have any of course. Anyway, a man of your talent could bring all the colour of the thing right back here to New York,' and Clarence Diver laughed loudly, 'so long as the colour you bring isn't yellow of course. I guess New York knows about all it wants to about yellow fever.' Matthew responded with a weak smile. He would be the one out there. 'Tell it so that so that New Yorkers can almost feel the heat and see the jungle. Make 'em sweat, Matty, make 'em sweat.'

Matthew tried to look enthusiastic, which he was, of course, but he was the one being invited to go to this heat and this jungle that Diver had just referred to as a hell-hole and a white man's grave so his enthusiasm was somewhat mixed. But, despite the obvious dangers, he decided as soon as he heard the offer he must accept. It wasn't just newspaper work, it was what he had felt coming, an adventure, a chance of glory. Going to Panama and sending New York the story of how the Panama Railway was built would be his chance to chronicle a piece of history in the making. It wasn't the death of a president,

162

true, but it was the birth of a railway and a new age.

Clarence Diver went on.

'Aspinwall's raised a considerable amount money for this railroad, Wall Street has backed him to the hilt. The company floated with a million dollars they tell me.'

Matthew was impressed. Such a vast sum was hard for him to comprehend.

'A million?'

Diver nodded solemnly.

'So you can guess the sort of people who'll have their tongues hanging out to hear how it's going down there. There's swamps, raging rivers, mountains, jungle, and God knows what else. Personally I don't doubt for one minute that it will get built, but with all that has to be overcome I guess there'll be plenty of folk here who will think it's by no means a sure thing. And if it doesn't get built Wall Street will take a knock that'll make 'Thirty-seven look like a Sunday-school treat. If the right man covers the story as it unfolds it could be the making of him. There wouldn't be a paper in America, Europe even, that wouldn't pay top dollar to sign him up. Well, Matthew, what do you say? Is it Panama for you or should I get out that young cannon of mine again?'

And once more Clarence Diver laughed.

Matthew responded in kind, though this time his laughter was not so very forced.

'When do I sail?'

It had been as he knew it would ever since his meeting with Sam Grant. He was to be a newspaperman again, and not the least of them, by God, not at all the least of them.

Chapter Twenty-three

That evening Matthew went to his parents' house and broke the news of his offer of a job, but he did so in the way Clarence had suggested to him.

'Of course your parents must be told. But better to leave me out of it. Just say that you had an approach from the Associated Press and decided to accept.'

'You mean lie to my own parents?'

'Not lie, no. It's more a question of adjusting what you say so as to protect the greater good.'

'Greater good?'

'To the world you'll be working for the New York Associated Press, as indeed you will be. Only you and I, Matthew, must know that you are also working for the government. These things are sensitive and not easily understood by what I might call the lay mind. Tell people only what they need to know. I've found it usually suffices.'

'I suppose so.'

And Diver had proved correct. Matthew's mother accepted at once that her son's undoubted talents had been recognised and the offer of a job as special foreign correspondent was no more than he deserved. It was a confirmation of what she had held all along, that her youngest son was someone above and beyond the commonplace. As to Panama she was less certain. It sounded, she said, horribly foreign and a long way from home. Still, as she and her husband had begun life together by striking out into the unknown to a far-distant foreign land, she was sure that Matthew would be as successful as his father had been, do great things, and come home rich and famous. Matthew felt that his mother's view, though perhaps a little biased in respect of his talents and abilities, chimed in nicely with his own estimate of the eventual outcome of his adventure but he was careful not to make any mention of hell-holes or white man's graves. Instead he mentioned that he understood Panama could be hot and sometimes quite wet. His mother said that if he could take the New York summer heat then he could take any heat anywhere and, remembering her childhood and youth in the west of Ireland, that a little soft rain never hurt anyone.

Matthew's father remained strangely quiet but at the end of the visit he went to the door with Matthew and, when the goodbyes to his mother had been made, took out his pipe and lit it.

'Mat, I haven't much advice for you, you're a grown man and must make your own way based on your own decisions, but I'll tell you one thing, if you're going to lie, then learn to lie well or not at all.'

Matthew thought about it. He could challenge his father's position but, as he had indeed at least bent the truth, and it seems done it badly, he preferred to seek more of his advice.

'How did you know?'

'It doesn't matter. Let's say I've been taught by experts so I know. Tell your story any way you like, Mat, but make it a good story.'

'How?'

'Stick as near to the truth as you can. Only change what has to be changed and that only as little as it needs.' Despite himself Matthew was impressed that his father, to him a simple, illiterate, honest man, was so well-versed in such things. 'Go and tell your news to Dan, and this time make him believe it. Dan's nobody's fool. If you can convince him you can convince anyone.'

'Thanks, I will.'

His father knocked out and put away his pipe.

'And one more thing. Do you really know anything

166

about Panama, the weather and such?'

Matthew hesitated, but then decided the truth was best all things considered.

'Only that it's a hell-hole and spoken of as the white man's grave.'

'And rightly so, son. They asked me to go down there and work on the railway. Offered me so much money that it made me curious so I looked into it.'

'And?'

'Have you made a will yet, Matty?'

Matthew was surprised and not a little shocked at the question.

'Of course not.'

'Then do so, son, and leave it here in New York.' And with that last cryptic piece of advice his father took his hand and shook it solemnly. 'Good-bye, son, and may God go with you.'

Matthew stood for a moment after his father had gone back into the house and the door had closed. It was not that the farewell had been so solemn, but that it had seemed so final. It disturbed him.

Then he turned and set off. He would tell his news to Dan and he would take his father's advice. He would tell Dan that he'd had a disagreement with Frederic Hudson and had resigned and that he had tramped the streets trying to get a job. That he'd kept it to himself out of embarrassment that he'd been so foolish as to give up a good position simply to make a point. He'd tell Dan of his interviews and of his rejections and he would tell him that finally he had gone to the Associated Press who had offered him the job because it had been turned down several times already because of Panama's dangerous climate. By the time he reached his brother's front door he felt confident in himself and his story.

And his confidence was not misplaced. Dan accepted what he told him. Like their father he knew about Panama.

167

He also had been offered a job on the railway and had also refused for the same reasons as his father. But went further than their father and tried, vainly, to dissuade Matthew from setting out on this venture.'

'You'll like as not die down there, Matty. Many a stronger man than you already has. It's a fever trap, little more than a cemetery. For God's sake stick it out here and keep looking. If it's just a question of money ...'

But it wasn't.

It was more than money. Much, much more.

Chapter Twenty-four

William Henry Aspinwall was a commercial force, a man to be taken seriously, and regarded by all whose opinion mattered as someone of consequence. His company, Howland and Aspinwall, built and ran some the fastest clippers on the seas trading with Europe, South America, and the Far East. Besides being an extremely wealthy man he was also considered by both friends and rivals alike as an unusually lucky one.

Two years previously he, with a group of fellow New York merchants, had launched a new venture, the Pacific Mail Steamship Company. This line was to be served by brand new, steam-driven paddle-wheelers and had been granted a contract by the government to carry mail from Panama City to that rapidly burgeoning port, San Francisco. However, the discovery of gold in California, almost coincidental to the launch of the line, meant that from the very first voyage the passenger lists of his ships were over-subscribed and sailed crowded to capacity with fare-paying passengers as well as mail.

A most fortunate turn of circumstances, said his friends. A man singularly well-informed, said others. There were even a few who dared to say, but only among trusted friends, that the source of Aspinwall's luck, or if you preferred, his information, could only have been Washington. Aspinwall, they pointed out, had been a great friend and supporter of President James Polk, a dynamic man who, with others, was fervently convinced in the divine right of America. Polk's great propagandist, John L. O'Sullivan, editor of the influential *Democratic Review*, had suitably clothed this theory of divine right in words:

We may confidently assume that our country is destined

to be the great nation of futurity. It is so destined because the principle upon which a nation is organized fixes its destiny, and that of equality is perfect, is universal. It is by the right of our manifest destiny to overspread and to possess the whole of the continent which Providence has given us.

Manifest Destiny!

Only two words, yet they would shape a country for ever. Manifest Destiny. Divine Right. God's will. Gott mitt Uns. The eternal cry of the religious zealot.

The genocide of indigenous peoples, aggressive war, annexations, conquest – all the will of Divine Providence. President James Polk had set out to make sure that America fulfilled its destiny and he had succeeded. America was now a nation from ocean to ocean, united under God.

Critics, and there were not a few, had been almost silenced by success. Almost, but not quite.

There were those members of Congress who suspected President Polk of using the Contingent Fund to finance *agents provocateurs* in Texas and California. They suspected incidents had been carefully arranged to provoke Mexico into responses which would enable America to go to war and thereby acquire Texas and California for the Union. President Polk had even been called to account for his use of the Contingent Fund, to submit to legitimate Congressional oversight the disbursement and purposes of its secret monies. Polk responded boldly.

The experience of every nation on earth has demonstrated that emergencies may arise in which it becomes absolutely necessary for the public safety or the public good to make expenditures, the very subject of which would be defeated by publicity. In no nation is the application of such funds to be made public. In time of war or impending danger, the situation of the country will make it necessary to employ individuals for the purpose of obtaining information or rendering other important services who could never be prevailed upon to act if they entertained the least apprehension that their names or their agency would in any contingency be revealed.

And his rebuttal stood.

Congress might be able to strike down the ideology of Manifest Destiny now that it had served its purpose, but realised it could not enforce oversight of the Contingent Fund, not without fatally harming its essential purpose.

And so Congress left the Contingent Fund alone and America went on under President Zachary Taylor, himself no friend of Manifest Destiny, to consolidate its new acquisitions however they may have been obtained. Taylor was a pragmatist through and through and, being pragmatic, set about turning his predecessor's gains to his own purposes, to forge, by force if necessary, a nation at peace with itself and united under law. To that end he made sure that envious minds were not allowed to raise any awkward questions of the Polk administration such as: was it not very convenient that William Aspinwall had set about building his ships for the Pacific Mail Line so very near the time gold was discovered in California? Just in time, in fact, to benefit from the ensuing gold rush. That matter, like the Contingent Fund, was left alone.

So it was that William Henry Aspinwall was free to go from success to success unhindered by any taint of special government preferment. His Pacific Mail Line flourished thanks to Californian gold and he had even begun a rival shipping line to the main mail carrier on the eastern coast run. This run went from New York to Havana and New Orleans and now, since the gold rush and the opening of the Oregon Territories, carried on to Chagres on the Caribbean coast of Panama. Finally he had begun the last link in his trans-continental chain, the Panama Railway.

As to people who quietly wondered how much his good fortune was due to Lady Luck, how much to an astute business brain, and how much to powerful, well-placed friends, well, money talks, they say, and what it usually says is, "mind your own damn business".

Oh yes, William Henry Aspinwall had been lucky all right. But luck can change as do presidents and President Taylor, although he suppressed any hint of government favour or preferment, proved not at all as favourably disposed to William Aspinwall as had been his immediate predecessor James Polk. If Manifest Destiny had been the driving force of the Polk Administration, Taylor's had been peace between states in the newly expanded Union. Taylor was lukewarm, even indifferent, to the success of shipping lines and railways, even ones that connected the two great oceans. He saw his duty as president to make sure the question of whether the newly acquired states were slave states or free was peacefully resolved and the Union held together.

Indeed, he had been sufficiently cavalier about the prospects of the Panama Railway as to conclude a treaty with Britain, the Bulwer-Clayton Treaty, which freely and clearly gave away any American destiny, manifest or otherwise, in Central America. Taylor's eyes had been firmly and exclusively fixed on the maintenance of the Union as he had inherited it and any expansionary visions into Central America shrivelled to nothing in the hard frost of his indifference.

William Aspinwall bided his time. Taylor was altogether too powerful a personality and a president to challenge. But on the death of President Taylor Aspinwall felt emboldened to write to President Millard Fillmore and remind him of President Polk's promises concerning the Panama Railway. He even went so far as to make a barely veiled threat to withdraw from the project and leave it abandoned unless previously given assurances as to the future of the railway were confirmed. And his judgement of President Millard Fillmore had not erred. The Polk Plan

172

was to be resuscitated and William Aspinwall, reassured by Secretary of State Webster of Washington's full but totally deniable support of his aims and objectives, continued the construction of his railway. Investors on Wall Street and elsewhere went about their business and slept soundly at nights unaware that behind closed doors in Washington, a small skirmish had taken place. Manifest Destiny might indeed be dead as an ideological driving force in the domestic politics of the Union, but in Panama, the northernmost state of that sovereign and friendly country, New Granada, a small rearguard action would still be fought. The question was, would it be won?

Chapter Twenty-five

Matthew filled the days following his bizarre interview with Clarence Diver by more walking and thinking. What else was there? Diver had insisted that they both maintain their respective routines so none in the boarding house might suspect that anything had changed with either of them, and his thoughts on these long, empty days were unsettling to him. That this whole thing was not straightforward he already knew but his romantic view of himself diminished somewhat over these days of waiting and he was no longer so sure that it was a kindly fate which was looking over him. He thought hard about the dramatics employed by Diver. Why would anyone go to all that trouble? Why put on such a theatrical performance? And the job? How would Diver manage to obtain a position for someone whom no newspaper would employ, and with an organisation not only as prestigious as the Associated Press but one which was intimately allied to all the papers who had so solidly combined to refuse him work?

Matthew knew of the Association of course. A brilliant initiative of the six main New York papers to use the pony express to get news of the Mexican War back to New York and onto the streets in the shortest possible time. But now the horses and dare-devil riders had been retired in favour of the Morse magnetic telegraph, and only the year before the telegraph line had been completed between New York and Halifax, Nova Scotia. Why Halifax? Because it was the first point of contact for ships crossing between England and North America. At Halifax incoming ships from England could drop off the British papers carrying the latest European news, not the least of which were share prices from the London Stock Exchange.

Prior to the telegraph the greatest coup achieved by the Associated Press had been the announcement of the British Cabinet's decision on the British-American Oregon boundary dispute. The details of this momentous event were on the streets of New York hours before the official despatches had even arrived in Washington never mind been opened and read by the secretary of state, and it had all been done on a mixture of horse relays, boats, and carrier pigeons. What did the future hold for the newspaper industry now that the telegraph was spreading across the country and soon would even be under the Atlantic ocean? The Colt revolving-chamber pistol might be the shape of things to come in small arms but the Morse telegraph would, in its own way, prove to be the more powerful weapon in changing the face of America and the civilised world. He thought about it and finally came to a simple but inevitable conclusion.

The conclusion that emerged from Matthew's speculations was that for some reason which he could not fathom Clarence Diver was playing him for a mark or a dupe, but why *he* had been chosen he could not understand. He had no money, nor did his family. He had, to his knowledge, nothing to steal which made it worth anyone's time and effort setting up an elaborate confidence trick. It followed, therefore, that he was being set up to do something which was almost certainly illegal and, when the deed was done, whatever it was, he would be left to face the consequences by himself. What else could it be? True, Clarence Diver had played his part as he said he would and at the Bigane Boarding House been nothing other than his normal self. But, Matthew reasoned, if Clarence Diver was indeed some sort of clever and accomplished criminal who had built up a solid front as a government accountant, then surely he would want to maintain that fiction intact? When whatever he was planning in Panama was over he would want to be in a position to deny any collusion or, better still, probably make sure Matthew wasn't in any position to tell his side of things. As Diver had already displayed a ready familiarity with firearms Matthew rather favoured the latter of these two options.

Such then was the burthen of Matthew's thoughts as he had walked the hot, summer streets, with nothing to do but think and pass the time and wait for Diver's next move.

The move, when it came after three days, brought Matthew's' conjectures (which had been solidifying into certainties) crashing down. Diver had come to his room after dinner and told him that next morning at ten o'clock they had an appointment with Associated Press to confirm his position.

It was hardly credible that the New York Associated Press would either involve itself in a conspiracy or be taken in by a confidence trickster, no matter how accomplished.

Matthew made his thanks in something of a daze but finally accepted that he was, after all, to become a real newspaperman again, and went to bed puzzled but happy. Fate was still on the job.

At ten the next morning Clarence Diver was as good as his word and took him to the offices of the New York Associated Press.

There they were passed at the reception desk as expected visitors and Clarence took Matthew up to a first-floor room where he introduced him to a sallow, sad-looking man who wore pince-nez, had thin black hair, a small, spade beard, and a neat moustache.

'This is Matthew O'Hanlon, the young man I told you about.'

The man behind a desk had not risen nor had he offered any greeting on their arrival. At Diver's introduction he turned his sad eyes to Matthew. Matthew's smile of enthusiasm seemed to do nothing to lift the man's gloom. He turned his look back to Clarence Diver.

'Well, he's here so I guess he'll do. Does he know what's expected and about the money?'

'I'll explain all that later. When can he start?'

Matthew began to feel a little aggrieved at the way these two men spoke of him as if he weren't there but couldn't make up his mind whether to intrude on their conversation or not and, if he did intrude, what he might say, so the sad man answered Diver's question uninterrupted.

'As far as I'm concerned he can begin as soon as he can get a berth and be on his way.' He removed his pince-nez and looked down at some papers on his desk. 'Now, if you'll excuse me, I have work to do.'

Matthew finally spoke.

'I'd like to thank you for this chance, Mr, er, Mr ...' The sad eyes looked up at him but no words came. 'I won't let you down.'

Under the moustache the lips moved. It was as if the smallest of smiles had formed.

'No, you won't let *me* down, son. I'm sure of that.'

And the eyes went back to the papers on the desk.

Matthew was a little disconcerted by this enigmatic response but Clarence took his arm.

'We'll be on our way then.'

Matthew paused, thinking to bid his benefactor farewell, but the head never rose so they left the office and returned to the street where Matthew stopped.

'Who was that?'

'The foreign editor. He seemed to like you. I was worried about that. He's not a man who takes to everyone. Come on, we've things to do.'

They walked away with Matthew wondering how the foreign editor, whatever his name was, reacted to people he didn't like. Still, he had a job: he was now a special foreign correspondent for the New York Associated Press.

'Shouldn't I have some sort of identification? Something to let people know who I am?'

'I'll see to that. I'll see to everything. All you have to do is pack your things and be ready to sail as soon as I can arrange a berth. What have you told your family? Did you tell them about Hudson dismissing you?'

'No, at least not quite. I told them I'd had a falling out with Hudson, a disagreement about a story, and that I'd quit and gone to the Associated Press and they'd offered me a job.'

'What else did you tell them?'

'I told them about Panama. Everyone who has anything to do with construction knows they're building a railway so, other than that, there was nothing else to tell, was there?'

Clarence Diver stopped.

'No. Nothing for anyone else. But there is a little more you should know.' They were standing not far from a bar. 'Let's go in there and I'll tell you.'

It crossed Matthew's mind that it was a little odd that all his instructions were coming from Diver and nothing at all from the foreign editor of the Associated Press. But Diver had fulfilled his promise. They had been to the Associated Press and they had met an editor. The meeting had not been quite as odd as his experience at Diver's office but neither had it had been straightforward, not at all what he had expected. However, it had happened and now he was determined that his confusion should be brought to an end. Once the waiter had brought their coffee he would demand some sort of coherent explanation.

The coffee came and the waiter withdrew but before Matthew could begin the confrontation Diver spoke.

'I guess you're wondering what this is really all about? I wouldn't blame you if you were to think it some sort of a clever charade to put something over on you.' He took a drink and Matthew thoughtfully followed suit. 'I can see how you might. But let me assure you, Matthew, this is all on the level, well, almost on the level. As on the level as these sort of things can ever be.'

Matthew decided to assert himself. It was now or never.

'What sort of things?'

Clarence Diver sat back and looked around. The place wasn't busy and no table near them was occupied. He sat forward again, leaned his elbows on the table, and spoke confidentially.

'Government things. Things the government wants doing but can't be seen to do. Those sort of things.' And he looked at Matthew, who was thinking hard what to say next. About ten different and urgent questions seemed to be clashing around at once in his head each demanding immediate utterance with the result that he said nothing. 'I see you're confused. Who wouldn't be? Let me explain.'

Clarence Diver took one more look around the room, satisfied himself that they would not be heard, and began.

'William Aspinwall is building a railway across the Panama Isthmus. When it's finished it will cut eight thousand miles off the sea journey round Cape Horn and will be vital to the opening up of our new territories in the west. There's the gold rush but that will pass. What we need are settlers out there and the settlers will need supplies and lots of them if California and Oregon are to grow. That railroad is the fastest and safest way to get everything that's needed over there.'

Matthew, who had been expecting something – he didn't know what – but something more than this obvious statement about the railway, was both disappointed and annoyed.

'That's hardly news and still doesn't explain ...'

'I know, I know, but hear me out. We've got the Oregon territories now but if we're to keep them they have to be settled and settled by Americans. I'll be straight with

180

you, Matty, because I know you're sharp. We got Texas by pushing in American settlers and making sure they wanted to stay American. Once they were established all we had to do was create a bit of a fuss here and there, set up some situations that got the Mexicans' backs up, and push them until they picked a fight with us. Once they'd done that we knew that Texas and California would drop into our lap.'

Sam Grant's words came back to Matthew, that the Mexican War was, from start to finish, a conspiracy to acquire territory. At the time he hadn't paid much attention, dismissed it as some sort of frustrated distortion of events which only a military mind could understand. Yet here was Clarence Diver expressing exactly the same view.

'You mean we went to war simply to get their land.'

'Not simply, Matthew, by no means simply. These things are never simple nor straightforward. They take time, planning, money, and men. And that's what's worrying Washington at this very moment. What we did to the Mexicans the British could well try to do to us. If we don't get our settlers into Oregon they will sure as hell start getting theirs in and when they've got enough they might try the same game, cause a fuss, get us to respond, and then bring in their troops at the request of their settlers to ensure their safety. The game works, we know that, we just don't want it to work when we're on the wrong end of it.'

Matthew thought about it but he still couldn't see what his role might be. Panama was a long way from the Oregon Territories.

'So what am I supposed to do in Panama, become some sort of a spy?'

'No, no. Nothing like that. But we need to know what's going on. We need to know who's coming through Panama and heading off up to California and Oregon. What I told you back at my office is ninety-nine per cent straight. New York and the whole of America want news of the railroad they're building down there. They want news of settlers coming in and gold going out. They want to know what's happening in California and Oregon. It would all be genuine news, Matty, all newspaper stuff. But if you kept your eyes open, your sharp newsman's eyes, and if you spotted anything not quite right, then you'd get whatever it was back to me.'

'But how would I know if something was not quite right? I've never been outside of New York. Dammit, I've never been outside of Manhattan except the odd trip across the East River to Brooklyn and I doubt if Panama is much like Brooklyn.'

Diver gave a short, dutiful laugh.

'Don't worry, Matty. Once you're settled and get the feel of the place you'll be able to spot anything that doesn't ring true. I'll tell you what to be on the lookout for and all you need to do is keep your eyes open.'

It didn't sound right but Matthew couldn't quite put his finger on what was actually wrong, so he changed his line of enquiry.

'But wouldn't it be easier for the British to send any settlers in from their own territories in Canada? Why send anyone all the way round through Panama?'

'Oh there'll be settlers coming in across the new border all right. We can't stop that, the border's just a line on a map at the moment. There's nothing to stop people coming and going as they please. But those aren't the settlers we're worried about. They'll be ordinary farming folk with no particular wish to do anything except stay alive and make some sort of living and not be much interested on which side of any line they do it. What we're worried about are the organisers, the ones who arrive and start getting folks thinking.'

'You mean *agents provocateurs*?'

'Exactly. The frontier is a hard and unforgiving place

182

and it wouldn't take much to make people up there feel they've been forgotten by Washington and everyone else back in the comfort of the big cities in the east. We know from experience how easy it is for a few well-placed agents to stir up feeling.'

'But why Panama? Why send these agents all the way from the east coast of Canada down to Panama and then back on up to the new territories?'

'Because Oregon isn't where the trouble will start. It'll start in California. San Francisco is only one step up from a rough house and there's precious little law beyond. The British will send men trained for this kind of work, trained to organise discontent. Then they'll send in settlers who'll carry the thing on up in Oregon. Like I say, Matthew, it works, believe me. You don't need an army, just a few hundreds of the right sort of settlers.'

'And that's what I'd be looking for? A few hundred apparently ordinary people slipping through with thousands of other genuinely ordinary people?'

'No. If the British try anything they'll have to have someone permanent in Panama to get their own people safely through and get any information that comes back from the territories out to London. That's what you'll be looking for. Is there some respectable, permanent resident who gets an unusual number of visits from people passing through, passing both ways? I know it sounds as if you'd be looking for a needle in a haystack but you won't be. Real travellers will come into Panama and get out as quickly as they can and they'll spend as little as they can manage. The people you'll be looking for will stay a while with their contact. They won't be short of money so they might spend enough to get noticed.'

Matthew was trying hard to believe, but Diver wasn't making it easy for him.

'And the rest of the time, when I'm not creeping about spying on respectable residents?'

183

'You'll do what you want to do, be a newsman. You'll send reports on the railroad, the settlers, and the prospectors, the men coming home wealthy and the men coming home broke, the successes and the failures, the dreams and the nightmares. It's all there, Matty, the gold rush, the new frontier, all it needs is the right man to tell it. You.'

Matthew had to admit it all sounded plausible, but then, he told himself, why wouldn't it? What the hell did he know about spies and international intrigue? But the part about the railway, that was all true and would indeed make a great story to send back, lots of great stories: the prospectors, the settlers, the new frontier. If he could do that, why, maybe he would come back to New York, spit in Fred Hudson's eye, and go and take that job on *The Sun*. But there was still the other side of it all, the secret side.

'Well I don't know. A newspaperman is fine. But an agent, a secret agent?'

Diver laughed.

'No, Matthew, you'll be no agent. You've no training nor experience. You'll be a reporter, that's all. Now, what do you say? Now that I've told you all of it I need to be sure you're still willing and I need to make arrangements.'

Matthew knew it was decision time.

'Who are you? Who do you work for exactly?'

'I'm Clarence Diver and I work for the government of the Union. To be exact I work for the office of the Contingent Fund of Foreign Intercourse set up by Congress in 1790 at the request of President George Washington and despite its fancy name the office of the fund is, in plainer terms, our secret service. There, now you have it, Matthew. I really am what you would call a secret agent.' Diver sat back and smiled at him. 'You've known me for a reasonable time, Matthew, what would you say? Do I look like a secret agent?'

No, thought Matthew, if I were to say you looked like

184

anything I'd say you looked like an accountant. But he didn't frame the thoughts into words.

'No? Not your idea of what an agent should look like? Well that's the point, see. A good agent doesn't ever look like one. Remember that, Matty, the man or woman you'll be looking for won't hang out any sign. That's why I chose you. I needed someone with a nose for a story. Someone who can see past the surface of things. Come now, as I said, it's time to decide. Are you the man for me? Will you go to Panama and tell America how the railroad gets built and how the West is being opened up and keep an eye open for what I want at the same time?'

As Diver had been talking an almost dead idea was rising from the ashes of itself. This would be an adventure. This was something that didn't happen to everyone, only to the chosen few. Was he being offered, here and now, his own personal chance for glory? And if he didn't take it, would another chance ever come his way? He looked at Clarence Diver waiting. Then he reached across and held out his hand.

'I'll go.'

Diver took his hand and shook it.

'Good man, Matthew, I knew I could rely on you. Welcome to the fund.'

Chapter Twenty-six

The whole of the family gathered at Matthew's parents' house to bid him farewell, including his honorary Auntie Nora. He drank, but not to excess. His father, remembering his own voyage all those many years ago, warned him.

'Enjoy yourself tonight, son, but go easy. Some people don't take well to the sea. I didn't myself and it took me almost a week to pull myself together. If you start off tomorrow with a head on you'll regret it.'

Matthew listened and was comparatively abstemious.

However, the next morning, the siren sizzle of bacon had fatally tempted him. His mother had insisted that his sister cook him a substantial breakfast. Somehow she had got it firmly rooted into her head that her youngest son would be starved on the journey and she was determined that he start his voyage filled with enough food to get him safely through the first two or three days. Matthew tried to do justice to the mighty meal as his mother and sister stood over him but finally he had given up and pushed the plate away.

'Any more, Ma, and I swear I'll burst.'

And the two women dutifully laughed and cleared away.

The handshakes and goodbyes were made at the door of the house. The docks they all knew would be much too crowded for his family to make any proper farewells so they stood, waving, crying, or both, as he had departed, his trunk on a handcart pushed by his eldest brother, Dan.

New York docks, as was usual, were a scene of almost utter chaos. Everywhere was a mass of humanity on the move. Every outgoing ship was crowded to capacity. There were many families of settlers going to a new life, but more numerous by far were the men gripped with gold fever. As the *New York Herald*, before dispensing with Matthew's services, had recorded,

"... vessels are being filled up, societies are being formed, husbands are preparing to leave their wives, sons are parting with their mothers, and bachelors are abandoning their comforts; all are rushing head over heels toward the El Dorado on the Pacific."

Dan put a chain and padlock from the wheel of the cart to its handle then pulled down Matthew's trunk and hauled it along, following his young brother through the press of men, women, and children in the great sheds that stood between the last of the city streets and the quays. It did indeed look as if the whole of New York were on the move and one felt that, when the last ship of the day had set sail, Manhattan at the very least could be no more than a ghost town.

The individuals which made up this heaving crowd, this throng of mobile humanity, were various in their appearance. There were the shiny, black, tall hats of those men who intended to take sophisticated fashion with them. These bobbed alongside cloth caps of men who had never come within sniffing distance of fashion. Then there were the slouch hats of the shifty, worldly wise gentlemen. Here and there were tough, wide-brimmed hats suitable for the tropic sun worn by the careful and well-informed. Added to that were all the exotic contrivances supposedly suitable for far-away climes which New York stores had imported to service the insatiable demand of the gold-fever victims. And among all this variety of male headgear moved the ladies. Bonnets were, of course, universal, and the mamas, together with their daughters, managed to make the crush even worse, if that could be imagined possible, by insisting on travelling in wide crinoline skirts. True, only a small number of ladies were sufficiently affluent to use whalebone frames to achieve the desired bell-like effect but, for the rest, what multiple layers of flared petticoats could do had been done. Though utterly impractical for any sort of voyage Dame Fashion had been paid her necessary due.

Passing through the great, dark sheds which were for the most part roofing only, Matthew emerged to a forest of masts and rigging which stretched out in the sunlight in all directions. Ships not only lined the quays but were out into the harbour riding at anchor awaiting their place at the dockside. It was like some grand naval ceremonial. And there, by the quayside, standing out from the mass of sailing ships stood the Cherokee, massive and majestic, a miracle of modern marine engineering, the great paddle-wheeler was a wonder to behold. As big as a building and, even in repose, a monument to the unimaginable power of steam. It had been Clarence Diver who had made all the arrangements for the passage and he had managed a comfortably equipped first-class cabin on the *Cherokee* which Matthew would share with only one other traveller, something of a luxury on such a crowded boat. Matthew found his way to the gang-plank with Dan dutifully following. Here Dan handed over the trunk to a porter to whom Matthew gave his cabin number and the two brothers readied to make their final farewells. Matthew was keen to get on board for, he felt, with the deck of an ocean-going ship beneath his feet, he could feel as if his adventure had truly begun.

Dan paused to get his breath back.

'Look after yourself, Matty, and write.'

Matthew laughed.

'Of course I'll write, it's what I'm going there to do.'

Dan smiled at the joke but once again became serious.

'Ma and Pa will want to know how you are. We'll get someone to read your letters to them and I'm sure they will treasure them, Ma especially so.'

Matthew assumed a seriousness he found it hard to feel.

189

He wanted to be on his way.

'I'll write. I'll send the first letters back with the purser on the *Cherokee* and Mother will have it as quick as is humanly possible.' He held out his hand. 'Now I must be on my way.'

Dan took his hand and shook it, then turned and was soon swallowed up and lost to sight in the crowds. Suddenly Matthew felt alone and somewhat unsure of himself. It was an adventure, certainly, but was it more than that? *A hell-hole. A white man's grave.* The words came back. Then he pulled himself together. Others were enthusiastically flowing up the gang-plank, men, women, and children. Matthew joined them. If women and infants dared to make the journey what could there be to fear? Besides, whatever Panama had in store for him he had a pleasant ocean voyage to look forward to and he intended to enjoy it.

Once on deck he made his way to his cabin, established that his trunk had arrived, then went back out onto the deck where he along with not a few other gentlemen passengers strolled about trying to look as if they were old hands at this sea-going business. He stood aloof from the obvious *ingénus* who crowded the rails on the seaward side of the ship then hurried about looking everywhere and at everything. They called to one another in admiration at the tall, majestic funnel which rose from the superstructure amidships between the fore and aft masts, and squealing or gasping in amazement when, finally, the great paddles began slowly to rotate and the ship finally got underway.

As the *Cherokee* passed Manhattan the shoreline was lit by the late afternoon sun and Matthew got a completely new view of his native city, replete with fine villas whose extensive gardens ran down to the very water's edge. The *Cherokee*, leaving those palaces of the wealthy behind, he looked out on Brooklyn which, from a distance, seemed all charm and serenity. The ship then skirted Staten Island and entered the Hudson Narrows with its mighty fortifications, passed Sandy Hook, and finally, the breeze freshening a little, headed for open water. The great adventure was at last begun.

Chapter Twenty-seven

Matthew was on deck making his final farewell to his homeland and trying to adjust his mind to what lay ahead. He stood alongside those other passengers who were still crowded at the rail watching New York slowly recede. To his left, halfway along the ship, one of the great paddle wheels churned through the grey-green waves of the Atlantic driving the *SS Cherokee* forward. She was one of the new, steam-powered, paddle-wheelers used by the US Mail Line. Fore and aft of the funnel were two masts which carried just enough sail for the unlikely emergency of the steam engines failing. She was fast and comfortable, and Matthew was pleased that Clarence Diver had managed to get him passage on such a vessel rather than on one of the many sailing ships which still plied the route.

He looked up. The mighty funnel, almost as high as the masts, was pumping out black smoke which drifted away quickly on the wind. Magnificent! Was there no limit to what human ingenuity could achieve? This was indeed the dawning of a new age, the days of sail and horse were over, on both land and sea this would be the Age of Steam. Above and beyond the funnel's smoke dark clouds were threatening rain but in the distance, past the great wheel and beyond the bow of the ship, the sky on the horizon was clear and blue. They were headed for fair weather. He turned and looked back again at the land. It was already noticeably further away. He gazed in wonderment. What speed must they be doing?

Matthew left the rail and began to walk along the deck towards the front of the ship. There was nothing to see but the sea, but he wanted to look forward not back. Out there, over two thousand miles away, lay his future. New York, home and family were behind him now, part of his past.

He arrived at the bow of the ship where other passengers lined the rail and stared out at the vast, empty expanse of water as the *Cherokee* ploughed on beginning its journey to Chagres and Panama. Matthew stood for a moment then began to realise that an odd sensation was creeping over him.

When the ship had cleared the shore and made some distance a steady swell had begun to make itself felt and the *Cherokee* began to roll. The roll was indeed only very slight, neither paddle-wheel came even close to lifting clear of the water, but now, well out from land, it was providing enough motion for Matthew to feel it rather keenly. He left the rail and made his way back towards his cabin. But he didn't reach it. Suddenly he was overwhelmed by a feeling of nausea. He turned, made his way quickly to the rail, roughly elbowed aside the passengers there, stood for a second, then, pausing only to grab off his hat, leaned over the rail and gave up his breakfast to Neptune and the deep.

Near him, three young men looked on and laughed. Two women whom Matthew had pushed to one side exchanged glances, then turned away in disgust as if Matthew had been some drunk paying the price of over-indulgence on the sidewalk.

Matthew, however, was unaware of either the laughter or the censure. He heaved once more and more came up. He hung across the rail of the ship, weak and helpless. He stiffened and retched once again but this time very little came. Once again he hung limply, feeling worse than he had ever felt in his life. Through the profound nausea his brain centred itself on this sudden, inexplicable and almost total collapse of his condition. He must have contracted some illness, some colic, some bilious ... Suddenly a great terror overcame him. It was cholera! He was going to die! No one could feel as he did and live. He strained again as another retch wracked his whole body, then sagged back on the rail once more. For a moment fear of death contested with a sadness for a young life cut short, but both soon lost out to another bout of futile retching. Matthew tried to stand up straight, failed, and hung again on the rail. It was impossible, he knew, but, if anything, he was beginning to feel worse. Slowly another fear began to possess him, that he might not die, that this awfulness, this terrible awfulness that had so suddenly come upon him might keep him in its grip and torment him for … how long? How long could he stand it? Matthew, completely lost to all that was around him, had entered into that surreal nightmare world, the second stage of sea-sickness. Just over two miles out Matthew lay hanging over the rail, mostly praying for a quick death but between times dwelling sorrowfully on the state of his immortal soul.

The adventure, which he had so eagerly sought, was providing him with his first new experience. It would be one of many, but not, alas, the best of them.

Chapter Twenty-eight

Eventually something resembling life returned to Matthew's stricken body and, having decided that his boots were not, after all, waiting to come up and follow his breakfast, he slowly and with infinite care made his way to his cabin. Once inside he dropped his hat, which he found still gripped in his hand, on the floor and fell onto his bunk. He had never, ever, in the whole of his life, felt so bad.

Matthew's cabin companion was a medical man, Doctor Robert Tomes by name. An American employed by the Pacific Mail Line, he was returning to Panama after a few weeks leave and had come on board at the very last minute so neither men knew anything of each other except their names and that they would be cabin companions on the journey. Tomes stood up from the table at which he was sitting reading a book, picked up Matthew's hat, put it on the table, and came to the bunk.

'Sea sick, eh? Well, if it all came up and there's nothing left maybe you'll pull through in time for dinner.' At this monstrous suggestion that, if he lived, he might ever eat again, Matthew groaned and turned his face to the wall. 'Shall I give you something?' This further assault, this repeat of the idea that anything, anything at all, medical or otherwise, should pass his lips almost brought words to Matthew's mouth but they were hustled aside as something else pushed its way to the fore. He leaned his head over the side of the bunk and retched. Tomes stepped lightly back, but his quick footwork proved unnecessary. All that could come up had been given to the ocean, all that was left now were violent but impotent spasms.

Matthew lay back and groaned once more Dr Tomes

took out his pipe and tobacco pouch.

'I guess you'd prefer me to smoke outside?' Matthew gave his travelling companion a look. Apparently this fiend in human shape, this devil, although being a doctor and therefore well aware that he was in the presence of pain and death, could smile and talk as glibly of smoking pipes as he could of eating meals. Martyr-like, Matthew turned away from his tormentor. Tomes smiled. 'Well then, I guess I'll leave you and take a turn about the deck.'

He took up his own hat and left the cabin slamming the door shut in a manner which to Matthew, in his disturbed state, felt like a deliberate blow.

When, some half an hour later, Robert Tomes returned Matthew was fast asleep and he remained that way for almost three hours. When he awoke his companion was once again sitting at the table reading his book. Tomes looked up as Matthew slowly put his legs over the side of the bunk and pushed himself up into a sitting position.

'Ah, back from the grave?'

Matthew was about to make a suitable reply when, to his surprise, he realised that although he felt far from well, he was no longer *in extremis*, as he had heard priests sometimes refer to the final state before life's passing. He even found he could speak.

'God, I felt awful. I was as sure I was going to die as I was of anything in my life. I still feel bad, but, thank God, not quite so bad.'

'It can be a little trying, sea-sickness. They say Horatio Nelson was a great sufferer and had to spend the first few days at sea confined to his cabin.'

Although Matthew was undoubtedly better, he was in no fit state to enjoy any erudite discussion on the medical condition of famous British naval men. With an effort he stood up.

'I think I'll get a breath of air.'

Tomes handed him his hat which was still on the table.

'Good idea, take a few turns round the deck and clear your head. We'll get to know each other when you get back.'

Matthew took his hat and left the cabin. The breeze had strengthened, as had the swell, making the ship roll more noticeably, but Matthew felt distinctly better walking in the fresh air and feeling the breeze cool his flushed face. Going to the stern he looked back across the empty ocean. The overcast sky had been left behind and above the ship there was now clear blue with the sun beating down warmly. Far off in the distance was a bank of low clouds, all that was left of New York and America. He continued his walk to the far side of the ship where, not far from the mighty paddle wheel, a young man suddenly arrived at the rail and grabbing his hat in his hand he leaned over the rail. Matthew, as he passed on, looked at his heaving back sympathetically. Unbeknown to him this was one of the very same young men who, only a few hours before, had laughed so heartily at his indisposition but, unaware of this, the young man's plight touched him. A survivor of the ordeal himself, waves of compassion floated from him for he knew from bitter experience what awaited the young man once his initial tribute to the sea had been paid.

Matthew returned to the cabin after three turns round the deck a new man. He had forgotten what, at the time, had seemed the calculated callousness of his travelling companion and was ready to meet him and, as the other had put it, get to know one another. They would be much in each other's company on the journey which, depending on the weather, might take up to two weeks. If it proved at all possible, he would prefer to spend the days in the society of someone he could get along with.

There was a distinct spring in his step as he approached the cabin door. This was indeed an adventure and he proposed to give himself up to it wholeheartedly, beginning with finding out all he could about Panama from this Doctor Robert Tomes into whose company a kindly fate had thrown him.

He opened the cabin door and Tomes looked up at him from his book.

Chapter Twenty-nine

The journey proved long, hot, and tedious for, as a US Mail ship, the *SS Cherokee* had to make stops at Charleston, Savannah, New Orleans, and Havana before going on to her ultimate destination, Chagres.

Many of the sailing ships hurriedly pressed into service to ensure the supply of berths met the demand made the run direct as they carried settlers heading for the new American territories and men on their way to the Californian gold fields. All were in a hurry, the settlers to get to their new homes and the prospectors to make their fortunes with as little delay as possible, so no ports of call were necessary.

In his temperament Matthew was in sympathy with the California-bound brother adventurers; in his own way he was also a prospector. Like them he was looking to make his fortune with as little delay as possible and, feeling as he did, he found the mail stops somewhat annoying. However, what cannot be avoided must be endured so he went with Robert Tomes who, being medical and having made the journey twice before, knew the value of getting ashore, having a hot bath, and eating at least one good meal made from fresh, local produce. He also insisted on bringing back to the ship fruit, a couple of bottles of wine, and other provisions for the next leg of their journey. Matthew suffered these stops with a good grace. He bathed when Tomes bathed, ate a good meal with him and, once back on board and underway, willingly shared in the provisions and wine his companion brought to their cabin. It was, he felt, the least he could do to repay Tomes for all the valuable information he had given him on the nature of their destination.

Another fortunate result of these stops was that any serious fever cases, of which on the *Cherokee* there were only two, might be taken ashore so as to prevent spread of contagion among the passengers and crew. Not an inconsiderable number of settlers and prospectors travelling on cramped sailing boats that made the run non-stop learned the hard way that the mixture of poor ship's victuals, heat, and over-crowded and unhealthy conditions made fever, if it broke out on board, as dangerous as any shipwreck, and many poor souls found their hopes already dashed by ill-health by the time they landed at what they had hoped would be the gateway to bountiful future or El Dorado.

Matthew had discovered from the beginning of the voyage that his cabin mate was a ready source of information on Panama, if somewhat forthright in the manner of his speech.

'Chagres is a hell on earth, as foul a spot as God created anywhere on earth. It's little more than mouldering shacks built on a swamp. How they ever intend to get a railway to run over that ground – what there is of it – defeats me. But each man to his own trade and mine's medicine, not engineering, so I suppose they must know what they've let themselves in for.'

Many evenings, when the heat of the day had moderated, they walked the deck, Tomes smoking his pipe and talking of California and how, in his opinion, San Francisco – though admittedly little more than a rackety port at the moment – would one day become a place of some consequence.

'If you're looking for a story then let me take you up to San Francisco some day. It gets pretty lively on the waterfront sometimes and what goes on there would fill more than a few pages on its own. But there's more than that, a lot more. California is opening up and it's not just the gold, although God knows you might not think so from the men that crowd through to get out there looking for it. On the Pacific Line we call the harbour "the graveyard"'.

'Why so?'

'Because it's crowded with ships that are going nowhere.'

'How do you mean? They must be going somewhere.'

'Nope. When they arrived the crews straight way skid-daddled off to the gold fields, now they're stuck. The place has become a graveyard for ships that are perfectly seaworthy but can't find a crew. The Pacific Mail has to pay top dollar to be sure its men stay on board and make the return journey.'

'I hear fortunes are made every day. That there's gold nuggets as big as a man's fist just lying about waiting to be picked up.'

Tomes had smiled at that.

'Sure, everybody just walks out there, picks up as much as he can carry, then heads back home a millionaire.'

Matthew was suitably chastened though a little annoyed at his companion's satire.

'Well, I didn't exactly mean it that way.'

'No, sure you didn't. But there's plenty of fools who've read the same stories and high-tailed it off thinking it was exactly that way.'

'I suppose there is.'

'Oh there's money being made in California all right and plenty of it, and it isn't all being dug out of the ground. Out in the gold fields a single egg can cost as much as a dollar and I heard that a feller called Sam Brannan who runs a store in Sacramento has pulled in as much as a hundred and fifty thousand dollars a month. Of course it can't last, but even when all the gold hullabaloo is over California has prospects, fine prospects. Why I suppose there's more …'

And Matthew, knowing little or nothing of Panama, California, gold fields, or even the price of eggs, had listened with interest.

Finally, after leaving their last port of call, New Orleans, and having been in all twelve days at sea, they sighted land at about four in the afternoon. The ship had reached its destination, Chagres. Despite the tropical sun that blazed down from a clear, blue sky, Matthew left packing his trunk and stood, bareheaded, without a jacket, his shirt loose and open at the neck, for over an hour at the crowded rail gazing out at the land which grew bigger and more defined as the ship approached and finally entered Chagres Bay.

He felt his excitement rising. All his old enthusiasm was returning. Soon he would be there, his feet on dry land, and the real adventure, his adventure, could at last begin.

Chapter Thirty

To Matthew's surprise, when he returned to the cabin to finish his packing and get ready to leave the ship, Tomes seemed in no hurry to disembark. He was sitting at the table reading and smoking his pipe. When Matthew appeared in the doorway he looked up from his book.

'Good God, Matthew, how many times must you be told, put your hat on if you're going to stand out on deck. That sun could boil water.' He stood up and went to Matthew's bunk where his hat and jacket lay. He picked up the hat and tossed it to him. 'And wear it all the time you're out there. God knows what you're so busy looking at. It's jungle, all jungle, and nothing but jungle.'

Matthew caught the hat feeling annoyed at the paternal tone Tomes had used, as if he were a child to be cared for, someone who needed to be looked after by an older and wiser head. However, his head did ache and it was no doubt caused by the sun so he said nothing and went to his trunk. He folded the last of his shirts and put them on top of his other clothes. Now, apart from a few bits and pieces, he was ready. He looked across at Tomes who was again sitting reading and smoking his pipe.

'What about your packing? You don't seem to be nearly ready.' He gestured to Tomes' half-filled trunk. 'You're barely half done and we'll be dropping anchor any minute.' He stood for a moment listening. 'The engines have stopped. We must have arrived.'

Tomes' looked up from his book, took his pipe out of his mouth, and listened.

'You're right.'

Then he resumed his reading and his smoking.

Matthew, annoyed at his companion's indifference

205

went to the cabin door, but Tome's voice stopped him.

'Hat.'

Matthew shot him an angry look, wasted as it was still buried in his reading, then went to his bunk, snatched up his hat, which he jammed anyhow on his head, and left to go on deck.

The scene had not noticeably changed except that the rail was now almost clear of passengers who had all gone about the business of getting ready to disembark. He looked out across the bay at the low silhouette of the land, so near and yet still so far.

The *Cherokee* lay about a mile out from the shore which, as far as Matthew could make out, seemed to have little or nothing in the way of any town or harbour that he could make out. What he saw was a far distant horizon formed by grey-blue mountains. Below this horizon and forming another was a dark green irregular wall of dense verdure which came down to the sea. Set at the bottom of this massive and intimidating tangle of growth was a stretch of land with what looked like a scattering of low sheds and huts. There were one or two structures of more than a single storey which could pass for buildings, but from where he stood the place looked more like some abandoned and derelict ruin than the exotic town of his imaginings.

A haze of heat hung about the ship and what little sea breeze there had been whilst they were still in motion was now no more than a sensation of hot air stirring around him, and Matthew realised for the first time how hot it was going to be once he was on land. He had never known, even at the height of a New York summer, such heat.

Then Tomes was at his side.

'Well, there you are, Matty, that's Chagres and Panama, that's what you travelled over a couple of thousand miles to see. Worth it, would you say?' And before Matthew could answer he gave a small laugh. 'But

206

don't worry, it gets worse. In fact this is the best way to see it, from a distance, and the greater the distance the better it gets. Why, from two thousand miles Chagres might even look like some sort of tropical paradise.'

And he laughed again and once again Matthew was annoyed at his superior and patronising manner.

Who, he felt like asking, had appointed Dr Robert Tomes as his guardian and guide. But before he could form the right words for some stinging reply Tomes' manner changed. He was looking at the sky, then took out his pipe and pointed with it.

'Over there.'

Thomas looked to see what Tomes was pointing at. There was nothing, or almost nothing. The sun was beating down fiercely from a clear, blue sky onto the flat calm where the *Cherokee* lay at anchor. True, he could there were some dark clouds moving into the sky from over the distant mountains. But they seemed nothing of consequence.

'You mean the clouds?'

'It's late in the day and those clouds rolling up mean rain within the next couple of hours.' People were now busy collecting on deck, hauling their baggage behind them, getting ready for the disembarkation to begin. 'We're better situated here on the boat than anywhere we might find on shore so we might as well stay as comfortable as we can while the boat's emptying. They'll soon be coming out to start ferrying passengers ashore and when they do things will get hectic here, and in Chagres and when the rain comes it will get worse. I suggest we stay put until everybody's off, then, when the rains are over it will be cooler for a short while and we can walk about and try and pick up any evening breezes that might come. At least we'll have the boat to ourselves.'

The idea of not going ashore appalled Matthew. He hadn't made this journey to sit on a boat and waste his time. But before he could speak he realised his headache had become much worse and with it there was a touch of dizziness. He suddenly felt weak and unsteady. He reached out and held onto the rail. Tomes looked at him with concern.

'Feeling bad?'

Matthew nodded but stopped at once as a piercing pain shot through his head.

Tomes took his arm. The deck was now quite crowded and it was only with difficulty that Matthew, even with Tomes' assistance, managed to stay on his feet and make his way against the tide of humanity disgorging from within the ship out onto the deck. The two men pushed and elbowed their way back to their cabin, picking more than a few curses on the way, but they made their destination, where Tomes took off Matthew's hat and gently eased him onto his bunk where he sat, his headache worsening.

'Lay down, Matty.' Matthew took the advice and lowered himself onto the bunk. Tomes stood over him for a moment. 'I was afraid of this when you came back without a hat on. An hour out in that sun for somebody not used to it can be cruel. I've known men die.' He bent down and placed a hand on Thomas' forehead, then took up his wrist, pulled out his pocket-watch, and measured his pulse. 'Well, it looks like a touch of the sun. I'll give you something to make you sleep. When you wake you should feel better.'

Matthew watched Tomes' back as he busied himself with his medicine box. Why such concern? All through the voyage he had been careful of him, been like some sort of guardian angel. Why was that?

Tomes returned holding a glass of some grey liquid. He put an arm under Matthew's shoulders, lifted him, and helped him to drink. Then gently laid him down again. Matthew watched him again as he went back to his medicine box and began to put things away. Was it because he was a doctor, the natural wish of a medical man to see to a travelling companion's health? Or was it something more personal? But the draught, whatever it was, began to work and Matthew felt drowsy. Tomes was now sitting watching him. Outside the cabin there was still the noises of passengers and baggage but within a couple of minutes Matthew's eyes closed, for him the sound diminished and became silence, and he slept.

Tomes looked at the sleeping figure. His face was concerned. It was not fever, of that he was sure, but a bad case of the sun could do plenty of harm and he didn't want Matthew on land in a weakened condition. Chagres was bad enough to a man in the best of health, to a man in a low condition and not used to the tropics it could be like walking into your own grave. He decided to have a word with the captain and arrange for them both to stay on board overnight and go ashore tomorrow; that way he'd get a good night's sleep. If, by tomorrow, he wasn't fully fit then something else would have to be arranged. Maybe a day's delay in taking on new passengers. That might prove tricky. The captain had been well paid and would accommodate him, he knew, but only up to a point. Still, with a good night's rest and, if necessary, the right medicine, Matthew would probably be ready to land tomorrow. Quietly he stood up and put his hat on, went to the cabin door, took one last look at the sleeping figure, closed the door behind him, and went in search of the captain.

Chapter Thirty-one

Matthew took out his handkerchief and wiped the sweat from his face. A waste of time, of course, firstly because the handkerchief was already thoroughly damp and secondly because the sweat immediately returned.

The two men were still in the cabin, Matthew on his bunk, awake but still feeling dreadful and Tomes once again reading. Matthew had slept but his sleep had brought him no relief. It had been crowded with strange and frightening visions in which he was desperately trying to force his way through dense undergrowth to escape some horrible thing that pursued him remorselessly. Closer and closer it came, slower and slower became his progress, and always the heat, the terrible heat. Just as he felt the beast upon him he woke with a start and forced himself to sit up.

The cabin door was open and the noise of passengers above on deck disembarking was diminished but still considerable. Tomes, lost in his novel, ignored it but to Matthew's agitated nerves the cacophony of raised voices, boots, and trunks being dragged, bumped, and dropped was like red hot nails being driven deep into his skull. The worst thing about it all, thought Matthew, was that there was no way he could escape. He was trapped in this oven of a cabin and if he left and joined the noise and bustle outside it could only be worse. The thought made him shudder as Tomes glanced across.

'Here, Mat, you shaking?'

'No, it's just the heat and that noise. I swear it's making this damned headache worse, a thing I would have said couldn't be done. How long did I sleep?'

'Not long enough.' Tomes put down his book and came across to Matthew. 'Let me have a look at you.'

Tomes began to examine him and Matthew felt a tinge of alarm. Words spoken more than once, *a hell-hole, a white man's grave* came to him once again.

Tomes felt his forehead, looked closely at his eyes, made him stick his tongue out, and once more took his pulse.

Matthew's alarm increased. Both Dan and his father had warned him. The fever! Good God, he had succumbed already. He was as good as dead.

Tomes stood back and looked down at him.

'Nothing. As I thought, just a nasty touch of the sun. Try to remember that down here you always keep your hat on if you go out and take plenty of fluids. Water's best but mind you know where it's come from. The stuff the natives drink down here might as well be prussic acid for any new arrival. If you can't get clean water then bottled beer is best but avoid spirits. In this heat and what with everything else spirits can be as lethal as the local water. Best lie down for a while. In an hour or so I'll give you another sleeping draught. That should get you off for an hour or two and by then the worst of the noise and fuss will be over and we'll have the ship to ourselves.'

'But what about us getting off?'

'Don't worry, that's all taken care of.'

Matthew's mind, such as it was in his present state, forced questions into his consciousness. How taken care of? When would they disembark? But as he was also suffering agonies of pain he put aside such queries and lay back. However, one question forced itself into words.

'You're sure it's just the sun? I feel pretty awful, you know.'

'Just the sun.'

'Not fever?'

'Not fever.'

Matthew relaxed. Not fever. Thank God. He lay back once more, closed his eyes, and spent all of his available energies in pushing the pain in his head away into some corner. All he sought was oblivion.

A hand shook his shoulder. He opened his eyes and looked up. Tomes stood over him.

'You've slept. Best thing that could have happened. Means you're on the mend.'

Suddenly Matthew realised that his headache was almost gone and that the noise of passengers had ceased. There was a strange quiet. He sat up. He felt hungry.

'I feel better.'

'You look it. But remember what it was like because you can't let it happen again. This sun can kill someone who's not used to it.' A vague memory drifted unasked into Matthew's mind. Frederic Hudson had said it was the sun that had killed President Taylor, the sun combined with cold cherries and buttermilk. Why had that come back to him? Then he realised why. Because he'd called it horse shit. But that was in New York where a healthy man dying from the sun seemed an impossibility. Now he wasn't so sure. 'Come on, Matty, let's take a turn on deck and get out of this oven of a cabin. We'll have it all to ourselves apart from the crew. Who knows? There may even be a breeze. But don't count on it.'

Matthew once again wondered about Tomes' concern for him, now and throughout the journey, was he wrong to think it odd, overdone? Had he been wrong about President Taylor and was now wrong about Tomes? He dismissed the question from his mind, whatever the reason, Tomes had proved a godsend when the heat-stroke had hit him, and he was right now. There would probably be no breeze but it would be cooler on deck than sitting in the stultifying heat of the cabin. Matthew stood up and waited to see if the dizziness returned. It didn't.

The two men went up onto the deck where Matthew gratefully found it less oppressive than the cabin. But any

213

pleasure in the diminishment of heat was qualified. There was a smell in the still evening air, the smell of rottenness. No, more than that, the odour of decomposing flesh. Matthew had been used to the clean sea air and even Tomes' pipe-smoke in the cabin, once he had become used to it, had not been offensive. But there was a hint of death in the odour of decay that drifted from the dark shadow which was now all he could see of the land.

The sun had set and the fierce heat of the day had moderated, but only slightly. Even now, at nine o'clock, it was still almost unbearably hot, but at least the boat was clear of passengers and their noise. Only Tomes and himself remained on board along with the crew who, Tomes assured him, would still be busy for another two hours getting the ship ready for tomorrow when the mail would be brought on, the returning passengers would board, and the run could begin.

There was a half moon and the sky was full of stars, the sea was a flat calm, and the air was still. The land was a low, dark mysterious shadow and the whole scene, viewed from the rail of the *Cherokee*, could have been deeply romantic. Except for the smell.

Matthew, from the moment he had agreed to go to Panama in Clarence Diver's New York office, had been slowly building his own mental image of the country he was going to and during the repetitive days of the journey he had done just as Tomes had said, he had dreamed up his own picture of Chagres as some sort of tropical paradise. In his imagination lightly clad, dark-skinned maidens figured prominently, and a vague idea that he, as a white man, would somehow be treated by the simple natives as a spoiled favourite, cooled by fans and fed delicate but delicious foods. Such, he had now begun to realise, was probably not going to be the case.

The combination of the heat and the noise, the headache, and now this faint but definite odour of decay

214

had erased any idea of paradise or dusky maidens from his mind.

He turned to Tomes who stood beside him at the rail pulling on his pipe.

'Won't the captain mind us staying overnight?'

'No. I'm a doctor and I'll give a look over to any of the passengers that come aboard who might show signs of fever. He doesn't want any cases on board when he fills up with his return load and heads off. There's always a few who, when they come aboard, are not in such a very bad way but are close to becoming so. I'll give the new arrivals a good look and any who would be a problem on the voyage the captain can put back ashore.'

'Isn't that a bit brutal, leaving the poor devils behind?'

'Perhaps, but practical. You've made the journey now and you've seen how most of them are packed together. Panama fever, yellow fever, or any other fever that got aboard in an advanced stage would run through the ship before it made its first port and it wouldn't just be passengers. He'd lose crew and he'll need them all fully fit to get through the journey. No, you don't knowingly let fever on board, Matty, not if you can help it. Those that fall ill during the voyage are hard enough to deal with.'

Suddenly Matthew noticed that, as they had been talking the moon and stars had gone as had the dark shadow of land and the night had become black. The crew had lit lanterns to carry on with their business.

'It's very dark suddenly.'

'Clouds. They come up quick. Best we go back to the cabin.'

Tomes knocked out his pipe on the rail and the two men went back to their cabin where a sailor was just coming out.

'Lit the lamp in your cabin, gentlemen. Thought you'd be heading back when I saw the clouds come up.'

Tomes thanked the man and he left.

215

Almost as soon as they had returned and sat down there was a sudden, loud noise, as if many hands had started throwing fistfuls of pebbles at the decks above them.'

'Good God, what's that noise?'

'Rain. But that's Panama for you, one minute you're scorching under a clear blue sky, the next you're in a communal shower-bath. This is the rainy season and I'd have avoided it if I could. It could make the river tricky and the paths will become pretty nasty. Still, it was take your leave now or lose it, so I guess we'll just have to do the best we can.' And he took out his pipe once more and began to fill it. Matthew didn't doubt what Tomes had said but found it hard to believe that mere rain could make such a confounded noise. Tomes looked at him and grinned. 'You slept through it last time but take the lamp if you like and go and have a look. Even in the dark it's something to see if you've never seen it before.'

Matthew took his hat and the lantern, leaving Tomes in the pitch black of the cabin, and went to the stairway that led up to the deck. Before he reached the top he stopped and held up the lantern in front of him. Through the open doors where the stairway opened onto the deck he could see what looked like water being poured from an enormous watering can. A not inconsiderable amount was splashing in through the doorway and running across the upper steps of the stairs. Pulling his hat tightly on his head he went up the last few steps of the stairway and stepped out onto the deck. In an instant he was thoroughly soaked. He held up his lantern and, with the light of two or three others set out for the crew, he could see that it was just as Tomes had said. It was rain and nothing but rain, but not rain as he had ever seen it before. The air was full of water. Visibility was almost nil. From the hot, dry, timbers of the day the deck had suddenly become a sheet of water which leapt and danced as if alive. Matthew stood for a moment spellbound, then turned and went back down the stairs to the cabin.

Tomes was already undressed and in his bunk with his pipe in his mouth. He looked at him as he entered.

'Worth seeing, eh?'

Matthew stood in the doorway dripping.

'I couldn't see much but, well, I've never seen anything like it. It's as if we've been caught in a waterfall.'

He took off his wet hat and threw it beside his bunk then put the lamp back on the table. Tomes picked up a taper which he kept by him, lit it from the lamp, and then lit his pipe.

'Don't worry, you'll get better views, believe me, and plenty of them. Best take off your wet things and dry yourself. You've had a touch of the sun I wouldn't want you to follow it up with a chill.' Once again the nagging question of the reason and sincerity of Tomes' concern for his wellbeing surfaced. But the advice, as always, was sound so Matthew followed it and began to remove his clinging shirt. Tomes nodded towards the table where a cloth covered something. 'There's some cold meat and bread on a plate there and there's wine still in the bottle. I've already eaten and I thought you might want something before you turned in for the night. Things will be starting early tomorrow and it'll be all go for a few hours. I'll arrange for you and our luggage to go ashore on the first boat, the one that brings out the mail. Once I've finished going over the new arrivals I'll join you and we can sort out transport for the river. Now I'm turning in.'

Matthew felt a sudden small spasm of alarm. Somehow the idea of landing alone worried him. He had grown used to Tomes, had enjoyed listening to him, and even now, despite the nagging doubt of his sincerity, had come to view him as a sort of personal guide who would take him to Chagres and then over the mountains to Panama City. He had naturally expected Tomes to take the lead on arrival, he was the one with experience of the country. Yet

217

here he was proposing to send him off on his own. This new casualness confused him. He couldn't actually accuse Tomes of anything but he rather felt that his attitude was almost a dereliction of duty at a critical moment and the idea of going to Chagres alone unsettled him.

The truth was, it was finally dawning on Matthew how very far from home he was and how very different and even dangerous was the place to which he had come. An experienced companion and guide, no matter if his *bona fides* might seem a little questionable, was something Matthew felt essential at this stage of the journey.

'I could stay on board until you're ready.'

'No you couldn't. You'd get in the way. The sooner you and our luggage are gone the better.'

'I see.'

Tomes knocked out his pipe onto his hand, dropped the ash onto the floor, and put the pipe under his pillow. He then pulled up the sheet, and turned over.

'Put out the lantern when you're ready.'

Matthew sat and looked at his back.

That was that then. Tomorrow he would land at Chagres alone.

Well, it was what he had come for, an adventure, an encounter with the unknown. He sat on the bunk, slowly unlaced his boots, and pulled them off and then pulled off his socks. He tried to cheer himself up by reminding himself that this was the beginning of his search for glory, a new stage in his life. He couldn't very well expect to achieve any degree of fame if he was constantly in the care of someone else. At some point he must strike out for himself. These thoughts revived his spirits until he remembered the smell of decay and the tiny flame of renewed enthusiasm, like his dream of paradise, was snuffed out.

Matthew took off his trousers and drawers, dropped them on his boots and socks beside his wet shirt, then went

218

to the bottle of wine, poured himself a glass, took it to the table and uncovered his meal. There wasn't a great deal of food and he was hungry so it was soon gone, and what wine there was left in the bottle only half-filled his second glass. As Tomes' breathing had achieved that regularity which indicates sleep he decided that there was no more he could do so he turned down the lantern, went to his bunk, and lay down under his sheet.

He stared out into the blackness. All was silent, as silent as the tomb which in many ways, thought Matthew, was exactly what the cabin suddenly felt like.

These morbid thoughts, however, were interrupted by a loud snore. Tomes as a rule didn't snore, but it was not completely unknown. Strangely the noise coming out of the darkness comforted Matthew. At least he was not alone. The small flame of enthusiasm managed to re-ignite. It was still an adventure and it was still *his* adventure. Another snore came. Matthew smiled. Suddenly he was rather glad he would be going alone and first, he was also pleased that he was able to cast Tomes' concern for his health and comfort in an equivocal position. It made the whole situation all the more fascinating. He wasn't yet asleep but he was already dreaming. He had a job to do for Clarence Diver and his country. He was alone in what was possibly enemy territory. He was a man with a mission, a man working against the odds. Not a secret agent perhaps but, well, as near as dammit, and he closed his eyes and waited for his daydreams to be replaced by the those of sleep.

Chapter Thirty-two

Matthew was wakened by Tomes who was already up and dressed.

'Come on, Matty, time for you to be up and off. The boat with the mail will be alongside within the hour and you have to be ready to be on it when it goes back. The water's still warm enough to shave if you're going to bother.'

Matthew rose, washed, shaved, and got some dry clothes from his trunk to replace the things that had been dropped the previous evening on the floor and were still damp. He dressed then poured himself some coffee from the pot on the table which was still hot. He looked around the cabin. His trunk was already gone but Tomes' still stood by his bed. He finished his coffee, put on his hat, threw his jacket over his arm, and went up on deck where he took a deep breath of morning air and at once regretted it. His lungs filled with the same smell of putrefaction that he had first encountered the previous evening and his deep breathing turned to coughing. Tomes came to him.

'Heavens, Tomes, what is that awful smell?'

'You'll find out soon enough. Look, the boat's already on its way, sooner than I expected. If they're starting early there must be plenty waiting to board. Looks like she'll be full going back. I guess plenty of the gold-diggers found it isn't just a matter of picking the stuff up and bringing it home.'

Matthew went and stood by his trunk which was beside a small gantry at the rail. From this gantry hung ropes attached to the end of a narrow gangplank. The other end of the gangplank was by the rail where it opened and, thirteen days ago Matthew had boarded to begin his

221

adventure. He tried to forget the smell and watched the sailboat carrying the sacks of mail nearing. As it approached more crewmen appeared, opened the rail and the gangplank was lifted, at one end by ropes and pulleys attached to the gantry and the other end by crewmen's muscle. It was put over the side, at the rail end made secure to the deck and at the gantry lowered it so that it sloped down along the side of the ship. The mail boat pulled alongside, made it secure, then two of the crew went down, the mail sacks were handed over, brought up and taken away by other crewmen. The day's loading had begun.

Matthew gazed down into the boat as the two crewmen hurried up and down the gangplank. Apart from the mail sacks about twenty passengers stood towards the rear of the boat, and once the mail was gone they slowly climbed up the gangplank and began to arrive on the deck.

They looked a sorry sight to Matthew. All were men and the majority dirty, ragged, and none too healthy. Only two of them who came aboard first looked clean and in good health. Tomes came to his side as the last few came aboard, one being helped up the ladder and onto the deck by two others.

'There you are, Matthew, that's what the gold rush produces. Two men who might have made a fortune and the rest will be ones it's probably broken for life – and one or two it's killed, although they'll take a few more days or weeks to die.'

'You mean the one who was being helped?'

'Yes, but at least three others I'll need to check just from watching them come on board. That one being helped won't last more than a few days if that. I'll get him off as soon as I can. I hope to God too many of the others haven't picked up the fever from him. Still, it's not my problem, I won't be on her during the return journey.' He noticed the look of alarm on Matthew's face. 'Don't worry, I'll not send any of them back with you. You'll be on your own going ashore. No sense in asking for trouble is there?'

While they were talking the two sailors who had brought up the mail had placed Matthew's trunk in the waiting boat. Tomes held out his hand.

'Well, I'll see you when I've finished here. Welcome to Panama. I hope it turns out to be all you expected or wanted.'

They shook hand, Tomes turned away, and a voice called from the waiting boat.

'Come along, sir, we've got six more boat loads to get onto her this morning.'

Matthew went down the gangplank into the boat which was untied, pushed away, caught the breeze and sailed towards the land. Matthew looked back at the vast bulk of the *SS Cherokee* and then turned to look at his destination. The smell once again forced itself onto his attention and, even though the heat of the day was already building, felt a chill of apprehension run through him as they neared the shore.

Chapter Thirty-three

Matthew was supposed to be a writer by trade, a journalist, a wordsmith. Yet there were no words he could find for Chagres, other than 'appalling'. The place was utterly appalling. The smell that yesterday had drifted out to the boat had only been a whiff of what he found on arrival. The smell had grown as the boat neared land and Matthew's first impression of the place as seen from the *Cherokee* was slowly confirmed. It was not a harbour in any meaningful sense. It was certainly not a town, and only by stretching the definition to its most elastic could it be called a village or settlement. It stood beyond a rubble-strewn, muddy beach to one side of a river mouth which discharged brownish water out into the sea, turning the blue of the Caribbean murky as far out as the *Cherokee*. What he could see of the actual settlement consisted of small, single-storey, haphazard thatched huts beyond which rose a wall of dark jungle.

The heat beat down on the place where they landed, a rackety wharf at the river's edge which looked as if, at any moment, under the weight of the men and baggage crowded on it, would slip from the mud into which it was built, fall into the river, and drift out to sea with its sorry-looking cargo of defeated humanity. Beyond the men waiting to board the boat were more of the huts with mud or rubble walls, a few made from what looked like the remains of wooden packing cases. All were roofed with a mass of straggling thatch which must have been made from some sort of local vegetation.

And there was the smell.

Matthew climbed out of the boat onto the wharf and two of the men from the boat followed him with his trunk.

The waiting crowd parted for them and closed again behind them. None of the faces registered interest and no one spoke. The crewmen put the trunk down and returned to the boat. Matthew stood on the wharf by his luggage and watched as the crowd of men began to shuffle forward and those at the front began to board. Then the smell forced itself to his attention once more. Wherever it came from the heat seemed to suck up the foul odour and smear it over everything and everywhere. He was wondering if the smell was going to cause him to throw up when a sailor from the boat who had helped bring the trunks onto the wharf pointed past him. Matthew turned and looked. A black man wearing the remains of a shirt and equally ragged trousers stood by a donkey which was hitched to a flat two-wheel cart, and was looking at him and grinning. The man from the boat called out.

'I'll help you load if you like, sir.' He climbed out of the boat and came to Matthew's side. 'Ready when you are, sir.'

Matthew turned his attention from the black man and his cart to the sailor and it suddenly dawned on him that this sailor expected him to load his own trunk. He turned back to look at the waiting black man.

'Who is he?'

'Ask him, sir. That would be the best way.'

Matthew walked across.

'Who are you?'

The man gave him a wide grin and he nodded.

It was a response. But it was no answer.

'Who sent you?'

The grin remained and several nods were added.

An idea occurred to Matthew. This was, he reminded himself, a foreign land.

'Do you speak English?'

The man spoke.

'English,' grinned and nodded several more times, then

226

spoke again, 'English.'

Then he then rattled off something which Matthew not only couldn't understand but couldn't even identify as any language he might ever have heard even in such a polyglot city as New York.

The black man fell silent.

Matthew mentally cursed Tomes for having placed him in this position. If he put his possessions on the cart and trusted this negro he might lose everything. If he sent him away how was he to move the trunk? More importantly, where was he to move it to? The sailor came up.

'I've got to go, sir. We'll be loaded in a few minutes. What's it to be? You going with the cart or not?'

Matthew made a decision.

'Load the cart and get this man to help you.'

The sailor knuckled his forehead, pointed to the trunks and beckoned the man.

'Look lively, you idle black bugger, and give me a hand with that bloody trunk.'

The black man dropped the donkey's tether which he had been holding and joined the sailor. If he resented the sailor's mode of address he didn't show it. True, the grin had gone, but that was all.

Matthew felt rather pleased with himself, that he had done rather well, taken command of a difficult situation. He stood and watched as the two men loaded the trunk onto the cart. When it was done the sailor came to him, knuckled his forehead, and stood looking at him expectantly.

'Oh, yes. Thank you and take this for your trouble.'

Matthew handed across a few coins. The sailor looked at them, then at Matthew, then put the coins into his pocket, turned, and left to rejoin his boat. Matthew watched him go and noted that the boat was loaded and the sail once again hoisted, then he turned and saw that the black man was already on the move and moving quickly with his trunk on the cart.

'Hi,' shouted Matthew but the man either didn't hear or chose not to listen. 'Hi there, stop.'

A small boy, black and naked except for a broken straw hat, arrived from nowhere. He looked at Matthew for a moment and then started to laugh. Matthew frowned at him. The little boy stopped laughing. Matthew turned his attention once more to the cart and was about to shout once more when something hard hit him in the side. He looked at the boy who was about to throw another stone. Matthew made a dash at him.

'You little devil. I'll teach you ...'

But the urchin was gone. He jumped off the wharf onto the muddy beach and disappeared under the timbers. Matthew stood for a second then turned again to see the back of the cart turn a corner and also disappear.

'Good God. My luggage is stolen.'

He looked for aid at those men who had not boarded the boat which was already pulling away from the wharf. What he saw was a blank indifference. These men neither knew nor cared what had happened and no help would be forthcoming from any of them.

Matthew turned away and began running. Once off the wharf the street, if you could call a stretch of mud between dilapidated huts a street, was not easy going but Matthew had no choice. He soon had to give up trying to run through the mud that came over the tops of his boots in favour of walking as briskly as he was able. He came to the turning where he had lost sight of the cart and stood, looking down the street into which it had turned. It had stopped at the far end and the negro had disappeared. Matthew set off keeping his eyes on the cart but still able to note that the buildings on either side of this thoroughfare, though all single storey and in no way prepossessing, resembled real buildings, most of them having windows, several having doors and some recognisable roofs of corrugated tin. He returned his attention to the cart. The black man had reappeared and stood beside it talking to another man, a white man who was wearing a light suit and broad-brimmed hat. Matthew came up to the cart. The black man looked at him and the white man who, on closer inspection, was not so very white, looked also. The suited man stepped forward and put out his hand.

'Mr O'Hanlon?'

Matthew paused for a moment, surprised. Then, with relief that he was expected, took the offered hand.

'Yes, O'Hanlon, from the *Cherokee*.'

The man smiled.

'Well as she's the only boat out there in the bay you could say I'd guessed that.'

Matthew gave a polite laugh.

'Of course.'

'Come inside out of the sun. Newcomers sometimes find it troublesome.'

Matthew was grateful for the invitation. Now that the problem of his trunk and cart had been resolved he was indeed finding the heat something of a problem, especially as he was wearing not only his hat but also his jacket. He followed the man into the building, which was built of brick and was two storeys in height, something of a monster compared to what Matthew had so far seen of Chagres.

Once inside Matthew felt distinctly better. Coming in suddenly from the sunlight his eyes took a moment to adjust but he soon found that the slatted shutters, although closed, allowed the fierce sun shining on them to create bright bars of light between the slats which were sufficient to make the interior visible but kept it dark enough to give the impression of coolness.

The suited man shouted something in the same language Matthew had heard the cart man use and another black man came through a door at the back of the room. The suited man spoke to him briefly and the man disappeared through the open front door.

'Juan will help Diego get your trunk upstairs.' He gestured to two comfortable-looking wicker chairs that stood in a corner either side of an upturned wooden crate which obviously served as a table. 'Let's sit and have a coffee shall we? Unless you'd prefer beer?'

Matthew had taken off his hat and was glad of the chance to sit. It was still only about nine thirty but the choice his host had presented to him was a difficult one. It was very early to take anything alcoholic but hot coffee somehow didn't appeal.

'Do you know, I think a beer might be just the thing.'

'Good man. I'll join you.' The man called out once again and this time in English and the face that came through the door this time was not black but oriental. 'Two beers, Henry.' The oriental nodded and disappeared. The man turned again to Matthew. 'My name's Da Silva, Francisco, so most English call me Frank.'

'How do you do, Mr Da Silva.'

Da Silva smiled revealing at least three gold teeth.

'Frank, please.'

Matthew smiled back.

'Well then, Frank.' Matthew paused as the two black men, Juan and Diego, came through the front door carrying his trunk and took it through the door at the back of the room. 'Tell me, Frank, were you expecting me?'

'Yes. Tomes sent a note on a boat that came three days ago that there'd be the two of you next time the *Cherokee* came down, so I made sure a room was ready and sent Diego down to the wharf with the cart. Robert still on the boat?'

'Yes, he's giving the new passengers a look over.'

'Thought so, he often does.'

'Often?'

230

'Oh yes. Robert does the journey every two or three months. Seems doctoring on those Pacific Line ships is pretty much a part-time occupation. Maybe they're lucky and carry less fever patients than the ships on this side.' He gave Matthew a sly smile. 'Or maybe he has a few lady-friends in the ports the mail boats put in at. Wouldn't surprise me. Very energetic and resourceful man, Dr Robert Tomes. What I would call full of life energy.'

Oriental Henry came in with two mugs of beer on a tray. He put the drinks on the crate and left. While waiting for Henry to deposit the beers Matthew gave a quick thought to what Frank Da Silva had just told him. If Dr Robert Tomes had met him for the first time on board the *Cherokee* nearly two weeks ago how could he have sent any message about his arrival on some previous boat? Yet it seemed he had. The man sitting with him not only knew he was coming but knew his name.

Frank Da Silva leant forward and picked up his mug then nodded to Matthew's.

'Go ahead, Mr O'Hanlon, Chagres isn't New York but I can vouch for the beer. I have the casks sent down from up north. It's good German beer and I've had a cellar built to keep it cool.' Matthew picked up his mug and took a drink. Da Silva was right. The beer was delicious and almost cold. He took another deep drink then wiped his mouth with the back of his hand. 'Good?'

'Very good.'

Da Silva smiled and took a drink himself.

'You'll find different rules apply down here and one of them is that it's never too early in the day for a cool beer. Now, if you'll excuse me for a moment I must get Diego to go back to the wharf and wait for Robert's trunk to come ashore. Just shout for Henry if you want a refill.'

Frank stood up and disappeared through the back door. Matthew took another drink and thought about the situation.

231

What did it all mean? Had Tomes lied to him about the frequency of his journeys? Why on earth would he? But then again why would Da Silva make such a thing up? And the message, had it come from Tomes? Or had perhaps Clarence Diver sent it to see that someone was waiting for him when he arrived. That made more sense. He took another drink. It was indeed very good beer.

Frank Da Silva returned and sat down.

'Are you sure it was Dr Tomes who sent the message of my arrival, not someone called Diver, Clarence Diver?'

'No, it was Robert all right. In his own hand and signed. It was in his letter making arrangements to get you both over the mountains and on to Panama City. It was with another letter from him to be forwarded. Can't remember the name, French I think. I sent it on. Probably doing the same there as he did here, making arrangements for you. You must be good friends for him to take so much trouble,' he smiled a wide golden smile, 'either that or you're important. Which is it, Mr O'Hanlon? Or shouldn't I ask?'

Matthew, somewhat confused by the question, could think of nothing to say so he tried to smile knowingly and took a drink of his beer.

Da Silva seemed to accept his reserve, took a sip himself, and waited.

'You say Dr Tomes often stays to look over passengers?'

'Usually, most times. I think he must have some sort of arrangement with the Line or maybe with the captain. He always prefers to travel on the *Cherokee* if he can.'

Matthew finished what little was left of his beer.

'I see.'

Although, in truth, he didn't. No, he didn't see at all. And that worried him.

232

Chapter Thirty-four

After they'd finished their beers Frank Da Silva took Matthew upstairs. There was a narrow, rather rickety staircase immediately beyond the door through which Oriental Henry had appeared and disappeared and through which Matthew's trunk had passed. At the top of the stairs Frank Da Silva stopped in the light of a doorway although Matthew, only a few steps below him, could see no actual door.

'Best room in Chagres, after my own, of course. Even the manager of the railway construction hasn't got a better.'

Matthew climbed the last few steps and followed Da Silva into the room. It was a bare place. The walls were covered in a thin lime-wash through which the brick-work clearly showed, the off-white was stained in places with damp and liberally scattered with insects of various sizes. The floor was bare boards and the only furniture two black, iron bedsteads with what looked like hard, horse-hair mattresses. The trunk stood beside one of the beds and there was a storm lantern on the floor in the middle of the room floor.

And that was it. There was nothing else, not even bedding.

There was one large window which filled the room with light. Unfortunately it also filled the room with heat as it lacked curtains and frames, never mind any form of glass. It was just a large square hole in the wall. Matthew looked up. The ceiling was the sloping, corrugated tin roof of the building around the edges of which, from the amount of webs, lived colonies of spiders.

'Pretty fine, eh, Mr O'Hanlon? Better than you

expected or hoped for.' And when he saw the look on Matthew's face he hurried on. 'By our standards down here I mean. This isn't New York,' he laughed, 'but I guess you've already noticed that. Mostly the shacks and huts here are mud-built and rat-infested. If the roof falls in or the walls fall down they don't even bother to repair them, they just put up another. They're lazy people and dirty, but you'll be fine here.' Matthew, he could see, was still far from convinced. 'Dr Tomes has never complained.'

'Hasn't he?'

Da Silva gave up. If the young man didn't realise his good fortune then let him go somewhere else. He'd soon find out his mistake.

'If you're not satisfied perhaps you'd like to look elsewhere.'

Matthew adjusted his mind to his new circumstances by the simple process of remembering the dwellings he had passed when following the cart. This room was awful, but from what little he had seen he was willing to settle for awful as the alternative was more awful still.

'No. This will do. I doubt we'll be here long.'

'Just tonight. Tomorrow you go up-river. It's all arranged.'

'Who by?'

Da Silva laughed.

'Me of course. Didn't I tell you? I run the transport here, boats out to the shipping, canoes up to Gorgona, and then mules over the mountains. It's usually not more than two days' journey depending on your luggage and the weather, and I've made sure you have a place at the hotel when you stop overnight. Won't be as good as this but after a day going up the mountains it'll suit I think.'

'A hotel?'

'Sure. The Washington. I'm part owner. Now, if you'll excuse me I have things to do. Robert should be here in an hour or two. There weren't many fever cases going out, only six or seven that I saw. Everything you need is downstairs. Come down whenever you like and if I'm not there just shout for Henry. He'll look after you.'

And with that Da Silva left Matthew to himself and his thoughts.

Matthew, free from the obligations of courtesy, took off his jacket, threw it onto his trunk, and went and sat on the bed. It was as he suspected. The mattress *was* hard.

He turned over in his mind the conversation with Da Silva. What was going on? Why had his arrival been announced in advance by Tomes? And if Tomes knew he was coming why had he played the stranger on the boat? More importantly, what should he do about it now he knew, keep it to himself or confront Tomes when he came?

All tricky questions.

Matthew pulled off his mud-coated boots, lay back on the bed, and gazed at the ceiling, and, without noticing it, dozed off.

He was woken by Juan and Diego bringing in Tomes' trunk and dropping it by the second bed. Neither man took any notice of him as he sat up. Matthew picked up his jacket, took out his watch, and found that Frank Da Silva had been pretty accurate in his estimate; he had been asleep for nearly two hours. As he put his watch away there were footsteps on the stairs and Robert Tomes came into the room. He threw down his hat on the floor, followed it with his jacket, sat on the bed, and unlaced his boots which he then kicked off and lay back.

'Five. We had to turn five off. The poor devils will die in this God-forsaken hole if I'm any judge, but they'd probably have died anyway on the journey and maybe taken at least twenty or thirty with them. I managed to get one fit to travel, as far as New Orleans anyway. If he gets looked after there he may even live.' He turned to

Matthew. 'Well, Matty, what do you think of our accommodation? Even if you've only walked through the place from the wharf you'll know we're pretty well set up. It may not seem much but believe me, this is high living compared to what else is on offer.'

Matthew found that he had still not come to any decision on whether to confront Tomes or not.

'This fellow Da Silva. What's he like?'

'How do you mean?'

'Well, who is he? He says he runs the transport, that he'll be taking us up-river and over the mountains and on to Panama City.'

'Not himself, he won't. He doesn't stir much out of Chagres. Too many boats coming and going and too many people wanting passage both ways. But he does run all the transport, up and down the river, mules over the mountains, and out to all the boats, and he's part owner of the ruin in the mountains he calls The Washington Hotel. God knows how much money he's made out of the gold rush, not to mention the settlers coming through. I wouldn't be surprised if he's not already worth a million US dollars.'

Matthew was surprised and impressed.

'He didn't seem much to me.'

'No? Well I don't suppose he looks the part of a millionaire, certainly not the New York sort anyway. But Frank Da Silva is a big man in these parts. If it comes through Chagres, gold, people, goods, whatever, Frank gets his cut. And he's got the concession for supplying the railroad workers with accommodation and food. You saw the hovels back there down by the river?' Matthew nodded. 'Well, compared to what the men who come here to build the railway get, they're palaces. Mostly all he's done is rig up poles and roof them over with greenery. Not that it keeps anyone dry when the rain really comes. But it's better than being in the open, not much, but better, at least there's some shade. As for food, you've caught the smell I guess?' Matthew nodded again, he'd caught it. 'That's mostly Da Silva again. He gets cattle and pigs here, God knows how, has it all slaughtered, takes what he wants to supply the railroad, and the rest is just left lying around to rot in the sun. The locals pick at what he leaves, there's the dogs as well and the alligators that come up out of the swamp. And then there's the rats and whatever comes out of the jungle after dark so the stuff gets fairly well spread about. One way or another the locals add their fair share to the unholy mess and you get that distinctive perfume known as the odure of Chagres. But don't worry, we'll be off soon after first light and it'll all literally be behind us. The next boat isn't due in until Thursday. That gives Da Silva two days to get us over the mountains. By that time this place will be a bedlam house again with the new arrivals wanting to get forward and the ones who've had enough wanting to go back. Right now it's peaceful. Those who came on the *Cherokee* with us are gone and those going back are on board, but the place will soon start to fill up again. Take your ease here while you can, Matty, once we get past Gorgona the travelling will get tough and you'll think fond thoughts of this room and these mattresses.'

'Do you always use this room when you're passing through?'

'I don't know about always. This is only the third time I've taken any leave in two years but being a doctor in this climate gives you pretty big pull so Da Silva looks after me. Oh, he's the unofficial postmaster by the way. Any letters or reports you want to send back, get them to Da Silva. He'll see they're safely on the next boat back.'

So, thought Matthew, everything in and out of Chagres goes through Frank Da Silva who just happens to take great care of Dr Robert Tomes.

'Just taken leave twice before?'

'That's right. The Pacific Line keeps me pretty busy.'

'I see.'

But once again he didn't. Either Da Silva was lying to him, or Tomes was. But which? And just as important, why?

Chapter Thirty-five

The noise was like the end of the world. Suddenly, out of nowhere and into the blackness, a million men with hobnailed boots were stamping across the tin roof. Then Matthew, staring into the blackness remembered the rain that he had seen on the boat. That same torrential rain was now falling on the tin roof above their heads. Matthew sat up. From the dark a voice spoke.

'Nothing you can do. When it comes it's like nothing on earth, and you have to put up with it. With luck it'll be over by dawn. It'll be better if we don't have to start in the stuff although we're bound to catch it a few times on the journey.'

Matthew lay back on the mattress. He couldn't remember going to sleep. The last thing he'd known was lying naked on the mattress sweating in the heat. Not even a breath of breeze had entered through the window. Now he was awake again.

He heard movement.

'I'll light the lantern. We'll get no more sleep with that noise going on. Might as well get dressed, it'll be dawn in about an hour.'

Matthew looked towards the window. He could see nothing at all.

'How can you tell?'

'You get like that, you sort of feel the time. During the day even if you hadn't a watch you could look at the sun. At night you have to sort of guess. But after a while it comes.'

The lantern suddenly cast a light across the room. Tomes was naked, squatting by it adjusting the flame, then he stood up and went to the window and calmly urinated out of it. Matthew looked on, shocked.

'What the hell are you doing?'

Tomes' head turned and, seeing Matthew's face, laughed.

'You don't think anyone's down there do you? And if they were how would they notice my small contribution? Take your turn when you're ready or, if you'd prefer, go downstairs and out back like we did last night.'

Matthew swung his legs off the bed, got up, made his way to the window, and relieved himself. When he'd finished he looked down from the window. There was the noise of the rain, blackness, and nothing else.

'Come on, Matty, the sooner we're ready the sooner we'll be on our way.' Matthew returned to his bed and began to dress. From downstairs there began to be noises. 'That'll be Henry setting out the breakfast.'

When they were both ready Tomes took the lantern and they went down to where, already, there was the smell of bacon filling the room.

To his surprise Matthew found he could eat a hearty breakfast, not least because Henry was an excellent cook and the heat had not yet become too intense to take away any appetite. By the time the meal was over dawn was beginning to spread its light in the sky, the rain having suddenly stopped as if turned off at a tap by some unseen hand.

The trunks were brought down by Diego and Juan and loaded on the cart which then set off to the wharf. The street was a mixture of deep mud and water and the mule had to be repeatedly and savagely beaten to keep the cart going. Matthew stood in the doorway and watched it go until Tomes called him.

'Here, Matthew, Frank has something for you.'

Matthew went back inside. Frank Da Silva walked to him and pointed at his hat.

'A fine hat for the city, Mr O'Hanlon, or a pleasant ocean voyage, but it'll be nothing but pulp if you wear it going over the mountains.' He then looked at Matthew's feet. His boots were still mud-caked from his arrival. 'And as for those, I'm surprised they lasted your walk from the river to my house.' And Da Silva beckoned to Henry who came forward carrying a wide, stiff-brimmed, leather hat and a pair of calf-length, lace-up boots. Over Henry's arm was a heavy waxed cape. Henry handed them all to Matthew who stood looking at them. Da Silva patted him on the shoulder smiling his golden smile. 'There, now you are equipped.'

Matthew looked across at Tomes who he found now had on a similar hat and had his trousers tucked into his laced-up boots. He was also wearing his cape, thrown back over his shoulders.

'Is all this necessary?'

Tomes nodded.

'Essential.'

Matthew looked again at the outfit. Dressed as Tomes already was he felt he would look ridiculous, like some sort of stage bandito.

'Come, Mr O'Hanlon. Take off your fancy boots, you can get new ones in Panama City. As for your hat, leave it or carry it as you wish.'

'Yes, get a move on, Matty, we want to be on our way.'

Matthew, reluctantly, did as he was bid but refused to put the cape on and sling it over his shoulders as Tomes did. Instead he threw it over his arm.

Da Silva held out his hand.

'Goodbye and good luck, Mr O'Hanlon. May God go with you.'

Matthew shook his hand then, with Tomes, went out into the street and set off to the wharf.

As Matthew walked beside Tomes he soon felt the benefit of the boots. The mud came up well past his ankles and the going was slow and heavy. However, useful as the boots might be, he felt irked by the hat and the heavy cape slung over his arm. The sun was not yet visible above the trees but already the water from the rain was beginning to rise from the ground in a sort of miasmic vapour and the cape seemed an unnecessary burden which he hadn't asked for and, at the moment, could have happily done without. That turned his thoughts to a question – who had paid for it all? He had not been asked for money and had not seen Tomes pay for anything.

'Who paid for our room and board and for this equipment?'

Tomes smiled at him.

'Courtesy of the Pacific Mail Line. You might say it was from William Aspinwall to you, almost personally.' When Matthew looked puzzled, Tomes continued. 'I can put in for travel and equipment. Two hats, two pairs of boots and two capes don't come to much and I'd arranged the room anyway so the second bed might as well get used.'

'And the food?'

'I told you, I'm a doctor. We're scarce round here and therefore much in demand. People like doing me favours. Don't worry though, Da Silva will find some way of setting the account straight. He's no philanthropist, believe me.'

At the wharf there were already twenty or thirty dishevelled and tired men lounging about aimlessly. They were so filthy and so weathered their faces that it took Matthew a few moments to realise they were white men. Tomes cast his eyes over them.

'Came in at first light and waiting here for the next boat out. More of those who found that California wasn't a place paved with gold. If they've got the price of passage they're the fortunate ones.'

None of these men took any notice of Matthew or Tomes, indeed they seemed incapable of taking notice of anything, such was their condition.

Matthew remembered his fellow travellers who had disembarked from the *Cherokee* only two day before. When they landed he had heard the noise of guns being discharged and their whooping and cheering even from the boat. One of the sailors had been passing at the time and stopped.

'Sounds like a few of them are celebrating as if they'd already struck it rich.' Then he'd shrugged. 'Poor fools, they should wait a short while and see what they've let themselves in for before they waste ball and powder so freely.'

And he had gone about his business.

Waiting alongside the wharf was a long canoe with eight black rowers and a black steersman. Their trunks were already loaded so Matthew and Tomes got in and sat, one behind the other, in the middle of the craft. As soon as they were settled the rowers pushed off and the canoe began to move forward easily in the wide, sluggish waters of the river mouth. Two hundred yards from the wharf, to their left, the swamp began and stretched for what must have been nearly a mile to the more solid ground where the jungle began. Along the edge of the swamp were several huts built over the water on stilts, and about three hundred yards beyond the huts was the first evidence Matthew had seen of the construction of the railway. Men, too many to count, were working on what looked like some sort of causeway which had already made its way about half-way across the swamp.

'What you're looking at there, Matty, is the Panama Railway. They say they're going to build the line through that swamp onto the solid ground on the other side, through the jungle, and then over the mountains.'

Matthew looked again at the construction then at the swamp. Its flat, vegetation-coated surface extended away beyond Chagres as far he was able see. And these men were going to build a causeway capable of carrying a railway all the way across it? Madness, sheer madness. And this lunacy was what he was supposed to write about for the New York papers?

'But that's madness. It can't be done.'

The canoe slid onwards away from the men toiling on the low spit of land they were creating.

'In that case I guess you'll have one good story and then be out of a job. But don't worry, it'll get built all right, and it will keep you busy with plenty of stories. Do you know, in the early days a boat came in carrying about five hundred strong Irishmen fresh from Ireland. Within a week not one of them was still on his feet. I think about thirty survived the fever to get a boat back out of this place. The rest became permanent residents and for all we know that pile of dirt sticking out into the swamp may be their burying ground.'

Matthew gave a small shudder at the thought and remembered what Dan had told him, that both he and his father had been offered high wages to work on this railway. Thank God they had refused them.

'But if the workers die so easily how on earth do they expect to get the thing built?'

'Things have gotten better, not much, but some. They make sure they have the right sort of medicines and now they've got blacks, Chinese, and even Hindoos working here. They still die, but not so quickly. Like I said, you'll get your stories and one day there'll be a railway line. That's modern engineering for you, almost as miraculous as modern medicine.' Matthew turned away from the swamp and looked ahead at the river. Coming towards them was a large canoe very much like their own. As the two boats passed each other he could see it was filled with men in a similar sorry state as those already gathered on the wharf. Tomes watched the canoe go past. 'More who've had enough. You'd think the sight of them would put the new arrivals off but it never does. That's real lunacy for you, the madness of gold-fever. Just one more fever to add to all the others of this pestilential country.'

The canoe slid forward and on either side nothing was visible except the dense jungle that came down and spilled over into the water. Suddenly Matthew realised that the air smelled fresh and clean. The stench of Chagres was behind them. The rowers dipped their paddles in the settled unison of skilled men and the jungle slipped by. Where the river made a gap between the trees sufficient to look up into the distance, Matthew could see the blue, hazy mountains which, when visible, dominated the skyline. He had never seen mountains before so he was of course no judge, but even to his untutored mind they looked considerable.

That's where we're going, he thought, and that's where the railway is going. Across that swamp, through this jungle, then up and over those mountains. Good God! It couldn't be done, could it? Yet back there were the men making it happen and growing out into the swamp there was the beginning of their causeway. Perhaps, after all, with American know-how …

Then out of nowhere the rain came.

The river surface began to jump and boil. Tomes pushed him in the back.

'Get your cape on.'

Matthew grabbed the cape which he'd dropped in the bottom of the canoe. It was heavy, stiff, and difficult to unfold from the bundle he had made of it. By the time he had got it over his head and his hat back on he was soaked to the skin.

About ten minutes later the rain stopped, the clouds cleared as miraculously as they had arrived, the sun shone, and the heat hit Matthew like a slap. Under the cape he felt hot, wet, and uncomfortable. After a few minutes he could take it no longer. He pulled off his hat, scrambled off his cape, and replaced his hat. In less than a few seconds his clothes were steaming in the fierce heat. Twenty minutes later the clouds came back out of nowhere and once again he was soaked to the skin before he could get his cape on. This time the rain lasted for about forty minutes before the clouds went and the sun returned hotter than before, a thing Matthew would have sworn couldn't happen. Two rowers bailed out the rainwater that had collected in the boat and then returned to their places and with the others paddled on, unconcerned with the rain and the heat alike. Matthew pulled his cape back and let it hang over his shoulders down his back as Tomes had done.

Nothing changed as they travelled along, the jungle on either side was the same, and the mountains, when he caught sight of them, were the same and not noticeably nearer. The air was sometimes filled with bird calls and the occasional alligator slipped from basking on the bank into the water as they passed. Matthew was fascinated but after a while it all seemed to become somewhat dreamlike and he let his mind wander to musing on Chagres and the railway, on Da Silva and Tomes, on Clarence Diver and himself. Something more than reporting on the railway was going on and something more than he'd been told by Clarence Diver. But what? What was going to be his role in all this, whatever it was? The air on the river was pure, sweet even. The last vestiges of Chagres had totally disappeared. Despite the heat and the burden of the hat and cape he suddenly felt happy and excited. He was in a canoe on a river going through the deepest jungle. And if that wasn't enough of an adventure it was now spiced with mystery and perhaps even danger. Had Tomes deceived him or was Da Silva lying? He was glad now that he had not confronted Tomes after Da Silva told him about the message. He had alerted neither of them to his suspicions. He felt he had done well so far. He had shown, even if only to himself, that he could play as deep a game as Tomes or Da Silva, or possibly both. He would become a deceiver and, he decided, not the worst of them.

Chapter Thirty-six

The rowers rested briefly at around midday and took whatever food and drink they had brought with them. Matthew and Tomes stretched their cramped legs on the sandy shore and to Matthew's surprise, as he hadn't thought of it himself, Tomes produced from somewhere under his cape some bread and cheese wrapped in a handkerchief and a flask of water.

'It's all right to drink. Frank's water is about as clean as you'll get in Chagres but I boiled it anyway.'

Matthew took it gratefully and, everyone having eaten, drank, and done whatever else was necessary, the journey resumed until by late afternoon, after more bursts of torrential rain and having passed two more laden canoes on their way downriver, the rowers finally brought them to shore.

The small settlement of Gorgona was, in some ways, not dissimilar to Chagres. The heat was certainly the same and another wooden wharf rose from the mud of the river's edge, though smaller than that of Chagres. There were several of the same style of mud huts thatched with vegetation, although these were all in a better state of repair and one or two were even lime-washed. A single track from the wharf led through the settlement to its centre, obviously well trodden. Beyond the dwellings and rising up behind them was the jungle. Tall trees from which and through which spilled the same tangled mass of growth. But there was no swamp and most importantly to Matthew no smell. In fact the place looked comparatively clean and, compared to Chagres, welcoming.

It was from Gorgona that newly arrived passengers from the latest boat would set out on the trail over the mountains. Those who could afford it hired mules here to carry them or their luggage. Here also, in the centre of the village, the ragged refugees from California who had made it across the mountain trail bargained or begged for a place in one of the canoes to complete the final stage of their humiliation and get back to Chagres where they had once arrived so full of hope and ambition.

The rowers pulled the canoe alongside the wharf, tied up, and unloaded the trunks which four of them then carried through the settlement to one of the lime-washed huts. Outside the hut stood a large black man with no shirt but wearing clean white trousers and a wide-brimmed straw hat. On seeing Tomes his face split into a big grin and he held out his hand. Tomes took the black man's hand and greeted him in what Matthew recognised was Spanish. Then Tomes turned to him.

'This is Fernando. He'll be taking us over the mountains with a couple of his men.'

Fernando stepped forward and held out his hand. Matthew paused for a second, unsure of how to react. He had never, ever, in his life shaken hands with a black man. Other than trying to give orders to Diego when he had met him at the wharf he had never, so far as he could remember, spoken to one. Somehow he felt that treating this man as he would a white man, even one as off-white as Frank Da Silva, was some sort of transgression. The smile disappeared from Fernando's face. He let his hand drop, said something in Spanish to Tomes, and walked away.

'Well, Matthew, that was about as foolish a thing as it was possible for you to do. This isn't the American South, nor is it New York, and a man's colour here doesn't signify like it does in those places. Fernando was to take us over the mountains and without him and his men it's an even-money bet a new arrival like you, used to city ways and city comforts, might not make it all in one piece. If it had been me on my own I guess I could have made it but now, if we're to get you to Panama City safe and sound, I'll have to go and square him.'

Matthew was stung by the rebuke, not the criticism of his manner to Fernando, but of his ability to cross the mountains without some sort of nursemaid. Why, women and children among the settlers made the journey, plenty of them. To imply that he, a grown man, might suffer. Ha! It was no more than a gratuitous insult to his intelligence.

'If it means more money I'm quite prepared to ...'

'Money?' Tomes gave a dismissive laugh. 'No it's not money, it's pride. And Fernando's pride will take some mending. I'm pretty sure I can keep him from killing you but I'm not at all sure I can get him to take us over the mountains. Still, I'll do my best.'

Now it was Matthew's turn to give a dismissive laugh.

'Kill me? Don't be ridiculous.'

Tomes looked at Matthew steadily and there was no laugh this time.

'I won't be. I'll just tell you how it is so you'll not make the same mistake again. Look around you, go ahead and look. See any law? See anything that looks like the civilisation you're used to? You've insulted a man who's important and respected in this God-forsaken place. To stay important and respected he has to repay that insult. How do you think he'll do that? Take you to court? Bar you from his club? Write a strong letter to the local paper? He'll cut your throat and leave your carcass in the street for everyone to see and the buzzards to pick at.' He saw Matthew's reaction of disbelief. 'Believe me, that's the truth. This is a place where men make up their own law and justice is quick and violent. Now wait here and if I bring him back put out your hand first, and damn well smile, the biggest, best, and brightest you can manage. Remember, your life might depend on it.'

And Tomes set off in the direction Fernando had gone.

Then the rain began again.

Matthew stood by the trunks. Several black men, oblivious of the torrential rain, sauntered past obviously to have a look at him and the idea that Tomes had planted in his mind of a sudden and lethal revenge by Fernando began to sink in and take root. This was, after all, a wild and desolate place.

Then, through the rain came Tomes accompanied by Fernando and it seemed to dawn on Matthew for the first time what a very well-developed specimen this particular black man was.

Matthew smiled and held out his hand.

Fernando stopped in front of him.

'So very pleased to meet you, Señor Fernando.'

Matthew kept his hand out and cranked up the smile another notch. Fernando waited, unsmiling, for just long enough, then he took Matthew's hand and shook it. But there was no smile. Matthew was relieved, but not completely so. His hand had been taken, true, but Matthew had noted Fernando's eyes and they disturbed him, disturbed him considerably. For the eyes told him quite a different story from the handshake.

They ate roast chicken in the evening in front of the hut by the light of a storm lantern and drank beer which Matthew thought he recognised as the same as he had been given by Frank Da Silva.

'This is the same beer I had back in Chagres in Frank Da Silva's, isn't it?'

Tomes nodded and finished the food in his mouth.

'It is. He sees that Fernando gets a couple of kegs wherever his latest shipment arrives.'

'Payment in kind? Seems a bit lavish to me to send such good beer to such a primitive place.'

'No, not payment in kind, a present to show his esteem for the man. For God's sake get it firmly fixed in your head, Matty, that until we reach Panama City you're in a different world. I told you, Da Silva is a big man here, wealthy and powerful. If he chooses to keep on good terms with Fernando that means he's a big man too. Not so rich but still powerful, and what's more his word is law with most of these people. They rely on him for work and he treats them fair. If anyone could be said to be a chief in these valleys and mountains it's Fernando.'

And Tomes went back to his meal.

Matthew had finished his meal, which he had found excellent and he now finished his beer. He felt rather sulky at Tomes' tone and words. What did it matter to him if Fernando were some petty lord in this place? It was only two days to their destination and then he could forget Fernando.

Later they lay inside the hut on the earth floor in their clothes and slept. Matthew's sleep was troubled and restive. The floor was hard and he dreamt of being pursued by a giant black man armed with an enormous knife, which seemed all too real, but despite his troubled sleep when he woke it was already daylight outside. He got up and went out of the hut to find Tomes smoking his pipe in the hot sunshine.

'Go into the jungle and do what's needful. Our trunks are loaded and we're ready to go.'

Matthew went into the nearest jungle, relieved himself, cleaned himself with some leaves, and returned to find Fernando and two more men standing by the hut. Each holding the halter of a mule. One of the mules carried the trunks, one on either side of it. The load seemed impossible for the animal to carry any distance. The other mule carried nothing.

'Why two mules?'

'One's to carry you if it becomes necessary.'

Once again Matthew was stung by this slur on his strength and ability.

'No, dammit, there's no need. I'm fit and strong and if

251

women and children can make this damned journey ...'

Fernando, ignoring Matthew's outburst, spoke to the men and they began to move off.

Robert Tomes began to follow.

'Come on, Matthew, and don't make any more trouble, you've managed enough already. Just do as you're told and try to keep up.'

And Tomes set off behind the second mule. Matthew stood for a moment then followed. What else could he do?

Then the rain began again.

Chapter Thirty-seven

Even to Matthew's untutored eyes the pathway through the jungle was clear. From much use it had been widened and kept clear of any jungle incursion. But being clear to the eye did not make it sure underfoot. As soon as the settlement of Gorgona was left behind the path began to climb quite steeply. It became narrow and rocky and was criss-crossed with endless narrow waterways through which the torrential rains ran down to the river. These waterways laid bare the rocky ground and what little surface soil the rainwater had not removed human traffic had cleared. The result was that the trail underfoot was mostly bare rock, slippery and dangerous. Added to this the great trees to either side were festooned with creepers, which combined with the canopy of leaves to shut out most of the sunlight. This lack of sun, however, did nothing to reduce the oppressive heat, making the trail dark, steamy, and difficult even for the sure-footed mules.

The path rose upwards, sometimes steadily, sometimes precipitously, but always upwards. Sometimes it was necessary to ford wider watercourses where the fast-flowing streams went well over the tops of the calf-length boots Matthew and Tomes wore, and time after time as they climbed the rain hammered down and poured from the canopy of the trees. Matthew, as he struggled on, wondered how on earth settler families with women and children and baggage had managed such a difficult trail. On several occasions small files of men coming down from the mountain passed them wordlessly, more returnees from the gold fields, and as usual almost all were in a sorry state. Late in the morning the mule carrying the trunks lost its footing and fell. One of the trunks, Matthew's, broke loose and the lid burst open as it hit the rocky ground, spilling his clothes onto the wet ground.

Fernando, who seemed incapable of tiredness or fatigue in leading the group, stopped and began to speak. Matthew knew no Spanish but that was no barrier to understanding the gist of Fernando's words. He swore first at the muleteer, then turned his attention to the mule which, while swearing, he and the two men kicked, beat and goaded until it had struggled to its feet. Matthew's trunk was roughly repacked with the stained clothes, the lid secured, and re-loaded onto the mule. All the while during this enforced halt Matthew sat on a rock trying as best he could to regain some energy. He was grateful that Tomes, who had also sat down, seemed to be as ready for a rest as he was and was not inclined to conversation, both men preferring to save their breath for the continuance of the journey.

When the mule was ready Fernando came to them and spoke to Tomes.

'He says do you want to ride on the spare mule? He thinks you look as if you've had about enough.'

Matthew was about to make some sharp rebuttal of this slander on his condition but he caught Tomes' eye which said wordlessly, don't make any more trouble.

'No, thank him but say I'll continue on foot.'

Tomes translated, Fernando returned to the mules, Matthew and Tomes stood up and the party got underway once more.

Although they must have climbed some considerable distance in altitude the heat never abated and the heavy leather hat and cape became almost intolerable to Matthew. Around one o'clock Fernando finally called a halt and they sat down to rest and eat. Fernando had been carrying a large, leathern satchel slung across his shoulder and from this he now produced their meal, two loaves of coarse bread which he broke and handed out, and then a can from which he removed the tight-fitting lid and handed to Matthew. It contained a mess which seemed to consist mostly of beans. Matthew looked at it then at Tomes.

'What am I supposed to do with this?'

'Dip your bread in, get as much as you can onto it then pass the can on.'

Matthew looked once again at the mess inside the can. Hunger, for he was very hungry, fought with what was left of his city sensibilities. He had walked through a street up to his ankles in mud, ruining a perfectly good pair of boots. He had slept naked in a room without windows, door, or bedding. He had urinated out of the window. But this as food? Fernando said something in Spanish. Tomes interpreted.

'He says get a move on and take what you want. Others are waiting.'

Matthew pushed his bread into the can stirred it round and handed the can on to Tomes who did the same and again passed it on until all five men had taken their share, Fernando last and wiping the can clean.

To his surprise the mess, whatever it was, tasted quite good although Matthew was tempted to put this down more to his appetite than to any culinary art and now that it was gone he wished he had made a little more effort with his bread when he had the chance. Fernando then passed round a case-bottle in which was water laced with a little rum. Each man took a drink, wiped the bottle, and passed it on.

After the meal, such as it was, the journey resumed and Matthew, finding his second wind, felt easier in the climbing. The small party toiled on up the mountain trail through the heat of the afternoon and, mercifully, were spared any more rain.

Then they came upon the dead body.

A man, obviously a Californian returnee, ragged and dirty like so many Matthew had seen, was sitting on the ground with his back to a rock by the side of the trail. His head, hatless, rested forward on his chest and his arms lay by his sides as if in sleep. Fernando stood by the man and gave his leg a hard prod with his boot. The man slipped slowly sideways, rolled onto the ground, and lay there.

Fernando turned to Tomes.

'Finito.'

Tomes nodded and they all began to move on. Except Matthew.

'Here, Tomes, we can't just leave him like this.'

Tomes stopped and looked back.

'What do you suggest? He's dead.'

Matthew looked at the man. He had never seen a dead body before.

'Maybe he's fainted.'

Tomes came back and looked down at the inert figure. Then shook his head.

'Nope. He's dead. Fever maybe or exhaustion. Probably both. There's nothing we can do.'

'But if he's dead shouldn't we bury him?'

'What, here? How do you propose we do that? Even if we had spades we wouldn't get more than a few inches through any ground round here before we hit solid rock. Leave him, Matty, maybe someone going down to Gorgona will take him along, if not the buzzards and the whatever else there is round here will pick him clean. Whatever happens he's past caring.' Fernando called to them. 'Come on, Fernando wants to get to The Washington before dark.'

Tomes walked off and, after one last look at the body, Matthew followed him. It was a brutal country all right and now he knew it was literally the grave of at least one white man.

Fortunately, as the daylight began to fail, the trail levelled off somewhat, the jungle became more open, and the going comparatively easy. More than once since the

256

trouble with the trunk Tomes had asked Matthew if he wanted to ride on the spare mule but Matthew's pride had so far managed to prompt a refusal, but the last few miles of serious climbing had almost broken him. He had never felt so weary and exhausted in his life. His legs ached, his back ached, and his feet hurt. His whole body, it seemed, had begun to throb with pain and he knew he was holding the group up as they slowed their pace to accommodate his failing strength. So when Tomes turned once more, concerned about the failing light, and offered him the mule he accepted. The muleteer helped him to mount and Matthew, holding onto the mane, sat astride the beast and the journey resumed. It was chronically uncomfortable but as he could not have walked more than a few steps he accepted his humiliation and suffered in silence.

Night had fallen for nearly an hour when they reached their night's resting place but they had been fortunate covering the last two miles of the trail by the light of a moon unobscured by clouds and shining from a star-filled sky. What spirits were left in Matthew rose when he saw the great fire that had been lit in a space of ground by The Washington Hotel. All around this blaze were groups of men whom he recognised in the light of the fire as yet more returners. Then he looked at the hotel and his spirits sank once more. Admittedly he was seeing it mostly by the weird light of the great bonfire which gave it a somewhat fantastic aspect but even despite this distortion he could see it was a rambling, ramshackle place, more like some hastily and badly assembled farm outbuilding than anything else.

The muleteer helped Matthew to dismount and set him on his feet, Fernando gave orders to his two men who went off to see to the mules and he then led Tomes and Matthew to the doorway of The Washington and left them there. Inside it was lit with two or three oil lanterns which gave just enough light for Matthew to see that the interior was like some vision from hell. There seemed to be just one vast room throughout which, between the posts which held up the roof, was filled with sets of three-tier bunks, roughly made, with canvas stretched across the frames. This, then, was the hotel's accommodation: at least a hundred bunks in a dark airless room with an overpowering smell of unwashed humanity. However, as far as Matthew was able to make out every bunk was occupied.

'My God, I'd rather sleep out in the open than in this hole.'

Tomes nodded.

'Pretty foul I'll grant you, but these men have all paid two dollars each for those cots and consider themselves to be the lucky ones. If it rains, which it likely will, they'll be inside.'

'But the smell?'

'They've known worse, I doubt they even notice it.'

Then it dawned on Matthew that if they weren't to sleep in this charnel-house they must sleep outside and, as Tomes had pointed out, it was indeed most likely to rain. Fernando came back and spoke to Tomes.

'Come on, Matty, Fernando's got our accommodation ready.'

Matthew followed Tomes and Fernando who led them round the back of the hotel where, at a small distance from the building, he made out a large tent. Fernando pulled open the flap and inside was a lighted lantern, two bedrolls already laid out, and beyond the bedrolls their trunks. Matthew went in with Fernando and looked round. The tent was big enough for them to stand upright in the middle between the bedrolls. The flap opened, Tomes came in, and Fernando left.

'My God, Tomes, this is wonderful. I thought back there we might have to sleep on the ground.'

'Yes. You might have mentioned as much to Fernando,

maybe even thanked him. There's over a hundred men out there round that fire who'll have to sleep in the open tonight and any of those with money, and there must be at least a couple, would have paid handsomely, damned handsomely, for this luxury.' Almost to reinforce Tomes' words, as he finished speaking there was the sound of heavy rain on the canvas. Matthew was ashamed and annoyed. Ashamed of his failure of gratitude and annoyed that Tomes had been so quick to point it out.

'Well, he's paid isn't he?'

'Yes, he's paid, but that doesn't make him a servant, and he resents being treated like one. I'm afraid he has not developed any great liking for you, Matthew, and I hope you can get to Panama City without making things worse with him or you might never get there at all. I told you how it is out here. Now let's get some sleep, we'll be off at first light.' And with that Tomes took off his hat and cape, stretched himself on the bedroll, and pulled the cape over himself. 'Cover yourself with your cape. This canvas is good but if the rain lasts it will start to come through.'

Then he leaned over and turned out the lantern. Matthew stood in silence for a while then realising that his body was screaming out for rest he also took off his hat and cape, lay down, covered himself, and within minutes, to the dull drum of rain on canvas, sleep came.

Matthew woke suddenly trying to scream, but the scream would not come because there were fingers round his throat. He tried to struggle but something was holding him tight and he couldn't move. He tried vainly to shout or to free himself but, struggling for air, he felt himself losing consciousness and words formed in his head that his mouth was unable to frame.

'Mother of Mercy, I'm being murdered. Is this how it all ends for me?'

Then a bottomless pool of inky darkness filled his mind and he slid into it.

Chapter Thirty-eight

Matthew knew he was lying on his back, without the ability to move, his arms and legs useless. And above him, looking down on him, very close and breathing hotly on his face was a hideous black monster, a visage with terrible eyes full of hate. A devil's face. Oh my God, he thought, I am dead, and I am in hell!

Then Matthew's mind cleared.

It was the face of Fernando!

His first thought was that Fernando was the one trying to kill him. Once again Matthew tried to scream and this time succeeded. Fernando immediately placed his hand over Matthew's mouth and said something. Matthew grabbed the hand and pushed it away.

'Help, help. Murder.'

The words should have been shouted but they came out more as a croak and a vicious pain ran through his throat.

Fernando drew back and said something. Then Tomes' face appeared looking down over Fernando's shoulder. He was holding up the lamp and Matthew saw there was a trickle of blood from his hair running down his forehead into his left eyebrow and from there on down his cheek.

'Easy, Mat, you've been attacked and your throat's in a bad way. Don't try to speak.' Fernando stood up and stepped aside and Tomes knelt down. He held the lamp closer and gently examined Matthew's throat. 'You're damned lucky. I heard him coming in but he knocked me cold before I could do anything. If Fernando here hadn't been outside the villain would have done for you.'

Matthew croaked out the words before he remembered Tomes' injunction not to speak.

'The villain?'

'One of the men out there, probably broke and desperate, saw we had this tent and took his chance. Fernando was on guard not far away and heard something. He came in and finished him but not before he'd had a good go at strangling you.' Tomes stood up, his examination complete. 'It'll be damn sore for a while but as far as I can see there's no permanent damage done.'

Matthew pulled himself into a sitting position held his throat gently and croaked.

'Where's the man?'

'Outside.'

'Under arrest? Guarded?' Tomes shook his head. 'Not escaped?'

Tomes smiled. With the blood and the lantern light coming from below his face took on an unearthly almost diabolical look.

'I told you, Matty, there's no law out here. Fernando says he pulled the man off you, dragged him outside, and cut his throat. His body's still there if you want to see for yourself.'

'Dead?'

'Fernando didn't spare himself, he made sure of it. I checked. He's cut from ear to ear.'

'My God.'

'It'll be dawn in about an hour so there's no point in going back to sleep even if we felt like it. Best get ourselves ready. If our visitor had friends out there they might take exception to the welcome he got on his visit. If we're gone before they miss him we'll avoid any unnecessary trouble.'

Matthew couldn't believe what he was hearing. Unnecessary trouble! Someone had tried to murder him. Surely they couldn't just pack up and move on as if nothing had happened. He forced himself to speak.

'But we must report it. He tried to murder me. Someone must be told.'

262

'Who? Why? He's dead and you're not. Nobody cares except maybe his friends if there are any.' Tomes turned to Fernando and said something in Spanish. Fernando nodded and left the tent. 'Fernando will pull the body somewhere out of sight and then get the mules sorted out. With any luck we'll be well on our way before his body's found.'

Matthew scrambled to his feet.

'But when they find him won't they follow us?'

'What for?'

'Revenge.'

Tomes smiled again. Matthew was a difficult pupil who didn't seem able to accept the world he had come into.

'Once they find him, if they find him, we'll be long gone. They'll forget him and move on. They're bound for Gorgona and Chagres and one man more or less won't deter them. All they want is to get on a ship and head back to wherever they came from and put the infernal gold rush behind them. No, if we get away at first light we'll have no more trouble. Oh, and by the way, Fernando saved your life. You might give some thought to how you will say thanks to him.'

And Tomes bent down, put the lantern on the floor, picked up his hat and cape, and left the tent.

Matthew stood for a few minutes gently massaging his throat. Fernando had saved his life. He had never known anyone who had done anything so heroic before. How on Earth did one say thank you for such an action, especially as Fernando appeared to speak no English and he had no Spanish. Then his fingers touched something.

Matthew stood outside the tent. It was still dark but the sky was just beginning to lighten. The fire they had seen on arrival had somehow been kept burning all night despite the rain and now had been built up again and was blazing. From the light of the fire Matthew could see that there was movement all over the encampment as men made ready to be on the move.

Tomes came up with Fernando.

'The mules are over there. Let's be on our way.'

Fernando turned to go but stopped as Matthew stepped forward and caught his arm. Fernando turned and looked at Matthew. The light from the large fire showed that the look on his face was anything but pleasant. Matthew let go of his arm and began to take something from round his neck. Then he held it out to Fernando.

'Thank you.'

Fernando looked down at Matthew's' hand then slowly took what was being held out to him. He held it up so that firelight fell on it. It was a thin gold chain with a small gold medal on it. On the medal was the image of a woman holding a child in her arms. His mother had given it to him on the occasion of his First Holy Communion and he had worn it ever since. Indeed he had never until this day taken it off.

Fernando looked again at Matthew. This time the look on his face was different, almost reverent. He turned to Tomes and said something in Spanish. Tomes translated.

'He wants to know what it is.'

'It's a holy medal, it has the Madonna and Child on it. It was given me by my mother at my First Holy Communion. My mother told me that the priest said it had been blessed by the Pope himself in Rome. I want him to have it to say thank you for all he has done, leading us, getting this tent, and saving my life.'

Tomes turned and gave Matthew's message to Fernando who listened patiently then held up the medal and looked at it again. Then he blessed himself slowly, put it round his neck and held it again so he could look down on it. Then he looked at Matthew and blessed himself again. Matthew felt he ought to say something but before he could Fernando stepped forward, said something in Spanish, then grabbed him by his shoulders and kissed him square on the mouth. Matthew pulled himself away and

264

wiped his mouth with the back of his hand before he had time to think but, having done it, he realised that once again he had probably mortally offended Fernando. But Fernando laughed, stepped forward once again, grabbed Matthew's arm, took his hand, and shook it vigorously, talking all the while. Then he turned away and headed off, fingering his new medal.

'Well whatever it is it seems to have made some considerable impression. Come on, we're off,' and they headed after Fernando. 'I'm no Papist, Matty, just a poor Protestant in a superstitious, idolatrous country, but I'll tell you this, you have a friend for life now in Fernando. He thinks what you gave him is big magic, the biggest. You being a Roman might understand how that works more than I, but you've put yourself square with him, square and beyond.'

Matthew smiled as they caught up with Fernando who was standing by the mules showing his medal to the two muleteers both of whom on seeing it crossed themselves twice as he had done then both held up a hand and saluted Matthew who, not sure what to do, stepped forward and solemnly shook each of them by the hand. At this they and Fernando all looked at one another then burst out laughing. Matthew, not at all sure why, joined in.

'Can we break up the party and get going?'

Fernando, obviously understanding Tomes' words, gave instructions and the group moved off.

Matthew fell in at the rear, pleased with himself and the old thrill of adventure surged through him again. He had travelled over two thousand miles down the Atlantic and in a short while he would have crossed from the Caribbean to the Pacific. He had travelled through jungles and climbed over mountains. He had shaken hands with black men and even been kissed by one. This last was not something he had wanted nor enjoyed, true, but something different and outrageous, something far beyond the ordinary. He had survived a murder attempt and made a friend of a man recently disposed, if Tomes was to be believed, to hate him rather than love him. He felt now as he had when talking to Sam Grant, that he was indeed exceptional and a man bound for glory.

The dawn was coming up quickly behind the trees and in not more than a few minutes there would be enough light to see the trail clearly and avoid any danger. They were about to go down the mountain, a journey Tomes had said was easy compared to the climb up. By the end of the day they would finally have arrived, they would be in Panama City, their destination.

Chapter Thirty-nine

Panama City had been established as a port by the Spanish to receive their gold from Peru and send it over the mountains along the well-maintained Camino Real, the Royal Road, to the Caribbean where it was loaded onto Spanish galleons at Portobello. From there it set off into the Caribbean and became prey to the likes of Drake and other sea rovers.

The mule trains carrying gold from Peru still crossed the mountains over the now ill-kept and treacherous trail, but now the gold was the property of European companies with headquarters in London or Paris. It was these mule trains that gave some of the prospectors making their way to California their first sight of the yellow metal they sought, slung in ingots across mules. To see so much gold out in the open re-kindled plenty of appetites and reinforced the fairytale that told how the yellow metal simply lay about waiting to be picked up. A long, badly victualled sea journey in cramped conditions, to arrive at the dispiriting landfall of Chagres, had dented its fair share of enthusiasm. From Chagres to Gorgona paying extortionate rates for travel and crossing the steep mountains led many a man to wonder if the expedition he had entered into with such hopes and expectations would indeed lead to a happy outcome. But the sight of real gold, and plenty of it, re-fired many a waning dream and after the gold had gone on its way down to Chagres it was with uplifted hearts such men found the going easier and the spirit stronger.

Occasional attacks were made on these gold trains protected as they usually were by one white man with a brace of pistols, riding his own mule, and a few natives with dilapidated muskets walking behind. But inevitably the gold, if taken, was found not many yards away in the jungle, the weight making it impossible to carry more than a few yards and the bandits, if found, were shot in Panama City's main square for their trouble.

Matthew and Robert Tomes were sitting at a table outside the best hotel in the city drinking an evening glass of wine before having dinner. The topic of gold and its theft had come up in their conversation because the next morning three men would be executed by firing squad in the square, having made such an attack on a gold train a month previously.

'Do you know the weight of a bar of gold?' Matthew shook his head. 'Too much for any man to carry for more than a few paces.'

'Why not take the mules?'

'And if you did, stole the mule and its whole load, where would you take it? To the north and south of the trail is nothing but miles of jungle and mountains, the mule would be more of a burden than a help.'

'Why not down to Chagres or back here?'

'Because everyone would know the gold was stolen. How could it be disposed of, always assuming the thieves managed to travel the trail without being taken? An unlikely scenario, you will agree.'

Matthew agreed.

'So the gold is safe out there in the open where everyone can see it? Strange. I might write a piece about it.'

Matthew leaned forward to the table and took up his wine. He felt relaxed and comfortable. His journey was over and he had arrived safely. On their arrival the previous evening Tomes had taken them to this hotel where they had once again shared a room, but this time a proper room with furniture, bedding, a window with shutters, a chamber pot under each bed, and hot water for washing and shaving delivered to their room in the morning. Luxury. The bill, Tomes had told him, was, as usual, down to the Pacific Mail Line as Matthew was his guest.

'The line keep it on permanently for any officials or officers passing through or any big bugs, politicians, shareholders and the like, who may be travelling through on their way up to California or beyond.'

Matthew looked out across the square. It was wide and cobbled and surrounded by imposing Spanish colonial buildings. Palm trees were dotted around the sides of the square and in one corner was an ornate fountain. The evening could not be said to be cool but the fierce heat of the day had subsided and had brought out locals and visitors in substantial numbers.

'It seems a busy place.'

'It is. Panama City has become a halfway house for anyone doing the journey east to west or the other way. If you want a boat north you have to wait here for it so the place is permanently full.'

Matthew looked out on the square. The moon was bright in the sky, there was light in the windows of the cafés and bars, and outside lamps burned. This was more like Matthew's dream of paradise even if there were no dusky, half-clad maidens to attend on him.

'I like it. I think it has charm. I might write a piece on it.'

'Oh it can have charm all right, especially in the evening when you can't see the real condition of most of the buildings.'

'I suppose so. I must say I wasn't impressed with what I saw when we arrived yesterday.'

On their arrival Matthew had taken in the place he had travelled so far to come to and, as he told Tomes, he had not been favourably impressed.

The main street seemed to consist entirely of hotels and

269

bars, none of which looked overly enticing. The buildings were old and many had once been of some magnificence but their grandeur had long ago faded as the fortunes of Spain's empire had faded and the façades had obviously suffered from time and neglect. However, the place had suffered a revival with the coming of the gold rush, and, not unlike a battered and aging prostitute, the main street had hurriedly applied as much make-up as it could and dressed itself with a garish, gay front and set out to capture as much as it could from the men waiting there for the ships that would take them away to wealth and success.

'It can be a passable town if you stick to the right places but for the most part this place lives pretty much off those passing through, and it can be a rough passage believe me. Outside the city there's a camp, we passed it remember?' Matthew nodded, he remembered. It reminded him of the camp outside The Washington Hotel. 'It's filled with men who found that Panama City had so much charm that it emptied their wallets and when that happens the only way of getting a berth is by working your passage. Which is fine if you're a butcher, a cook, a carpenter, or had any other trade useful on board. But if you had no ship-board skills to offer the only thing left is to go and join the other destitutes and pick up what you can from any new arrivals that still have a little trust or innocence left.'

'You mean rob them?'

'Rob them, steal from them, do whatever was necessary to get them parted from their money. Down here you have to learn quick and if you're a slow learner you usually take your lessons to the grave.'

Matthew would have laughed at such theatrical language back on the *Cherokee* but now he knew better.

'A dangerous place then?'

Tomes nodded.

'But interesting. Like I say, with the sort of men going

270

up to the gold-fields parts of it can be rough, damned rough, especially Little America.'

'Little America?'

'That's what the locals call the camp. If you go there to get a story see that you go with some good strong company is my advice, Matty, company that knows how to use firearms. What happened back at The Washington could easily happen again in that camp and you'll need someone as good as Fernando at your side, and more than one would be better. Now, to business. Tomorrow afternoon I leave Panama City on the *SS California* and we need to get you settled in some decent accommodation. You can't stay on in this hotel and there's precious few places where you might make yourself both safe and comfortable.' Once Matthew would have bridled at this suggestion but experience had finally taught him to listen to Robert Tomes and trust his judgement in such domestic matters whatever other reservations he might have. 'Let's go in and eat, and over dinner I'll tell you of a place I think would suit you down to the ground as far as accommodation goes.'

Chapter Forty

The next morning Tomes introduced Matthew to Dr Aleksandar Couperin, who arrived at their hotel at ten thirty. They found him waiting in the lounge, a neat, well-dressed little man with thinning jet-black hair smoothed over a dome-like head, complemented by a thin moustache and finished off with a neat little beard. Matthew took an instant dislike to him, not least because he felt the blackness of his hair owed more to chemistry than to nature and, though he could not actually smell any, suspected him of being the kind of man who would use perfume of some sort. Tomes, however, greeted him warmly.

'Thank you for coming, Dr Couperin. This is my companion Matthew O'Hanlon, foreign correspondent for the New York Associated Press, down here to cover the new railway and anything else that he thinks may be of interest to the people back in New York.'

Dr Couperin smiled and held out his hand to Matthew.

'I'm pleased and honoured, Mr O'Hanlon.'

Matthew shook the offered hand which was damp and soft. Dr Couperin looked at him expectantly and Matthew had the distinct feeling that he ought to say something, but as to what that something might be more than the usual form of greeting he was at a loss, with the result that Tomes continued.

'Come, let's all sit down and get acquainted.' Tomes led them to a table. 'Would you care for coffee, Doctor?'

'Thank you.'

Tomes beckoned a waiter.

'Coffee.'

The waiter nodded and left.

Matthew looked around. On their arrival the previous day he hotel had been busy, bustling even, but now it seemed deserted.

'We seem to have the place to ourselves this morning. Everyone seems to be gone or be otherwise engaged.'

'Yes, and there is a reason, Mr O'Hanlon. Everyone has gone to the main square to watch the execution. Not much of interest happens here in Panama City in the usual course of events and if there is an execution, especially a multiple execution, people tend to make a holiday of it.'

'The gold robbers?'

'Yes.'

'I'd forgotten. What time does it take place?'

'Noon, but people like to get out there early and get a good view. It is one of our few big social events so almost everyone will be there seeing and being seen. The ladies especially enjoy such occasions as they can dress up and show off their best clothes.'

Tomes joined in.

'I hope the rains keep off. Wouldn't want the ladies' finery ruined by a sudden downpour.'

The doctor shrugged.

'We are used to it and are prepared.'

'Will you go, doctor?'

'No, Mr O'Hanlon, I would prefer not to be associated with the event.'

'See too much death in your business for a few more to be of interest?'

The doctor seemed puzzled by Matthew's question.

'I'm sorry, I'm afraid I don't quite …'

Tomes intervened.

'Dr Couperin is a doctor of law. He's a lawyer, not a medical man.'

Matthew apologised.

'Sorry, I just assumed that doctor meant a medical doctor.'

Couperin raised a hand.

'No apology necessary I assure you. It is an understandable mistake. As to my reasons for not attending the ceremony, I defended the men at their trial. Obviously I failed them or they would not be going out there today to be shot. Having failed them I do not wish to be part of the spectacle of their murder.'

'Murder?'

The doctor shifted uneasily in his chair.

'My apologies, I had not meant to speak with such force but the truth is, this matter has touched me deeply.'

At this point the coffee arrived and was laid out by the waiter on the table. Dr Couperin leaned forward and poured himself a cup, added sugar, sat back, and took a drink. To Matthew all of this was done in the manner of someone collecting themselves together. Tomes and Matthew both poured their coffee and waited. Obviously Tomes had noted the doctor's manner as well.

'Gentlemen, I'm afraid I spoke hastily and without thought.' Couperin forced a weak smile. 'Not a thing any good lawyer should do and, if having done it, admit to.' He waited for his little joke to sink in and Matthew smiled dutifully. 'The three men who will be shot today are all young, the oldest is only twenty. The evidence against them was, to say the least, flimsy and circumstantial. In any civilised court of law the charges would have been thrown out never mind a guilty verdict being found. But here, as you will soon find, Mr O'Hanlon, things are not always civilised. There is a smooth surface of order here and below that surface ...'

He stopped speaking and rose to his feet. A man in a rather grand military uniform with a peaked cap and carrying white gloves had come into the lounge, heading for the main door. Seeing the group at the table he made a detour and on arriving at the table spoke in Spanish to Dr Couperin. Couperin answered briefly and whatever he said

275

seemed to amuse the newcomer because he laughed loudly. The military man then looked at Tomes and Matthew smiled and saluted then turned and left. All three watched him leave and when he had disappeared through the front doors Dr Couperin sat down. 'That was Colonel Hernandez, our chief of police. I'm afraid he is not only the guardian of the law here he is, unfortunately, also the judiciary. If he chooses he can be judge, jury and executioner, but of course not visibly so in the court. Such was the case with the men I defended. They were effectively judged and sentenced before the trial began. However, I am monopolising the conversation and my legal troubles were not the reason you asked me to come, Dr Tomes. How can I be of assistance?'

'Mr O'Hanlon needs accommodation. I wondered if you might be able to offer him a room in your house for as long as it takes for him to get settled?'

The question seemed impossibly abrupt to Matthew. Tomes was calmly asking this man to take an utter stranger into his home for an indefinite period. He was struggling to think of something that he might say to make it a little less of a command and more of a request when Dr Couperin responded.

'Of course. Mr O'Hanlon will be most welcome. I would be honoured to have him as my guest for as long as he wishes.'

Then he turned, beamed a smile at Matthew, and awaited his response.

'Thank you.'

It seemed weak to Matthew but what else could he say?

'That's settled then, Matty. I have to be on the *California* by three this afternoon so if you two don't mind I'll go and get on with my packing and leave you to get acquainted and make all the necessary arrangements.' Tomes stood up and Dr Couperin and Matthew followed suit. 'Well, this is goodbye, Matty, at least for the time being. I'll look you up when I'm next down here if I may and maybe we'll dine together and you can fill me in on all the news.'

Suddenly it dawned on Matthew that Tomes was going. He had come to look on him as someone permanent, a sort of colleague and guide, and hadn't given any real thought to the fact that once they reached Panama City Tomes would move on and be gone from his life.

'Certainly. Certainly, Robert, and may I thank you, thank you most heartily.'

Tomes waved away the thanks.

'No need. Enjoyed every minute of it.' He turned to Dr Couperin. 'Thank you, Dr Couperin, I know that you and Matty here will get along famously.'

'I'm sure we will.'

The men shook hands and once more Tomes turned to Matthew.

'Goodbye, Matthew, and good luck.'

Matthew felt an odd tightening in his throat and, unable to actually speak, took Tomes' outstretched hand and shook it.

Tomes then turned, walked away, and was gone. Matthew found that he actually felt worse on this parting than he had done when leaving his mother, father, and family in New York. It was as if some guardian angel was suddenly gone and he was alone.

Then Dr Couperin spoke.

'Perhaps you would like to accompany me to my house and see your room? My wife and daughter will be there. They will not go to see the execution until later. I have made arrangements to have satisfactory places reserved for them.'

Matthew stood slightly dazed for a moment then realised he was being asked to leave the hotel and go with Dr Couperin.

'Oh, ah. Yes. Yes by all means. That would be fine.'

277

And they put on their hats, left the hotel and went out into the heat of the day and began to walk.

'Tell me, Doctor, have you known Dr Tomes for long?'

'No, not so very long. In fact this morning was the first time we have ever met.' And Couperin bowed gracefully removing his hat as two very elegant ladies went past arm in arm. Matthew's mind was in a whirl. This morning! The first time? Yet here he was being taken into this man's home. 'But of course I have known of him for some time and we have several mutual friends. His visits here are brief, naturally so given the nature of his work, but he is very highly spoken of. You are fortunate to have such a friend, Mr O'Hanlon, are you not?'

'Yes, I suppose I am.'

But there was a certain reservation in Matthew's agreement as he added yet another piece to the puzzle that was Dr Robert Tomes.

Chapter Forty-one

Walking beside Dr Couperin Matthew was able to observe him more closely without giving any offence. He was a neat, slightly built man, dapper rather than smart in his light-coloured suit with a pair of pince-nez attached to his coat lapel and lodged, when not in use, in the breast pocket of his jacket. He carried a Malacca cane with a silver top and his age, Matthew guessed, was about forty though he may have been a well-preserved fifty. As they walked Doctor Couperin kept up a flow of inconsequential small-talk, giving Matthew information on the history of Panama City, which he followed by talking with an easy familiarity of the current leading lights in society. He then gave Matthew his view on the current financial state of Panama City in particular and New Granada in general. He pointed out one or two of the more notable buildings they passed and regretted their condition which, he said, was all too common. He stopped when they arrived at the corner of the plaza on the opposite side of which stood the cathedral. It was a truly impressive building dominating the square with two massive, white towers flanking an ornate façade.

Matthew stood beside Dr Couperin and gazed at it for a moment.

'Good heavens, it's quite breathtaking.'

'Yes, it is our best building from the colonial period and, thank God, has been well preserved.' Couperin gave a small laugh. 'I say, thank God, but please understand it is no more than a figure of speech to me.' They continued walking. 'I am a confirmed atheist, you understand. Are you a believer, Mr O'Hanlon?'

'Roman Catholic.'

'Indeed! As an American I would have thought that if

Christian at all it would have been Protestant.'

'My parents are Irish.'

'That would, of course, explain it. I have always understood that the Irish were, forgive me, as superstitious in their beliefs as are the people of this country. I refer of course to those of Spanish blood not the indigenous natives.'

'Are the natives not Catholic? I understood that mostly they were.'

'Oh they profess Catholicism, but in truth I can assure you they are still pagans. It may seem strange to you that an atheist should make such a statement so authoritatively.'

'Not at all.'

Matthew's response was no more than a cold politeness. He objected to his own faith, that of his family and of Ireland, being dismissed as superstition. His manner, however, seemed not to be noticed by Dr Couperin.

'Though an atheist who rejects all religion, I have a thorough understanding of Christianity. I was born in Paris and my mother, who was Russian, was particularly devout to the Russian Orthodox Church. For some generations my father's family were closely associated with the Roman Catholic Church most notably through the church of St Gervais.'

'Were they?'

Matthew's response was still formally polite.

'Tell me, does my name, Couperin, not seem at all familiar to you?'

'No.'

'Ah, then you are not a music lover?'

'Not at all. I like music.'

'Yet the name Couperin is not familiar? Well, it is of no matter.' Although his tone betrayed the fact that he thought it rather did. 'My family gave France one or two rather well-thought of composers. But as I say, no matter.'

And a silence fell between them as they walked on.

Matthew was puzzled by this man. In the presence of Robert Tomes he had been courtesy and politeness itself. Now that Tomes was gone he seemed to have changed, to have become somewhat superior, condescending even. Or was it just his imagination? Matthew reviewed the morning's proceedings at the hotel. Couperin had explained about not being personally acquainted with Tomes, that he was a known and well-respected figure locally. But was that enough to agree to admit a stranger in to your home? Matthew allowed he was a foreigner here, unused to local ways, so perhaps in a place like Panama City the say-so of someone like Tomes was enough. Would his parents have done as much if say, some priest whom they knew by sight and reputation, had asked the same of them? Put like that, put into some context he could relate to, it all seemed plausible. No, he decided, there was nothing he could put his finger on. But still, if nothing was actually wrong, things were not altogether right either.

Matthew was still pondering this when Dr Couperin stopped at the door of a large, fairly modern house quite unlike the Spanish colonial buildings he had pointed out earlier in their walk. The street was not far from the cathedral and the centre of the city but they had been walking quite steeply uphill and turning and looking back one could looked out across the rooftops into a wide, blue bay. The buildings on this street were similar to the one in front of which they stood, rather dull to Matthew's mind, not unlike any number of modern houses in Manhattan, in fact. But he had to admit that the view was quite impressive especially as the expanse of water he looked out on was now the Pacific Ocean.

'A fine view, yes?'

This time Matthew's response was warm and genuine.

'It is indeed.'

Dr Couperin turned back to the house.

'My home and my office, Mr O'Hanlon. Please come in.'

'Thank you.'

The interior of the house matched its externals, modern and rather dull, but even to Matthew's inexpert eye everything looked rather expensive. Dr Couperin's law practice, despite his failure with the men to be executed today, was obviously flourishing. A black servant girl came to them in the hallway and took their hats and Dr Couperin's cane.

'My wife and daughter will be in the sitting room.'

Couperin went to a door, opened it, and Matthew followed him in.

The shock was considerable and Matthew almost let a gasp slip from his mouth. Couperin's wife and daughter stood up on the men's entry. Madame Couperin was about her husband's age but Matthew was still impressed. She was darkly beautiful. However, his attention to her was fleeting compared with that which he gave to the young woman at her side. At once she captured all Matthew's attention. Indeed, perhaps she had captured a little more than his attention. Matthew, of course, knew himself to be a hard-bitten newsman and scorned such a romantic notion as love at first sight but even so he had to admit that strange and unusual feelings were surging through him, not altogether unpleasant but definitely unsettling.

Suddenly he realised that Couperin was once again speaking and that Madame Couperin had held out her hand.

'Oh, quite,' was all that Matthew could manage as he took it.

'And my daughter, Edith.'

Edith shouldn't have smiled.

But she did, and it was of course fatal. It was incredible

but Matthew knew at once that the impossible had happened. He was in love, head over heels and hopelessly. And he didn't care.

Chapter Forty-two

'*Enchanté.*'

Quite why Matthew had spoken French he did not know. Was it bravado or confusion? Probably both. Whatever the reason it was a success. True it was Mama who spoke, but it had undoubtedly gone down well. She answered him in French.

'You speak French? How delightful. I speak English, and Spanish of course, but Edith speaks only French and Spanish. This means you two will be able to converse. It will be nice if ...'

There was an edge to Dr Couperin's voice as he interrupted his wife in emphatic English.

'But perhaps, my dear, Mr O'Hanlon speaks Spanish as well as French. We have not asked him, have we?'

A look of annoyance clouded Madame Couperin's face.

'Of course, I just assumed ...'

And once again Couperin cut her short.

'Do you speak Spanish, Mr O'Hanlon?'

His wife shot him a thoroughly nasty look but Matthew, uninterested for the moment in either Doctor or Madame Couperin failed to notice either the tone or the look and smiled at Edith and gave his answer to her in French.

'I fear not and, as for my French, it is only the school-room variety so I fear I will prove a poor conversationalist.'

Edith returned the smile.

'In that case, M'sieur O'Hanlon, I will teach you Spanish and you can teach me English. And if we both prove to be poor pupils we will be able to fall back on French.'

It was not a passionate speech nor was it long. It was also true that the words actually spoken could not bring the smallest blush of shame to the cheek of modesty. But for Matthew it might have been something Shakespeare had penned for Desdemona or Juliet and then thought too molten even for the coarse groundlings of a Tudor audience.

Matthew could not have felt happier.

He was about to speak when Mama intervened.

'I fear Mr O'Hanlon will have little time for conversation, my dear, or for learning Spanish. He is here to report the news back to New York. He is a man of some consequence and will have much to see and do.'

'But Maman, if he cannot speak Spanish how will he collect his information?'

The question suddenly seemed blindingly obvious to Matthew, and yet it had never occurred to him. This was Panama and the language here was Spanish. Yet at no time had anyone, not Clarence Diver nor the editor at the New York Associated Press nor even Robert Tomes had asked him if he could speak it. Why? And why had he not thought to bring it up himself?

'My dear Edith, you know as well as I that with the recent rush of Americans through the city even most of the most common of people now have some English. People like shopkeepers and saloon owners have to be able to speak it quite well. How else are they to make their living?'

'Really, Maman? I can't say that I'd noticed.'

'That is because you always speak Spanish, my dear. Why should anyone speak English to you?'

As they spoke in French, probably from politeness to their guest, Matthew decided there might be something in this explanation. After all, if you want to skin a tide of humanity rushing on its way through, hurrying to be elsewhere, the least you would need to be able to do is

286

speak their language. But then he looked at Edith again.

'Still, I think if I had some little knowledge of Spanish it would be a great asset to my work. And if you would be so kind as to assist me in my learning, mademoiselle, then I think the time would be well spent.'

Edith smiled once more and Matthew felt himself slipping into total confusion and embarrassment. It was Dr Couperin who saved him, in English.

'However, Mr O'Hanlon, all of that can be for another time. If you are to stay with us you must see your room and I regret we men must stoop to mercenary matters.' Couperin turned to his wife. 'You will want to be setting out, my dear, if you and Edith are to be settled in time for the executions. Your places are waiting, all is arranged through Colonel Hernandez, but do not forget your parasols. I have no idea if there will be adequate shade.'

'Oh yes, Maman, come, we must hurry, we must not miss anything.' Matthew had to remind himself that the event which caused such anticipation in Edith was not some festival or holiday but a public shooting. However, he resolutely told himself that this was a foreign country and things were done differently here. As a newsman he could not and would not sit in judgement. He was there to report the hard facts as he found them. He had to be cold and dispassionate. 'Will you be going to the execution, M'sieur O'Hanlon?'

In his current confused state it came as something of a blow to Matthew that he had not thought of this himself, but before he could formulate some sort of response to Edith's question Dr Couperin answered for him.

'No, Mr O'Hanlon will not be going. The execution of common thieves is not important news in the great city of New York.'

'I see. Well, we must go, but I am glad you are coming to stay with us, M'sieur O'Hanlon. I have thought ever since Maman told me of your coming how nice it would be to have …'

But Maman obviously thought it not the right time for her daughter to share her feelings on Matthew's arrival.

'Come, Edith.' It was almost a bark and Edith looked at her mother a little surprised. Mme Couperin forced a smile and her tone changed. 'Come, my dear, we will be late and your father and Mr O'Hanlon have much to discuss. Good day Mr O'Hanlon. I am so pleased Aleksandar has brought you to our home. I know we will all get along together famously. But now we must go. Come, Edith.'

And mother and daughter left the room.

Dr Couperin looked a little uncertain, as if he expected Matthew to say something, but Matthew said nothing so he proceeded.

'If you will be guided by me, Mr O'Hanlon, I think it would be most unwise to attend today's execution.'

'And why is that? If what you told us at the hotel is true then I would have thought it was just the place for me to go, see for myself, and ask questions.'

'And if you do that Colonel Hernandez would certainly have you deported and your career here would come to an abrupt end. Is that what you want?' No, thought Matthew, that was the last thing he wanted. 'Besides which, you speak no Spanish, so how will you ask your questions and who will you ask? Mr O'Hanlon, believe me, today's shooting is not the place to begin your work; it must be left as just another execution of common criminals. As I said to my daughter, hardly the sort of story you have been sent here to report on. It is your decision, of course, I simply offer the advice of someone who wishes you to prosper while you are among us.'

Matthew thought for a moment. He didn't like the idea of passing up his first chance of a story, but was there a story? Other than what Dr Couperin had said in the hotel what was there to say the execution was anything other than what it appeared to be? Then there was his lack of

Spanish.

'Well, perhaps you're right.'

Dr Couperin walked to the door.

'I think you will like your room. It has an excellent view out over the ocean.'

Obviously he felt the matter closed.

Matthew followed Couperin out of the room and up the wide staircase. But he wasn't thinking of any ocean view. He was again wondering what on earth was going on. Edith had been told he was coming so clearly the family knew, yet Couperin seemed determined to indulge in some sort of play-acting. Why?

Couperin opened the door of a large, bright room, comfortably furnished and with a substantial window which did indeed give a wonderful view out onto the Pacific. Matthew noticed that, beside two armchairs, and against the wall opposite the fireplace where the sunlight would fall on it, was a writing desk with all the accoutrements for writing on it. There was also a swivel chair which looked new.

'As you can see I sometimes use the room for writing but rarely so. However I think you will find it comfortable. I will have a good wardrobe brought in and there is plenty of room for a bed. If you are satisfied and we can agree terms I will have everything brought in this afternoon while you arrange for your things to be sent from the hotel.

Matthew looked at the room. It was excellent, almost as if it had been arranged for the very purpose of accommodating him. As to terms, he was quite sure that they be able to come to some agreement. Clarence Diver had arranged for him to receive what seemed a very generous salary from the Associated Press and had made it clear that if funds were needed for any matters of a non-journalistic nature they would be forthcoming through arrangements he would put in place at a local bank.

But as to whether he was satisfied the answer must be,

289

no, he was not. He was definitely dissatisfied. Edith was obviously expecting him yet both Couperin and his wife indulged in this pretence that they had known nothing of his arrival before he had met Couperin at the hotel. Under different circumstances he might have said something, confronted Couperin and demanded an explanation. Forced the truth from him.

But then there was Edith.

Hmm.

Matthew paused for only a moment.

'And what are the terms, Dr Couperin?'

Couperin smiled.

'Come down to my office and we will draw up a little agreement. Nothing too harsh I assure you.' And he gave a small laugh. 'But as a lawyer, you understand?'

No, Matthew didn't understand. But he would. He promised himself that this puzzle would be solved. In the meantime, however, there was always Edith and learning Spanish.

'Of course, Dr Couperin. Please lead the way.'

'And while we are in the office perhaps I can give you help with any report you might wish to send.'

'Help?'

'The railway construction company is one of my clients. I have all the facts and figures you might need to let your Associated Press know how things progress. I assume you are keen to get some report off as soon as possible?'

'Yes. Yes, of course. Anything you can tell me will be most helpful.'

'Good. Then we will go to my office.'

And Matthew followed his new host downstairs.

All neat and tidy and wrapped up in a ribbon for me, he thought. A room with a desk, facts and figures for a report. Whatever is going on someone has gone to a lot of trouble to get it ready. A lot of trouble indeed.

Chapter Forty-three

The Yellow Oval Room of the White House, October 1850.

'*The subject of the annexation of Canada to the United States is beginning to assume a shape of importance if we are to judge from discussions that are going on in the province itself, the mother country, and the northern section of our own confederacy. Has the South no interest in this issue that she seems to be asleep at her post?*'

President Millard Fillmore, having read these words out loud, threw the copy of *De Bow's Review* on his desk and looked up at Daniel Webster.

'Well, Daniel, has the South any interest in the proposition that the United States should annex Canada from what De Bow calls its "mother country" and propel us into a war with Britain which, if it went badly, might well allow the British to take the whole of the Oregon Territory and perhaps annex California as well? As president of this country, both northern and southern, I feel I may be allowed some little interest in the matter and I hope my secretary of state has not been, like the South, asleep at his post.'

Webster scowled.

'It's claptrap, mere rabble-rousing claptrap. Why should I waste my time on such nonsense?'

'*De Bow's* is a respected financial and agricultural journal that circulates widely throughout the South. There are many who will read this and not see it at all as claptrap or nonsense.'

'Then they're fools.'

'True, very true. But being a fool has rarely stood in the

way of men becoming highly influential in the land of ours. Many people would say we have a fool as president at this very moment.' The president smiled and pushed the journal to one side. 'But I'm sure you're not one of them, Daniel. The point is that there are people, fools perhaps, but powerful fools nonetheless, who are hell bent on driving a wedge between North and South and will use anything that comes to hand, even something as ludicrous as this,' and President Fillmore gestured dismissively at the journal on his desk, 'the point is, do you intend to do anything about it?'

'What do you suggest? To pay it any attention at all is to give it a credibility it doesn't deserve. And where can it go? Nowhere.'

President Fillmore look at the newspaper again.

'Well, perhaps you're right. I hope so. However, it was not really the annexation of Canada that I have asked you to come and talk about.'

'I'm grateful for that.'

'How are things progressing with the Panama Railway?'

'You mean with the railway itself or matters associated with the railway?'

'On whichever you have information for me.'

'Two weeks ago there arrived from a man in Panama City who is acting as foreign representative for the New York Associated Press a report, the appropriate part of which was passed to the *Tribune* and used in one of its articles. As far as everyone in New York and, I presume, in Panama City is concerned, he is a bona fide American journalist. There was a short supplementary report which was received by our man in New York and, he says, proved satisfactory. The representative of the Associated Press is established and accepted and has begun to ...'

The president interrupted.

'I do not wish to know what he has begun. You have

292

informed me that the New York Associated Press has a representative in Panama and that he has sent a report which was used, in part, in the *Tribune* newspaper. Good. That being the case I want a detachment of troops sent at once to New Orleans, enough to secure the safety of American citizens and property if either or both are threatened.'

'Threatened by whom?'

'By anyone. Have them officered by a good, reliable man but one of no significant seniority. As far as the officer is concerned, or anyone else for that matter, they are being made ready to be sent to establish a military garrison to protect the goldfields and support, where necessary, the civil administration. But they must be held in New Orleans and be at twenty-four hours readiness to depart by sea.' There was the smile again. 'If it proves necessary of course.'

'And you think it might prove necessary?'

'Don't you, Daniel? You are secretary of state. What is your opinion?'

'There is always wisdom in readiness.'

'How true. See that they are sufficiently supplied to pursue a short but vigorous campaign and to do so at short notice.'

'Very well. And the rest of it?'

A look of surprise came to the president's face.

'What rest, Daniel? Having taken your advice on the wisdom of readiness I am approving a force of troops to prepare itself to go to our new territory of California via Panama. A sound and sensible move. There is no "rest" that I know of, unless of course there is something going on of which I have not been informed and must therefore be unaware.'

'Just as you say, Mr President.'

'Good. Now, on to other things. That young hot-head Gadsden is up on his hind legs again.'

293

'I know. Apparently he's not satisfied with trying to get South Carolina to secede because California was admitted as a free state. Now he's out there agitating to get the place cut into two halves so one can operate slavery.'

'But people are listening to him, Daniel, people are listening, and if he's allowed to go on he'll cause more trouble than the tariffs of '28, and he's not peddling nonsense like this Canada business. He's dangerous.'

'I agree.'

'So what do you suggest?'

Daniel Webster thought for a moment.

'Well, he's something of a madman and lets himself get carried away. I'm fairly sure that some of what he says would lay him open to a charge of treason.'

'No, not treason, Daniel. That would be too risky. Gadsden's got important friends and there's already too many points of friction between the North and South. The Compromise has only been law a month and I need time to see that it works through to a satisfactory conclusion on the ground. But he must be stopped.'

'Aye, stopped, but how?'

'Come now, Daniel, yours being a first-rate mind and you a man of wide experience surely you have some suggestion?' Fillmore waited hardly a moment. 'No? Then we'll have to do it my way.'

'Which is?'

'By railroad.'

The president sat back well pleased that his answer had obviously confused his secretary of state who thought for a moment then, with a bad grace, gave up.

'You'll have to explain.'

'Everyone agrees we need a transcontinental railroad.'

'They do.'

'The North want a northern or central route linked into their industrial centres. The South wants a southern route to expand and diversify their economy.'

'If they do they've been very quiet about it.'

'Well, when I say the South I mean Gadsden and a few like-minded friends.'

'I see. But even with a federal land grant any southern route would have to pass in some part through Mexican territory. The way Mexico feels to us at present it would make any southern route unworkable.'

'Very true. So the necessary Mexican Land must be acquired.'

'Acquired? Good God, not another Mexican War.'

'No.'

'And not another Polk Plan. One is bad enough.'

'No, nothing like that. A simple commercial venture. I want you to see to it that we persuade enough men in the Mexican Government to be sympathetic to the idea of the United States buying the tract of land necessary to make a southern route viable. I meanwhile, will appoint James Gadsden to be our ambassador to Mexico with the task of exploring, on behalf of the government, the purchase of all Mexican land from Las Cruces to Yuma.'

Webster looked down at the president with a grudging admiration.

'It might work. It would keep Gadsden and his friends occupied and make them believe this administration is well-disposed to the interests of the South.'

'And it will keep the Compromise intact and deflect Gadsden from his trouble-making in California. If you can buy the right men in Mexico and Gadsden is even a halfway-able negotiator we might acquire peacefully and for a modest price a substantial increase in land. Who knows, maybe one day a southern transcontinental railroad may even get built.'

Webster smiled. He could never like President Millard Fillmore but he had come to respect his ability to keep the country from plunging into the civil war on the brink of which it seemed always to be tottering.

295

'And if Gadsden succeeds he will no doubt get his name into the history books as a man of consequence rather than the wild-headed fool he undoubtedly is.'

'Perhaps. But as I said, being a fool has never been a debarment to fame and preferment, not here in America, nor anywhere else as far as I know. Now, Mr Secretary, I think that's enough for you to be going on with. Get my Mexicans so I can get rid of the Gadsden nuisance, but get my troops to New Orleans first so you can get me what I want in Panama.'

'The safe completion of the railroad?'

The president looked up with the same false look of surprise. Then smiled.

'Of course. What else is there?'

Webster still hated that smile.

'What else indeed, Mr President?'

Chapter Forty-four

Fevers and other sickness prevail at Chagres as seems always the case. The workmen and those engaged in constructing the railroad in that district are falling victim to its pestilential malaria by the score. Three or four engineers, four carpenters, and about as many axe men returned on the Cherokee *with hardly enough life in them to last them to their homes. One man died on board as the ship arrived at Kingston.*

Matthew read these words proudly. They were only a few lines in the main text, the last few lines, and the name at the foot of the article was 'Californian', not surprisingly seeing as most of the five hundred-word article dealt with California. But those last lines were his, taken from the first news report he had sent to Clarence Diver. And now here they were in the *New York Tribune*. Wonderful.

Matthew had taken the room in Dr Couperin's house and based the news section of his report on the information provided by Couperin. As a matter of cold fact the words in the *Tribune* were almost all supplied by Couperin, given to Matthew after they had agreed terms. Matthew's own contribution had been a rather vivid account of his arrival in Chagres and subsequent journey from Chagres to Panama City. He had included the attempt on his life changing it only slightly by eliminating Fernando's part in the struggle and featuring himself as the one who repelled his assailant. He thought it rather well written and it was with some regret that, when Diver had sent him a cutting of the article, he found his six hundred words had been reduced to these few sentences. Still, it had appeared in print, that was the main point.

The rest of that first report, that supplementary element which was for Clarence Diver's eyes only, he had deliberately kept vague, that he was now accepted as the representative of the Associated Press, had taken a room with a local, well-respected lawyer and had arranged to take Spanish lessons, and that another report would follow soon. He also asked Diver to institute enquiries into one Doctor Robert Tomes who had been his cabin companion and had gone out of his way to strike up an association, that it might be prudent to check his bona fides. In writing this he had felt quite the secret agent, bold yet cautious, daring yet careful.

Dr Couperin had arranged for the report to be put with his correspondence and be sent back to Chagres for transportation on the first ship. Matthew knew it could not reach New York for at least three weeks and that any reply would take as long to get back to him so he had settled down in Panama City. The world at large saw him as a newsman, in his own eyes he was an agent of the US Government.

His first report sent Matthew at once set about searching for the person Clarence Diver had told him to look for, some respectable local who had a steady stream of foreign visitors, possibly English-speaking, who stayed for more than the short while necessary to find passage north. He walked a great deal being observant, sat outside bars and cafés keeping a keen eye open, and after no more than twenty-four hours his efforts were rewarded with a clear outcome.

He was wasting his time.

How on earth did one set about discovering this person? Panama was not New York, nor even Manhattan, but it was large enough and sufficiently supplied with transient people to make finding one local who was well supplied with visitors utterly impossible.

What to do?

His next approach was to make enquiries of tradesmen. This too brought quick results. Firstly that it was not easy to frame any suitable questions. 'I'm looking for someone local who has an abnormal number of foreign visitors, perhaps English-speaking' about summed up what he wanted to ask, but it soon got completely lost if concealed in any subterfuge. His second discovery was that Madame Couperin had considerably overestimated the locals' ability in the English language. The tradesmen he targeted had little or no English. Once again he retired from the field of endeavour frustrated. But all, he realised, was not lost. If he was going to find this person he had to speak at least some Spanish and that meant spending time, rather a lot of time if his progress was to be at all rapid, in the company of Edith. This he set about doing and was pleased to find she was willing and even seemed quite happy to accompany him on walks, spending no small part of her days with him. He even managed to make some progress in acquiring the language.

Whilst involved in this very necessary but undoubtedly pleasant activity Matthew rather forgot about his supposed position as foreign correspondent for the Associated Press but his failure to gather any further news for his second report was brought home to him one morning when Madame Couperin, who turned out to be a particularly avid member of that rapidly increasing phenomenon, female readers of sensational fiction, brought something to his attention at breakfast.

'I don't know if it would be of any interest to you, Mr O'Hanlon, but we have a celebrity in Panama City at the moment.'

'Indeed?'

'Yes. A writer and the son of a writer. Mr Frank Marryat.'

Matthew, never a great reader of fiction, searched his memory but came up empty.

'I'm afraid the name means nothing to me.'

'Indeed? You have not heard of Captain Marryat, the English naval officer and author?'

Something stirred.

'Captain Marryat. I seem to remember hearing that somewhere.'

'I understand he writes tales of adventure. I believe his book *Mr Midshipman Easy* enjoys a considerable popularity.'

'Oh yes, I've heard of him. Some of the fellows at school seemed to think highly of the novel although I myself never actually read it.'

'Nor I. My tastes lie in works that deal with the more profound and serious aspects of life. The book I am reading at present, *The Scarlet Letter* by Mr Nathaniel Hawthorne, for instance. I may have mentioned it to you.' Matthew started. Indeed she had mentioned the damn thing, and more than once. In fact one evening she had cornered him after dinner in the living room and talked almost non-stop on its main subject, a fallen woman. 'It is a most beautiful work, so deep, so penetrating. It lays bare ...'

Matthew interrupted hurriedly. Anything but another lecture on sexual sin and subsequent redemption.

'And is this Captain Marryat in Panama City?'

Madame Couperin paused, obviously irritated at Matthew's lack of interest.

'No. His son, who is also a writer, is passing through on his way back to England. We had the pleasure of meeting Mr Marryat when he first came through on his way to California. A charming young man. If you wish I can arrange an introduction.'

'Thank you, that would be most kind.'

'Not at all.'

Now it may seem that the son of a well-known English writer of naval adventures, even if he himself is a writer, is hardly the stuff which either a foreign correspondent or a secret agent of the US Government immediately latches onto. And in the normal course of events Matthew, in both of his capacities, would have declined Madame Couperin's offer. But the truth was that Madame Couperin had touched Matthew's conscience. He was being well paid to deliver regular and full reports to the Associated Press and so far had done so only once. In addition, apart from learning Spanish, he had done nothing constructive in his role as secret agent.

But this latter, he felt, was not altogether his fault. It was all very well for Clarence Diver to tell him to look out for some local person who seemed to have a steady stream of visitors who might be agents of the British Crown. In New York it had sounded plausible and exciting. Here, after almost two months in the country, it seemed well-nigh impossible. The British agent might well be operating at full speed with a steady flow of British spies no more than a street away but Matthew would not have known. Many parts of Panama City were no more than a bedlam of a place with prospectors and settlers piling in from Chagres, waiting for the next boat out, and then leaving. As for some established local, he had no access to the houses of anyone who might fit Diver's description and he could hardly stand outside houses and count the people who came and went. How, he asked himself over and over again, did one begin? As for railway news, there wasn't any. At least nothing new. The story was the same week in and week out. The railway progressed slowly and a steady stream of men fell victim to the pestilential climate. It looked likely that the figures given him by Dr Couperin and sent in his first report could, with only slight variation, be repeated as more or less accurate for each successive month.

This son of Captain Marryat might not be real news but it was something.

The following day Madame Couperin told Matthew at breakfast that she had arranged for him to meet Mr Frank Marryat that morning at his hotel which, by coincidence, was the one at which he and Robert Tomes had stayed.

'He is passing through on his way home from California and will set out for Chagres tomorrow. I fear it is very short notice for you and if you have other urgent business I can let Mr Marryat know that ...'

'No, no, not at all. I shall be delighted to call on Mr Marryat this morning.'

Edith seemed quite excited about the meeting.

'May I accompany you, Mr O'Hanlon? I have never met a writer. I may decide to become one myself one day and if I do I'm sure he would be able to help and advise me.'

This sudden and unexpected question discommoded Matthew more than somewhat. They were now firm friends and he was sure that, given time and the right opportunities, their friendship might ripen into something more. However, much as he usually desired her company, he felt that taking an aspiring young lady writer to an interview being conducted in his role as foreign correspondent was not quite the appropriate way to conduct his business. He sought for some kind of answer to her request other than a flat refusal but was saved by Edith's mother.

'Of course you may not, Edith. What an absurd request. This is not a social visit. Mr O'Hanlon will be conducting an interview to be sent back to New York. You would only be in the way.' Edith, obviously abashed, accepted her mother's decision in the matter and Matthew, seeing her disappointed, felt at once both relief and regret and tried desperately to think of some compensation that might revive her but before he could say anything Madame Couperin continued. 'I suggested ten o'clock. I hope you find that suitable?'

Matthew dragged his attention from Edith to her mother then glanced at the case clock that stood against the wall of the breakfast room. It was almost nine.

'I see. Well, in that case I'll get myself ready and be on my way.' He stood up. 'And thank you, Madame.'

In the hall he met Dr Couperin, who breakfasted earlier than his family and his lodger.

'Going out on business, Mr O'Hanlon?'

'Yes. Madame Couperin has kindly arranged an interview …'

'With Mr Marryat. She told me yesterday evening. Well, I can't say that it seems the sort of thing that will set New York back on its heels but it is something I suppose. I fear Panama City may have come as a disappointment to you as a source of news. Despite all the comings and goings and sometimes violent behaviour of our more transient visitors it is essentially a quiet place.'

'Yes, perhaps so. But now I must …'

'Although, if one knew who to talk to … There is a side to Panama that few visitors see. That few visitors are allowed to see.'

'I really must …'

'Ours is not a happy country, Mr O'Hanlon, nor yet a free one.'

'I'm due at …'

'But I see I am delaying you. Perhaps we might talk this afternoon.'

'Quite, this afternoon. Glad to. But now I really must …'

'At three?'

'Three. Excellent.'

'In my office.'

'Quite so. But now I must …'

And, at last, he did.

Chapter Forty-five

Frank Marryat was twenty-six with long black hair, a flowing moustache, and a beard trimmed to a point. He was deeply tanned, lean, tall, and well-built. Apart from the fact that his clothes were of the latest fashion and extremely well cut he looked exactly what he was: a wealthy writer, artist, and explorer. Two years previously his first book, *Borneo and the Indian Archipelago*, had appeared in print in London chronicling his travels in those remote and dangerous regions. He had come to Panama some months previously on his way to visit California to gather information for his next book. Now he was back in Panama, his researches completed, making his way home.

The interview took place in Marryat's rooms as the hotel lobby and lounge were busy and not conducive to conversation.

'No, I have no title for the book yet. To be utterly truthful I'm not at all sure what sort of book I'll write. The material is so abundant but so diverse that various titles have suggested themselves but none do full justice to the scope of the thing, and a title, I always feel, must encapsulate the essential spirit of the work. Do you not agree, Mr O'Hanlon?'

'Yes, I suppose so.' The interview was not going well. Marryat was quite willing to answer Matthew's questions but did so in a vague and offhand way with the result that Matthew found it hard to seek out and develop any subject which might be the basis for his article. He tried a new tack. 'And Panama, what are your thoughts on it and the railway?'

Marryat didn't answer but for a moment but looked at Matthew, who sat with his pencil poised over his notepad.

After what had become, to Matthew at least, an embarrassingly long silence, Marryat leaned forward.

'Now look here, O'Hanlon, tell me truthfully, as man to man, what are you really up to?'

The question took Matthew completely by surprise.

'Up to?'

'Yes. I don't mean this nonsense of interviewing me. As if anyone here or in New York would give a damn about what I've been up to in California or what my thoughts on Panama or anywhere else might be. What is it you really want?'

The completely blank look on Matthew's face and his total lack of a ready response seemed to puzzle Marryat.

'I can assure you, Mr Marryat, that I am exactly what I say I am, the resident foreign correspondent of the ...'

Marryat waved this assertion aside.

'Yes, yes. I'm sure you have all the papers and were I to write to the New York Associated Press someone from there would confirm what you say. I dare say you even send stuff back now and then ...'

'A part of my last report appeared in the New York *Tribune*.'

'Part?'

'Some dozen lines.'

'I see. This Associated Press of yours has forked out a considerable amount of money to locate you here in Panama City so you can, off and on, send them a dozen lines.' He shook his head sadly. 'Really, Mr O'Hanlon, one doesn't know whether to weep or laugh.'

And Matthew realised that, stated as baldly as Marryat had done, it did seem odd.

'It was my first report. There will, of course be others and on more important matters.'

'Like me passing through and my thoughts on California and the railroad they're building here? No, Mr O'Hanlon, let us put aside this charade.' He sat back and considered Matthew for a moment. 'If I were to hazard a guess I would say you were here on covert business for someone, the American Government perhaps, or some commercial interest?' He suddenly sat forward with an eager look. 'Dammit, it's not the canal is it?'

Matthew, deeply disturbed by Marryat's penetration of his real purpose in being in Panama, tried to assume a dismissive manner.

'What canal?'

His answer was greeted with a laugh.

'Good God, man, be cautious by all means but don't carry it to ridiculous extremes. It only makes you look foolish. Come now, what are you up to? Who sent you here?'

Matthew tried desperately to get some contempt into his reply and almost succeeded.

'To do what exactly?'

Marryat smiled and carried on, not in the least deflected by Matthew's tone.

'Ah, there you have me. If you were really a secret agent of some sort it might be one of several things.' Once again Marryat sat back and considered Matthew. 'But that's the problem I have you see. You are so patently *not* a secret agent, so it all puzzles me.'

This time Matthew was stung by Marryat's assertion that he was not what in truth he was.

'And why am I so patently not an agent? Not that I am, of course.'

'Of course. Well, there are several things but I'll just take two. The first I've already touched on, no reason for being here that would convince anyone who cared to give it any thought. The second that you have made yourself so obvious. If I can stumble on you without even looking you can't be exactly blending in, can you?'

And here Matthew remembered something Clarence Diver had said and felt he now had the upper hand with this rather arrogant Englishman.

'I see. But if I am so patently not an agent might that not mean that in truth I am a very good one?'

Matthew felt the barb had gone home for a second, until Marryat threw back his head and laughed out loud.

'By God, O'Hanlon, you may not be an agent but you can surely make a fellow laugh.' And he laughed again then composed himself. 'But seriously, I wondered about you as soon as I heard you wanted to meet with me so I agreed. I thought it might be worth my while to try and find out what you might be up to. But having met you I freely admit to being at a loss. Whatever you are you have the advantage over me.'

'Are you saying that it was because you thought I was an agent that you agreed to our meeting?'

'What other reason? An interview for the New York newspapers was as nonsensical as the story of you being here reporting for them. I would probably have gone to New York on the same boat as the report or even before it so, in the unlikely event of anyone really wanting to interview me for the New York papers, it could be done much more easily there. And then there was the source of the invitation. It came from the house of Dr Couperin. Now there *is* a man worth watching. If Couperin has his finger in something here then His Majesty's Government would want to know all about it.'

Now it was Matthew's turn to laugh.

'Dr Couperin, an agent? What nonsense. I've lived in the house for almost two months, I know him and his family.'

Marryat shrugged.

'Ah, in the face of such overwhelming evidence I must, of course, be wrong. But a little advice, Mr O'Hanlon. Be very careful of Dr Couperin, he is a clever and I think a ruthless man.'

Any laughter had now gone and Marryat was so

obviously serious that Matthew tried to inject a sneer into his reply.

'And your opinion in these things of that of an expert is it?'

'In a way, yes. You see, I really am a secret agent. That is, I have acted in that capacity for the British Government from time to time. In fact, as I was coming to Panama, I was told to try and make the acquaintance of Couperin as I passed through on my way to California. I was also told to make what enquiries I could about him, obviously without alerting him. London is convinced he is up to something here and has been for some time but they do not know what. I met all three of the family socially including that rather pretty daughter of theirs. I also made what enquiries I could. My time, unfortunately, was limited and my resources scant so I discovered nothing. But what do I find on my return? That a stranger has arrived and been installed in their house. That this stranger has put it about that he is a foreign correspondent for a consortium on New York newspapers. Interesting and worthy of further enquiry. But my time here once again is strictly limited, no more than a few days. What am I to do? Then a golden opportunity is dropped into my lap. Mrs Couperin conveniently asks me to meet you. Of course I agreed, what else could I do? And here we are and I'm still none the wiser. Are you sure you won't enlighten me, Mr O'Hanlon? I assure you that Britain's interest in this region of the world is not in any way at odds with that of America. If Couperin is working for anyone my guess would be the French.'

Matthew wanted to dismiss this accusation out of hand. But the idea had lodged. He had no objection to casting Couperin in a dubious light, nor even Madame Couperin. But not Edith. He absolutely drew the line at any possibility of her involvement in anything underhand.

'This is all nonsense, positive claptrap.'

'Is it? Well if you say it is, it must be. As you say, you've been here such a long time, nearly two months. But it does illustrate quite vividly the problem of being a spy doesn't it? Is what I am telling you no more than a pack of lies? How are you to know for certain? That's the problem with the whole business of being an agent, you can never know whether what you're being told is true or false. And even if it's true are you being told for a reason? Is the truth being used to manipulate you? Even a deliberate and obvious lie can be a ploy. It is a world of eternal grey. Black and white just don't exist. All a spy can ever really trust for certain is information gained by himself from a perfectly unprejudiced source, and such information is, I assure you, as rare as a golden-hearted whore. Take for instance the poet Keats ...'

'Who?'

'John Keats. A chap rather well thought of in the poetry line. Yet in his poem, 'On First Looking into Chapman's Homer', he writes,

Or like stout Cortez when with eagle eyes
He star'd at the Pacific – and all his men
Looked at each other with a wild surmise-
Silent, upon a peak in Darien.

Damn fine poetry of course. Damn fine.'

'So?'

'Well it wasn't Cortez was it? This place, Panama, known then as Darien, was conquered by Balboa not Cortez. Yet because Keats is such a respected poet it becomes a sort of truth.'

The door of the room opened and a man entered leading three large hounds. Marryat's manner changed, signalling to Matthew that the interview, such as it had been, was over. 'Ah, my manservant with the hounds. Are they well exercised, Barnes?'

'Yes, sir.'

'Good, then feed them.'

310

'Very well, sir.'

Barnes, the manservant left the room and the dogs, unleashed, came to Marryat and gathered round him. Matthew was unsure what to do. The whole matter of Couperin had been left somewhat hanging. He looked at the dogs who were all three standing looked intently at him. One muttered a low growl. Matthew, neither familiar with dogs nor fond of them, sat a little more upright but made no other move.

'Silence, sir. Sit down.' The dogs looked at their master, then, having apparently lost interest in Matthew, lay down around his chair. 'Well, Mr O'Hanlon, we seem to have run out of anything to say to one another.' He stood up and held out his hand. Matthew looked at the dogs doubtfully. Marryat smiled. 'Don't mind them, they won't bite, not if I don't tell them to.'

Matthew stood up and shook hands, put away his notebook and pencil, and picked up his hat which was beside his chair.

'Thank you for your time, Mr Marryat.'

Marryat walked with him and opened the door while the dogs looked on.

'Not at all. You are an interesting fellow, if something of an enigma. Had I the time I think I would value getting to know you. But alas, *tempus fugit*.'

Matthew's response was as cold as Marryat's had been condescending.

'I hope you have a good journey home.'

'So do I. And remember what I told you. Couperin is clever and he's up to something. If you are indeed an innocent in this then please be very careful. Good day.'

The door closed. Matthew put on his hat and walked away thoughtfully.

Had he done well or badly? He didn't know. Should he believe Marryat or not? He didn't know. Did he think Couperin a spy for the French? Yes, he might well be. But

311

in that case what on earth should he do about it? He didn't know. And with these thoughts jostling in his brain he walked out into the harsh sunlight and headed back to the Couperin's house where, he remembered, Dr Couperin had said he wanted to tell him something.

Chapter Forty-six

Matthew sat opposite Dr Couperin in his office.

'Do you remember, Mr O'Hanlon, when we first met there was an execution about to take place?'

'Yes. And you said the men were being murdered.'

'So I did, and so they were. You see, Mr O'Hanlon, there is a civil war going on here in Panama. It is unacknowledged by the government and goes utterly unreported, but nonetheless it goes on.'

'A civil war.'

'Well, that is an exaggeration perhaps, but not much of one. Those men who were shot on the day you arrived were not bandits but revolutionaries, men fighting for freedom.'

'Whose freedom?'

'The freedom of Panama. You are not fully acquainted with the country but I assure you that there are many here who long to see their own flag flying over Panama City and to have it as the capital of a free and independent state. New Granada is a vast country and we are at the very northern tip, separated by mountains and jungles, for the most part forgotten and ignored. Panama is a poor place, but it need not be. The people work hard but their labours are but poorly rewarded. What money is not taken by officials in taxes goes in bribes to those same officials. Bogotá gets much from Panama I assure you, but Panama gets very little from Bogotá. The people find it difficult to survive never mind live happy and fulfilled lives.'

Matthew refrained from pointing out that the Couperin's home seemed a long way from poverty and mere survival. 'There are those of us who try to bring about change. Some have chosen armed struggle. You yourself saw what happens to them. They are branded bandits and shot after a sham of a trial which is always a forgone conclusion. I myself, do what I can. I represent the men brought for trial. But it is very little and rarely brings about any mitigation of the result. There is only one case in which I have been involved where the death sentence was not handed down, and that was because the man was the son of a wealthy citizen who was able to buy his acquittal.' Couperin shook his head sadly. 'No, my poor efforts are going nowhere, yet I cannot bring myself to see violence as the only solution. These poor lands have already seen too much bloodshed so I seek another way.'

'What way?'

'You.'

'Me?'

'Yes.'

'What can I do?'

'You can tell the world of our plight and of our struggle. You can make people pay attention. The power of the press, especially the American press, is well known. If you could bring our story to your New York papers it would soon be taken up all over America and across Europe. We would no longer be alone and could no longer be ignored by the politicians in the Bogotá.'

'But I have seen no evidence of what you are telling me.'

'The executions?'

'But, if you will pardon me, I have only your word for that. For all I know the men shot that day were indeed bandits.'

'True, and how very sensible of you. But I expected no less. Had you accepted my unsupported word I would have doubted your sincerity. But I had to be sure you were impartial, that your only interest was in bringing the news to the wider world. I said to you this morning that Panama is, under the bustle of the gold rush, essentially a quiet

314

place. That is true, but only for a very good reason. The police here have spies and informers everywhere. Anyone who speaks openly in support of the rebels brings down on themselves the attentions of Colonel Hernandez. He is the most powerful man in Panama. As I told you in the hotel when we met him he is, in effect, judge, jury, and executioner. The people fear him and rightly. But you are an American, you have the protection of your government. Once I heard that a foreign correspondent was being sent from New York I own I began to lay my plans.'

'Plans?'

'I have told you, Mr O'Hanlon, I do not wish to resort to violence but I support Panama's fight for freedom. I, myself, hold Mexican citizenship, but as soon as Panama is free I shall become a citizen of this country. I made it my business to see that your companion Dr Tomes was made aware that hospitality would be available at my house, I arranged that he was advised by people he knew and trusted to approach me. That is why I agreed so readily to accept you, a stranger, into my home. I was awaiting you. You, Mr O'Hanlon, and the New York papers that you represent, are my plan.'

And Dr Couperin sat back, folded his hands, and waited for Matthew to reply.

'I see.'

'I am glad. I have placed all my hopes in you.'

'You were expecting me?'

'Yes.'

'How?'

The question threw Couperin's calm manner slightly and he frowned.

'I regret I do not understand.'

'I set off from Chagres the morning after I arrived. I was not delayed at all. How could you have known of my arrival and made the plans that you have just outlined?'

'I see. A good question. There was a letter sent by Dr

315

Tomes some weeks before your arrival.'

'To you?'

'Oh no. I have told you, I am not acquainted with the good doctor. I met him for the first time at the hotel in your company. The letter was to the agent of the Pacific Mail Line here in Panama City. It said that Dr Tomes would be coming around a certain date and would be travelling with the new foreign correspondent of the New York Press Association who would be located here.'

'And this agent of the Pacific Mail told you of our travelling together and the date of our arrival?'

'No, not directly. His wife told my wife. They are great friends. They share an interest in literature.'

'I see. Does your wife share your sympathies regarding Panama?'

'To a certain extent, yes. But she knows nothing of my plan.'

'This plan is your and yours alone?'

'It has to be. It is the only safe way.'

'I see.'

Matthew reviewed what Couperin had told him. It could be true, that there were indeed revolutionaries, freedom-fighters, as he said. This part of the world seemed to have been in a constant turmoil of revolution ever since he could remember. And the proposal to make the world aware that Panama was at this very minute fighting for independence also made some sort of sense. Publicity could do nothing except help such an endeavour. And there had indeed been a letter. Frank Da Silva had told him as much on his arrival at Chagres. That he had received a letter announcing their arrival and another letter from Tomes had been forwarded to Panama City. It all seemed to hang together, just. Then the words he had heard this morning from Frank Marryat came back to him. '*All a spy can ever really trust is information gained by himself from a perfectly unprejudiced source.*'

And whatever else Couperin might be he was, by his own admission, definitely not an unprejudiced source.

'Assuming I believe you, that these revolutionaries exist and you are working for the independence of Panama, what exactly do you propose?'

Couperin lent forward eagerly.

'That you see for yourself. That you meet these men who risk their lives. That you go into the jungle and meet with their leader and his lieutenants.' He sat back once more. 'I warn you it will not be without danger, and danger from both sides. If the rebels think you are a spy or that you might in any way, even without meaning to, betray them, they would not hesitate to kill you. If the fact that you even know of the existence of revolutionaries comes to the ears of Colonel Hernandez he will take action. At the very least he will have you expelled. If he finds out you have actually met with them and that you propose to publicise their cause then I feel sure you will fall victim to either some fatal accident or contract some sudden violent illness which will prove just as fatal. I tell you this, Mr O'Hanlon, because I wish to be open and frank with you. I have espoused the cause of an independent Panama, you have not. To you, I know, it would be no more than a news story. It is for you to decide whether such a story is worth your life, for that is indeed what you will be risking. The choice, as I say, must be yours and your alone.'

Chapter Forty-seven

Three days after his talk with Dr Couperin the doctor invited him once again into his study in the afternoon and informed him that the revolutionary leader would meet with him in two weeks. Matthew chafed at the idea of so long a wait but apparently the leader had insisted; a necessarily cautious man, he wanted to be sure of Matthew and so had instituted enquiries.

'That he has agreed to a meeting at all is entirely due to the fact that he trusts me as a friend of the revolution. But his trust does not go so far as to take my word alone nor would I wish it to be any other way. Now we have made contact we are in deadly danger. If a word of our intentions were to get to the ears of ...'

'Colonel Hernandez. I know, you already told me. But two weeks.'

'I'm afraid he was adamant and I cannot risk any further contact. You must be patient.'

Matthew tried to be patient and managed it only because Edith seemed keen to spend time in his company, showing him the city and trying to teach him Spanish while he tried to teach her English, both efforts resulting in much French, a not inconsiderable amount of laughter, and some very telling compliments which drew from the young lady more than one welcome blush. On those occasions when Matthew was not enjoying the company of Edith he gave thought to whether to send a report to New York or not. On the one hand it was, he presumed, exactly the sort of thing Clarence Diver would want to know about. On the other hand there was no news, other than the continuing death and sickness toll of the railway, which would hardly justify a report to the Associated Press. In the end he decided to risk sending a brief message. It read:

"The railway construction project takes its usual toll on the life and health of its workers although the end of the rainy season at least improves the conditions in which the work progresses. The causeway across the Chagres swamp is almost complete and the company confidently expect to be able to open the first part of the line next year to carry passengers at least halfway up river on their journey to Gorgona.

For the attention of C. D.

Contact made with group who may be seeking to make Panama an independent country. Further information to follow."

Once the report was written and sealed into its envelope Matthew realised that since sending his first report he had not established some more secure means of forwarding his information. He now regretted this. The content of his first report had been innocuous, containing as it did only the information about the railway and stating that he was now settled and accepted as the representative of the New York Associated Press. Had eyes other than those for which it was intended seen that report it compromised nothing. The same could not be said of the addendum to this brief report. It was for Clarence Diver's eyes only, even as cautiously worded as he had tried to make it. He regretted now that he had not been given some sort of cipher to use.

Then he thought of Fernando. Why not send his reports via Fernando and ask him to see that they were placed in the safe hands of an officer, preferably the purser, on the next outgoing ship? If what Tomes had told him were true, that Fernando, having been given the medal, was now a loyal friend, that was surely the safest way to get his reports out of Panama.

Matthew had seen Fernando a couple of times leading in parties of more affluent travellers to the hotel he and Tomes had used. Both times Fernando had waved a greeting and he had acknowledged it. However, it might be some time, weeks even, before another such party hired Fernando and his men and were brought right into the city. Normally he would leave his charges at Little America. It would be a nuisance, of course, to have to loiter anywhere near Little America but it was undoubtedly the quickest way to get his report off.

Matthew remembered Tomes' warning about Little America being a dangerous place and searched for a vantage point sufficiently far from the camp so as to be able to watch new arrivals yet not draw attention to himself among the desperadoes who inhabited the place. He found what he was looking for in a small café where he could sit at an outside table under the shade of an awning. From his table he had a sufficiently clear view of the new arrivals from the mountains.

He had spent rather a lot of time in the company of Edith and, thanks to a natural aptitude for languages rather than any teaching skills on the part of the young lady, he had surprised himself by gaining a basic mastery of the Spanish language. He was, of course, limited by a lack of suitable vocabulary, his conversations with Edith were not designed for any workmanlike purposes, but he could now make himself understood in simple conversation.

It was on the third afternoon of his vigil, as he sat keeping company with a cup of the café's rather vicious coffee as it went cold, that he espied Fernando.

He got up and walked to where he and his two men were unloading baggage from the mules while the owners of the baggage waited.

Fernando turned and saw Matthew who was almost up to them. His face split into a grin and he strode forward. Matthew stood and held out his hand almost defensively, ready to do his utmost to repel any attempt at a kiss. Fernando took the offered hand and pumped it joyfully speaking rapid Spanish only fragments of which Matthew was able to catch and interpret. With his other hand he took hold of the medal and held it for Matthew to see.

When Fernando's enthusiastic greeting had died down Matthew began, haltingly, to speak.

'I come as a friend. As a friend of the heart.' That Matthew had addressed him so and in Spanish seemed to impress Fernando profoundly and he stood, listening in a suitably solemn manner. Over the last three days of waiting and watching Matthew had had plenty of time to rehearse his speech. 'I want a letter taken on a ship leaving Chagres. The letter is most important. The letter must be safe.'

Fernando nodded slowly.

'I understand.'

Matthew took out his report in its envelope. It was stamped and addressed to Clarence Diver at his office in Greenwich Village.

'Here is the letter.' Matthew handed it over. Fernando took it and, without looking at the address, put into the satchel he wore. 'Give it to an officer. Now I must go. Thank you, my friend. I thank you from my heart.'

Fernando said something, which unfortunately missed Matthew's ability in Spanish by some yardage, so he smiled, said thank you once again, turned, and set off. After walking about twenty paces he glanced back. Fernando was once again busy with the baggage. Matthew relaxed and walked on, pleased with himself. He was getting the hang of things. He now had a safe and secure means of getting his reports out of Panama City and onto a ship. Yes, he felt, he was getting the hang of things nicely, and if a meeting with these freedom fighters could be arranged then maybe he would soon have something quite startling to put in a report, something that would make Diver realise what a good choice he had made. And once he had alerted Diver he could see no reason why he shouldn't use the thing as a genuine news story. As

322

Matthew made his way back into Panama City he felt rather pleased with himself both in his role of foreign correspondent and as an agent for the Union. He wished that somehow he could make Sam Grant aware of what he had done, how he had successfully taken his first steps on the road to glory.

Chapter Forty-eight

The jungle was very much the same as that which had surrounded Matthew on his journey from Chagres. Thankfully the rainy season was almost over and the rain held off but the heat and dank atmosphere combined to make the air thick and unwholesome. Had Matthew been at all interested in botany his current journey would have been one fraught with interest. The trail over the mountains from Gorgona was so well used that the vegetation which had pressed around them was only that of the most coarse and tough varieties which could survive the constant passage of humanity. Other more tender species had retreated some small distance from the trail and were not so easily visible except to the more observant and interested traveller of which Matthew had not been one. Here, where there was no trail, at least not one apparent to Matthew, the jungle in all its infinite variety brushed against them, plucked at their arms, legs, and hats, and tenderly coiled itself around the legs as they forced their way onwards.

Matthew had agreed to this meeting with the leader of the revolutionaries taking place in the jungle. How could he not? But now that he was actually forcing his way behind his guide, he began to wonder if he had been wise. Perhaps he should have insisted on some more neutral, safer place. A place where he would not be so very cut off and alone. But his thoughts of the story he was heading towards gave him strength and encouragement. If what he had been told by Dr Couperin was true he would be the first to report a new civil war in the region, an emerging nation's first painful struggle for freedom. He would bring the voice of the revolution's leader to the world. It was what he had come to Panama for. This was a story which would get headlines on the front page, not be tucked away on some inner section at the tail end of someone else's article. And there on that front page would be his name for all of New York to see. Why, if he delivered this story he might be able to go back to New York and yes, spit in Fred Hudson's eye, go to *The Sun* and demand that job.

However, as elated as the possibility of breaking a great story made him feel there was another reason for his feelings of elation. In one of his pockets he carried a letter. It had been delivered to him at Dr Couperin's by hand. The man who delivered it, a prospector headed to the gold fields, could only say that he had been paid to bring it from Chagres and, as it bore no stamp, Matthew assumed that it had originated from that foul place.

On opening the letter his curiosity had at once been satisfied:

My dear Mr O'Hanlon.

On arriving in Chagres I made further enquiries about you and, as you are familiar with the place, you will appreciate what a compliment to you it is that I delayed my departure even for a few days in this fever hole. However, it appears you are worth it for I find that you arrived with a certain Dr Robert Tomes and that he and you travelled together from New York. My dear sir, I salute you. I had marked you down as something of a fool, certainly no one who might be involved in anything of concern to His Majesty's Government despite your association with Dr Couperin. Yet here you are, revealed as the close confident of Dr Tomes. Well, sir, it appears that it is I who am the fool and you who are the cleverer man and I should have taken more note of your observation that looking so unlikely an agent made you an exceptional one. But my warning to you concerning Dr Couperin stands even though I now see that you have no need of it. As to what you are involved in, I own I have discovered no more here in Chagres than I did in Panama City. You have been too many for me, sir, and I once again salute you. However, I must make a report of what I have discovered to my government. Panama is too valuable a strip of land to fall into the hands of any agency or government which might be ill-disposed to the British interests in the region. I name no names you understand. All I say is that if, having reached the Pacific in California and the Oregon Territories, the American Eagle turns it would be ill-advised to turn towards Darien. That things will change I do not doubt, but for Panama to be added as the next state of your Union would be an unacceptable outcome to His Majesty's Government. If it is your own government for whom you are acting I suggest you make known to them that the situation as it presently stands will very soon be relayed to London. American and British interests aside, however, I am minded to think that Panama will not stay as it is for very much longer, and when the railway presently under construction reaches its destination I have no doubt that before long the flag that will float from the citadel will not be that of New Granada. In fact, in my judgement, it may well be a new flag to add to the community of nations. If that is where your involvement lies then I look forward with interest to the outcome of your endeavours and remain, sir,

ever yr. humble servant,
Frank Marryat.

Matthew had no idea what the reference to Robert Tomes meant but Marryat's sentiments, especially those that showed that he believed Matthew the better man, had gladdened his heart. As for the notion that America might consider some form of forcible occupation of Panama, well, the idea was preposterous and confirmed Matthew's opinion that Marryat's superior manner when they met had

327

no basis in any actual talent for deception and intrigue. However, the letter's last sentences had strongly reinforced Matthew's opinion that Panama might well be in the process of bringing about its independence from New Granada. Marryat wasn't a disinterested source of information, true, but even so, that his assessment should chime in so nicely with Matthew's own gave him considerable satisfaction. With these thoughts streaming through his head he followed the guide who hacked their way through the jungle.

Dr Couperin had taken Matthew as far as the outskirts of the city and there he had been handed over to another man who had taken him to the edge of the jungle. There this guide had been waiting. The guide was an indigenous native who spoke almost not at all and when he did only in a few words of barely understandable Spanish. But he seemed to know his job, for although Matthew could see no obvious path through the undergrowth they had made steady progress which seemed to indicate they were in fact following some sort of trail.

After about an hour, around mid-afternoon, the guide suddenly stepped out from the tangle of the jungle into a clearing. Matthew followed and there, standing looking at them, stood four men, the most ghastly assortment of villainous bandits that Matthew could have imagined in his wildest dreams. Dirty, bearded, and with battered headgear, they each carried a firearm and every one of them could have modelled for one of the more sensational illustrations in the popular violent novelettes about the exploits of daring frontiersmen and adventurers. The guide stood to one side and one of the band of men came towards Matthew, holding a large pistol pointed directly at the third button of Matthew's waistcoat.

'Welcome.' To Matthew's surprise the man had not only spoken in English but with an American accent. 'You are Mr O'Hanlon, I take it?'

'I am.'

The man lowered his pistol and held out his hand.

'Welcome to the revolution, my friend.' Matthew took the offered hand and, as they shook, the man turned, said something in rapid Spanish at which his three companions broke into cheering, one waved his hat, and one fired his musket into the air. 'See. My lieutenants also welcome you. Come, we will go and sit down and I will tell you all you want to know about our struggle.'

The man turned and began to walk to a side of the clearing. Matthew followed. The lieutenants also moved away and Matthew saw that the Indian guide had produced a large flask from the satchel he carried and handed it to the three men who immediately sat down and began to pass it round and take sips of the contents.

The leader stopped by a log a distance away from the drinking men and indicated that Matthew should also sit.

'My lieutenants are celebrating your arrival. They know that this is a great day in the life of the revolution. That with the American press on our side victory will be assured. The government of New Granada will no longer be able to hide our struggle from the world. Now, my friend, what is it you want to know?'

The interview lasted about half an hour by which time the flask was empty and the three lieutenants asleep. The leader, who insisted Matthew refer to him as El Liberator and would give no other name, said he had been born in Panama but moved to New Orleans at the age of fifteen, worked there for fifteen years, at what he would not say, then returned to Panama to work on the railway. Soon after arriving he got to hear of the revolution and immediately left his work and joined the fighters in the jungle. That had been two years ago. He had risen in the ranks of the cause by his bravery and cleverness and was now the leader. As to his plans he would soon issue a manifesto laying out his vision of the future for his country. Once that was done he would issue an ultimatum to the government of New Granada to grant independence to Panama or face an armed uprising. He hoped, he told Matthew, that the use of force would not be necessary but he had five hundred trained and equipped men under his command in the jungle, all ready to die for him and the cause, but if it was at all possible he wished to avoid any more bloodshed.

'Too much blood has already been spilled over this land. I seek a peaceful solution, but if I must sacrifice my life and the lives of my men then so be it. *Viva la revolución.*'

At which one of the lieutenants woke, gave a feeble echo to the cry, turned over, and went back to sleep.

The interview proceeded, but more because El Liberator seemed to enjoy talking about himself rather than providing any concrete information about plans or resources or what backing the cause might have among the local population, especially the middle-classes. On such subjects El Liberator was expansive but vague. However, as Matthew's experience of revolution and revolutionaries was equally vague he did his best to keep an open mind. He was far from convinced but neither was he totally sceptical. This rather comic figure and the lieutenants who were drunk and asleep now might be formidable fighters when sober and awake. How was he to know?

'When will you issue the manifesto?'

'Soon.'

'How soon?'

At this the man stood up angrily.

'No more questions. Enough. You need to know no more.' He smacked his chest with his hand. 'Only I, the leader, know all. That is how it must be. Soon there will be a manifesto and you will give it to the world so they know that El Liberator leads his country from the iron heel of New Granada to independence and greatness. Now go. Tell the world of what is happening here.'

And he strode over to his sleeping lieutenants, kicked two of them while shouting in Spanish, and then strode off into the jungle. His lieutenants struggled quickly to their feet, grabbed their hats and firearms, and also disappeared into the undergrowth leaving Matthew looking after them and the guide squatting impassively staring into space.

Chapter Forty-nine

Matthew arrived back to Dr Couperin's house as the sun was setting. The Doctor was waiting for him and led him into his office.

'Well, Mr O'Hanlon?'

'El Liberator, as he insists on calling himself, is not the most prepossessing of men, is he, and as for his lieutenants ...'

'There was a problem?'

'No. It's just that while we talked they got drunk and fell asleep and when you boil it down to hard facts El Liberator told me nothing.'

'What did you expect him to tell you?'

It was a good question.

'Well, something solid, something I could check.'

'I see. And if you had fallen into the hands of Colonel Hernandez? If you were followed or intercepted you would, of course, have refused to divulge any information about plans and strategies or any names you might have been given, names of influential people who have given support to the revolution?'

'Of course.'

'Even though Colonel Hernandez has powerful methods of persuasion at his disposal which he has never hesitated to use in dealing with those revolutionaries who have passed through his hands.'

'You mean torture?'

'Yes.'

'But I'm an American citizen.'

'That would hardly deter the colonel. When he had what he wanted your body would be found and he would institute a thorough investigation into your robbery and murder. Some poor devil would probably be shot for the crime. He would, of course, send his sincere condolences to your ambassador in Bogotá. Remember the executions on the day of our first meeting.'

Matthew thought about it.

'But if he could tell me nothing why agree to a meeting?'

'Did he tell you nothing?'

'Only some vague reference to a manifesto and that it would be followed by an ultimatum to the government.'

'And you consider that nothing?'

'Nothing solid.'

The doctor rose.

'In that case all I can suggest is that you wait and see what the manifesto says, if and when it appears.'

Matthew also stood up.

'Yes.'

'Will you send a report to New York?'

'I don't know. There's no story yet, nothing that any paper would publish. But I might send some background to sort of prepare the way in case anything actually does happen.'

'Good. I will inform the leader. He will be pleased. He would have expected no more at this stage. Now you must be hungry. I will arrange for a hot meal and some wine to be sent to your room. My wife, daughter, and I are dining with friends this evening.'

'Thank you, that would be most welcome. Could you arrange for a hot bath to be drawn before I eat? The jungle leaves one in rather a used condition.'

Dr Couperin smiled.

'A used condition. How very apposite, but then, words are your stock in trade are they not? A bath is already being drawn for you. I anticipated your request. Now you must excuse me, I must dress and then we must be on our way. Good evening.'

334

Matthew made his way to his room where a large bath tub had already been placed, half-filled with hot water. Towels and soap stood on the floor beside it. He took out his notebook and pencil, threw them on the desk, and began to undress. The door opened and a maid entered carrying a large ewer of hot water which she poured into the tub, curtsied to Matthew, and left. Matthew finished removing his clothes and then gingerly lowered himself until he was sitting comfortably in the hot water. He lay back and let the strains of a hard day ease from his body.

Had it been a success? He wasn't sure.

Would he send a report to Diver?

Yes, he rather thought he would.

Even if it all came to nothing it would show Diver that he was busy and had his finger on the pulse of things. But what exactly would he put into the report? He eased himself a little lower into the water, picked up the soap, began slowly to lather himself, and gave himself up to thought.

The door opened and once more the maid entered. She placed the ewer of hot water she was carrying by the tub, curtsied once more, and was gone.

Matthew, having covered his private parts with his hands during her visit, resumed his lathering.

How to word it? And then a thought struck him. Why not include a reference to Marryat's letter? Marryat's view that in the not-too-distant future Panama would have a new flag certainly seemed to support the idea of a revolution aimed at independence. It was a pity he couldn't use the stuff about him being the better man. He would have like Diver to see that. Then he had a brainwave. Why not send the whole letter, not a copy but the original. He could refer to the flag business in his report but Diver would then be able to see for himself Marryat's opinion of him.

Matthew lathered his hair enthusiastically.

Yes, by God, that was the way to do it.

Chapter Fifty

The Office of the US Secretary of State
Washington

'The British Envoy, Mr Secretary.'

The man making the announcement stood to one side of the doorway and the British envoy extraordinary to the United States, Sir Henry Bulwer, entered.

Daniel Webster rose to greet him.

'Please sit down, Sir Henry, it is as always a pleasure.'

Sir Henry sat down heavily.

'Not for me, sir, not today.'

Daniel Webster sat down slowly and prepared himself for what appeared would be a difficult interview.

'Then please share with me the reason for your visit, no matter how unpleasant it may be.'

'I'll be brief. Your government has placed an agent in Panama City. Of itself that might be of no serious concern, you can scatter your agents across the face of the globe as far as His Majesty's Government is concerned so long as you don't act against British interests. But to place an agent in Panama at this time, and taken in conjunction with all the other factors does, in the view of my government, class very much as acting against our interests. I have been asked, nay ordered, by London to state in the strongest possible terms, the strongest possible, that any direct intervention by the United States in Panama would be considered a breach, a severe breach, of the Clayton-Bulwer Treaty and His Majesty's Government would feel compelled to mobilise troops and ships from our Caribbean possessions to protect British interests and guarantee the continued sovereign integrity of New

Granada. There, sir, I hope that's plain enough and brief enough for you.'

Sir Henry Bulwer had been a diplomat for some time, and Daniel Webster was a little taken aback that such a seasoned practitioner of the art of diplomacy should have lowered himself to what was little more than bluster.

'My dear Sir Henry. I see that you are in a somewhat disturbed condition ...'

'Never mind my condition, sir. My condition is my own affair. What is between us, what *is* our affair, is the matter of Central America. Let us both be satisfied to concentrate on that, sir.'

'Very well. Firstly I reject completely and totally the claim you have made that the United States has placed an agent in Panama.'

'Name of O'Hanlon, Matthew O'Hanlon. Probably a damned Fenian as well as an agent of yours. Calls himself foreign correspondent of the New York Associated Press. Been in the damned place about a couple of months. Stays with a Dr Couperin.'

This battery of accurate information rattled Daniel Webster. What a diplomat was told was usually only a small fraction of what his intelligence service knew, and if that was so in this particular case the British knew a great deal indeed.

'But if he says he is the Foreign Correspondent as you say, why should he not be one?'

This reply and the pacific tone of its delivery seemed to calm Sir Henry somewhat.

'I don't doubt that he is what he says he is. My point, sir, is that's not all he is.'

Webster poured more oil on Sir Henry's troubled waters.

'I'm sorry, Sir Henry, I find your response a little abstruse.'

'Damn your games, Webster. I was the one who led the

negotiations on our treaty on Central America. The thing bears my name, so don't shilly-shally with me, sir. You want to build a canal between the Caribbean and the Pacific. Very well, so do we, so do the French. Now it seems that you have chosen the Panama route and are setting about securing America's grip on the place.'

'But it is not a canal that is being built. It is a railway.'

That drew a scornful laugh.

'Just as next year we will begin to build a railway for Pasha Abbas in Egypt and, when it is built and is the only link between the Mediterranean and the Red Sea, it will become inevitable that a British company will be chosen to build the canal.'

'I see. You think Mr Aspinwall's railroad is no more than a precursor to obtaining the rights to build the canal?'

'That is exactly what His Majesty's Government thinks. At this moment in time there are two places in the world that are vital to international trade, Central America and Egypt. As I have said, we will build the canal in Egypt. It is essential to our East India trade route.'

'And if a canal in Central America were just as essential to American interests?'

'American expansion has already taught us that when America turns its interest on to a territory, even if it be the sovereign territory of a friendly country, that territory can no longer be deemed safe and secure. If America turns to Panama we would, as I have said, support to our utmost the integrity of New Granada.'

Webster smiled.

'I see, and I am forced to admit that I cannot put your mind at rest on this matter, Sir Henry. A canal is indeed proposed and will be built and if London feels that may damage its interests or would be a threat to the sovereignty of any country in Central America then that saddens me, but it will not stop the project from proceeding.'

'Then, sir, I formally warn you. Panama is part of New

Granada and ...'

Webster held up a hand.

'I'm sorry, Sir Henry, you have misunderstood me. The project I refer to has nothing to do with Panama. I refer to the Rivas Isthmus route.'

'Nicaragua? But that route was dismissed by your Congress twenty years ago.'

'And twenty years ago no one could have built a railroad in Egypt. The steam engine in all its manifestations has changed the world, led, I freely admit, by Great Britain. What was deemed impossible twenty years ago is now manifestly achievable. Last year the Nicaraguan government signed a contract with Cornelius Vanderbilt for his company to build the canal.'

This seemed to discommode Sir Henry somewhat.

'The Lake Nicaragua route?'

'Following the San Juan River from the Caribbean.'

'And you can assure me, absolutely assure me, that the United States has no territorial ambition in Central America in general and in Panama in particular.'

Daniel Webster stood up.

'You have that assurance and if you wish I will give it to you in writing.'

Sir Henry stood up.

'No need, sir. The matter of the security and neutrality of transit routes across the region is fully covered by the Clayton-Bulwer Treaty. If an agreement has been entered into between Mr Vanderbilt and the Nicaraguan government I can accept your verbal assurance, Mr Secretary, and will see that it is conveyed to London.'

Daniel Webster held out his hand.

'Then good day, Sir Henry.'

The two men shook hands and Sir Henry Bulwer went to the door where he paused.

'And this O'Hanlon fellow. Our people seem damn sure he and Couperin are working for someone against the

340

interests of New Granada. Not you?'

'Not us, Sir Henry, and if it will calm London's mind I will do what I can to find out what, if anything, the man is up to. If it transpires that your intelligence service are correct and something untoward is going on I will see to it that it is stopped.'

'Good.'

The door closed, Daniel Webster waited a moment then rang his bell. His assistant entered.

'Get me in to see the president at once or as soon as possible, then find Jeremiah Jones and have him wait for me at his house. Take him there and keep him there by force if necessary.'

Yes, sir.'

The door closed and Daniel Webster spoke out angrily to the empty room.

'God damn and blast. How in hell's name did they find out?'

Then he sat down and began to decide in what words he would tell President Fillmore that the Polk Plan had just been effectively blown out of the water and how, having told him, he might then distance himself sufficiently from any further explosions that might take place here in Washington or in Panama.

The door opened.

'The president says he will see you at once.'

Daniel Webster stood up. It was going to be a difficult interview. Very difficult indeed.

Chapter Fifty-one

As it turned out there was no need to find Jeremiah Jones and certainly no need to forcibly detain him in his home. His health had already done that. Jeremiah Jones lay in his bed, dying.

'I am not a religious man, Mr Secretary, not in the way that term is normally applied. But I do believe in justice and I believe that we must all settle our accounts either in this life or beyond it. I have been directly responsible for the deaths of several innocent people. I am not proud of that but neither do I expect ...' and here he took a linen cloth from under the pillow and quietly expectorated into it. He replaced the cloth and took a bottle which, together with a small, silver bell, stood on a little table by his bed, poured some of its contents onto a spoon, and swallowed it. 'Laudanum. It keeps the worst of the pain at bay.' He replaced the bottle on the table and looked at it. It was half full. 'I doubt I shall get to the end of the bottle or the week. However, I am sure you did not come here, Mr Secretary, to listen to my views on the afterlife, nor discuss my health.'

Daniel Webster, gifted orator though he was, found it difficult to find the right words. This old man was dying. Yet he needed him to live long enough to do one last task. Only Jeremiah Jones knew the full reach and present deployment of the Polk Plan. Only he could bring about the abortion of the whole project in such a way that any debris from its destruction would not attach itself to the secretary of state. The man clearly had only a few more days at most and those days would be painful. To ask him to exert himself in any way, mentally or physically, would increase the pain and shorten what days were left.

'The Polk Plan must be stopped. You must stop it and you must see that no repercussions reach Washington.'

They were not the best of words, that much he knew, but they did the job.

Jones nodded his head.

'I suspected as much. It was all done too hastily and with inadequate personnel and resources. There was always a fair chance that it would fail.'

Webster didn't try to keep the annoyance from his voice.

'Then why the hell didn't you say so at the time?'

'I was not asked at the time. I was simply ordered, by you, to resuscitate the plan, which I did. Is the problem with our people?'

'No, at least not that I know of.'

'The young man I placed there has not caught fever or anything like that? I was most careful to see that his health and safety were suitably protected from the outset. We couldn't have him dying too soon, could we?'

'No, no one's caught any fever.'

'Is it the British?'

Webster nodded.

'I see. That was always a weak point. Sir Henry Bulwer negotiated the treaty. He would naturally have taken a particular interest that it was not contravened.'

'He came to see me this morning. I gave him my assurance that we had no ambitions territorial or otherwise in Panama and that our canal interests lay solely in Nicaragua.'

'Where, of course, our scope for action would be drastically more limited with the British camped on the Mosquito Coast and in Belize. Did he seem satisfied?'

'He seemed so. And now I want the Polk Plan terminated. Can you do it?'

'No.'

'No?'

344

'I am dying, Mr Secretary.'

'Damn it, man, I can see that. But the president has said that it must be terminated even if it means letting the British know that some rogue element with the government set the whole thing up.'

'Oh dear, that will be messy.'

'Not for the president. If he breaks the news and institutes a full congressional investigation he would, of course, be above any suspicion of involvement.'

'But you would not.'

'And neither would you.'

The old man's face crumpled and Webster for one moment feared he had sustained some sort of attack and the end was upon him. Then the old man's eyes turned on him and he saw the seizure for what it was. Jeremiah Jones was laughing.

Jones reached under his pillow, took out his cloth, found a free place, on it and coughed into it. He returned the cloth to its place and took two or three slow breaths.

'Really, Mr Secretary, to make me laugh is as good as taking a pistol to my head.'

'I see nothing to laugh at.'

'Do you not, sir? Do you not? Then pray let me enlighten you. You come here to my bedside and find me dying. Despite that, you demand my help. And then you threaten me. Do you seriously think I will be available to give evidence to any investigation?'

Daniel Webster had already realised his mistake and took the rebuke humbly. He needed this dying man.

'I apologise. But I ask you once again, for the good of the country if not for me. Can you stop this damn thing?'

'Not I. But I can do my best to see that what you want is done.'

'Can I help in any way?'

'Do you want to, Mr Secretary? Do you really want to be any more involved than you already are?'

345

Daniel Webster stood up. He had done all he could. His political fate was in the hands of this dying cripple.

'Is there anything you need, medically I mean.'

'No, Mr Secretary, but thank you for asking.'

Daniel Webster hesitated. What did one say to a man who had only days to live?

Nothing.

So the secretary of state for the Union turned and left.

Jeremiah Jones lifted the small bell from the table and shook it.

The door opened and a man came in.

'Send at once for a galloper then bring me paper, pen, and ink. When the galloper comes I shall have two sets of papers ready. They are to go by the fastest possible means to Panama City. Use whatever authority is needed. The fastest possible means, understood?'

The man nodded and left.

On the bed Jeremiah Jones lay back weakly and his eyes closed, but whether it was in sleep or death there was no one present to determine.

Chapter Fifty-two

Matthew never felt the blow when it fell. But he did feel it, and felt it considerably, when he came to. It was as if someone had started a small but fierce fire in the scalp at the back of his head. In addition to which his whole head throbbed with a deep, dull pain and his vision was blurred. Not that there was much to look at. The room was bare, the window shuttered, and what little light came through the shutters revealed nothing other than a table and two stools and a dirt floor. There was nothing more. Very slowly, so as to ensure that the pain in his head did not get worse, if that were possible, he hauled himself up into a sitting position then he leaned to one side and vomited. The feeling that swept over him was not at all dissimilar to the sea-sickness he had suffered on the *Cherokee*. He sat for a moment unable to move and waited to see if there was anything more to come up. The taste in his mouth was horribly sour but slowly he began to feel the nausea subside and he was left with only the pain in his head which was more than adequate to make him feel dreadful.

What on earth had happened?

A man had come to Dr Couperin's house and told him that Matthew was to meet someone who had a message for him from El Liberator. The doctor had told him of the visitor himself.

'The address is in a part of the city where it is inadvisable for a stranger to go alone, not far from Little America. Would you like me to accompany you?'

Matthew felt a little annoyed at the idea that he was not capable of taking care of himself. In order to meet with Fernando had he not gone to exactly that part of town several times?

'Did the messenger say I should come alone?'

'No, just that you should be at the address within the next hour.'

'Nevertheless I will go alone, but thank you for your offer.'

And he had set off, found the street, and stopped at the address Couperin had given him. The last thing he remembered was standing looking at the door of a shabby house, one of a uniformly shabby terrace, about to knock on the door.

Now he was here, wherever here was.

He slowly tried to stand up but he sat down again quickly as he felt the nausea return. His vision was clearing but trying to stand had made him dizzy.

The door opened and a figure stood silhouetted in the rectangle of harsh light. Matthew blinked at the sudden brightness unable to see anything but a dark silhouette. The figure, a man, entered the room and stood looking down at him. Slowly Matthew's eyes adjusted to the light and the figure became more clear.

'Good God, Diver.'

Matthew once again tried to stand and once again sat down.

'Bit groggy, I expect. You will be for a while. Concussed I should think. That fool with the cudgel damn near killed you. You've been out for almost twenty-four hours. At one point I thought we'd lost you.'

And indeed Clarence Diver had lost Matthew, lost him completely. What was Diver doing here and what was he talking about? And why was he taking it all so calmly?

'What the hell is going on? What are you doing here and what's all this about a cudgel and concussion?'

'Ah, if you're talking like that it's a good sign. Means you'll soon be up and about. I'm afraid you'll have to stay here for a while even when you're fully recovered.'

Matthew tried to stand once more and this time

succeeded in remaining upright, leaning against the wall. His vision was quite clear now and the pain in his head slightly diminished.

'Look here, Diver, when did you arrive?'

'Three days after you. I came on the *Falcon*, damn fine ship, fast and comfortable these paddle steamers, aren't they?'

'Three days?'

'Yes. I followed you over from Chagres and been in Panama City ever since keeping an eye on things.'

'Keeping an eye on what things?'

'You for one. Had to make sure you were all right. And then there were several other bits and pieces. But everything is in place now so I had to arrange to collect you. Sorry my man gave you such a damnable bump on the head, but the right sort of help is hard to come by down in this place and I'm afraid I had to make do with what was to hand. They're roughnecks mostly but they'll do.'

'Do what?'

But Diver ignored the question and carried on.

'The Couperins were put in place some time ago so at least we had a good base of operations and Tomes was available to nurse-maid you down here and get you settled. That was a stroke of luck him being available. He told me of your little skirmish at The Washington Hotel. Damn lucky that Fernando chap was so alert. According to Tomes we came within a toucher of losing you. Still, all's well that ends well, as the Bard so neatly said.'

Matthew, still at a total loss, lowered himself onto the floor once more.

'Diver, I haven't the vaguest notion of what you're talking about. None of what you're saying makes any sense and you're taking it damn lightly that I've been attacked and put in this place whatever it is.'

'An old store room on the edge of Little America. Stout enough in construction to make anything inside safe from

349

prying eyes and wandering hands. I'm afraid I had to eliminate the previous owner-occupier. He tried to get too high a price to vacate.'

'Eliminate? How do you mean eliminate?'

'I mean kill. Remember back in Manhattan? I told you it sometimes becomes an unwelcome necessity. Down here I'm afraid that necessity arose early on. Not that I minded because the fellow was a bit of a bad lot even by the standards of Little America, and disposing of him as I did sent my stock up among the inhabitants considerably. It ensured no one was likely to become too inquisitive about what I might want to do with my storehouse. I dare say a few men might have seen you carried in but they'll keep it all to themselves.'

'Are you saying that I've been kidnapped and that you organised it?'

'Got it in one. I always said you were sharp, Matty. The trouble was the whole project got re-activated at damn short notice and I had to find a suitable man quickly and you, thankfully, suddenly became available. Not that I'm complaining. As it turned out you were an excellent choice. If I'd had six months to find someone I couldn't have done better.'

But Clarence Diver's encomium of Matthew's talents did nothing to clarify the situation.

'But what's going on?'

'The Polk Plan is going on, Matty. A plan originally thought up by a man called Jeremiah Jones at the request of President James K. Polk.'

'A plan to do what?'

'Nothing too difficult. Just steal a country.'

'Steal a country?'

'Well, not a whole country. Only the important part.'

'What country?'

'Panama.'

'But Panama's part of New Granada. It isn't a country.'

'You're right. At the moment it isn't.' A jovial smile lit up Clarence Diver's chubby face. 'But it soon will be, my boy, it soon will be.'

'I can't believe what I'm hearing, that you would do these things.'

'Someone has to. And now, Matthew, I must be on my way. I have business to attend to at Dr Couperin's. That's why we had to get you out of the way a little early. There's things happening at Couperin's we couldn't let you know about so we thought it best to put you on ice as it were for a couple of days. You won't be very comfortable here I'm afraid but there'll be two buckets for you. One will have clean drinking water the other I leave for you to fill.' Diver gave a small chuckle. 'Don't get them mixed up in the dark will you? And don't make a fuss or try any heroics. There's two men on guard at all times. If you try to draw attention to yourself you'll get another knock on the head.'

'And what will happen to me in a couple of days?'

'Oh we'll let you out and you can do as you please. It's just that at this moment any premature action of yours might be of considerable nuisance to us. Once our business is concluded, three days at the most, you'll be as free as a bird. And now I must really be on my way. I have a rather important meeting to attend.'

And Clarence Diver left the storehouse, closing the door behind him.

Matthew felt his way and sat on one of the stools. The door now closed and the light it had admitted gone he sat in the dark trying to get his eyes adjusted to the sudden lack of light.

He had no idea what to make of the interview or what Diver had told him. It all sounded like the ravings of a madman.

The door opened and a man came in carrying two buckets, one heavy, the other not. He put them both on the dirt floor and left without speaking. Matthew recognised

351

him. He had been one of the lieutenants at the meeting in the jungle.

Matthew slowly got up and carefully felt his way to the buckets. One was empty, the other had cold water in it almost to the top. He cupped his hand and filled his mouth with water, washed it round, then spat it out. At least it had eased the sour taste. He cupped his hand again and took several sips. Then he carefully picked up the empty bucket and took it over to the window where the gaps round the shutters gave a little light. He put the bucket down, then felt his way back to the wall once again sat down.

His movements had caused the dizziness to return and with it had come the nausea. He felt ill, he felt afraid, he felt at a loss to know what was happening to him or why. He suddenly felt the almost irresistible urge to scream. He even managed to open his mouth. Then nature took over, he passed out, and crumpled to the floor.

Chapter Fifty-three

Matthew, although he was unaware of it, spent two days in and out of a delirium brought on by both his concussion and his incarceration in his ill-ventilated and stiflingly hot prison. There was no bed and the dirt floor was prone to dampness. Clarence Diver, concerned at his condition, visited him twice but on neither occasion did Matthew recognise him. In his fevered and confused state he lived half in and half out of a continuous nightmare world where people from his past as far back as his childhood blended in with the likes of the Couperins, Fernando, and Frank Da Silva. He was trapped in a place that was in part Panama City, part Chagres, and part the worst locations of Manhattan. There he walked or ran, constantly seeking escape from something horrible but unseen. Finally, Clarence Diver brought a doctor whose license to practice had been revoked due to intemperate drinking. The doctor had been promised much, both in money and access to liquor, if he could bring Matthew onto the mend and afterwards keep his mouth shut. Temporarily sober enough to see what was required, his ministrations were successful. Under his instruction a bed was provided with a mattress and blankets. Medicine was obtained and administered and, as the fever passed, Matthew slept the dreamless sleep of recuperation and finally awoke to find himself in the same storehouse. The shutters were still closed but there was a lamp burning on the table, and sitting in a chair by the table was Madame Couperin.

Seeing his eyes open she stood up, picked up a bottle that was on the table, and came to the bed.

'Mr O'Hanlon, I'm so glad you're awake. I hope you feel better. You have been rather unwell for three days.'

She put a soft, cool hand to his forehead. 'Better. You are not so feverish now. Here, take a little water.'

She bent down, eased her hand behind his neck, helped him to sit up, and put the bottle of water to his lips.

'What's happening?'

'I cannot tell you anything. My husband and Mr Diver brought me here when it became clear you were very ill. They thought you might die.'

'And did they bring a doctor to me?'

'Yes. He left medicine and instructions and I have been doing my best to nurse you.' Matthew tried to get his legs over the side of the bed but Madame Couperin stopped him. 'Please, Mr O'Hanlon, you are not strong enough to get up and walk unaided. Lie still and rest and I will go and let my husband know that the worst is over. I may even persuade him to send a carriage and move you at once back to our house. The water will be here by your bed. Try to drink it.' Madame Couperin put the bottle down and went to the door. 'Rest, Mr O'Hanlon, I shall return as soon as I can.'

The door closed behind her.

Matthew waited a moment then slowly and with difficulty got his legs over the side of the bed and sat up. The lamp was still burning and in its light he looked around the room. Stacked on the floor against the wall opposite were six long crates. Next to the crates were six smaller wooden boxes. In front of these stood what looked like three small gunpowder barrels. Matthew's knowledge of firearms was extremely limited but even he could make a guess that the long boxes contained muskets and the smaller boxes either pistols or ammunition. He forced his mind to work. Whatever Clarence Diver was doing he was going to do it using armed men. What was it he had said? Not a country yet but soon would be. What could that mean? Was he in charge of some sort of filibuster? Did he intend to invade Panama and take it for himself? Others

354

from America had tried to do as much he knew. But with ... and Matthew made a mental estimate of the number of weapons in the boxes ... thirty muskets and as many pistols, if that's what they were, was it possible? Of course there might be more weapons elsewhere.

The door opened and the man he had recognised as the lieutenant to El Liberator came in with a bowl. He brought it to Matthew and held it out. It contained some sort of broth. Matthew took it and the spoon which the man pulled from his pocket. He noticed that in his belt there was a large knife.

The man looked at him.

'Eat.'

Matthew's Spanish was good enough to understand the simple command and he began to eat, not so much because the man had told him to and was standing over him but because suddenly he realised he was very hungry.

When the bowl was empty the man held out his hand and took it and the spoon and went to the door. As he stood for a moment and looked back at Matthew the cudgel hit him, the bowl fell from his hands, and he fell to the floor. Fernando appeared in the doorway, stepped over the inert body and beckoned to Matthew.

'Come. We must go.'

Matthew tried to get up but his legs failed him and he fell back onto the bed.

'Help me.'

Fernando came forward, put an arm round Matthew's back, and pulled him to his feet. Matthew tried to help but Fernando was to all intents and purposes carrying him. It was several days since his eyes had been exposed to the fierce sun and, once through the doorway, he felt blinded and stood still. Fernando pulled him forward.

'Quickly. We must go.'

Matthew forced himself on and as his eyes adjusted he saw another body on the ground. Again one of the lieutenants from the jungle. This one stared sightlessly at them as they passed him.

Fernando forced Matthew on through the camp. Nobody gave them more than a casual glance. Matthew, unshaven and unwashed, was still in the clothes in which he had set out for his meeting, all of which had left him in a condition all too familiar among the dwellers of Little America. As for him having to be helped to walk, well, many men got into that condition if they were lucky enough to find the price of a bottle or two. Anyway, many of the men in the camp, the long-termers, knew Fernando by both sight and reputation as a man not to be meddled with.

Fernando got Matthew to the edge of the camp and there Matthew saw, thank God, a small cart with a mule harnessed in the shafts. Fernando scooped Matthew up and put him on the flat wooden bed of the cart then climbed beside the driver. Matthew, once more almost in a faint, felt the cart jolt forward. He did not care where they were going; it would be somewhere safe, somewhere he could get proper medical attention, somewhere he could recover. Fernando had once again saved him. He closed his eyes and tried to say a prayer of thanks and lost consciousness.

The cart jolted to a halt. Matthew woke, opened his eyes, and looked around. They were in a narrow street. Fernando dropped from the cart and came to Matthew's side.

'Over there. You must go over there. You will be safe but I cannot come with you.'

Matthew looked in the direction Fernando had pointed. At the end of the street he recognised the main square.

'Where must I go?'

Fernando seemed agitated and impatient.

'Go, go now. You will be safe if you go there now.'

Matthew forced himself to sit up.

'Go where?'

'To friends. Friends who are waiting for you. But you must go now. I cannot come. You can walk, yes?'

Matthew struggled to the edge of the cart and dropped his legs over.

Fernando caught him round the waist and lifted him down as if he was no weight at all then stood back and looked at him.

'Who will be there?'

'Friends. Trust me.' He took out the medal from his shirt, held it for Matthew to see, then kissed it. 'Trust me.'

Matthew nodded.

'Of course I trust you.'

'Then go.'

Matthew, slowly and with difficulty, set off along the street towards the main square. He was not at all sure his legs would hold out. He edged towards the houses and put his hand on the wall to steady himself and keep himself upright. His eyes began to lose focus, the street and the square beyond became blurred. There was a buzzing in his head and he had lost any feeling in his legs which now moved as if by some independent power. He was an automaton winding down. The spring inside him was broken. He would never reach the square where Fernando said his friends would be waiting, ready to look after him. He felt an overwhelming desire to simply stop and lie down on the flagstones of the sidewalk.

Then he said out loud,

'Get on, get there. Fernando has got you this far. Finish it.'

He took his hand from the wall and began to walk again and suddenly he was in the square, out of the shade of the side street and in the bright glare of the sun. He held up his hand to shade his eyes and looked about. Where were they?

Then he saw three uniformed men approaching him, looking directly at him. They were local police. He stood not knowing what to do and not knowing if indeed he could do anything. The three police stopped in front of him and their faces came into focus. One was unfamiliar but the other two he recognised, Clarence Diver and El Liberator.

Were these the friends?

Clarence Diver smiled at him.

'Hello, Matthew, thank God you could make it. You had me worried. But you're here now.' And he lifted the musket he was carrying as did El Liberator and the third man. 'Goodbye, Matty, sorry it had to end this way.'

Matthew gave up. He closed his eyes. It was all over. Somewhere far away muskets crashed out, there was a scream, perhaps it was him screaming. He didn't know, he was too tired. All he wanted was peace.

A deep blackness swallowed him and the peace that was oblivion closed over his head.

Chapter Fifty-four

'Is he going to be all right?'

'With care and rest he will, but it was too damn close. Far too close.'

Matthew decided not to open his eyes. He was happy where he was. He felt no pain.

But a hand shook his shoulder and a voice forced its way into his mind.

'Mr O'Hanlon. Are you awake? Can you hear me?'

It was Edith. No other voice on earth could have induced him to open his eyes except hers.

'Yes, Edith, I can hear you.'

And he opened his eyes.

He recognised the room. It was his own in Dr Couperin's house. He was in bed. And under the sheet he was naked!

Edith, as beautiful as ever, was looking down at him.

'It wasn't you who … You weren't the one who …'

Edith suddenly understood and the puzzled look left her face.

'Oh no.'

'Thank God.'

'That was Mama.' Matthew closed his eyes and a low moan escaped his lips. That was almost as bad. 'A black man brought you here and carried you up to your room.'

'A black man?'

'Yes.'

'Did he say who he was?'

'No. He put you on the bed and left.'

Robert Tomes appeared at Edith's side.

'Well, Matthew, you're back with us. A little weak, I'll be bound, but safe and sound now. Off you go, Edith, this young man and I have things to talk about. Close the door behind you and no listening at keyholes.' Edith gave a small giggle, giving Matthew a pang of envy then left, closing the door behind her. Tomes pulled a chair to the bedside and sat down. 'Now, Matty, I have to decide what to do with you. You're not out of it yet, not unless you have a damn good story to tell me. So, what's your story?'

Matthew looked at him.

'Story?'

'I brought you down here. I was at your side the whole journey. I looked after you in Chagres, brought you safe to Couperin, and got you installed here. Everything went like clockwork. No fever, no accidents,' he paused, 'except that little episode at The Washington. However, that's beside the point and the point is, I was told that you were a rather self-absorbed young man and none too bright, that you would make no trouble. I have to say that was also my assessment of you after we'd sailed down together. Now what do I find? You have single-handedly, as far as I can see, undone everything Diver so carefully set up with Couperin. You were supposed to die out there today, Matthew, not Diver and the other two. You were set up as the target. It's what you were sent down here for, that and your report. So, as I said, what's your story? Who are you really and who do you work for?'

Matthew tried to take in what he had just been told. He was physically worn out but there was no longer anything wrong with his mind. Obviously Clarence Diver had duped him from the very beginning. For some reason he needed a man, an American, to come down to this place and conveniently die and he had been chosen as that man. And Couperin was part of the scheme. It had all been arranged. Diver's recent visit to the storehouse came back.

'He's going to take Panama isn't he? Diver and Couperin have a plan to take the place for their own? They've mounted a filibuster.'

'No. Close but not quite, and now he's not going to do anything is he, except be buried? Colonel Hernandez's men shot all three of them before they had a chance to shoot you. So we'll leave him out of it shall we? It's you I'm concerned with.'

'Three of them?'

'Diver, Smith, and Clelland.'

'Americans?' Tomes nodded. 'But they were wearing local police uniforms?'

'Courtesy of Colonel Hernandez. Couperin thought he was on our side. He certainly took our money. And he was going to become a general, head of the army of Panama, when it was all over. I would have thought that would have been enough to secure his loyalty but it seems somebody persuaded him to change his mind.'

'Our side? Are you part of this?'

'In a way. As I said I was told to look after you, see you didn't die of fever or something before Diver could kill you in the right place and the right time.'

'But why me and why did I have to die here?'

'Because if an American, a prominent American, was brutally slain by local government soldiers as part of their attempt to suppress an uprising then Henry Aspinwall could ask Washington to send troops to protect other Americans working on the railway. The troops, needless to say, are ready and waiting at New Orleans.'

'I was to die just so Aspinwall could have troops to look after his damn railway.'

Tomes shook his head sadly.

'No, Matthew. You had to die so that when Dr Couperin declared himself head of the Provisional Government of Panama with the full support of Colonel Hernandez, American troops would be here to protect the new country as soon as Washington recognised the government, which they would do almost at once.'

'Couperin? But he's French.'

'Mexican actually. He took out citizenship when he went to live there.'

'All of this simply to hand a country to Couperin?'

'Yes, because then Couperin's government would grant Henry Aspinwall the contract to build the canal with suitable guarantees of American interests on either side of the canal, while not actually giving up sovereignty of course. It gets round the Clayton-Bulwer treaty quite neatly. Panama gets independence and we get our strip of it, a canal zone. It was a very good plan, almost foolproof. Until you brought the whole thing crashing down.'

'But I didn't. At least, I don't think I did.'

'Well somebody did, so I was told that the project had to be terminated forthwith and I was to terminate it. I was also told that all possible compromising elements which couldn't be safely disposed of in any other way were to be eliminated.'

That word again.

'You mean killed?'

'If you prefer it. Smith and Clelland were too much of a liability to just send them on their way. They knew what it was all about and who was involved so they had to go. I was sorry that Clelland couldn't be got out. He was ex-army, a good man mostly, but too fond of drink. Smith was just a violent thug. He came here from New Orleans to work on the railroad, got into a fight, killed a man, and ran to Little America where he holed up. It was just an oriental he killed so nobody bothered to look too hard for him and he managed to steer clear of trouble here. He recruited the men from the camp that Diver needed to take care of any possible opposition until the army could get here and do the thing properly. He would have had to go once his job was done anyway.'

'Which one called himself El Liberator?'

Tomes laughed.

'Did he call himself that? Typical. That was Smith.'

'And what about me? Do I get eliminated?'

'That was my plan. Diver and the other two were provided with police uniforms by Colonel Hernandez and shot you in a public place. That was all as originally intended. The difference was that as soon as they'd done it I arranged for Colonel Hernandez's men to shoot them. Neat and tidy. All the loose ends gone.'

Matthew couldn't believe that this man whom he had regarded as a friend could talk so calmly to his face about arranging for his death.

'Then why am I alive?'

'Ah, that was something I hadn't allowed for. It was a rushed sort of operation so I had to use what came to hand. Hernandez was willing enough to get rid of anyone who knew his part in it all. Once he knew the original plan was finished he didn't want anyone left around who could tell the whole story any more than we did, and of course we paid him. But you were a problem. You were too sick to make it on your own to the square and I was running out of time. Couperin was supposed to get you there but I had to get him out of Panama quickly. There was no way I wanted him dealt with by Hernandez. Couperin is too important to us. That meant using someone else and the only person I knew who might do the job was Fernando. I contacted him, explained and he agreed, for a price, a very high price. He kept fingering that damn medal you gave him and saying he was betraying a sacred trust and putting his soul in danger. But in the end we agreed a price. Catholic souls, it seems, come mighty high and he wanted it paid in silver.'

'Silver?'

'He said if he had become a Judas the money had to be silver. My God, you Papists are a funny bunch, thank heaven I'm a Protestant.'

'But if Fernando took your money …'

'Oh, he took it. And then when everything was set his

men took me. They made me write a letter to Colonel Hernandez saying that at all costs Diver and the others must be shot before they could kill you. They told me that if you died Fernando would come back and I would die, and they made it clear it wouldn't be quick but it would be painful. Of course I wrote the letter. Then they tied me up and we all waited. That was a long wait, Matthew, a damn long wait. I wasn't sure Hernandez would do as I'd told him and even if he tried, Diver might kill you before his men got their chance. I tell you, Matthew, I'm not an especially religious man but all I could do was pray so I prayed, prayed like I was a little child. Then Fernando came back, stood in front of me and took out the silver, counted thirty coins, and then threw them at me and laughed. And that was that. His men untied me and they went on their way. I came here and found you asleep in your bed. And that brings us to where we are now. So, Matthew, you've heard my story, now let me have yours. And like I said, it had better be good, because you're still a loose end, there's no Fernando around any more to tie me up, and I still have my orders.'

'You mean you would still kill me?'

'Those are still my orders. Of course I wouldn't do it personally, it's not my line of work. But I doubt it would be difficult to find someone down here who would be happy to do it for a small fee. Perhaps even Colonel Hernandez might arrange something. He's an amenable sort of man.'

'But I don't know anything. All I know is that I was sent here for the New York Associated Press. You came with me on the boat and ... wait. There was one thing. In Chagres Frank Da Silva said you had written to him saying I was coming.' Matthew forced his memory to dredge the brief conversations he had had with Da Silva. 'Yes, that's it. He said you had sent two letters, one to him and one to be forwarded to Panama City. He didn't remember the name but said he thought it was French.'

Tomes was obviously surprised.

'He told you that, did he? Why didn't you ask me about it?'

'Well, I wasn't sure. You were so friendly on the boat and so careful of my health. It did cross my mind that you were perhaps too friendly, too careful. But why? Even when Da Silva told me about your letter I still couldn't think why. Then, when I got here, Couperin seemed so very willing to take me in, simply because you asked him to. But he explained that, at least he had an explanation. There was something going on, but I was never sure what.'

'And then of course you met Edith.'

Matthew flushed slightly.

'Yes.'

'And she sort of filled your available time, I suppose?'

'In a way.'

'Yes, she was supposed to. You would have to have been a very dull brick indeed not to have suspected something if left on your own to think too much. She was asked to occupy you and keep your attention. But you still got that report out without Couperin knowing.' Matthew felt a little better. 'You used Fernando.'

'Yes. How did you know?'

'Couperin told me you had slipped out a report without him knowing.'

'But if he didn't know ...'

'Da Silva told him. He was on our payroll. There was always the chance you'd try to bypass Couperin and nothing comes in or goes out of Chagres that Da Silva doesn't know about, I told you that.' Tomes stood up. 'I'm afraid your story is proving somewhat thin, Matthew. You say you know nothing. You want me to believe that you're an innocent in all this. Yet Diver and the others are dead and so is the project. Somebody must be responsible and if not you, who else is there?'

Unfortunately Matthew was forced to agree with Tomes' conclusion. Who else was there?

'Couperin?'

'Oh no. He did his job well and right up to the end. He'd sent your last report on the rebel's declaration of independence and was writing the report about your death when I arrived and told him ...'

'My report about the rebel's declaration? I never wrote any such report.'

'No, Couperin did. Not that it matters now. As I say, up to my telling him the plan was finished he did his job. Anyway, Couperin wouldn't betray us. We need him too much and he knows it, and he's a lawyer so I'm sure he's tucked away some fairly damning stuff about our activities here and in Mexico. No, there was no way we would eliminate Couperin. As we speak he is safely on a Pacific Mail boat which will sail at first light tomorrow. In a few days he'll be back in Mexico where no doubt we will find some suitable work for him to do. I'm afraid you'll have to do better than that.'

Matthew had a sudden flash of memory.

'Marryat.'

'Who?'

'Frank Marryat. He's a writer, came through Panama on his way to California. I met him on his way back.'

'Met him how?'

'Madame Couperin told me about him. She arranged a meeting.'

'A meeting? What for?'

Marryat's words came back to Matthew and to his regret he found that now he fully agreed with his assessment of the newsworthiness of Frank Marryat to the New York Press.

'It was an interview.'

Tomes obviously shared Marryat's opinion of his newsworthiness.

'An interview?'

'I know. But nothing else was happening and I … well it seemed a good idea at the time.'

'You're not helping yourself with this sort of nonsense, Matthew, you know that?'

'He said he was a British spy.'

Tomes laughed.

'Did he, by God? And if he was, why on earth would he have told you?'

'Well, he seemed to think that if he told me he was a spy I might tell him what I was doing here in Panama.' The look in Tomes' eyes told Matthew all he needed to know. 'Yes, I know, it sounds ridiculous. But dammit, this whole thing sounds ridiculous. Why was I brought here? What was Clarence Diver actually up to? Why the men and why the guns in that storehouse? If I wasn't part of it, if I hadn't seen it all happen around me, I'd find it all ludicrous. But Diver and those other two are dead. I nearly died. And everything I told you did happen exactly as I said.' Matthew had raised himself up on one elbow but now he collapsed back onto the bed and closed his eyes. He had had enough. If it was finished it was finished, he wanted no more part of it. 'I've had enough, Tomes. If you don't believe me that's your problem. I've told you what I know and you must make up your own mind about it, whatever you think it's the truth so do what you must and if you decide you will kill me I hope your filthy soul rots in hell.'

Tomes sat looking at Matthew for a moment.

'Heavens, either you're the most consummate liar I've ever met, and I've met a good few, or you are indeed telling the truth.' Matthew opened his eyes. 'Well, Matty, I'm not sure where this leaves us. I have my orders and they are quite explicit. My only problem is whether you do after all constitute a compromising element. I'll give it some thought. Meanwhile I have to think up some story to

367

cover this mess. Three American citizens, albeit dressed in police uniforms, have been shot in public by the local constabulary. Questions will be asked, Matthew, both here and in Washington and perhaps in London and Paris. I need an explanation, something to cover the facts so far as they will become known, and I'm damned if I know where to start. Making up stories is not in my line, but ...'

Matthew, suddenly revived, pushed himself up.

'Look here, Tomes, perhaps I can help.'

Chapter Fifty-five

Matthew felt much better as he lay in bed the next morning. The previous evening Edith had brought him his supper with her own hands. He decided that he would get up and go down to breakfast. Whatever her part in this thing he had decided that his future, if he had one, included Edith. And even if Tomes carried out his threat he wanted Edith to know of his feelings for her and perhaps let him know that they were reciprocated. Knowing that, knowing Edith loved him, he felt he could face up to, and yes overcome, whatever Fate might hurl at him. Then a terrible thought struck him. What if Edith was gone? Hadn't Tomes said that Dr Couperin was on board a ship which left at first light? What if, last night, Madame Couperin and Edith had joined him in his flight. He was sure that they were not involved, not so deeply involved, in this business. But would Couperin leave his wife and daughter alone, without protection after what had happened? Surely not.

Matthew dressed hurriedly and went down to the breakfast room. There sitting at the table was Madame Couperin. She looked at him and picked up the coffee pot.

'Good. I felt you were much better and after a good night's sleep I thought you might feel hungry so I made sure a place was laid for you.' She put down the coffee pot and placed the cup and saucer by his place which was set. 'Do please sit down.'

Matthew had been standing looking at the table. Madame Couperin was alone and only one other place, his own, was set.

'Where is Edith?'

'She breakfasted a little early today and now she is

getting dressed and packed. She is going away.'

The words struck into Matthew's heart. Edith. Going away.

'Going away?' Then a thought struck him. 'But if Edith is going then why are you also not getting ready?'

'Because I'm not going anywhere, Mr O'Hanlon. I decided that after the terrible events of yesterday it would be best for Edith to go away from Panama City for a while. Colonel Hernandez has kindly arranged for her to go and stay with his sister in Santiago.'

'But is she not going with her father? Are you not going to join your husband?'

'My husband has already left, Mr O'Hanlon, his boat sailed this morning some hours ago. And in answer to your question, no, I will not be joining my husband. I will stay on here in Panama City.'

The maid entered and put a plate of food before Matthew.

'Then Edith will be staying also?'

'Of course, when she returns from her visit.'

'Thank goodness.'

'I'm glad you are pleased but I don't see why you seem surprised. Of course Edith will return here. And when she is married ...'

'What? Married? Did you say married?' Madame Couperin was obviously annoyed by both the interruption and the question and her look was not lost on Matthew. 'Sorry, but as you have mentioned marriage I must speak. As Dr Couperin is unavailable I must tell you that I love your daughter. I have loved her since I first saw her. With your permission I intend to tell of my love and propose to her.'

There, it was out. Matthew waited as Madame Couperin stared at him.

'But that is impossible, Mr O'Hanlon. Edith hardly knows you. I hardly know you.' Matthew was about to

370

interrupt again but Madame Couperin held up her hand. 'But even if I knew you well, it would still be impossible. Edith is already engaged.'

'Engaged?'

'To Colonel Hernandez's nephew. He works for the government in Bogotá. A fine young man with considerable prospects. As I said, Edith is going to stay with his mother, Colonel Hernandez's sister.'

The news stunned Matthew.

'I see.'

He spoke mechanically and in the same manner took a distracted sip of his coffee.

'And if none of that were the case I would never let Edith marry you, or anyone like you.'

Matthew looked up. Madame Couperin was looking at him with what appeared to be hate in her eyes. The look shocked Matthew. Did she hate him? Why?

'Anyone like me? I don't understand.'

'An American, Mr O'Hanlon, I would never let my daughter marry an American.'

'But you're American, you said that you came from ...'

But the name escaped him.

'I was American. I took Mexican citizenship when I married Dr Couperin.'

'I'm afraid I don't understand.'

Madame Couperin gave a nasty laugh.

'Of course you don't, that is because you are stupid, Mr O'Hanlon. You come to our house all swagger and self-confidence, and all the time you are nothing but a puppet, my husband's puppet. And because a pretty face is dangled before you, you cannot see what is all around, that you are being used, that you are disposable. You see Edith and because you are an American you think you can possess her. We laughed at you, Mr O'Hanlon, behind your back we were all laughing at you, at your arrogance and your stupidity.'

371

Many things can kill love and humiliation is one of them. They had used him, even Edith. As love died in Matthew's breast his mood changed. She was right. He had been a fool and blind, he had indeed let Couperin treat him as a puppet. But now he was different.

His voice was calm.

'You are right, Madame. Dr Couperin used me and he was not alone. You played your part and, apparently, so did Edith and may I say that you both performed magnificently. However, I must remind you that your plan, whatever it was, has failed and it is your husband's confederates who are dead, not I. It is your husband who has had to run away, not I. I think we may agree that the puppet's strings are now cut and my eyes are wide open, that I have won and Dr Couperin, and you of course, have lost.' He picked up his coffee cup and held it as if for a toast. 'I wish your daughter well in her marriage, Madame.' He drank and put the cup down. 'And as for you …'

And Matthew stopped. He had been ready for anger, for hate, for any sort of furious outburst. What he had not expected was a genuine laugh.

'My dear, Mr O'Hanlon, how wrong you are, how very wrong. The strings are still firmly in place and your eyes still firmly shut and you are still a fool who cannot see what is all around him. I wish I had known that you were such a fool from the beginning, I would not have involved Edith in my little scheme and waste her time on such a blockhead.'

'Your scheme?'

'Oh yes, and from the beginning. You see, I hate America. I hate Americans with their dollars, their arrogance, and their glorious hypocrisy. I was born there, I grew up there. Oh I know America, Mr O'Hanlon, know it for what it is. Know it as you do not. But I escaped from America, left it behind. I wanted rid of it. I wanted to go away and forget its taint. I met Dr, Couperin in Mexico City. I needed a husband and he wanted a wife so we married. He was a lawyer, that was all I knew of his work. He did well, we had a house, money, servants. I was content. Then I found that America had followed me and sought me out. It seeped back into my life like some odious gas. My husband worked for the Mexican Government, had friends among the most influential people. But I discovered that he was also in the pay of the Americans, that he was their spy. What could I do? Leave him? Impossible. Edith had just been born. So I had to stay and watch him as he dripped the American poison of treachery into the very hearts of men who held Mexico's fate in their hands. He bribed and he blackmailed and I watched how America stole what it wanted. I saw at close quarters how your great Declaration of Independence is no more than hollow words when the American eagle turns its hungry eyes on land that belongs to others. Then, after the war, we came here. I suspected Couperin was here working once again for the Americans but nothing happened and slowly I began to believe that America had finally given me up, had let me go. Then he told me that you would be coming from New York and would be staying in our house. America had come back to torture me again but this time I swore on my mother's grave that it would be I who would torture America.' Once again she laughed at Matthew, but this time the laugh was more of a sneer and Matthew felt it like a slap on the face. 'And you are so stupid that you still think you are the winner? No. You have lost, America has lost. Go back to New York with your tail between your legs, Mr O'Hanlon,' she smiled, 'if Dr Tomes lets you live.' She stood up. 'I am finished with you, you have served your purpose. You should leave.' She walked to the door. 'Goodbye, Mr O'Hanlon.'

Matthew sat looking at the door. He tried to put

everything Madame Couperin had said into some sort of order alongside everything else he knew. That she was speaking the truth he didn't doubt. But why had she done it? Why had she betrayed her husband? Who was she working for? The only other person in the whole sorry mess was Marryat and if she was working for or with him then that meant she was working for the British. But where did that get him?

Nowhere.

Then he remembered Tomes. Tomes needed a story to explain what had happened and explained in a way that there seemed to be no American involvement.

Matthew's brain began to turn. For the first time in a long time his mind began to run like a reporter's. By God, it didn't matter a damn what the whole thing had really been about. All that mattered was what someone told the world what it was about. It was a story, that was all, a story that needed telling. At last he could do something he was trained to do and good at. At last he was in charge and he could pull the strings because it was *his* story. Matthew got up, hurried upstairs to his room, sat at his desk, and began to write.

Chapter Fifty-six

The Yellow Oval Room, The White House, Washington

December 11th 1850, 11 a.m.

'Good morning, Mr President.'

President Millard Fillmore stood at the window looking out over the South Lawns. On Daniel Webster's greeting he turned.

'Well, Daniel. I hope you bring good news. I could do with some.'

'I do indeed, Mr President. Sir Henry Bulwer has just left my office.'

'A satisfactory meeting?'

'Very.'

'Good. What did he want?'

'I asked him to come in so that I could apologise.'

'Apologise? What the hell have we done that needs an apology to the British Envoy?'

'We have done nothing. I had to apologise for slightly misleading him over that little matter down in Panama.'

President Millard Fillmore looked coldly at his secretary of state.

'I know of no matter, little or otherwise, down in Panama. A consortium of American investors is building a railroad. I wish them well. But it is not a government-sponsored project. Other than that, I repeat, I know nothing.'

Daniel Webster smiled a satisfied smile. He was a well-educated man and felt that, as the poet had so soundly observed, he was so armed with a good story that the president's look passed him by like the idle wind which he respected not.

'Of course, Mr President. It is, as I said, a very small matter and would not in the normal course of events be brought to your attention but, as it impinged on the Clayton-Bulwer Treaty, I felt you should be informed.'

President Fillmore's manner did not, however, thaw.

'Then pray inform me.'

'I had to tell Sir Henry that I had slightly misled him when he called to register his government's concern about a man in Panama who they thought an agent of the American Government, a certain Matthew O'Hanlon. I had denied he was an agent. This morning I admitted that he was indeed working for the United States.'

The president's voice froze a little more.

'Did you indeed?'

'Yes. I explained that it had come to our knowledge that three American citizens, led by a man named Clarence Diver, a sometime minor official of a small government department, had organised a filibuster attempt against New Granada in Panama. Our agent, Matthew O'Hanlon, was sent to Panama City and told to find out how far their plans had progressed. He found they had smuggled weapons into the country and were preparing to arm men for an uprising. They had printed a manifesto and intended to send an ultimatum to the government of New Granada, making some sort of impossible demands. Whatever the response from Bogotá the ultimatum would be used as the signal for the rising. New Granada has no troops in Panama and there was only a small force of local police led by a certain Colonel Hernandez. O'Hanlon, at great personal risk and having been wounded by Diver's men, managed to alert Colonel Hernandez at the very last minute. The leaders of the filibuster had disguised themselves as police and were about to give the call to arms. They resisted arrest and fired on the police. Colonel

Hernandez had no choice. They were all three shot and killed.'

A smile slowly spread over the ample features of President Fillmore.

'So? Our agent frustrated an attempted filibuster by Americans against a friendly country? Excellent, Mr Secretary, too often American citizens have ignored our Neutrality Act. It is right and proper that this Clarence Diver's attempt was brought to nothing with the assistance of the United States Government. It shows everyone that we will be rigorous in observing our neutrality in the region and protecting the sovereign integrity of our neighbours.'

'Yes, as you say, excellent. I also told Sir Henry that in his report O'Hanlon praised the support and assistance he had received from a British citizen, a Mr Frank Marryat who may have, on occasion, acted for their government in similar sensitive matters.'

A smile began to steal over President Fillmore's face.

'Better still. A joint venture in Central America by the United States and British intelligence services. What better proof of our commitment to the Clayton-Bulwer treaty?'

'What better indeed? Sir Henry made the same point.'

'And went away satisfied?'

'Oh yes.'

'And New Granada?'

'They have been informed. I await their response.'

'And this Colonel Hernandez?'

'Our report ...'

'From this O'Hanlon?'

'No, not exactly. The name on the report was Robert Tomes. It is my belief O'Hanlon used it as a cover name. There *is* a Dr Robert Tomes who is a medical man employed by Aspinwall's Pacific Mail Line. But he could have had nothing to do with this. O'Hanlon undoubtedly used it as an alias.'

The president's smile widened.

'No doubt, no doubt. He sounds a brave and resourceful man.'

'Yes, that is how it sounds doesn't it?'

'But I doubt O'Hanlon will be able to stay on in Panama.'

'No. I think that would be inadvisable.'

'So what will happen to him? Having so ably thwarted an incident which would have been highly embarrassing and even damaging to the country's relations with our South American neighbours I feel some sort of appreciation should be shown. A medal perhaps?'

Now it was Daniel Webster's turn to smile.

'No, Mr President. This whole business has been somewhat unfortunate even if there has been a happy outcome. I don't see that it would be in the best interests of either the present administration nor that of the country to make the matter more widely known.'

'Perhaps you are right, Mr Secretary. But such resource and bravery need to be recognised. I quite understand that our agents are of necessity self-effacing men who avoid any publicity. But that shouldn't prevent O'Hanlon himself knowing that his services have been noted and appreciated at the very highest level. What do you suggest, Daniel?'

'Well, as it happens, a vacancy has arisen in New York. I believe O'Hanlon actually comes from there, from Manhattan. A posting like that would I am sure be most welcome to him especially after his arduous service in a difficult climate.'

'Is it an important post?'

'No. I am assured by the comptroller that from now on the work of the Fund for Foreign Intercourse will be substantially diminished. In fact, for the foreseeable future, it will become primarily administrative. The comptroller suggested that on his return Mr O'Hanlon act as press liaison in New York until some other more fitting appointment should arise.'

'Excellent. Who knows, if he does well he might decide to leave the service of the fund and go in for journalism on one of the New York papers. They are, I am sure, always on the lookout for talented young men.'

'Yes indeed.'

'Good. See to it, Mr Secretary.'

'Yes, Mr President.'

'And now we must turn our attention to other more pressing matters.'

And so the president of the United States and his secretary of state turned to other business. The wheels of government ground on once more, as they always must and as they always will.

Postscript

The Panama Railway was completed at a cost of some $8 million, eight times the original budget, and the first commercial run was made in January 1855. The death toll of those who worked on the railway's construction is not accurately known but is estimated at between five to ten thousand and may well be more. What is known is that so many workers died during construction that the company started a lucrative cadaver trade. Bodies of workers who died with no known next of kin, and that would be the majority of the labourers, were pickled, put in barrels, and shipped abroad where there was an increasing demand from medical schools and teaching hospitals for anonymous corpses. The money from this gruesome trade provided enough income to the company to maintain its own hospital, so the grim business did have some sort of crazy logic to it.

The settlement of Chagres was developed and became the home of the American colony associated with the railway. It was given the name Aspinwall by its American inhabitants and Colón, in honour of Christopher Columbus, by its Hispanic population.

The British, meanwhile – Mr Robert Stephenson having supervised the building of their Egyptian railway – tried to frustrate any attempts by anyone but themselves to build a canal from the Mediterranean to the Red Sea. However, their hopes of gaining the license to build the canal failed and it was Ferdinand de Lesseps, with backing from Paris, who gained the contract and built the canal. America fared no better in Panama than the British had done in Egypt. Having built their railroad in Panama they failed to obtain the contract to build the canal which was given, once again, to de Lesseps and a French-backed company.

Strangely, it was the existence of the US railroad which spurred on de Lesseps and his backers. They hoped to use the railroad to move much of their equipment and men. However, when they learned of the charges that would be levied on them they thought it cheaper to simply buy a controlling interest in the railroad which the Compagnie Universelle du Canal Interocéanique did in 1881 and began work. However, the Isthmus of Panama proved too much for de Lesseps and after eight year's work in 1889 the project was abandoned.

America, even after de Lesseps was awarded the contract, did not lose interest in a canal and continued looking at an alternative route. However, in 1902 the Spooner Act authorised the purchase by the US of the assets of the defunct French Canal Company "provided a treaty could be negotiated with Colombia [previous New Granada] to complete the canal." This provision meant that the Nicaragua option remained open and under active discussion. There was even a Sanchez-Merry Treaty, signed between Washington and President José Santos Selaya's Nicaraguan Government, just in case the Panama option fell through.

From 1899 Colombia had been in a state of civil war, the Thousand Days' War, as it became known, involving the Liberals against the Conservatives with fighting not infrequently breaking out within both factions. It was this state of chaos that persuaded Washington that a workable treaty with any Colombian government, if and when one was formed, would be inherently unreliable. What was needed was a stable and sympathetic government in an independent Panama. By 1902 the Conservative faction was strongest in Panama but on January 20th the Liberal warship *Admiral Padilla* defeated and sank the *Lautaro*, a Chilean warship loaned to the Conservatives. President Roosevelt saw his opportunity. He didn't send troops as Millard Fillmore had arranged to do, he sent ships from the

US Navy on the excuse that he needed to protect American citizens and US interests in what was now universally known as the Canal Zone.

As both sides in the civil was now realised that a clear victory was beyond either of them a peace treaty was signed in October. However, fighting continued and under US pressure a second peace treaty, the Treaty of Wisconsin, was signed on the US battleship bearing than name.

Once a government existed again in Colombia the US wasted no time. In June 1903 secretary of state John Hay signed the Herrán-Hay Treaty which Congress then duly ratified. This treaty gave the US total control in perpetuity of the Canal Zone, a strip of land three miles wide on either side of the canal. The payment agreed was $10 million and an annual rent of $250,000 paid in gold. However, Tomas Herrán, the Colombian Chargé d'Affaire in Washington, seems not to have kept the Colombian Government very well informed of the details of the treaty he was signing on their behalf because when it was put before the Senate of Colombia the treaty was rejected.

With Colombia's failure to ratify the treaty, rather than settle for the Nicaragua option, the US government decided to use a variation of the old Polk Plan.

So it was that on June 13th 1903, with the approval of the White House, the *New York World* newspaper published the following communiqué:

Information has reached this city that the State of Panama, which embraces the Canal Zone, stands ready to secede from Colombia and enter into a Canal Treaty with the United States. The State of Panama will secede if the Colombian Congress fails to ratify the Canal Treaty.

Panamanian independence was declared in November and the new government was led by Dr Manuel Amador Guerrero, who just happened to be the chief physician of the American Panama Railway Company. As president

383

one of Guerrero's first acts was to appoint as ambassador to the United States a French engineer and sometime soldier who had worked on the original, failed canal project, Philippe-Jean Bunau-Varilla.

Without any formal consent or approval of the new Panamanian Government and only two weeks after Panama's declaration of independence Bunau-Varilla signed a treaty with US secretary of state, John Hay, which once again effectively ceded the Canal Zone to the US Government. Bunau-Varilla had not lived in Panama for some years and he never returned. He did, however, own a considerable holding in the New Panama Canal Company which had taken on the assets of de Lesseps' failed venture and which, on the signing of the treaty, was paid $40 million under the terms of the Spooner Act!

In 1903 the Stars and Stripes were hoisted and the United States, without firing a shot and untainted by any charge of imperialism, were granted in perpetuity all rights and authority, *"which it would possess as if it were sovereign territory"*.

What Presidents James K. Polk and Millard Fillmore had attempted, President Theodore Roosevelt finally achieved.

The Polk Plan worked!

President Zachary Taylor

The body of President Taylor was taken from the public vault of the Congressional Cemetery to Kentucky where it was buried in the family plot on their Louisville plantation known as 'Springfield'. But the story didn't end there. In 1991 Prof. Clara Rising, after some years of studying the circumstances of Taylor's death, persuaded his closest living relative, who also happened to be the Coroner of Jefferson County, Kentucky, to order an exhumation and examination of the remains. The results, those made available to the public, did not support poisoning by arsenic. However, at the time and subsequently, there has been a persistent body of opinion that there is enough evidence from the event itself, the contemporary circumstances, and the results of the exhumation and examination, to support a conclusion of assassination. The question of what caused President Taylor's death will probably remain, as President Millard Fillmore always intended that it should be, buried and unanswered, but not, however, forgotten.

President Millard Fillmore

Millard Fillmore was one of the founders of the university at Buffalo and its first chancellor. He retained that role while serving as vice president and president and returned to it after leaving the presidency. As he had predicted his Whig Party passed him over as their presidential candidate in the next election in favour of Major General Winfield Scott who was, however, beaten by the Democrat Franklin Pierce. In 1855 Fillmore left America and toured Europe. He was offered an honorary doctorate in Civil Law by

Oxford University but declined on the grounds that he lacked the literary or scientific attainments to justify such a degree. He also pointed out that, lacking a classical education and not able to understand Latin, he was not inclined to accept any degree which was written in a language he could not read. By the next presidential election in 1856 the Whig Party had disintegrated over disputes on the slavery issue and was, for the most part, replaced by the Republican Party. Fillmore, however, joined the anti-immigrant, anti-Catholic, American Party, the political wing of the Know-Nothing Movement, and ran as their presidential candidate in the election polling over twenty-one per cent of the vote which still stands as the best third-party candidate result in any presidential election. He died in bed as the result of a stroke in 1874.

Daniel Webster

Daniel Webster made one last attempt to gain his ultimate goal, the presidency, by seeking the Whig nomination in the 1852 presidential election but was placed third behind Winfield Scott and Millard Fillmore. Not that it mattered, because before the election he fell from his horse and suffered a serious head injury. This was complicated by the fact that he suffered from cirrhosis of the liver and was already an old man. He died on October 24th 1852. His reputation, however, has lived on and his name is remembered due in no small part not to the glory of his own legal, political, or oratorical achievements, but to a short story by Vincent Benét which appeared in the *Saturday Evening Post* in 1936, *The Devil and Daniel Webster*. It was a re-telling of a story of the same name by Washington Irving and based on the Faust legend. The story was well received and adapted by its author into a folk opera in 1938. In 1941 RKO Pictures released it as a film starring Edward Arnold as Daniel Webster, Walter

Houston as Mr Scratch, the Devil, and James Craig as Jabez Stone, the Devil's victim. The film was very successful and won an Academy Award. This Oscar probably did more to secure for Daniel Webster the place in American popular history he desired more than any or all of his speeches.

The New York Gangs

It is hard to imagine the Manhattan of today as the breeding ground of the New York gangs, yet it was, and remained so well into the 20th century. In 1915 P. G. Wodehouse featured the New York gangs in his humorous novel, *Psmith, Journalist*, and his shock at the state of the Manhattan slums is obvious if muted. He even had to write a short preface to convince his British readership that such places and people did indeed exist. As Lemuel Possett had predicted the book, *Gangs of New York*, was written, by Herbert Asbury in 1928 and in 2002 was made into a film which was nominated for the Academy Award for Best Picture. During America's gangster period Al Capone, before he migrated to Chicago, and Lucky Luciano were both alumni of the Five Points Gang. Today Manhattan is world-famous as a place of wealth and sophistication; the slums are gone. But for anyone interested or curious as to what the place looked like when the gangs of New York thrived, some of its buildings and streets still exist in what is now Chinatown.

New York Associated Press

This co-operative, founded in 1846 by the five big New York newspapers of the day, eventually became the Associated Press, a not-for-profit news agency which is still owned by the US newspapers, radio stations, and television companies who use the news written by AP staff reporters and who also contribute news to it. Its services are also used by non-USA media who pay a fee to become subscribers. As Matthew O'Hanlon survived his assignment in Panama if fell to Mark Kellogg to be the first AP reporter to be killed in action. In 1876 he was accompanying General George Custer on his campaign and was with him at the Little Bighorn. His final despatch read: *I go with Custer and will be with him at the death.* It is doubtful he meant either Custer's or his own.

Ulysses S. Grant

Grant's career as a soldier from 1850 onward became somewhat chequered. He was given several different postings in a period of six years including one when, in 1852, President Millard Fillmore did indeed send an American force to the Oregon Territory which required its commanding officer, Grant, to take his troops to Chagres and across to Panama City. Cholera struck the troops while they were there and he recorded that men were dying every hour.

In 1854 he was forced to resign his commission due to bouts of heavy drinking, although nothing was officially recorded against his name. He had several difficult years trying, and largely failing, to provide for himself and his family in civilian life at different business ventures. The commencement of the Civil War, however, saw him back in the army. The rest, including his rise to the presidency, are well enough known not to need any repetition here.

Dr Robert Tomes

Apart from his medical career and service on the Pacific Mail Line Robert Tomes was a prolific author, publishing books and articles and translating works from French and German. In 1865 he was appointed US Consul at Rheims in France and served in that role until 1867. He died in 1882.

Matthew O'Hanlon

Matthew O'Hanlon took up the post of government press liaison with the New York Associated Press in an office supplied by them. A year later he was offered a position on the *Herald* which he accepted. He married a girl he had known from childhood, had three children, and passed into total obscurity, something he never regretted. He died in bed at the age of seventy-eight surrounded by his family.

Dr Couperin and Family

Dr Couperin returned to Mexico City where he once more took up the practice of law. He still had many friends and connections and worked tirelessly behind the scenes to encourage the Mexican government to accept the Gadsden Purchase, which went through in 1853.

Edith Couperin married Colonel Hernandez's nephew and went to live in Bogotá. After the birth of their first child, a daughter christened Seraphina, she contracted cholera and died. The nephew re-married a year later.

Madame Couperin stayed in Panama City and became a writer of sensational romantic fiction. Her first novel, which people say is always to a great extent biographical, told the story of a young octoroon slave-girl whose mother had been bought by the widow of a wealthy Boston lawyer. He had died while his wife was in the early stages of pregnancy and the widow wanted a maid for herself and a little girl to grow up as a companion to her child. However, as Boston was not conducive to slave-owning, the widow moved to Baton Rouge where she had grown up as a girl. The slave child grew up as one of the family and the girls became as close as sisters. Indeed, because the slave-girl's father had been a plantation owner, as had been her mother's case, she could pass for white and the two were able to go out together and be treated as if they were indeed sisters. However, when the daughter was aged sixteen the widow announced that she must now take her proper place in society and would no longer require a companion. The slave-girl would be sold either as a house servant or as a plantation slave! The girl, spirited, proud, and refusing any longer to accept the condition of a slave, ran away and after many brave and daring adventures reached Mexico where she met a dashing cavalry officer of noble Spanish blood who fell passionately in love with her. Despite her origins, which she did not stoop to conceal from him, they married and lived happily ever after. The novel was a great success in Central and South America but alas was never translated from the Spanish so remained unknown in America even to the present day. The title, in English, was, *The Very Different Daughters of Madame Marie Macleod.*

The Nicaragua Option

The idea of a second canal across Central America using the Nicaragua route never disappeared completely and in recent times has re-surfaced as a viable option. So much so that in 2012 the Nicaraguan Government signed a memorandum of understanding with a newly formed, Hong-Kong based company, HK Nicaragua Canal Development Investment Company, which committed the company to financing and building the Nicaragua Inter-oceanic Canal with an estimated total investment of $40bn. In July 2013 the China Communication Construction Company contracted to carry out the necessary feasibility study and President Daniel Ortega has since announced that construction will begin in 2014.

And so it goes on …

Other titles by James Green

The Jimmy Costello Series

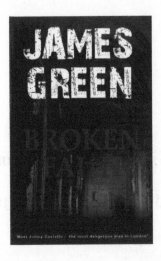

Corrupt ex-copper and fixer for the Catholic Church, Jimmy Costello, is sent to Spain to investigate when a senior cleric is accused of being part of ETA, the Basque terrorist movement.

Unsurprisingly, perhaps, a murder occurs as soon as he gets to Santander, and it's not the last as Jimmy encounters some unwelcome reminders of his violent London past.

His enigmatic boss in Rome may not approve, but Jimmy, as always, decides to see things through to the end ...

For more information about **James Green**

and other **Accent Press** titles
please visit

www.accentpress.co.uk